THE
SILK MAP

ALSO BY CHRIS WILLRICH

The Scroll of Years.

THE SILKMAP

A GAUNT AND BONE NOVEL

CHRIS WILLRICH

an Imprint of **Prometheus Books**
Amherst, NY

Published 2014 by Pyr®, an imprint of Prometheus Books

Cover illustration © Kerem Beyit
Cover design by Nicole Sommer-Lecht

Inquiries should be addressed to

Pyr
59 John Glenn Drive
Amherst, New York 14228
VOICE: 716–691–0133
FAX: 716–691–0137
WWW.PYRSF.COM

18 17 16 15 14   5 4 3 2 1

Library of Congress Cataloging-in-Publication Data

Willrich, Chris, 1967–
    The silk map : a Gaunt and Bone novel / by Chris Willrich.
      pages cm
    ISBN 978-1-61614-899-7 (pbk.)
    ISBN 978-1-61614-900-0 (ebook)
    1. Missing person—Fiction. 2. Fantasy fiction. 3. Maps—Fiction. I. Title.

PS3623.I57775S54 2014
813'.6—dc23

                         2013047298

Printed in the United States of America

For my parents, who've always been ready to walk a thousand miles for us.

CONTENTS

PART THREE: TANGLE

A NOTE ON DISTANCES:

For simplicity the distance unit *li* is assumed to be roughly three miles.

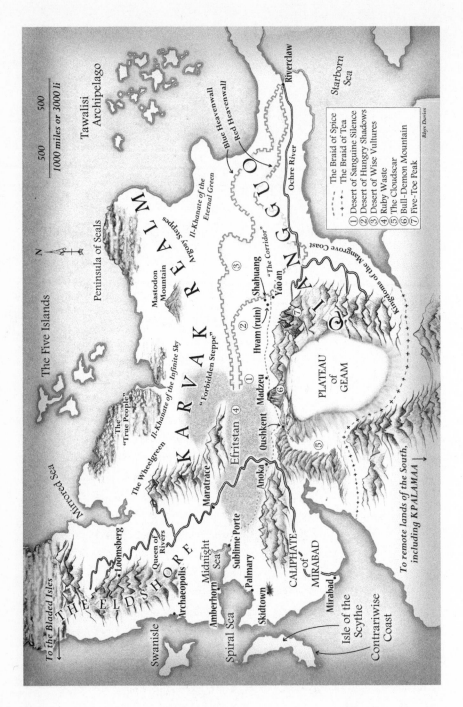

The Five Islands

Tawalisi Archipelago

Peninsula of Seals

500
1000 miles or 3000 li
500
500
N

Mastodon Mountain

Il-Khanate of the Eternal Green
Argosy Steppes

KARVAK REALM

Il-Khanate of the Infinite Sky

The "True People"

The Wheelgreen

Mirrored Sea

To the Bladed Isles

THE ELDSHORE

Swanisle

Loomsberg

Archaeopolis

Queen of Rivers

Amberhorn

Midnight Sea

Spiral Sea

Palmary

Sublime Porte

Skidtown

Maratrace

Efritstan ④

Oushkent

Madzeu

Anoka

CALIPHATE of MIRABAD

Mirabad

Isle of the Scythe

Contrariwise Coast

"Forbidden Steppe"

③

① Hvam (ruin)

② Shahuang

"The Corridor"

Yaoan

Kingdoms of the Mangrove Coast

LIANGGUO

Blue Heavenwall
Red Heavenwall

Riverclaw

Ochre River

Starborn Sea

⑦

⑥

⑤

PLATEAU of GEAM

To remote lands of the South, including KPALAMAA

Rhys Davies

- - - The Braid of Spice
— · — The Braid of Tea
① Desert of Sanguine Silence
② Desert of Hungry Shadows
③ Desert of Wise Vultures
④ Ruby Waste
⑤ The Cloudscar
⑥ Bull-Demon Mountain
⑦ Five-Toe Peak

PROLOGUE

MONKEY MIND

Spinning in a twilight world between darkness and light, earth and sky, Being and The Other Thing, Monkey flees.

In her dreams she's flying again over Qiangguo and the lands that encircle it, bright emeralds of the Mangrove Coast, green sprawl of the Argosy Steppes, browns, reds, and grays of the deserts where the great trade road meanders like a thread woven by a trembling hand. Monkey would tremble too, if it were all real. Once she truly leapt across clouds and made Heaven shake; now she can't even scratch her nose.

Yet in her mind she's free. And she sees things, and she hears.

Things that certain parties wish she hadn't.

She winks over her shoulder at the dozen dark shapes that dog her, careening through the sky like black meteors. Although meteors really shouldn't have arms, claws, and three blazing red eyes.

They are intimidating, these dream-monsters, but she is Lady Monkey and she's not about to hide at home, not when her curiosity's aroused.

As she descends from her cloud-leap, she hears the whispering of the Heavenwalls, those twin fortifications that cross the land like coiling dragons, meeting at Qiangguo's capital in the east and in the heart of the desert in the west. There an eternal firestorm swirls in the sands where true dragons go to mate.

And Monkey, because she is Monkey, hears the hiss of their power, their breath, as it is siphoned into the Red Wall and the Blue, and drawn across the land, absorbing still more vitality from the land itself as it goes. At last this accumulated *chi* converges at Qiangguo's capital and whorls through the Purple Forbidden City, unheeded by the inhabitants save as a gust of wind here, a rumble of stone there. Having swirled and mixed, the chi flows back to the Heavenwalls' tails, and the cycle continues. Back and forth the power travels, unguided, for it is as yet unmastered, waiting for someone to give it shape.

There is something uneasy about its whisperings today.

Monkey's dream-form descends near the earth, where three of the clawed shadow-shapes catch up with her.

One slashes, and Monkey's blood falls upon the nearest Wall, the red. A second does likewise, and blood falls upon the water of a nearby lake. The third's three eyes flash in expectation.

"You will perish here," it says, voice deep and urgent as an avalanche, *"and be poisoned in the waking world."*

Its words are full of refined loathing, the kind ordinary mortals only aspire to. Anybody can hate, but it takes multiple lifetimes of caustic living to become a Charstalker.

Monkey, she has to admit to herself, might be in a bit of trouble. Still, she is the dream-image of a power that shook Heaven.

As she falls past a juniper tree, she stretches her sky-metal staff to catch a branch, thinking thoughts of lightness. The branch groans and swishes back into place, throwing Monkey in a new direction. She somersaults as she moves, surprising one Charstalker with a bash to the shadow-cranium.

The creature becomes a billow of black smoke, snaking its way west and south toward its master. There are sounds of alarm from a nearby village, as dreaming people sense the battle.

A second Charstalker veers in for a slash, but Monkey's free hand shoots out and grabs the thing in what passes for the neck. It rakes at Monkey like a housecat being given a bath. This might not have been a good idea. The third Charstalker spoke true; these wounds might poison Monkey's own chi.

However, at that point they collide with the bricks of the Red Heavenwall.

The Charstalker, triple-eyes flashing with rage, becomes a smoke-trail, following its companion. There are shouts from a guard post atop the Wall, as dream-soldiers sense the conflict.

"You will not get to do that to me," says the third, and Monkey feels claws digging into her neck. *"You are dream-stuff, not stone."*

Monkey falls down the wall, losing a branch. She hits ground hard but rises and grabs at the Charstalker.

"You can't get rid of me. I'll take too much of your flesh with me. If you die in dreams, you'll be an empty shell. To live, you must accept the poison and become like me."

"Wondrous Lady Monkey is not like anyone!" she answers, and runs beside the Wall.

She came to this spot for a reason. It's the heart of the unease she's sensed in the Heavenwalls' chi. There is an old, great fissure here in the Red Heavenwall, beside a huge pond amid the junipers. Here an Emperor died alongside his daughter, she who founded the secret society of the Forest.

Monkey runs across the water and leaps inside.

"*No—*"

Entering the Wall is like stepping into a gale. Ordinary mortals would not notice a thing, except perhaps a sense of heightened anticipation as they stood among the terra cotta soldiers in this modest tomb for an emperor. But here the chi of the land courses, its path swirling and twisting in this wound.

Before its power, the Charstalker cannot maintain its dream-form. It comes apart, and shreds of it whip beyond the chamber, passing through the stones. Monkey can't know what will become of it, but it's too weak to poison the mighty chi of Qiangguo.

The chi of Qiangguo . . . now Monkey, rubbing her neck in its midst, feels all around her the unease that she scented before. She scowls a dream-scowl. It is as if she's forgotten something, having slept so long . . .

"You're up to something," she addresses the life-force of the land. "What is it? You can tell wise Monkey. When have I ever troubled you?"

It's as if a blast of air roars down from cold mountains. It knocks dream-Monkey off her feet. She collides with the toppled statue of an emperor, broken by tomb-robbers.

She lands on one hand and sneezes.

"*You're* looking for an Emperor again, aren't you? You still won't consider me?"

Again the wind howls; she somersaults out of the tomb, across the water, and onto a treetop, perched upon her staff.

She sniffs and smirks. "I scent it. An outlander? You're not trying *that* again? Your last three couldn't even figure out what was happening, let alone survive the trip. And of course, the Forest keeps hiding the home-grown candidates. No, you're just going to have to accept it. No chi-wielding Emperors for you."

She flips, leaps off the waters of the pond, and arrives back in the shadow of the Wall. Dream-Monkey breathes deep, taking in the air from the fissure.

"No . . ." she says. "You picked *that* one . . . but as I scent him, I know him.

The son of ne'er do wells. It's against his blood to rule anything. Perhaps not even himself. You can't be so crazy. Unless . . ." She sniffs, sensing a tendril of chi leaving this place for a remote land. "You're in cahoots with something . . ."

Dream-Monkey glances to her right, and sees Charstalkers swarming around her staff like nine scholars' scattered ink.

This won't do.

She sighs, turns to the fissure, and sucks in as much air and chi as a super-natural simian can. Turning, she *foofs* a blast of vital breath to the east.

Charstalkers scatter like spooked pigeons. They're all still present, however, and Monkey has just one chance. She leaps and rolls and snatches the staff. She is vulnerable for just one moment, as she gathers strength to cloud-leap once more. Claws slash, and dream-blood flies.

Screeching, she launches herself across the world. Just like in the old days.

Whenever her blood drops near a dreaming village, sleepers imagine they can fly.

Monkey passes over meandering rows of desert dunes, over the fires and light-ning strokes of the Dragonstorm, over forests of endless shadow and snowy mountains that seem draped in light.

At last she descends to a gray ocean of the far West, a place where true dawn hasn't quite begun, where three immense, craggy islands spear through the gloom.

She lands upon a titanic promontory that resembles a dragon's head, petri-fied just before rending another stony dragon on the opposite side of a narrow, sheer-sided strait. An extension of the third island is also present, stretching like a draconic head lowered beneath the other two, its skull forming skerries breaking the white waves two thousand feet below Monkey.

Down there are men. They ride dragon-prowed longboats, warring amid the skerries with spear and axe. They are a peculiar lot, pale as though imbued with the elemental essence of snow, their hair and beards often an outlandish red or yellow. Their blood is as red as any mortal's, however.

But the warriors aren't what truly snatches Monkey's interest. What she perceives most is the chain.

A vast coil of steel wraps around the "neck" of the stone dragon she stands upon, stretching across the strait to loop the similar rock formation opposite. In between, it plunges into the waters, and she can perceive how it also snares the dragon-shape beneath the waves.

She can perceive it—because of the invisible chi crackling through the links.

Monkey is so overcome, she does a backflip.

"Oh! Oho! He's not really to be Emperor at all, is he? He's bait, for . . . oh, that's *crazy*. I like crazy." Monkey frowns. "Though I do feel sorry for the kid, a little."

A cold breeze cuts across dream-Monkey's nose, and she shakes her head. Somewhere down there a warlord raises the severed head of his adversary, becoming the "master" of the Great Chain. Until next time.

"I get it," Monkey says. "It can't work unless we get him out of the trap he's in . . . and the best tools for that are his very own parents. It's time for Monkey to earn again her reputation."

She prepares to cloud-leap, but the nine Charstalkers have found her.

Monkey plunges off the promontory just in time, splashing among the dream-warriors. She doesn't know how conscious they are of the dream-state, but they do notice her, babbling in some barbarian tongue Monkey can't bother to take the minutes to learn. They jab spears and hurl axes, so Monkey doesn't feel too sorry for them when she plucks nine dry hairs from the top of her head and blows them hither and yon with the last Heavenwall chi in her lungs.

Each hair lands upon a pale warrior, and each warrior's appearance blurs and becomes the spitting image of Monkey.

When the Charstalkers land, it isn't pretty. They rend and bite and poison, and mortals can't shrug such things off. Here in this cold land, nine brutal men will awaken with darkness in their hearts.

But this is not Monkey's problem. Bracing herself against a rocky underwater shelf, she cloud-leaps again.

The world rushes past her in a white-green-blue-gray-brown blur, until the great mountains of her continent stab the sky below her feet.

"You have no idea," she whispers to the unhearing tiny figures of Persimmon Gaunt and Imago Bone. "You have no idea he'd be far safer where he is. But I can see it now . . . it's him or the whole world, kids. Even Wondrous Lady Monkey has to fall in line on this one. But she's going to turn it to her advantage; she always does."

As the world rushes toward her and her dreams turn dark, she murmurs, "Forgive me."

PART ONE

BRAID

There's no trace of people but this mountain road
Like a stone offering to granite gods
And no voice but the wind through the ridges
And rocky rivers roaring with thaws
And no one dwelling with nature
In farms or cabins or tents
And no time when you can nurture
Self-importance
It's too cold for that
And the mountains too many and wide
And the clouds no longer seem separate
Vast as the blue they disguise
Till moonlight shears weird and wondrous
Flaring the early rain
Striking your skin in the windfall
Of an awe that is cousin to pain.

—Gaunt, untitled,
composed in the Worldheart Mountains

CHAPTER 1

FOOLS OF FIVE-TOE PEAK

In hindsight, it was perhaps foolish to awaken the sleeping demigod.

Gaunt, Bone, and Snow Pine might have turned back after the third warning, but there was something about the trio of skull-adorned markers, embellished with old bloodstains and croaking unkindnesses of ravens that had aroused their professional ire. The road to Five-Toe Peak had been a route to inspire either despair or stubbornness. The three rogues were constitutionally inclined toward the latter. Of the former they had a sufficiency.

Thus they'd taken in stride the forest of the poisonous Zheng-bird, and the crags of the one-footed booming Kui-monsters, and the wasteland of elephant bones sliced with the tracks of giant Bashe-snakes who consumed elephant flesh.

Now, although Snow Pine was a child of the East, she'd long since stepped beyond the realms of her personal knowledge, and likewise passed the perimeters of scholarship and hearsay and drunken ranting. For they now skirted those mountains that defined the southern boundary of the Braid of Spice, which led to the dubious Western lands. Gaunt and Bone themselves hailed from the exotic empires of the sunset, where pale-skinned folk like themselves were the norm. But they'd taken the sea-route to the East, and knew even less than Snow Pine of this frontier.

Thus none of them knew what to make of the first marker, rising from its skulls.

It was a large boulder chiseled with the characters of the Tongue of the Tortoise Shell, the language of Qiangguo. The inscriptions were darkened with a suspicious-looking substance. By now, after a long sojourn in the Country of Walls, Gaunt and Bone could read them along with Snow Pine. This didn't put any of them at ease.

THE GREAT SAGE IS BUSY. COME BACK IN TEN THOUSAND GENERATIONS.

Around the stone, arranged rather like bulbs in a flower garden, lay the craniums of monkeys.

"At any rate I assume they're monkeys," said Persimmon Gaunt, considering the one in her palm. Her sun-bronzed skin and tattooed face (portraying a web-shrouded rose upon her right cheek) might lead a quick observer to judge her some barbaric marauder. In fact she was a poet and a scholar and—as circumstances warranted—wily tomb-plunderer and thief.

Her husband Imago Bone scrambled onto a neighboring boulder and perched there, scanning the land. "Do you think, as we are not monkeys, the message doesn't apply?" He was a lean fellow, veteran of many a mansion-theft and crypt-crawl, with scars upon either cheek, one from blade, one from flame. There was something jovial about even his fiercest scowl, something sinister about even his warmest smile.

Gaunt snorted. "You look rather like a monkey to me, up there." Her tone was not entirely warm.

Ravens squawked at them. Snow Pine shook her head at her friends. She was a wiry bean-pole of a woman, with short, straight black hair, wearing a gray tunic that seemed to defy any attempt to scrutinize her, as a nondescript boulder might shelter a glittering chameleon. Her eyes regarded all the wild nature about her coolly, trying to peer beyond surfaces into the interplay of contrasts that gave birth to the physical world. Such meditations helped soothe her in the midst of trouble.

But of late Gaunt and Bone seemed to exemplify that clash of contrasts, and their arguments did not inspire calm.

"You two can always head back to civilization," Snow Pine ventured. "I won't be offended. Whatever the Great Sage is, he—or she, or it—belongs to these lands. Like me. This might be something I should try alone."

Gaunt shook her head, though her expression softened. "Our child is just as imprisoned as yours. Together we've braved the Ghast Emperor's tomb, and the Goldfish Kingdom, and the Geomancer Gangsters, seeking an answer. We must dare the demigod. You said it's our last hope."

As she spoke Bone looked west toward the rising mountains, and toward the tangle of alpine forest blazing green like a jade necklace entwined with pearls of clouds, and toward the sun plunging behind those clouds toward the fabled cities of Madzeu and Qushkent and Anoka—and toward many other sights in that moment that weren't the eyes of his wife.

"I said," Snow Pine replied, "the Great Sage, Equal of Heaven, is the last chance I know of. There could be others in the wide world. I can only offer the knowledge I've got, such as it is. And my knowledge is fading as fast as that path ahead."

"We might as well continue, Snow Pine," Bone said mildly, scrutinizing the five-peaked range blazing like an icy weapon ahead. "We can help you dodge a few more monsters, if nothing else."

"All right," Snow Pine said.

"All right, all right!" mocked a raven, before Gaunt threw a monkey skull.

After they had frightened away the nine-headed Jiufeng-bird by mimicking barking dogs, and fled from the gibbering Fei Lian that seemed a mix of serpent, stag, leopard, bull, and sparrow, Snow Pine led them gasping to a second marker, appointed much as the first.

GO BACK. THE GREAT SAGE DECLINES ALL VISITORS.

"Hell," Bone said.

"Hell!" a raven agreed.

"These surroundings lie," Gaunt said.

"Oh?" Bone asked.

"They indicate great antiquity and neglect, Bone. Yet these markers have a perfect grisliness to them. Too perfect. I don't trust the sudden appearance of ravens."

"Hell!" said another bird.

"You feel we're being mocked," Bone said.

"I do," said Gaunt. Snow Pine thought Gaunt was studying Bone for signs of mockery of his own. Gaunt continued, "This Great Sage must maintain the warning through some magic. The demigod may even be aware of our approach. I find this annoys me."

Snow Pine said, "You'll keep going, then?"

"Of course," said Gaunt, and "Indeed," said Bone.

In truth, Snow Pine felt better for their companionship. Still, she hoped they could rise above their own troubles when they ascended the mountains.

The third marker did not manifest until they had reached the very slopes. By then the proliferation of bizarre wasteland creatures had acquired a certain charm. Not all were harmful. The trio marveled at strange, one-horned, goat-like creatures climbing the foothills, their shaggy coats rippling golden in the wind; and at a pair of one-eyed, one-winged birds with clawed feet intertwined, such that they formed one unit.

"Now there's matrimony for you," Bone said, whistling. "If either withdraws, both tumble."

"Pecking each other's still possible," Gaunt said.

"As well you would know," he muttered.

"I beg your pardon."

"Well, you have been throwing me looks like daggers the entire journey."

"Well, what do you expect? We're on a quest to rescue our son. And yet you act as if we're on a picnic."

He waved a hand airily. "A picnic among monsters and monkey skulls, Gaunt?"

"That's it, that's just it! You mock everything. Nothing's sufficiently serious for the untouchable thief Imago Bone."

"Says the poet Persimmon Gaunt. Who would rather wallow in despair than take action. Who thinks words matter more than deeds."

"Uh—" Snow Pine began. "Friends—"

She'd known them before they'd lost their son, and it hurt her to see them argue thus. She, who'd likewise lost a daughter, understood their grief.

But unlike Gaunt and Bone, Snow Pine had no spouse in which to seek solace or blame. She was a widow at nineteen. She sometimes wished her friends, in the midst of their bickering, would remember that.

She blinked at something salty she'd no time for. As her vision refocused on the foothills, she sucked in her breath.

"You've had decades to grow up," Gaunt was saying. "Don't you think it's time you got started?"

"Do you know where all injustice begins? It begins with someone declaring themselves a grownup."

"You speak of *injustice*, O thief?"

"Have you managed to overlook just how we've been *maintained*, O poet?"

"Friends!" Snow Pine repeated more urgently. "I think I know those horned goats. Unless I'm crazy, they're xiezhi. Empathic beasts. And they *hate* arguments . . ."

The xiezhi, their golden coats flowing, their hooves echoing like mad machinery through the foothills, were charging down in their dozens from the heights.

"Oh," Bone said.

"Will they attack?" Gaunt asked.

"It's said," Snow Pine said quickly, "they'll gore the person in the wrong, in any dispute. Unless either of you wants to live like a one-winged bird . . . run!"

They ran.

The three of them bore weapons, of course—Bone his many daggers, Gaunt similarly armed and with a short bow besides, and Snow Pine a curved dao-sword of Qiangguo. But they were none of them warriors. Snow Pine was perhaps the closest to a true combatant, with her hardscrabble upbringing and a little training from fighting monks and a warrior-woman of the wulin.

Now, if that wulin were here, perhaps they'd have a chance. But Snow Pine couldn't leap halfway to the clouds, nor shatter bones with her hands, nor disrupt the life-force of her foes. And Lightning Bug was as dead as Snow Pine's husband.

The ground ahead pitched and twisted with lurches and curves of granite, covered here and there with pebbles and fine silt. The treeline loomed on the right with its deceptive promise of sheltering woods but also gangs of tripping roots, trapping shrubs, swatting branches. The steep leftward slope looked ready to crumble into a minor avalanche at the first footfall.

A narrow path of firm untangled ground lay between. It led into a defile between vast rocks leaning like giants' abandoned playthings.

As they entered the passage, it bent left, and there they met a third marker, rising up from its own batch of skulls.

GO BACK AND HONE YOUR READING SKILLS. THE GREAT SAGE DOES NOT WANT YOU!

Ten crows flitted and squawked around the plinth. Each bird possessed three legs, and even with angry xiezhi on their tail, something about the birds made Snow Pine silent and wary.

But Gaunt and Bone gasped outrage at the marker.

"If there was any chance," Bone said, "that I would not . . . bother the Great Sage . . . that chance is done."

"Indeed," Gaunt said, "he has earned my spite . . ."

"If you want to hide on a mountain . . ." Bone said.

"Then hide on a mountain!" Gaunt finished for him. "Don't put up signs saying, 'Ha, ha, behold, I am hiding on a mountain.'"

"'Look at me, look at me, how reclusive I am!'"

They chuckled bitterly, leaning against one another. "We'd best prepare to be gored," said Bone, drawing a pair of daggers.

"Ha, yes," said Gaunt, with something near giddiness, as she prepared to fire an arrow.

As the spouses and their bewildered companion peered back along the path, they saw the horde of xiezhi sweeping toward them, horns aimed toward the defile like cavalry spears, less than a minute away.

Snow Pine drew her sword, and Bone's daggers were already out. For whatever good they would do. At least first blood would go to Gaunt, who raised her bow.

Looking at Gaunt's face, Snow Pine recalled the saying that dangerous as a tigress was, she never harmed her own cubs.

The xiezhi were in a sense between Gaunt and her cub. Snow Pine would not want to be them.

Persimmon Gaunt was sighting along the arrow, thinking, *I don't want to kill them. I don't want to kill anything, ever again.* The xiezhi were beautiful things; while they'd initially resembled goats, their gait was reminiscent of cats, and their eyes had the mournfully intelligent gaze of hunting dogs.

A ruthless part of her mind offered answers. Lovely pretty killers. At most you'll slay one. They're herd creatures; one death may disperse them.

When did I become such a cold thing? she wondered.

She fired, aiming for the ground ahead of the lead xiezhi.

The arrow raised gray dust, and the lead xiezhi snorted and blinked and growled.

Such is the last act of the adventuress Persimmon Gaunt, said the cold voice.

"Climb!" she told the others, and took her own advice.

Somehow she managed to keep hold of the bow as she hauled herself onto the huge, roughly shaped boulders defining the defile.

She slipped once, before Bone caught her arm. Of course he was already up here.

"Thanks. Where is Snow Pine—no!"

Their companion had not climbed. She was instead walking into the gap, sword raised.

The xiezhi rushed her. They were elegant but stank. Like moralists. Gaunt readied another shot, knowing there'd be no time.

Bone leapt.

Her idiotic glorious thief leapt.

Once again he survived something he truly didn't deserve to and landed on the lead xiezhi's back.

He yanked on its woolly neck, and it lurched about toward the heights. Bone was nearly knocked off. Yet miraculously he kept his hold around the neck, flopping to the xiezhi's left side as it hurled itself upslope.

He was well on his way to climbing Five-Toe Peak without her. About half the herd followed him.

The rest crowded before Snow Pine, snorting, stamping, looking confused. Snow Pine yelled obscenities and swung her sword in the air. They would not attack nor back off.

Somehow neither Bone nor Snow Pine were yet dead. *Goddess of Swanisle*, Gaunt thought, *I am not a lunatic, but I collect them.*

Light flared.

For a moment Gaunt assumed the sun had emerged from behind the clouds. Her crisp shadow fell upon the herd of xiezhi as if Krummara the Dead Huntress, a goddess of the West, had manifested here in the remote East. The xiezhi pounding the ground beside Snow Pine reacted as much, charging after their fellows toward the heights. Then Gaunt recalled that save for the clouds attending the mountaintops, the sky was clear.

The blazing light shifted and split, and Gaunt's shadow divided and whirled.

Gaunt whirled as well, arrow at the ready.

The three-legged crows from the marker had taken to the air. Along with this new liveliness their eyes had seemingly caught fire. Dazzling energies twisted in complex knots as the crows whirled and squawked. Gaunt's vision was soon a weave of searing threads, the rest of the world but a shadowy suggestion beyond.

"Sun-crows!" Snow Pine was yelling. "That's impossible! Sun-crows!"

"Back off!" Gaunt shouted at the birds, hoping anything so supernatural would have the gifts of language and reason.

Crows squawked and swirled around her, and lashes of light burned her way.

She dodged in a way that might have impressed Bone—had he not been busy playing with xiezhi—and kept her perch and her grip on the bow. Her skin felt as though she'd napped uncovered in a desert. She ignored her pain and fired at a dark shape concealed in a skein of light.

The sun-crow screeched its pain, and dark feathers fluttered toward the defile.

"Crows!" Snow Pine called.

Your mastery of the obvious, Gaunt thought, drawing a fresh arrow, *rivals my husband's*.

But Snow Pine was not addressing Gaunt. "Crows, behold the lineal descendent of Yi the Archer, he who shot your ancestors out of the sky! See how her line has been hidden in a benighted sunless land, for behold her pale skin, nearly the color of death! Now the legacy of Yi comes again. Where once there were ten suns, only one remains. How will you fare? Flee! Flee!"

Gaunt, who'd trained as a bard, felt a twinge of jealousy: cheering on a combatant was surely her job, and Snow Pine showed a knack for it.

Nevertheless Gaunt was the one with the bow.

She fired again, and this time luck was with her, if not sight.

A crow cried its outrage and flapped away on a damaged wing. Gaunt barely noticed the whips of crackling energy that descended upon her boulder—she tumbled off in a low roar of pebbles and dust, landing inauspiciously on her face.

Snow Pine helped her up, and Gaunt reclaimed the bow. Yet there was no need. With much invective in the manner of crows, the flock relocated to a cliff a quarter-mile away.

"Their eyes are still burning," Snow Pine said.

"So are mine," Gaunt said.

"You probably can't see Bone on his way to us."

"No, but I think I hear him."

"Run!" Bone was shouting from somewhere upslope. "Run!"

"What is he fleeing from?" Gaunt said, squinting. "I can barely see him, running down the slope."

"He seems to have found more xiezhi," Snow Pine said.

"He has a talent for finding things," Gaunt said.

"Maybe we should take his advice."

It might have been the light still blazing within her eyes. It might have been the return of violence, yet again, to her life.

Something dark and stony rose within her mind, and she stepped forward, as Snow Pine had done.

"Gaunt!" Bone was shouting desperately. "Run!"

"Persimmon?" Snow Pine was saying.

"You do not need to run, my friend," Gaunt heard herself answer, setting down her bow. "I realize now you were in no danger." The shadowy form of Bone came toward her, on foot now.

"I know! That's why I blocked the gap. They were attracted by you and Bone."

"I know."

"Gaunt!" Bone yelled, nearly in her face. She could barely see his beloved, vexing face. Golden forms rose behind him like a dark wave. She whispered a prayer that she was right and grabbed Bone, forcing him into a kiss.

"Mmmph?" he said.

"Shut up," she said, though it came out as "Shmp."

It was a good kiss. Standing at the edge of disaster was like that, sometimes. Nothing gored them.

When she opened her eyes, she saw more, and perceived Bone's astonished face and a herd of golden beasts nuzzling the ground for feed.

One by one the animals began snuffling away. Meanwhile the sun-crows' distant mockery blended with the wind.

"How did you know?" he asked when they pulled apart.

"I didn't, really," she said. "Well, perhaps I guessed when half the herd followed you and half stayed with me—until the sun-crows dispersed them. Since we were both at fault, I thought together we could mend things."

"Sun-crows?" He stared across the defile at the distant birds. She was beginning to make out his face. She liked it. Wilderness travel became him.

"You're burned," he said, touching her face.

"This comes of getting close to fires," she said.

Snow Pine said, "I'm glad you two put aside your troubles for now. No! Don't start! I'm sorry I said anything. So, how about we leave and come back in ten thousand generations?"

Bone smirked. "The Great Sage. I'd almost forgotten."

Gaunt shook her head. "I've advice to him on how to reword his markers. It begins with a hammer."

As they passed the third marker, Gaunt pocketed a fallen feather the color of obsidian. One never knew what might come in handy.

Bone led the way. *We altitude aficionados*, he mused, *have our uses.*

Up and up. Between the third marker and the shining ice of the five summits he saw a region of swift-moving clouds. Here and there the veil of white ripped to expose gray-tan contours of misty rock, perforated here and there by gangly trees. Bone should have been terrified. He was exhilarated. To have something to scale was a great mercy compared with the terror of stumbling through an ordinary day.

Stone steps rose into a whiteness that was almost an absence of form. Bone plunged in.

Now all the world was a pocket of ghostly shapes with three inhabitants upon a shifting landscape about three yards across. The steps narrowed and switchbacked.

Up and up.

A sudden shift of wind, and the world expanded, sun blazing upon a cliff inches to Bone's right, treetops far below like a green army's spears.

One misstep and I'll be even more gone than my son.

The thought drove Bone on. For the boy it was a magical form of *Gone* . . . and as such there was no giving up for Bone and Gaunt, they who, though husband and wife, still found it more comfortable to use old surnames than to abandon one of them or form a new or, outside of intimacy, to call each other *Persimmon* or *Imago*.

And the intimacy was a bit rare of late.

"I have the notion," Bone said to escape his own thoughts, "that when we reach the end of the path there will be only a marker. It will say, THE GREAT SAGE HAS GONE FISHING."

"COME BACK IN THE NEXT CYCLE OF THE EARTHE!" Gaunt added.

It was good they could laugh at something. Or grimace anyway. In normal times (to the extent that Bone had normal times) it was the glue between them. That and lust for new vistas . . . and lust for the bedroom—well, tent, inn floor, riverbank, graveyard, and on one memorable occasion—

"I wonder," Snow Pine said, "if he, she, or it can hear us."

"Or read our minds," Gaunt said.

The thought dampened his musings like mountain mist.

Now the steps strained for the vertical—practically a ladder carved into the mountain. Mist made it impossible to determine how far up it went.

They roped themselves together and ascended. Bone wished he had iron-silk; hemp would have to do.

A chilly half-hour blew past.

Breaking the cloud layer, they saw a wall of granite to one hand, a seeming infinity of blue on the other, and a floor to the world composed of golden, churning fluff.

He whistled.

This was why he had to succeed. To bring the boy back, to make his mother fully live again, so they could enjoy all these moments. The truest treasures any mortal could pinch from life's treasury.

"Bone," Gaunt said, voice all business. "Do you see it?"

Up there was a glinting of a more mundane treasure. Gold, or he was a guardsman.

"I see it. I think we're on the doorstep."

The alcove turned out to be big as a country teahouse, and Bone could not imagine how so much gold had gotten up here. There were gold plaques, and gold benches, and a golden doorframe with embossed characters in the Tongue of the Tortoise Shell.

The door itself was of iron, with a peculiar wooden knob, and a stone seal was set in its midst. There was also a window in the door, filled with translucent ice; through it, a dark passage was dimly visible.

"'*Om Mani Padme Hum*,'" Gaunt said, squinting at the inscription on the doorframe. "This is gibberish."

"It's not from my language," Snow Pine said, "but I've heard it. I'm not sure what it is, but the priests of the Undetermined use that phrase."

"The Undetermined?" Bone asked.

"You in the West may have heard of him as the 'Dust on the Mirror?' A legendary being of enlightenment who broke through the illusions of this world."

Bone remembered now. "He ended his own suffering and showed the way for others to end their own?"

Snow Pine nodded. "It's said about him:

> *The Undetermined*
> *Who won by losing*
> *Who is free of the chain of causes*
> *And has had great effect.*"

"Paradoxical," Gaunt said.

"Yes," Snow Pine said. "I don't really understand the Undetermined. And I say that as someone who's bashed her head against the Way of the Forest! But legends say he still appears now and then, with unmatched power and compassion." She pointed at the door. "Now, speaking of compassion, this phrase supposedly comes to us by way of a goddess of kindness and empathy. A holy man once told me it calls upon her name, but in our province we called the same goddess 'Guanyin.' So I don't know. A holy woman told me it means . . . aiya, can't remember. Something like 'generosity, patience, wisdom.' You know. Enlightened stuff."

"This door is most peculiar . . ." Bone reached out, and the stone seal blazed with a red inscription. Pain lashed his fingertips. "Ah!"

"'Monkey,'" Snow Pine murmured, looking at spindly red lines resembling a bamboo forest twisting in a fiery wind. They were already fading. "It means 'Monkey . . .'"

Gaunt studied the door. "There's a reason for the peculiarity, I think. Qiangguo's sages speak of five elements: metal, wood, earth, fire, and water. The door's of metal, wood, and earth. Bone has just discovered the 'fire' aspect."

"Thank you for the sympathy," Bone said, sucking his fingers.

"Poor thing. Now, if we interpret the ice as 'water,' we have the full set. There's some magical aspect to this door."

"Hm," Snow Pine said. "Is it to keep us out? Or keep the Great Sage in?"

"What do you know about him, again?" Bone said. "It may be important soon."

"I know only what Lightning Bug told me when she was teaching me this and that. There were so many things I only got pieces of, like shards of porcelain after an earthquake." She shut her eyes, remembering. "Once there was a great disturbance in the celestial court. An outsider came claiming to have power equal to anyone, including the August Personage in Jade. He, she, or it declared the title 'Great Sage, Equal of Heaven.' There was great commotion until the Jade Emperor gave the Sage the job of stablekeeper for the cloud-steeds. For a little while all was well. But at last the Sage understood the position was a lowly one and returned to mischief. Storms crackled in the sky. Meteors streaked and crashed. Heaven's angry generals at last won the day. Yet the Sage proved indestructible. Luckily the Undetermined himself was on hand. I don't know how the deed was done, but the Sage was kicked down to the mortal realm to dwell within this mountain."

"Hm," Gaunt said. "Kicked down to the ground. Five-Toe Peak."

"It's suggestive, sure," Snow Pine said. "There are always stories of wise folk on mountains, but maybe this folk is trapped *in* one."

Having already burned his hand, Bone saw no harm in trying the knob. It would not turn.

"Do you ever think before acting?" Gaunt said.

"I think while acting," Bone said. "And I think the door is locked. Moreover I think the lock is of the metaphysical, not the pickable, kind." He scratched his head. "Five elements. Perhaps we must match each element to its opposite. No, no, that only works in the Western system, where there are four . . ."

"Maybe," Snow Pine said, "we can use the hot stone to melt the ice somehow, and then . . ."

"The stone's already faded."

"Well, you could set it off again."

"Thanks so much for your encouragement."

"'Om Mani Padme Hum,'" Gaunt said while touching the knob. It turned smoothly, and the door groaned open. Although Gaunt needed give only a gentle shove, the noise suggested tremendous weight.

When the echoes had subsided, Bone cleared his throat. "Think before acting?"

"Well, you'd already tested the waters." Gaunt patted him on the shoulder. "The fires, rather."

They stepped into the Sage's realm.

Bone pulled out a torch, ignited it with one of Qiangguo's ingenious fire-starting devices, and led them into the passage.

The tunnel corkscrewed deep into the mountain, changing character as it went. At first it appeared hewn, a tomb-like passage. Later it seemed the result of natural processes, with a rugged floor and irregular walls, but with an improbable downward curve.

"I do not trust the geology," Gaunt said.

"I'm mistrustful of many things," Snow Pine said. "Governments, sorcery, criminal organizations larger than three, people who smile too much, men—"

"Ah, you wound me," Bone said.

"Should I trust you, master thief?" Snow Pine said. "As a general principle?"

"Point taken."

"But it's never occurred to me to mistrust rocks."

"You should," Gaunt said. "This mountain has the outward aspect of granite. But this tunnel has the look of limestone. Worst of all, we walk among stalactites and stalagmites, which in a limestone cave are the work of dripping groundwater. I doubt the ice of the summit could be responsible."

"It's wise to heed my wife," Bone said. "Geology is something of a hobby of hers. Along with trailblazing, tavern songs, polemics, practical mythology, wizard-taunting, and morbid poetry."

"Not true," Gaunt said. "Morbid poetry is a passion, not a hobby."

Bone smiled, yet Snow Pine tugged at her hair in a way that worried him. She said, "You think the tunnel is some sort of sham?"

Bone wondered, with a fresh wince of guilt, how Snow Pine managed. *We're stronger than you Westerners,* Snow Pine had said once, when he'd tried to broach the subject. *You're tough, you know how to fight. But we're tougher, we know how to suffer.*

"The whole mountain, perhaps," Gaunt was saying. "There is a degree of unreality about the proceedings, a mutability. I think some mind guides this environment, even if it doesn't dictate everything."

"The Great Sage perhaps?" Bone said.

"Or the thing that locked up the Sage," Snow Pine said.

"Wait," Bone said, halting. There came a distant, rhythmic noise in low tones, and in time to the rhythm a wind that fanned the torchflame. "It seems to me," he observed, "wandering about through underground passages was quite frightening enough when I knew the local folklore . . ."

"Well," said Snow Pine, "I may know the local folklore, but I have no idea what this is. But I can tell you one thing. It's snoring."

Snow Pine might have known her friends would find a way to turn anxiety into argument. Albeit a friendly one this time.

"I hadn't expected snoring," Bone said.

"I grow more annoyed with the Great Sage by the minute," said Gaunt.

"You snore as well."

"I have annoyance to spare."

"It's very delightful snoring . . ."

"I think we're here," Snow Pine said.

They entered a cavern that was a spelunker's dream. Vast blades of crystal stabbed all colors in all directions. Smaller cousins glinted in corners and jabbed underfoot. The travelers crunched gleaming wonders. Many crystals had a mirroring effect, and the trio were endlessly multiplied as they wove among the facets and edges.

From time to time Snow Pine glimpsed in the crystals a furry, simian face. "There is a beast in here. Be on your guard."

The snoring stopped.

"Beast?" someone murmured sleepily. The chamber echoed *Beast-Beast-Beast!*

They crept closer, their faces multiplying. Soon their three was joined by a fourth.

It was a monkey, such as Snow Pine had once or twice glimpsed in the forests.

Yet those monkeys had possessed black fur and tan faces; this monkey was all gray. Its eyes were closed, and it breathed in time with the fantastic snoring.

Sharing a silent look, the three proceeded until they came to the chamber's heart. The gray monkey lay upon the cave floor beneath a vast mass of crystal, granite, obsidian, limestone—a conglomeration of minerals fused with the ceiling. Snow Pine had the uncomfortable sense that a giant foot, complete with jutting crystal toenails, had pinned the monkey in place.

She crouched low, craning her head.

"I think the monkey's trapped," she whispered. "There's no room for it to move."

"Is it made of stone?" Gaunt exclaimed.

The monkey snorted and shifted at the sound, but its eyes remained shut.

"I think so," Snow Pine murmured.

"Is this the Sage?" Bone said, voice hushed.

"And should we awaken it?" Gaunt added in kind.

Snow Pine shut her eyes, thinking of a distant sea. "I think we have to. But I also think this is a creature of power. We may regret this one day. We should all agree."

"I say awaken it," Gaunt said. "We have come this far."

"I go where Gaunt goes," Bone said.

"No," Gaunt said, a distant look upon her face. "No, I don't think that is enough this time. I think you must choose."

Bone smirked. Snow Pine could sense he wanted to make light of the situation and could not, quite. "We can't command events," he said at last. "We can only do our best and hope our children prosper within the future we shape. Let's awaken the monkey."

Snow Pine said, "I'll do what I must. To give my daughter the world."

She stepped forward. "Monkey! Hello! Monkey!"

The snoring stopped and became set of agitated screeches, such as she'd heard in the forests. The bizarre creature sounded like a chimpanzee.

"I *had* heard the Sage referred to as a 'monkey,'" Snow Pine marveled to her companions, "but I never took that literally. I figured it was a nickname, or he was born in the Year of the Monkey, or something like that."

The screeching stopped. Gray eyelids rolled across onyx eyes. "Year of the Monkey!" called the stone simian. "Is that what this is?"

"No," Snow Pine said, wonder in her voice. "Actually it's the Year of the Snake."

"Feh! Missed it again! I can't stay awake longer than half a year at a time, and when I fall back asleep it'll be for at least half a cycle."

"You stay awake for six months at a time?" Bone said.

"Hey, hairy wildman, you try staying awake longer with a mountain on top of you." The mineral monkey sniffed the air. "No, I'm wrong. I thought you might be a fellow Monkey. But you're a Rat."

"I could have told you that," said Gaunt, unable to suppress a laugh.

"And a Snake! Hey, this is your year, young lady. Use it well." Another sniff. "Aha! There *is* a Monkey here, and it's you, girl of Qiangguo."

Snow Pine blinked. They'd never tried determining where Gaunt and Bone fell in the procession of years, because the calendars didn't match, and in any case Bone had forgotten the year of his birth. Western folk supposed their personalities were set by the stars, and that wasn't for her to argue. Yet she did not doubt the Sage's pronouncements. Like many people, Snow Pine scoffed a little at the old notion that personality was driven by the animal of your year.

But she *did* see something wise in Gaunt, and surely there was much that was opportunistic about Bone. As she recalled, Rat and Snake were not the best romantic match, and not the worst. Maybe that fit as well.

She herself never minded being a Monkey. *Girl*, however . . .

"Woman of Qiangguo," Snow Pine said.

The Great Sage laughed. "Who am I to deny a fellow Monkey her proper title? And a fellow female. But I would like it if you strangers would use one of mine. I think I deserve a little better than 'you,' don't you think?"

"Apologies, Great Sage," Snow Pine said.

"Equal of Heaven," the Sage added.

"Equal of Heaven," Snow Pine agreed uneasily.

"Wondrous Lady Monkey."

"Wondrous Lady Monkey . . ." Gaunt said.

"She Who is Aware of Vacuity."

Bone coughed. "She Who is Aware of Vacuity . . ."

"O Glorious Bedmate."

"What?" Bone said.

"Just seeing how far we could go with this," the Great Sage said.

"He has his faults," Gaunt said, "but he is spoken for."

"Ha!"

"*Lady* Monkey?" Snow Pine asked.

"Can't sages be female? Or simian? Or made of stone? Or dashing and gorgeous?"

"Apparently they can," Gaunt said.

"So, since you're clearly under-informed, what are you doing here? I haven't been awakened in a thousand years that I can recall. Must be something big. Is the Undetermined springing me?"

"I don't think anyone here qualifies for that title," Gaunt said.

"Ah, I had suspected," said the Great Sage. "Anyway, having been imprisoned in a mountain, I'd expect my release to be similarly dramatic. I deserve no less."

Snow Pine crouched beside the stone monkey head. Every time the Sage stopped speaking and assumed a distant look, it was easy to assume she was a statue. But swiftly enough she would blink, or sniff, or smirk. Each hair on her head was a separate mineral formation, like darker versions of the smaller quartz blades in the surrounding cave. Her eyes were black stones with clear impurities for pupils, like comets.

The comets swung toward Snow Pine. Granite lips revealed agate teeth. "You wonder how I can awaken. Surely I'm an artwork of sorts, you think, so how can I live? I concede it's a bit of a mystery to me also. Long ago, when there were many more moons in the sky, the quarrelsome god-clans of the Arctic and Antarctic warred over control of the sun and in the process changed its course."

"I have never heard of a pantheon in the far north . . ." began Gaunt.

"It became a pantheon of the far *west*, long before your people again emerged from caves, once the sun bent to its new path," said the Sage. "But that is beside the point, for the point was about me. Strange energies were unleashed in those days, and they fell upon a certain boulder in a magical place far beyond the Starborn Sea. I hatched from that stone, much as you see me now. And wonderful as I am, I'm no doubt not the most wondrous thing to be born when the sun changed course. Now. Tell me what has brought you so far to awaken me."

"Great Sage," Snow Pine said, glancing at her nodding companions, "we awakened you because we are in great need. We've lost our children."

The Great Sage frowned. "Children? Lost?"

"Our son," Bone said, taking Gaunt's hand, "and the daughter of Snow Pine here."

The Great Sage snorted. "Surely you don't need me to resolve this riddle. Haven't you considered that they might have eloped?"

Snow Pine strove to maintain her temper. "You are unaware of the circumstances. Our children are very small . . . were very small when we left them."

"Left them, lost them? Make up your mind."

"They were left in a safe place," Bone said, "so their mothers could join me in fighting a dreadful assassin from the West. The assassin is dead, but that haven is now lost . . ." His voice trailed off, and Snow Pine could see, for once, the guilt that lined Bone's face.

But the Great Sage was squeezing shut her stony eyes in exasperation. "I had thought people would only brave the wasteland to ask me matters of import! How to become immortal. How to vault through the clouds. How to assume the forms of animal, mineral, or vegetable. How to do battle with the Archon of Night, or rescue the Lost Moon, or face the Starwolf on the Day of Its Return. Lost children? Am I a village constable?"

All this time Persimmon Gaunt had been studying the Sage with narrowed eyes. Now she spoke. Fury lit her words.

"We are wasting our time! This weak one cannot help us. How could she do *anything* to recover a prophesied ruler trapped in a universe inside a scroll lost at the bottom of the sea? She cannot even shift a few rocks. Let's return to the village of Abundant Bamboo and consult the local wise-woman with her love potions and missing teeth. *There* is someone whose skills we can rely upon."

The Sage growled and opened her eyes. "I see what you're doing there. Playing to my vanity. What you fail to understand, bizarre woman with hair like fire and skin like snow, is that I have no vanity, only a true and honest appraisal of my own strengths. I know how to cloud-leap one hundred and eight thousand li—"

"The world isn't that big," Snow Pine said.

"Well, I may exaggerate a little for poetic effect. The point is, I'd be beyond the horizon, so how would you know? Likewise I can alter my form to explore the weave of atmospheric energies some mortals call the Celestial

Kingdom, or make my stone body molten to fathom the depths of the world. More prosaically I can become any animal, or turn as invisible as the wind."

"Yet you are trapped," Bone said.

The Sage scowled, but then she shrugged. "A triviality. I tangled with the Undetermined up in the ionosphere. He slapped me down, and threw a mountain onto me for good measure. A very special mountain. It's partly composed of my own stubbornness, so I can't directly shift it with my own strength."

"Interesting problem," Bone said, stroking his chin.

"Could you not dismiss it?" Gaunt said. "If it's a product of your own mind?"

"Sure," said the Sage, "if it were composed of fancy, love, anger, or a craving for fresh mangoes. Those feelings I could dispatch like mountain bandits. But I'm nothing if not stubborn. That means 'I' can never be rid of the mountain, because the mountain is essentially me. The harder I try to out-think the problem, the heavier the mountain becomes. Clever Undetermined! Either I become enlightened myself—fat chance—or I wait for him to release me. Anyway, why didn't you say at once that your case was so interesting! Children lost inside a magic scroll! Far more intriguing than losing them at the market. You will share what you know."

Snow Pine began, "I—"

"No, no, no," said the Great Sage. "Don't use words." She began to sniff. "Think about your loss, and your vital breath will do the rest." She continued snuffling, and despite Snow Pine's outrage at the Sage's manner, it was clear the endless boasts were not idle.

Loss, Snow Pine thought.

Once she'd been called Next-One-a-Boy—one of countless girls the world over neglected by parents in favor of sons. Perhaps hers were just more blunt about it. But there was a fire within her, and she ran away. She lived with a warrior-woman of the wulin. She lived with bandits. She took up with a bandit boy and led a gang in the capital. She might have made a life in crime but for the crazy foreigners and the treasure she'd stumbled upon, what she came to call the Scroll of Years.

The Scroll was a haven but also a trap, and when she and her lover got caught up in the troubles of Persimmon Gaunt and Imago Bone, they were trapped with pregnant Gaunt in the Scroll. But such a pleasant trap! There was a tower with friendly monks in the mountains within the Scroll, and as time passed swiftly there, it seemed the natural thing to marry her gangster and have a baby. She whom they called A-Girl-Is-A-Joy.

She remembered a two-year-old, a stomping, night-haired storm-cloud, rushing through the legs of bemused monks.

Try to sleep, Joy!
But I like noise!
Come inside, Joy.
I need a cliff!
Leave that alone, Joy.
I need to drop scrolls!

They had dropped the Scroll indeed. Her brash gangster was dead now, and her daughter was far away and under the sea.

Loss.

"Heady smell, you three," the Great Sage said. "It reminds me of something, like a remembered dream . . . ah, I've lost it. But let me ruminate a second." She shut her stony eyes and sneezed. "Okay." She blinked. "You got me. That is an interesting problem. It's not enough to get you to breathe water. You have to find the right spot, and the trail is cold. I could probably do it, but obviously, ha, I have another engagement. Let me think." She shut her eyes again, and only the lack of snoring confirmed she was still awake.

Snow Pine's stomach churned. She dared not believe they were on the verge of an answer. She could not stop herself from hoping. She felt the contradiction in her gut.

"Yes!" said the Sage, opening her eyes and chuckling. "Yes, I think that will do it. Simple and direct, really, if you know how."

"There's a way?" Gaunt asked, and now Snow Pine was the one to shut her eyes.

"There is. But you need some background here. Indulge your friendly Great Sage while I tell you a story."

THE GREAT SAGE'S TALE

A crow croaked this in my ear once.

I guess this happened three hundred years ago, more or less. Off in the heart of Qiangguo, in a green country between the Red and Blue Heaven-walls, there's a big lake with an island in the middle. An army guards the lake, but no one goes to the Island of the Iron Moths but Mandarins of at least the rank of Peacock—and *they* only go to bring back the ironsilk.

Hey, I see your eyes lighting up, Mister Rat! Yes, ironsilk, supple and steely by turns. Maybe you thought wizards made it, but it's a stranger story than that. It comes from the cocoons of the Iron Moths. There's a human clan on this island that tends to the Moths, keeping the immature caterpillars fed and listening to the adults' poetry.

Ye gods, that poetry! For yes, the Moths are sapient. They came originally from the darkness of space and in their hearts they've never left. Even the sun-crows visit the island to hear it, because they too crave tales of distant suns, maybe because we've only got one of our own.

There's the one about the star who got lonely for a planet to warm, and who chased and burned the fragile astral ships with their crystal hulls and nebular sails, pleading for news of any orphaned world.

And the one about the haunted lighthouse built atop a comet, last work of a dead people, whirling from sun to sun to guide the inhabitants of younger planets in exploring the starry realms—but woe betide those who dare enter the lighthouse itself!

Even one about the Pit Where Light Screams, where the Starwolf gnaws on the bones of old worlds. But I won't speak more of that.

The poems are beautiful. But they can make you strange. Maybe that's why the girls Jing and Xia got so peculiar. Jing was a go-getter; she was the one who figured that by boiling an unbroken cocoon in lava, you'd get long strands of ironsilk—far more valuable than broken strands from a perforated cocoon.

Now, those Iron Moths are strange. They marveled at this discovery, and even their caterpillars accepted the plan, some of them volunteering to be boiled alive. It's said that Jing's method was successfully applied to mundane silkmaking too. She was a hero. Her mother, a widow and head of the clan, gave her the best cottage on the island and a bunch of servants.

Now, among those servants was Jing's half-sister Xia, whom everyone accounted a dullard. *Xia* never came up with a million-yuan idea like Jing's. And Xia was a soft-hearted, maudlin type, mourning her dead mother and father, offering no respect to her stepmother. Just as bad, she was sorry for the volunteers in the caterpillar-boiling brigade. Xia just didn't have the spark, it seemed. Her future was going to be dusting and mopping and cleaning fireplaces.

But it turned out Xia had some loaded dice of her own. Sometime or other in her moody explorations of the island, she'd gotten hold of an Iron Moth cocoon that was neither hatched nor boiled. The pupa had somehow reached a twilight state between life and death, and for some strange reason it took a liking to Xia.

I told you this was a weird island.

The pupa wasn't hatching, but it did hatch a plan. The pupa would share all the poems the suncrows wanted, if the suncrows would carry Xia and a few cocoons off the island.

It was a wild notion, but suncrows like crazy plans, and sometimes so do human kids. It would take all the suncrows in Qiangguo; there weren't a lot of them, and they were scattered from the Mangrove Coast to the steppes of the Karvaks. It took a while to put things together. During that time Xia grew increasingly odd, and to tell you the truth, Jing and her mother were about ready to toss Xia in the lava. But at last one night the stars were blotted out by black wings.

Xia flew, suncrows clutching her gown, with a dozen cocoons in a pouch slung around her shoulder and her friend's cocoon clutched to her chest.

Shrieking of Xia's betrayal, Jing emerged from her ornate cottage with a bow and arrow. No stranger to martial things, Jing fired at Xia.

Now, to this day the suncrows swear the cocoon in Xia's grip shifted of its own accord to block the arrow. But the tip itself was coated in ironsilk; it pierced the cocoon. Whatever strange in-between life the pupa had, it ended right there.

Xia screamed and dropped the cocoon. By a strange chance it cracked Jing's skull and killed her.

The suncrows flew with the bereft Xia, far to the west, beyond the lands controlled by Qiangguo. Though the Heavenwalls stretched far toward the setting sun, in these remote realms the Empire could only clutch those lands immediately beside the Walls or between them. Nomads like today's Karvaks roamed and ravened in the steppes to the north of the Walls; trading oases and cities stood in the deserts to the south.

But nomads and traders could not help the cocoons. Only a volcanic mountain could do that. The crows knew of one.

And so they brought Xia and her prizes to a fiery mountain in a hidden land of the West, where new Iron Moths could hatch, beyond the reach of Qiangguo or Jing's clever boiling technique.

And if no doom has befallen them, I suppose they are still living there to this day.

When the Great Sage had finished, Bone said, "So, let's see if we understand. Perhaps the most valuable substance in the world, the greatest secret of Qiangguo, lies somewhere for the taking, somewhere to the west?"

"That's about the size of it," the Great Sage said with a wink. "Interesting, yes?"

"Yes," said Bone.

Snow Pine felt motivated to dim the fires of Bone's greed; she noticed Gaunt taking his hand with similar concern in her eyes. Snow Pine said, "But what does this have to do with our children?"

"It doesn't," Bone said. "We're being offered a bargain,"

"It can be fun doing business with a Rat," the Great Sage said. "He's correct. I'll offer you my services in recovering your kids. I know a great deal. Even before I learned the seventy-two transformations, even before I dazzled the energy-patterns of the Celestial Court, I was queen of the Mountain of Flowers and Fruit across the Starborn Sea. And many things have been whispered to me as I lay under my new mountain. If nothing else, it gives one time to think. And so, yes indeed, I believe I have an answer to your dilemma."

She paused.

Gaunt tapped her foot. "I confess to some suspense as to what that will be."

"She means to keep us in suspense, Gaunt," Bone said. "Until we bring her what she wants."

The Great Sage smiled.

"You want us to bring you ironsilk cocoons," Snow Pine said.

"Indeed. Though what I really want are the caterpillars. As many as you can get. And you'd best be quick about it."

"You claimed," Bone said, "you could stay awake for six months."

Gaunt said, "That may seem like a long time, Bone. But we don't know where this fiery mountain is or how to reach it. It seems logical to inquire upon the Braid of Spice . . ."

"But the Braid of Spice," continued Snow Pine, "is said to extend for nine thousand li. And we're no cloud-leapers. It can take a caravan years to cover that distance . . ."

"I recall accounts of sandstorms," Gaunt said, "bandits, demons of the desert . . ."

"Steppe warriors," Snow Pine added, "animated mummies, prehistoric monsters come to life . . ."

"And overpriced inns, no doubt," Bone put in.

The Great Sage yawned. "Oh, such fine bedtime stories. I feel myself tiring already."

"You are cruel," Gaunt said.

"I am myself," said the Sage.

"That's nothing to brag about," Bone said.

"Indeed? Many do not even achieve that distinction: to know one's self, and act upon that knowledge, even if it brings a mountain down upon you. But I am not entirely without pity. I give you a boon, to help you in your quest." The Sage tilted her stony, simian head. Something glinted between her ear and her skull. "See you the needle I keep, as a seamstress would? I invite the Monkey to take it."

Snow Pine hesitated. There was surely a trick, or a price to pay. And yet, though the Great Sage was callous, she did not seem malevolent, as such. And somewhere beyond the sea, and a greater gulf yet, a girl needed her mother.

She stepped forward and plucked the needle from the Sage.

When she claimed it, she felt a sudden weight, as though she'd attempted to grasp an entire planet. Her hand buckled and her fingers threatened to break.

All at once the Sage winked, and the needle suddenly had merely the heft due a splinter of metal. Yet it gleamed like a line of distant stars.

"What is it?" Snow Pine asked. Despite all that had come before, and all that lay ahead, she was not immune to wonder.

The Sage seemed to respond to her tone. "Ah," she whispered, "it was a gift from a dragon queen of the eastern sea. Its powers must remain my secret. But you could say it's a needle for weaving great events. Yes, that will do. Call upon it at dire need. But for now, tuck it into your robe."

Snow Pine did so, sliding it into an inside fold so it would stay near her heart. It pricked her finger, and she grunted in anger, for she half-suspected the thing had jabbed her of its own accord. When she patted her robe, the needle felt cold as a slice of midnight.

"It likes you," said the Great Sage. "Now, I suggest you be about your business. The year grows no younger."

Snow Pine wanted to ask the Sage many things. But she shared a look with Gaunt and Bone and understood that they wanted to be free of this presence as soon as possible. She could not fault them.

"Thank you, Great Sage," said Snow Pine, bowing not at all.

"I will not thank you, Monkey," said Gaunt, "but I acknowledge a bargain."

"Ha!" said the Sage. "You ladies are equally curt, in the manner of your own lands. How droll! And you, Mister Rat, I see that gesture you're making! I'd make one right back, but my hands are occupied."

"Why," Bone said, "I was merely scratching my nose, something you, alas, can never manage."

The Sage snorted, but there was less humor in the sound. "Begone, wanderers. I find you less amusing now. But a deal is a deal."

Maybe it took a woman of Qiangguo to hear the threat in that voice. Snow Pine took Gaunt and Bone's hands and led them back to the tunnel, a cold sensation over her heart.

The return to the doorway proceeded in silence; at least the snoring did not resume. The mountain descent was businesslike, for none of them wanted to dash their hopes by dashing themselves on the rocks. At last they reached the third marker, which was fortunately free of angry xiezhi or agitated suncrows.

Although they'd arrived from the east, from here they could just as easily proceed north, toward the commencement of the Braid. The same monsters would greet them either way.

They faced the path in silence.

Gaunt felt no hope at that moment. But she was used to living with no hope. If it came to a choice of no hope while moving, and no hope while standing still, she would move.

Bone's mind flitted among endless plans. If the Sage's bargain did not play out, why, at least they'd be closer to the West and the world he knew; there was a wizard he almost trusted, a pirate he was nearly friends with, a mermaid of his acquaintance . . . schemes pranced like xiezhi around the abyss in his heart.

Snow Pine silently told the ghost of her husband, wherever he might be: *I won't forget. Everything I do, everywhere I go, it's a way of saying, I won't forget.*

Bone broke the silence. "What's that saying? The journey of a thousand li begins with one step?"

"The proper drubbing of a proverb-quoter," said Gaunt, "begins with one kick."

Snow Pine snorted. "There's another saying, that reading ten thousand books isn't as useful as traveling ten thousand li."

"I suppose we'll find out," Bone said.

"I hope not," Gaunt said. "I fear I've only got nine thousand in me."

They walked north, and in that moment became the three newest travelers, following the thousands who'd gone before, who gambled everything on the Braid of Spice.

After the trio had departed, the Great Sage whistled.

A three-legged crow with fiery eyes landed on her head.

"Bring a piece of me to where the trail will be darkest," she said. "Whether it adds shadows or light, we shall see. Gah, that tickles."

The crow pecked at the Sage's head until it held in its beak a dark, crystalline hair. Without a sound it flapped away, and the Sage sneezed her farewell. She didn't like suncrows much, but they and she had a deal going, and by now she'd remembered a little bit of a dream that concerned Snow Pine, Persimmon Gaunt, and Imago Bone.

Sometimes crazy monkeys have to stick together.

CHAPTER 2

THE SECRET HISTORY OF THE SKY KHANATE

Lady Steelfox cast her falcon toward the dawn and aimed her bow toward the south. Blue seeped into the sky over the dew-spattered green of the steppe. She imagined for a moment she was sighting at the city of Yao'an, so many weeks' travel beyond the grasses and the deserts, and her pony snorted as if reproachful of such youthful whimsy. Lady Steelfox grinned. Such a shot would have been impossible even for Qiangguo's mythical Archer Yi.

And yet, she thought, *there might soon come a time when Qiangguo's cruel wall-builders consider me nearly as great a legend—if my pet inventor's tricks work as planned.* Thoughts of the future took wing like raptors as her eyes spied movement in the green.

A grasshopper twitched. She let fly an arrow.

The insect flew as well, but she'd anticipated its departure, and her shot bisected it.

Steelfox dismounted and sauntered leisurely to her kill. It was ungrateful to waste Mother Earth's food, so she popped half the insect into her mouth and crunched away.

A voice came murmuring upon the wind, as though a woman spoke from deep within a well. *You are surely improving, Lady. Though why you choose such bizarre targets, I do not know.*

Steelfox had trained herself not to jump when the shaman projected her words in this manner. "Haytham ibn Zakwan ibn Rihab," she replied, "claims he was once marooned upon a remote continent. He dwelled in peculiar pointed *gers* nearly as narrow as trees. He hunted vast buffalo on vaster alien plains. He smoked strange leaves that he hopes to cultivate upon our own continent. He says those foreigners and we Karvaks are much alike, though personally I cannot see why. But they did teach him that a good archer should practice by shooting grasshoppers, because if you can manage to shoot a grasshopper, surely you can shoot a man."

Steelfox searched the four directions for the shaman as she spoke.

To the south lay only the green steppes of spring. To the west lay more of the same.

To the north was her encampment, a row of thirty-six gers set in an east-west line, with five great wheelships rising behind, their sails bearing symbols in vertical script proclaiming the five elements. The fire-aspected sail belonged to *Redwind*, Steelfox's flagship, and it always pleased her to see it. Steelfox beheld much to make her proud. But no shaman.

To the east, obscured by dawn-glare rose the Great Khatun's temporary court, with the gray and white slopes of Mastodon Mountain rising beyond, feeding a meandering river that separated the two encampments. Steelfox could glimpse animals that way, but no nearby people.

Her falcon shrieked overhead, warning her of someone's approach. That was good, because apparently this morning Steelfox was perceptive as a rock.

Half that Mirabad madman's stories come out of his fever dreams, came the shaman's distorted voice, *and the other half out of his ass. If I hadn't seen his inventions for myself . . .*

"Yes," said Steelfox, shutting her eyes so she might touch her falcon's mind.

There was a moment when her thoughts, normally a disciplined herd, dispersed like a thousand wild horses. But she mounted one and rode it to the mind's horizon.

She was nine years old, and her father clutched her hand in his and placed it upon an egg the color of fire. "From the time Earth and Sky became two beings," Father said, "and learned both loneliness and love, our family has had the privilege of knowing animal minds. The talent is double-edged, as are all gifts. You may only choose one mind at a time, and each will mark you forever. Are you certain?" Father sounded so serious, but Steelfox had no fears. Despite her name, and despite the Karvaks' history with horses, it was the clouds, not the grasses, she longed to know. She nodded—

And in the next terrifying moment she was screaming, for she was trapped inside a shell . . .

Steelfox broke through the memory and all at once she was in the here-and-now and looking down upon herself, a little Karvak princess with her crown of black hair worn high and shiny with animal fat, in her thick, sky-colored tunic coat with its long drape and heavy sleeves: a drop of black-flecked blue in an ocean of green. The tiny woman shivered. The family gift gave her Qurca's perceptions but only a sliver of the mind that commanded them. Thus what was natural for him always disoriented her, for a time.

But only for a time. Soon she thrilled with the perceptions of the circling peregrine, swiftest of all beasts. Qurca was on his way to becoming an old bird, and she sensed a trace of stiffness in his wings, but he was agile yet. The steppe opened up before their eyes, a vastness of green to rival the immensity of blue above. Qurca noted slopes human eyes would miss, and burrows of ground rodents, and the occasional black of the sky-stones one found here and there in these lands. She would have to inform the Great Khatun of a few meteorites her smiths could harvest.

Far to the southeast was a temporary interruption of the green: a fleet of wheelships coming to greet the Great Khatun. They were at least an hour off, and Steelfox couldn't discern their insignia, but it was good to have this warning.

She coaxed Qurca to spy the land nearer at hand and soon spotted her quarry, a tiny human figure fording the river at an angle that placed it within the dawn-glare for little Lady Steelfox.

Qurca made an irritated shriek. Morning was a hunting time, and Steelfox was acutely aware of the movements of field mice far below, animals to which as a human she'd been oblivious. Qurca was too disciplined to stoop and slay, but she could sense his desire, a tension as great as any human ambition or lust. That he denied his appetite for her sake showed dedication that could shame a Karvak. She released him to his hunt.

A woman once more, she saw a bolt of feathers snatch a mouse from this world and fly to a place of feeding. She turned east and smiled. "Haytham's creation is a marvelous way to travel, shaman," she teased. "Better than wading through icy rivers!"

Bah, came Northwing's conveyed voice, obviously irritated by Steelfox spotting her. *Let the Karvaks, with their token single-animal bonds and their wheel-ships and their Wind-Tamers, say so if they want. I, a taiga shaman, can survey the land through the eyes of a whole flock of cranes. And there's no better way to greet the day than with cold water.*

Northwing strode out of the sun. She kept her hair short and her face bare of adornment. She wore a hunter's heavy gray coat and pants, her shamanic charms shining silvery over her coat upon half a dozen necklaces, and like Steelfox she carried a bow and quiver.

"I do not mean to insult you," Steelfox said. "Care for half a grasshopper?"

Bah.

"As you wish." Steelfox continued talking while chewing. "Why do you brighten my morning, Northwing?"

Your late husband treated me with more respect.

"Fear, you mean."

"Is there a difference, Karvak?" Northwing called in mundane fashion across the remaining span.

"Fear is for those outside the realm! I know you for an honorable vassal! I do not fear you!"

"Do you fear the Great Khatun?" came the shaman's answering bellow. "She summons you!"

This was insolent. With her outcry, Northwing had informed the sharper-eared guards that Steelfox's liege demanded her presence. Any delay now would be provocative.

Steelfox strolled with calm deliberation to her pony, mounted, and rode at a measured pace toward where Northwing stood with crossed arms.

"You may ride if you're done screeching," she said as she pulled up beside Northwing.

"I have legs."

They continued toward the river.

"Did my liege give a reason?"

"Does the khatun need reasons?"

"Is mighty Northwing a messenger boy now?"

"I go where I will, as any man might."

"Is mighty Northwing a man now?"

"I am a shaman, Lady. I walk between life and death, light and darkness, male and female."

"I'll never understand you Reindeer Folk."

"Do you not even realize, Lady, after all this time, that 'Reindeer Folk' is your name for us, not ours?"

Steelfox knew but answered, "And what is your name for yourselves?"

"'The True People.'"

"Well, fair enough." Steelfox held out her arm and Qurca alighted. He had a golden belly and gray wings, and a mix of these colors swirled upon his head, with his beak like the comb of a golden helmet dipped in ash. He swallowed the rest of Steelfox's grasshopper in one gulp, his chest puffing. Steelfox cooed and said, "But we're content to be Karvaks. 'Archers.' Let the world know us by what we do."

"Bah."

They crossed the river and rode past the Great Khatun's soldiers, beyond poles marking future encampments, for nobles arriving for the Parliament. They passed herds of goats, cows, and aurochs, who'd been relegated to this grazing to preserve the fields closer to the khatun's tents. Likewise they passed war-animals—ponies, mastodons, woolly rhinoceroses—before Steelfox even spotted the Great Khatun's gers and her two dozen wheelships.

The site sprawled over a territory far more vast than the khatun's own entourage required. Cauldrons big enough to cook an aurochs stood in rows before the tents, leading to a score of tree trunks dragged from the taiga and planted as posts for vast future pavilions. With few people stirring, the grounds had almost the look of a haunted and deserted spot, but rather than a place where humanity had once lived, it was a place where most people had yet to arrive.

"The Parliament of All is coming," Steelfox mused, "like it or not. . . . Northwing, in your wanderings between light and darkness, did you happen to pass *Redwind?*"

"You mean, did I look in on your mad inventor?"

"I suppose you could put it that way."

"Black smoke was pouring out of the wheelship's hold. The crew on duty were coughing and cursing the name of Haytham ibn Zakwan. Whether that was a good or bad sign, even a shaman cannot say."

"You do not approve of him, Northwing. But do you approve of my project? You have never said."

"Bah. It is not for me to approve or disapprove."

"But you do it anyway."

"You Karvaks will conquer the world. Or you will make it conquer you. That is nothing to me, nor are your unorthodox approaches toward that end— as long as you treat the True People well. Despite your many shortcomings, Lady Steelfox, you have always acted in our interest."

"I am glad you think so."

"If you are pressing me for advice, however, I do have a word for you. Pride."

"You are saying I have too much."

"No, Lady. You lack pride. The core of you craves praise, like a beaten dog. It leads you toward flamboyant action."

"Ha. Being Karvak is what leads me toward flamboyant action."

"As you wish. Here you are." They were before the gers. Northwing halted and looked around like a penned animal. "I find this encampment far too much like a city for my taste."

"Then go. Since you are so good with messages, tell Haytham to be ready for a demonstration as soon as fresh wheelships arrive. It will be within the hour. For that matter, you'd best be ready too."

"He'll pout like a child. He'll protest it's too soon."

"But he will do it. He has his own form of pride."

"As you wish, Lady."

As Northwing stalked away, Steelfox set Qurca to circling. Then she dismounted and gave her pony's reins to one of the khatun's soldiers.

The dome-shaped felt tents were arranged in a line, all doorways facing south. Fire-smoke puffed through the roof-holes. Most tents were the color of dry grass or cloudy skies or snow. The Great Khatun's was white with gold trim.

"You may enter, honored Lady of the Il-Khanate of the Infinite Sky," said the guard, "but mind you the Great Khatun speaks now with her poets."

The passage from outside to inside was a step from the most public of spaces to the most intimate. Light dimmed, sounds grew muffled, the chill tang of morning gave way to the warm earthy scent of the dung-fire. Movements had to be gentle in this place, for dried meat hung from rafters, cookware and supplies crowded the fringes, and the structure itself was always close at hand. Words in a ger were soft-spoken, for the tent was a crowded, hushed space, the defining opposite of the outside's eternal green and infinite blue.

The Great Khatun ruled a dominion comparable to Qiangguo in scope or to the Mirabad Caliphate in its prime. Yet instead of a palace she had this.

For a Karvak it was enough.

Steelfox prostrated herself, rose, and knelt beside the door on the western side. The old khatun nodded from where she knelt beside the fire. She who commanded the fates of countless lives was dressed and adorned much as Steelfox, with the exception that her hair rose taller and was more grandly greased and coiled. Her forehead shone with yellow makeup emphasizing her wise brow.

Her guests were not Karvaks but people of conquered lands. One was an Okcu, a relative of the far-flung folk of Qushkent and of the distant and possibly imaginary Sublime Sultanate. He wore furs, a sharply pointed hat, and thick mustachios. Around his neck was a simple charm of the Nightkindlers, an obsidian disk with an inset agate. Softly he said, "Great Khatun, I have spread word of your bloodless victory in the matter of the Peninsula of Seals."

"I hope you did not describe it as bloodless," said the khatun.

"Not at all. I composed many a stanza of slaughter and subjugation, and told of how the arctic sea grew so red that icebergs of blood will be seen from southern coasts for years to come."

"I am pleased. And you, Akinakhia?"

"I've told how you utterly destroyed the War Sages of the Five Islands," said a woman of the Oirpata, a tribe on the western fringe of the khatun's empire, where women dominated. Steelfox could not help squinting to see if the woman had indeed cut one breast from her body to facilitate archery, as some Oirpata were rumored to do. If so, Steelfox could not discern it beneath Akinakhia's tunic of golden plates. "I have described how the surviving army fled whimpering on their boats, to topple over the world's edge."

"That is well, since owing to bad weather we've barely been able to hold half of one island. And what word of the Northwest?"

A bearded man in chain mail and wolf's fur grinned. "Great Khatun, I have told how your annihilation of the city of Ingenstadt was reflected in the Mirrored Sea until the heavens wept at the devastation, accounting for the great hailstorm of last summer."

"I believe we acquired a small trading town called Ingen in that region," the khatun mused.

"That is all that's left! Of course, the story is more believable because I've spread word of wondrous Ingenstadt for three years now, even to the point of circulating curios."

"Ah, planning ahead. Well, I would be happier if you told of an actual battle. But we have not been able to mount much of an advance in your region, so it is understandable. I am pleased with your work, my poets and rumor-mongers! Go now to the Supreme Judge to learn of more recent events, and to consider how you may embellish them to strike terror in every soul."

The poets bowed to the khatun, and to Lady Steelfox, and departed the ger.

Steelfox prostrated herself anew. "I greet you, Great Khatun."

"Yes, yes, I am greeted," the khatun said rising. "Now come and hug your mother."

Steelfox embraced the most powerful woman of the known world. "I'm sorry I arrived only just last night, Mother. It's always difficult rousting enough Wind-Tamers to roll the fleet."

"Nonsense," said the khatun. "You're the first to arrive. Jewelwolf had best have a good excuse."

Steelfox felt a mix of rain and sun, as she often did at her sister's name. "A fleet is approaching," she said. "It might be her."

"I know."

"Our brothers are late too—"

Mother grunted. "Your brothers! They had desperately important drinking and sporting to do, I'm sure. I'm tempted to have my poets tell the truth about them. But that would be bad for the empire. The realm your father worked so hard to carve out of nothing. Well, no more of this. Are you hungry?"

Steelfox tried protesting that the ruler of the Four Directions shouldn't be making breakfast for anyone, but it was to no avail. Mother's habits were older than the empire, after all. Years ago she'd been no khatun but merely the wife of a minor chief, her clan on the edge of destruction. Much had changed, but not, in so many respects, Mother.

The fire was always going, and within the ger meat and vegetables were always close at hand, and soon mother and daughter were sipping soup and sharing news.

"It sounds as though the consolidation is going well," Steelfox said.

"Consolidation, yes. Expansion, not so much. Jewelwolf will likely have words for me about that. Her husband will too, though he's always careful with his words, that one."

"Jewelwolf speaks out of love for Father's dream. Not out of anger at you."

"What I love about you, daughter, is that you're always searching for the way out of the trap, social or physical. You don't want your family fighting, so you seek the verbal tactic to prevent it. You struggle at the limits of your assigned domain, half steppe and half taiga, and seek clever ways to enhance your position. I've heard about your pet inventor."

Steelfox let herself smile. "Soon you may more than hear."

"Intriguing! Earth and Sky know I could use diversion from the Parliament of All."

"I can well imagine."

"It is as it is. One never calls a Parliament for just one reason. There is the matter of a new Grand Khan, yes. But there are also marriages to arrange, armies to assign, delegations to receive, justice to be done. And love and sport, of course, as your brothers would remind me." This time the khatun did not sound so annoyed with her wayward sons. "Yet, none of these matters is as close to my heart as what I must say."

Dread filled Steelfox's own heart. She was about to be married off again.

Oh, there would be a pretense of choice, a dance of respect, but she and her mother both knew that Steelfox would ultimately accept the khatun's recommendation, for the good of the realm.

She hadn't chosen her late husband, a Reindeer Folk man, though in hindsight it had been a lucky match. He'd been kind to her, and she'd mourned when he perished in battle before fathering a child. She loved him most, however, for bringing her into the circle of his people—so different from the Karvaks but now so close to her heart. Steelfox had put off all other suitors, reasonably claiming she was unready, and that suzerainty of the Reindeer Folk and the bordering steppelands took all her time.

"Mother . . ."

"Hush, child. I'm not marrying you off. Although the eldest boy of the Cloud Arrow clan is brave and honorable, and worth a look—I am not yet food for scavengers, girl, so trust me on this—still. No, I am not corralling you, fox. I am giving you something to hunt."

Steelfox widened her eyes.

"I want you to see this." The khatun led her around the fire to a collection of chests, which even as a child she'd never been allowed to open. Her heart beat faster as the khatun opened the largest and most ornate, a lacquered, jade-inlaid chest marked with stylized cicada-shapes in Qiangguo style. Inside was clothing for moments of high import, weddings, funerals, treaties, and the anointing of khans.

The khatun rummaged through the clothing as though all the bright silks, velvets, and satins were just so many cleaning rags. Steelfox heard a click, and the sliding of some hidden panel. Her mother turned and raised up the strangest scrap of clothing Steelfox had ever seen.

It was the right sleeve of a dress, torn from its body by some unknown moment of violence, such that ragged tears still suggested the curves of shoulder and scapula. Its primary colors were green and brown and gray, and painted upon the shimmering fabric were suggestions of grasslands, deserts, and mountains, with blue rivers here and there, and dots for lakes, and dark pagodas marking cities, and the odd outlines of monsters. Many features were marked with a script, vertical like the Karvaks' but unreadable to Steelfox.

"Is it a dress, Mother? Or . . . is it a map?"

"It's perhaps both. I know a story about it. Not a true story, surely. But a story that may contain truth—a truth that may be of great importance for you. And your nation."

THE KHATUN'S TALE

When your father subjugated Madzeu, fox, I ruled there for a time. Now, your father mistrusted cities as he did dogs, mammoths, and men who swore only by Father Sky. Thus he stayed only long enough to secure the place and set off to conquer Qushkent. I wished our subjects to be happy so I promoted story-tellers and music. This is one story I heard sung.

Long ago there was a land beneath the ground, called Sham. In this place there was no light save what glowed from the magma pit at its heart or what shone from the magical crystals of the cavern roof. In this dim, ruddy gaze, human beings dwelled and harvested strange toadstools and stunted trees.

Into this land came one Bora, a girl of unknown origin. She was treated roughly by her adopted family, and so she dreamed of dancing at the Palace Outside, a citadel of crystal that peered up from the caverns of Sham, into the true light of day.

The kagan who ruled that palace announced a great gathering, and Bora dreamed of going, but her adopted family ringed her round with duties. Yet magical help came in the form of fire-fairies who wove her a dress of fire-spider webbing. And the dress had this wondrous property; it took on many colors and had the appearance of a map, showing the way Bora might take to journey to her unknown home. The fire-spiders meant by this to show Bora that her true journey did not end at the palace but would go on until she found her heart's desire.

Bora did not care about the fine points. Wearing this magical dress, Bora went to the great gathering.

In that place she danced with the kagan, a kind young man whom she loved at once. But she also beheld the upper world, gleaming green and blue and white like a vision from dreams. And because it was so unknown and so true, she feared it.

Bora fled from the Palace Outside. So panicked was she, she caught the sleeve of her dress in the gateway, and it tore, so that she had to leave it behind. It was all the kagan had by which to remember her.

As luck would have it, however, she left behind much more. For the gateway she'd found led not back into Sham, but into the very place that had terrified her, the wild outside world.

CHRIS WILLRICH   57

Now, the kagan is said to roam the world, carrying his heart in the form of Bora's torn sleeve, looking for the woman whose arm it fits. But of her fate, no one knows.

"This is clearly not fire-spider-whatsit," Lady Steelfox said after a moment of silence. "If that even exists. This is *ironsilk*."

The khatun nodded. "I believe the story takes many forms and has wandered many times up and down the Braid of Spice. It changes with each town and each year. I have even heard from Akinakhia one variation where the girl wears glass slippers. Yet I think there's truth in it. For I found within the royal treasury of Madzeu this sleeve."

"Why show it to me now?"

"A madman of the free desert town of Shahuang has this past year uncovered lost caves filled with paintings of times past. Among these is an illustration of a torn portion of this dress."

"Ah! Then the caves may point the way to more pieces."

"Indeed. And more pieces, together with mine, may just point the way toward a new source of ironsilk. News of this only just reached me via the poets, fox. I would send someone I trust to investigate this matter. You may consider it your last great venture . . . before I bind you to a new husband."

Lady Steelfox blinked. "I see much potential in ironsilk."

"Good. When the Parliament of All begins, my clever one, I want you to assign your vote to Jewelwolf, to use as she would."

"You trust her with this? Why should I not assign my vote to you?"

"I do not wish the Parliament to be troubled by any accusation of manipulation on my part. Jewelwolf is of the younger generation, and they will trust that your proxy is a well-intentioned one. Having done this you will depart on an errand I will concoct. But your true errand is the map. You and your sister have the keenest eyes and sharpest memories of all my children—and Jewelwolf is otherwise occupied. I must send you."

"I thank you, Mother. This is a true adventure, worthy of a Karvak. I won't disappoint you."

Mother nodded. "No, you will not." The khatun seemed to consider whether or not to say anything more. "I believe, fox, this Silk Map is more than a map. It is a story—the story of a woman's life. As such, I think it's an omen that the map is rent." She stood and stepped to the opening of the tent, looking south. "A woman yearns for a steady path through the years. At any rate, this one does. Yet there are always wars, sicknesses, famines, arguments. Deaths. There are moments when the sunlit path seems beset by storm, and the dark path lit by an unsuspected moon."

"Mother . . . I wish our customs . . . I wish you could remain khatun. Your rule's been wise. I wish we need not elect a khan."

The khatun turned. "Is that what you think I mean? Well. I thank you. But I was thinking of you. I think that to seek the Silk Map will be to experience such turnings and rendings. Perhaps sooner than you are ready for, my clever one."

This was Mother in her mystical vein, such as she'd indulged more and more often since the Grand Khan's death. Perhaps it was the burden of rulership. Perhaps it was age. Either way, Steelfox was impatient with it. She herself did not yearn for a steady path through life.

"I'm ready, Mother. If we can find the Iron Moths we'll have a strength that could make the world tremble. I can't yet tell you why. But I feel Mother Earth and Father Sky have brought me to this moment."

The khatun's smile was sad, and in that moment she seemed a very ordinary elder. "I don't think we are ever ready for what Earth and Sky have in mind. I acknowledge your courage, however. Your father would be proud."

"I wish I could believe so—"

She was interrupted by the ringing of a great gong. An officer walked into the tent. Despite the urgency inscribed in his stance, he bowed and shifted to the spot where Steelfox had waited patiently not long before.

"You may speak," said the khatun.

The man approached and prostrated. "Great Khatun, your daughter Jewelwolf is arriving."

"Thank you for your news. Make certain the encampment is prepared. Steelfox, go to your sister. Make her welcome."

That arrow's easier aimed than shot, Steelfox thought, but she said, "As you wish." She bowed and followed the soldier.

From the encampment the land rose gently toward the south. Steelfox bade her pony ascend. She saw Qurca's circling form drifting in kind. Her mind swirled as well; it was good to be in the wind again. She trusted her pony and loosened the reins, letting herself touch Qurca's perceptions.

The land receded below, like a collapsing green tent that puffed outward as it fell. The sun was well up as Jewelwolf's fleet came rolling in. Eighteen craft painted in bright colors, sails emblazoned with animal symbols, rolled upon their great wheels. Outriders on sabercats preceded the ships, mastodon-riders escorted the vessels, and the great mass of horsemen followed. Next came horse-drawn wagons carrying civilian gear, and last followed the woolly rhinoceroses and their brave riders, perhaps the toughest Karvaks of all.

The fleet could not have moved without the skill of the Wind-Tamers, one for each vessel. Steelfox could see them in their ribbon-bedecked coats, beating upon drums. The wind pulsed through the air like the invisible blood of the world.

Before the fleet even slowed, a woman leapt off the largest ship with a rope ladder, landing upon a pony brought up by group of riders bearing Jewel-wolf's red and gray standard. The riders galloped ahead of the ships and past the sabercats.

Steelfox broke her link to Qurca and halted, standing her ground against the advance of fleet and riders. As they reached her, she lifted her arm and Qurca alighted, screeching as the bannermen stopped, their ponies whinnying.

Only their leader's white mount made no noise but rather looked upon Qurca with a cold-eyed, nearly human appraisal. Aughatai had been Jewel-wolf's gift-beast almost as long as Qurca had been Steelfox's. The pony had much of Jewelwolf's character by now, and the two animals were never cordial.

"Lady of the Il-Khanate of the Eternal Green," said Steelfox.

"Dear Lady," answered Jewelwolf, dismounting.

They embraced. Jewelwolf dismissed her guards, who returned to the ships bellowing disembarkation orders.

"You are looking well," Steelfox said, as they walked toward Mother's ger.

"And you, elder sister," said Jewelwolf, "you seem well-favored as always." She smiled. "Shooting arrows at the sunrise again?"

"I have some catching up, to reach your level of skill."

"Oh, you're much too hard on yourself."

"I wish Father had heard you say that."

"I did tell him, frequently, though the winds of war roared loudly in his ear."

Once or twice, I'm sure, Steelfox thought. "How fares your husband Lord Rocklion?"

"He's well. Although he's somewhat preoccupied chastening the Xurian clans far to the east. While he dispatches them to Tawalisi across the sea, he dispatches me to vote in his stead." Jewelwolf sighed. "I suppose Mother would have preferred to see him, rather than me. With the exception of yourself, she's always preferred the conversation of men."

"Nonsense, sister. She'll be delighted to see you."

"Ever the diplomat. I admire your ability to rise above all frays. . . . So, she has not complained of my lateness?"

"Well . . ."

"Ah. I departed as soon as my husband could spare the ships, but I suppose Mother won't believe that."

"I believe you."

"Why, I thank you, elder sister." Jewelwolf's tone was airy and amused, as if implying Steelfox was surely insincere, but that Jewelwolf, as a true Karvak hero, would rise above it all.

It left Steelfox confused and irritated, as ever.

"You've added ships to the fleet," Steelfox noted, searching for a compliment.

"The four directions have sent me many Wind-Tamers," Jewelwolf said, a note of pride in her voice. "Dodderers and doubters claimed we couldn't form an organized school, but we found help on unexpected horizons. How fares your own fleet?"

"We do well enough," Steelfox said. *Of course you aim your words at my il-khanate's greatest weakness.* "I have an interesting addition myself."

"A new ship?"

"Something like that."

"Ah, Steelfox, always so many secrets. If you have something that can strengthen the realm, you shouldn't hoard it." Jewelwolf lowered her voice. "We've recovered from the disaster Father led us into. But vultures still circle the realm."

It always perplexed Steelfox that while Jewelwolf had been Father's favorite, Jewelwolf had, in the end, held the Grand Khan in contempt. "You'll see it soon. As for secrets . . . you're right, sister. I would speak of something before we reach Mother's ger."

"Oh?"

"Mother's sending me away on an errand." Steelfox could not keep the pride from her voice. "Something I must do immediately. She's asked me to give my vote to you."

"Me?" Jewelwolf sounded suspicious. "Surely she knows I'll support my husband as a spur supports a foot. And respect him though she does, she's never liked him. What does she scheme?"

"I see no scheme. Mother, as khatun, might well elect someone she doesn't like, if it were for the good, as you say, of the empire."

"But she's always championed Eldest Brother. That drunken lout who only wins battles by accident. There's intrigue here."

"You always think people are plotting."

"People always are. You, living among your Reindeer Folk, half animals themselves, have the luxury of believing otherwise. Mother is sending you away because of that. Because she knows you might emerge from Parliament disgraced. Or dead. That much makes sense." Jewelwolf nodded to herself. "You were always her favorite. What did she say, that you have some magical treasure to find? The First Forge of the Steppes? The Scepter of the Archon of Night?"

Steelfox's face burned.

"Aha!" said Jewelwolf. "Ah, sister. Still drunk on fairy tales like our brothers sucking down kumiss. But indeed I envy you. I'd love the opportunity to leave all my responsibilities and gallop off on a mad quest. Alas, some of us must consider matters of war."

It was hard to maintain composure around her younger sister. Keeping her voice steady around a shaman was comparatively simple. "I trust my khatun," Steelfox said. Yet she thought, *What if it's true? I'm a blunt instrument, and I do hate politicking. What if this Silk Map's something Mother invented to keep me busy? What if I'm just an idiot?* But she said none of this aloud, rather, "War? Do you mean something beyond your husband's 'chastisement'?"

"Our mother has a quiver of admirable traits, sister, but her bowstring's broken; she's too peaceable. With a new Grand Khan—and of course I mean for this to be Rocklion—we'll again be ready to invade the trading cities, and

Yao'an as well. This very year, perhaps this very season, we'll leave off the thin gruel of skirmishes and toss the poets some meaty war tales, as bloody flesh before wolves."

"As at Hvam?"

"Do you expect me to feel shame at that name?" Jewelwolf scoffed. "Have you forgotten Firegold?"

"I mourn the best of our brothers. But the truth is, the Hvammi got a lucky shot in. Heartened, they refused to surrender. In this, they behaved just as Karvaks would."

Jewelwolf made a dismissive wave. "City-dwellers have no more claim on martial honor than mice have a claim on the clouds. They choose to live as penned animals, and at our discretion they can be slaughtered as such. Your remarks reveal you've no heart for battle—as our father concluded. Don't feel ashamed. It's not for everyone, not even every Karvak."

Steelfox did not take the bait. "You seem different, sister."

"A good difference, I hope."

"You seem like a honed blade." *And a bloodied one.*

"Good. Yes, I have been learning much of the wider world. My horizons go on and on. I've seen the outlying nations at Rocklion's side. Like Mother, I've entertained poets and scholars." Jewelwolf hesitated before leaning close. "Unlike Mother, I've treated with sorcerers, and learned much from them."

"I will not repeat that."

"Thank you. I hoped you might understand, you who know the Reindeer Folk and their strange ways. I've searched for knowledge farther afield. I've encountered a cabal of sorcerers, one from the frozen North, one from the steaming South, the last from the stormy West. They've convinced me that an alliance might be beneficial."

"To whom?"

"Ha! Their lands are far too remote to threaten us, but my generosity aids them in securing various rare substances for their works. And they for mine. Already their assistance has improved the training of my Wind-Tamers. I could take matters further. Much further. But for now I think Mother would be squeamish." Jewelwolf shook her head. "Alas for foolish taboos. We're willing to lose thousands in battle, when a single human offering to higher powers could secure us a bloodless victory."

Something was agitating Qurca. His claws dug painfully through Steelfox's thick sleeve. She could hear her own heartbeat. "Father forbade such things."

"Sister, no one respects Father's memory more than I! But he tried the scrupulous path toward conquest. He failed. We nearly lost the empire. His methods will keep sacrificing honorable Karvaks to the cowardly schemers of Qiangguo and their ilk, time and again. Mother hides from the truth, but she knows the world laughs at us. Perhaps that is why she's willing to support Rocklion."

Qurca's mind was shrieking at Steelfox now. Images blew into her mind like evocative clouds ahead of a storm: a broken wing, a beak crushed against the ground, an egg cracked before its time, a peregrine turned to carrion. If she could translate the images into Karvak they might say, *Wrong, wrong, wrong!*

At the same moment, Aughatai was staring at the bird. Steelfox clicked her tongue and raised her arm, and after a moment's reluctance the falcon flew off.

"Trouble controlling your gift-beast?" Jewelwolf said.

"It is morning and I haven't been letting him hunt."

"He's always caused problems for you," Jewelwolf said thoughtfully. "I remember his hatching."

"Naturally."

Steelfox remembered the calm, grave voice, so much more devastating than any shout. *Look, my daughter, look how your falcon has emerged into the light. Let your fears ease. I know now, what I should have realized. You are not a baatar. Not a hero. There is no shame in that, my beloved girl. Take your bird and go now to your mother. Jewelwolf, attend me.*

"So here you are, sister, a baatar . . . talking of human sacrifice."

"Say what you will, our shame shall be ended, sister, whatever it takes." Jewelwolf paused and gazed south. "As it was at Hvam, so shall it be in Anoka, and Yao'an, and all the rest, if we are defied. And perhaps, for one example city, it shall be as Hvam whether we are defied or not. We'll claim their feeble fortifications and ring them round as we would the prey in a great hunt. All that breathes within shall live only at our sufferance. We'll let some escape: those with wit to flee and others who have talent. The rest we'll destroy, and the skulls of men, women, children, and animals will rise as monuments, and the smoke of their former flesh will writhe as a black banner upon the wind. For even the greatest army is weak if it cannot boast fear as its herald."

"Does your husband have a taste for such work?"

"He's learning. I consider myself a gifted teacher. I look forward to instructing my sons."

"The Grand Khan wasn't pleased with your handling of Hvam."

"Though you are my elder sister, it is not your place to criticize me in Father's name. You were never a baatar. He was right to send you to the taiga." Jewelwolf's voice softened. "You will always have an honored place, sister. But times are changing. You belong with your Reindeer Folk, not upon the grasses or the Braid of Spice. There in the shadows of the forests is where your destiny lies. Not in the bright glare of battle."

Something cold entered Steelfox's voice. "I may be no baatar. But I am our father's daughter. And I give him and our mother the respect you never did. If there's war, I'll distinguish myself in it. There is more than one way to prove one's worth."

She said these things, and perhaps Mother Earth and Father Sky heard her, or perhaps she'd already seen the shadows falling on the grass. Either way, the timing could not have been better.

Guards were shouting, and early risers among the children were pointing, as shapes emerged from behind Mastodon Mountain and climbed the eastern sky. Haytham ibn Zakwan had followed instructions and had positioned himself for a dramatic entrance. In fact, there he was in his white robe, waving theatrically down at the Karvaks beside the drumming Northwing.

I may be no hero, sister, but I can fly, Steelfox thought, as the shadows of the great balloons, carrying their flying gers, fell upon Lady Jewelwolf's astonished face. *All the way to the Braid of Spice.*

CHAPTER 3

IN THE ALLEY OF THE SCHOLARS OF LIFE

From a distance the city of Yao'an appeared to Gaunt as a squarish crystal covered in dust, some manner of mirror perhaps, shattered into myriad glass rhomboids and painted brown by the winds from the western deserts. Here at the northernmost foothills of the Worldheart Mountains, looking down on their destination, she fell to her knees. A month of hard travel had finally brought them to Yao'an, and this was only the threshold of their true journey.

Bone staggered up behind her and fell onto his face amid the dry grass. He coughed dust. "Well. We've arrived at the Jade Gate. We've accomplished that much."

"We walked, Imago," Gaunt murmured. "All we did was walk. We're good at that by now."

"Yao'an," said Snow Pine as she caught up to them. She sat cross-legged upon the hilltop. "When I was a girl I'd sometimes hear the saying, 'Beyond Yao'an, you will never taste springtime.'"

Snow Pine had said the Braid of Spice was not a literal road, for no authority had ever managed to maintain a highway all the way from Qiangguo to the Midnight Sea. But Gaunt did perceive three roads in this place at least. One stretched westward into dry country beyond a broad, willow-lined, muddy river. That river flowed north into a gray-and-tan expanse of desert before vanishing into a haze that blurred both horizon and sky, and a curve of the Red Heavenwall followed the waters north, with a narrow cart-path running between like a child running to keep up with her parents. To the east a broader road meandered beside the Heavenwall, passing into green grassy land dotted with scrub, eventually vanishing into better-watered territory patched with forests.

The travelers had emerged from similar country weeks ago to enter the wilderness leading to Five-Toe Peak. At that time they hadn't even come near Yao'an.

"A city," Bone mused in a voice he usually reserved for gems or gold. "Wine. Gossip."

"Food that isn't dry as sand," Snow Pine said, "or tough as sandals."

"A bath," Gaunt conceded.

Before long they were descending the hill as fast as they dared, billows of dust following them like a pack of thirsty, hungry, filthy dogs. At heart Gaunt was a city girl. She'd never let go her writing gear or at least three books, and crumbled in her pack was much-abused black clothing she considered her "escapade outfit," something suitable for both rowdy nightlife and the less-combative form of caper. She'd never wear it in a fight (unless a plan went very wrong), but it was worth the extra weight to clutch that much of her past.

Yet closer in, Yao'an revealed itself a doubtful source of rowdy nightlife. It was an orderly collection of thousands of buildings, laid out in the four-section pattern beloved of Qiangguo. Three high walls formed a *U*, closed at the top by the even taller rampart of the Heavenwall. The city lay at the spot where the Wall bent northward, so that no force appearing from the north or the west could afford to ignore it. Gaunt caught a glimpse of the two great markets—the Eastern, with its goods gathered from various provinces of the Empire, and the Western, with luxuries carried across the Braid of Spice.

Her heart hammered, and it was more than the plunge down the hill and onto the dry, cracked land bordering Yao'an. It was more than the thought of a few fleeting comforts.

Somewhere in this city, someone might know about ironsilk, and the story of Xia.

The walls loomed higher, and very few buildings rose outside. Most farmland here lay eastward. The few constructions to the west were caravanserais, filled with camels and merchants either newly arrived or soon to depart. Three stone watchtowers lay southward between the city and the foothills. One belched smoke as the travelers neared the Southern Gate.

Close up the city walls looked to be of brick and rising six yards overhead, topped with crenellations, flags, and soldiers. The guards at the gate seemed bemused.

"You came from the hills?" said their commander, imposing in steel armor formed of many small and interlocking bits that each resembled the three-pronged character for 'mountain.' "You don't seem like hillfolk, with their bright costumes and tasseled hats, smelling of yak milk. Now you," he continued, studying Snow Pine, "look like a girl from back east, in the Littoral. And you two, you look like death."

"Death's a country by the western sea," Bone said, "a pretty place, but never drink the water." But he said it in his native tongue.

"What are you babbling?" the guard asked.

"He says," said Gaunt, stepping on Bone's foot, "our caravan was hit by sandstorms and we're the only survivors. We stayed in the mountains out of sheer terror. That's where we found our guide."

"I got lost in the mountains months ago," Snow Pine said. "My poor parents were eaten by Bashe-snakes. May we enter the city, burn incense for the dead, and drown our sorrows in wine?"

"You need to pay to get in," said the guard. "Maybe a little extra because I don't trust you."

Luckily they'd left civilization with modest money belts, and one virtue of monster-infested wildernesses was that they were cheap. Gaunt plucked a few coins, and they clinked together in the commander's palm. He frowned and nodded, and led them into a guard shack where all their daggers and Snow Pine's sword were sealed into their sheaths with wax, a complicated imperial chop impressed into each. Gaunt's bow was bound with rope, every inch of which held similar calligraphy, and the knots were sealed with wax and pressed with the chops. The arrows were left alone.

"A weapon with a broken seal," said the guard commander, leading them back out, "is the mark of a miscreant and will make trouble for you. Seeing as you don't have travel papers, you'll want to get to the Western Market, and fast. Someone there might give you lodging. Otherwise the informal fees will stack up. That's free advice." He waved them through the gate.

"Do you need to pay to get out?" Bone asked in the Tongue of the Tortoise Shell, just as they were stepping through the gate.

"Not if you leave by the Western Gate," said the guard. He frowned as he realized Bone had understood him the entire time; however, by then they had mingled with a crowd of women in multicolored patchwork dresses and men in long-sleeved robes with circular collars. The guard grunted and returned his gaze to the mountains.

Gaunt and Bone attracted stares from the people on the wide stone street—nothing hostile, simply surprised attentiveness, as if a mated pair of tropical birds had suddenly descended and begun talking about the weather. Snow Pine, with her rumpled cloak and fierce expression, earned almost as many puzzled looks.

"Let's get to the Western Market," Snow Pine said. "That's the only place you'll blend in."

It was strange, Gaunt thought as they made their way toward the bell tower at the city's heart, they'd been dwelling much deeper into Qiangguo than this border city, and yet she hadn't felt so much appraisal as now. But they'd kept to small towns and rough corners of big ones, places where people were willing to overlook useful foreigners.

The sun was descending, and despite the stares they quickened their pace. Even Snow Pine wouldn't want to be caught unsheltered in this unfamiliar city's night. The noises and colors and scents were overpowering after so much time in the wild. It seemed to Gaunt she heard thousands of shuffling feet. She smelled sweat, dung, meat, spices. She saw crimson banners and roofs, golden doors, black clothing, and wood everywhere. It seemed Yao'an's people either loved wood or didn't expect to be staying in one spot forever. Only the frequently encountered walls of the city wards were of stone. These were four yards tall, gated and guarded.

Bone echoed her thoughts. "I feel as though I'm in a stockyard," he said.

"Yes," said Gaunt, "a giant stockyard, six miles on each side."

Snow Pine sounded uneasy. "This city feels more controlled even than the capital," she said. "Perhaps because it was built in a more warlike time, and it still guards against invasion."

"I'm surprised anyone dangerous lives out in that desert," Gaunt said.

"Well, beyond the desert, to the north, are the great grasslands. There are nomad tribes, some dangerous, some not." She ceased speaking as they came to a gate. This too called for an informal fee. Gaunt began thinking she was in the wrong business. They entered a ward devoted to the business of tradesmen and minor merchants. The rogues passed the shops of bakers, butchers, grocers, tailors, and carpenters. There were small gardens and peddlers' carts. They saw a low-rent alchemist's office with jars of peculiar substances stacked on shelves beside the street for passersby to marvel at. Bone lingered a moment, looking at flickering fire-gems, such as might be handy for illumination.

Gaunt took his arm, and Snow Pine said, "Those are unreliable-looking, Bone. Prone to explode." As Bone shrugged and went on, Snow Pine continued, "So, the fiercest steppe-riders nowadays are the Karvaks. In my parents' youth they conquered the trading cities to the west, but Qiangguo drove them out again. We know they could return. We're raised on bloodcurdling stories of their atrocities."

"And thus you must trust your protectors," said Bone, "and grease their pockets liberally."

"I don't love our rulers, Bone," Snow Pine said, "but I'm smart enough to know there's more than one source of evil in the world, and that they're not all equal."

As if to underline her argument, the next two gates let them pass without bribes. Twice they crossed gently sloping bridges where canals sloshed beneath. After the first crossing they saw more elaborate buildings—temples to various deities of the Celestial Court, buildings of civic administration, homes of the moderately prosperous. Here and there they saw an odd motif in the architecture. Three rabbits or hares were arrayed in a circle, as if they were running endlessly within the span of a wheel. The ears presented a subtle illusion. Each animal's ears pushed into the very center of the wheel, one swung backward, one swung forward. Each ear was shared with that of a different hare; the backward swinging one was also the forward swinging ear of the hare behind, while the forward swinging one was also the backward swinging ear of the hare ahead. Thus, while each animal seemed to possess two ears, the tableau of three rabbits portrayed only three ears in total, forming a sort of aural triangle at the picture's heart.

"Interesting," Gaunt said, after they'd noted a handful of these images. "Is there a special meaning to them?"

"Not that I know of," Snow Pine said. "I guess I've seen this motif once or twice before, but I never thought anything of it. There sure seem to be a lot of them here in Yao'an."

They zigzagged their way through the wards, some prosperous, some destitute, some welcoming, some suspicious. The sun became a half-circle sliced by city walls. A rich, heady smell crept into their noses as the shadows welled, that of thousands of cookfires all over Yao'an. Three stomachs groaned their way through two remaining wards until they found a gate to the Western Market. This called for a bribe even larger than the one at the Southern Gate, as though the guards sensed Gaunt and Bone were placing themselves in more danger with every new inch of afternoon shadow.

"Do you know what I hate most about petty corruption?" Bone said. "That it hardly ever has a central, plunderable vault."

"Hush," Gaunt said.

As the Westerners grumbled their way into the Market they were blasted by sound and color. Even with people departing the place to beat curfew, it was hard to find space to maneuver. There were some last, frantic trades being conducted at the top of the lungs, over such spices as nutmeg and coriander and saffron, over furs of otter and lynx and snow leopard, and glinting bottles of strange herbs, peacock feathers, and jewelry crafted from turquoise and gold and jade, parchments with rubbings from famous temples along the Braid, and glass marbles embedded with "evil eyes" of every hue.

There were griffin-hides and carapaces of giant ants. There were slabs with bizarre fossilized creatures within. There was a ship's wheel of immense size fashioned of black rock, carved along the rim with spidery glyphs. There was a clump of sand contained within a jar sealed with cork and a mysterious rune; the sand whipped and swirled like a live thing.

This was all bewildering enough to Gaunt, but by now much of the Market had transitioned from business to entertainment. There were stage magicians who were swallowing knives and spitting fire. There were sorcerers who were swallowing fire and spitting knives. There was a troupe of musicians performing with voice, flute, and fiddle from a platform atop a ridiculously large, and astonishingly patient, camel. There was a troupe of acrobats forming human pyramids, and walking on stilts, and juggling glass bottles filled with scorpions. The performers were cheered on by the denizens of the Market and by those elite citizens of Yao'an empowered to walk any ward at any hour. Gaunt had the feeling of a celebration only now commencing.

She looked around for someone to ask about it and found a grocer of Yao'an who was packing up her family's cart (she must have had appropriate papers for the gates.) "Madam," Gaunt said, or what she hoped was the equivalent, "is it always like this?"

"Huh?" The middle-aged woman looked a little dazed by a day at the Market. She took a moment to focus on Gaunt, and another moment squinting at Gaunt's auburn hair. She seemed suspicious. Bone took the opportunity to buy a few watermelons, and commenced handling them like an amateur juggler or a malfunctioning scale. The purchase seemed to ease the grocer's concerns. "No, respected outlanders," she said. "Business is down. It picked up today because Washing Day's tomorrow."

"Washing Day? What?" But by then the grocer had returned to her packing and corralling her helpers and children.

Snow Pine told Gaunt, "I should have remembered. This time of year they wash the images in the temples of the Undetermined." She pointed to three buildings at different corners of the Market, glinting with gold-plated statues. "They'll anoint the big images and bathe the little ones."

"The Undetermined certainly likes his statues," Bone said. "I suppose fame's no flaw if you're enlightened."

"Be respectful, Bone!" said Gaunt. He was normally an easygoing man, content to rob the rich and spend his gains among the poor. (Not give away, of course. Spend.) But he had a hard spot for religion, and as a wayward devotee of the Swan Goddess, at times that made her wince.

Moreover, they were surely surrounded by thousands of followers of the Undetermined, and she didn't want to test their serenity.

Snow Pine said, "Besides, Bone, most of those images aren't of the One himself. They're of his colleagues, the Thresholders, beings who compassionately help people toward enlightenment."

"I don't mean to mock," Bone said. "Everyone deserves a bath. Speaking of which . . ."

"Yes," Gaunt said, glad to be in agreement again, "we need to find an inn."

"One thought, if you don't mind," Snow Pine said. She began rapid, scattered conversations with people nearby that usually brought shrugs, but which sometimes resulted in pointing at various spots around the Market and beyond its Eastern Gate. Gaunt had a reasonable grasp of Qiangguo's language, but the speed of these exchanges left her far behind.

Snow Pine returned with a satisfied look.

"There are several sources for old legends hereabouts, but the best is one

Widow Zheng, who sells books not far down the great East-West Avenue. It's too late to consult her tonight, but she is out and about most days. Now, about that bath."

So they took up lodgings at the Inn of the Bright Future, only a modest step up from the Inn of Fond Remembrance next door, but at least the wood wasn't rotting. Having purchased a room and meals, they took bowls of noodle soup with pigeon eggs bobbing inside and sat on a bench outside the inn, watching entertainers and candlelight and the heavenly show of stars easing into view within the deep blue of evening. Bone sliced and shared one of his watermelons, and they felt warm breezes tickle the dribble down their chins.

For a time they could forget hope and worry for their children, and behave as children themselves.

At dawn they left the Market while its vendors were rising and some of its entertainers were snoring. They entered the city's great east-west road. Gaunt found it wider, cleaner, and more pleasant than the various paths they'd taken the day before, especially with a civic garden to their right. Peonies bloomed, their pink blossoms shining where the early sunlight caught them.

"It's the Fourth Moon of the year," Snow Pine said, head turned toward the flowers, "the Peony Moon." Something hard entered her voice. "The peony's a sign of love."

Gaunt had a moment's grief for her widowed friend, but in the next moment she'd seen something more beautiful to her than flowers. There were many peddlers' carts parked along the street beside the garden. One collection of three had a sign above that might as well have been written in blazing characters: WIDOW ZHENG'S KNOWLEDGE EMPORIUM.

The carts were covered with books.

Gaunt stepped closer, hesitantly now, hardly believing her eyes. It had been a while since she'd seen so many works in one spot. Not just codices, but also scrolls, paintings, tablets, pamphlets . . .

Widow Zheng herself was a spry elder possessed of gray hair and a face that had seen rain and sand and war. Her gaze twinkled like a fisherwoman who'd felt a tug. Though slight of build, she unleashed a voice that bestrode the wild territory between a noble's peroration and a carnival barker's shout. "Knowledge! Rumor! Accounts of Ancient Days! Tales of Bandits and Kings! Yours for a Pittance!"

"We do not have a pittance . . ." Bone cautioned a little hopelessly.

"These things can be negotiated," Gaunt said, drifting closer to Widow Zheng's treasures.

"Aiya," Snow Pine said, twisting her hair.

Gaunt's gaze flitted over a menagerie of books, some proclaiming their contents, some not.

"You may open them, my dear," said Widow Zheng, her voice now conspiratorial. "I know a fellow worshipper when I see her."

"You must understand," Gaunt said, "where I come from your cart would be considered a treasure-house." She quickly passed hands and eyes (and nose, oh, the scent of paper, leather, and papyrus) over such works from Qiangguo as *The Nightmare of the Crimson Citadel,* and *Lamentations of the Great Historian,* and *A Partial Reconstruction of the Classic of Music, from Such Fragments as Were Recovered from the Burning of the Books.* There were alien texts as well. Some were in the flowing script of the Mirabad Caliphate, which Gaunt regretted never mastering. Others were in languages she did not recognize at all. However, her mouth watered over foreign books translated into the Tongue of the Tortoise Shell: *A Mirror for Young Despots* and *A Discourse on Light and Darkness* caught her eye, as well as an absurdly fat codex titled *The Epic of the King Tutored by Wolves, the Savage Abridgment.*

"You have a lot of books for someone with no shop," Snow Pine dared to muse.

"Or outside a market," said Bone.

"Ah, well," Widow Zheng said, "I am fond of markets, but they are raucous places; here I can think. As for a shop, moving around a little protects customers who may not wish to be seen perusing the wares." She patted a book labeled *Precepts of a Moral Existence,* whispering, "Unconventional people such as yourselves might appreciate the forbidden novel *The Sweet Blossoming of Plums.*"

Snow Pine looked thoughtful, and Gaunt smiled. (Bone was poking around nearby, muttering something about treasure maps.) The book sounded intriguing to be sure, and she suspected many a respectable home boasted a discreetly shelved copy of *Precepts of a Moral Existence*. Still, they only had so much coin and pack space, and though drawn by such words as *Sweet*, her heart was stirred more by notions like *Nightmare, Burning, Wolves*. Such was her nature. Yet most of all they needed intelligence about the Braid of Spice.

"Do you have anything about the Western Road?"

"Hm. Not much, I admit." Widow Zheng plucked *Lamentations of the Great Historian* from the shelf. "This is probably the best. It includes a biography of the famous Envoy Da, whose four-year expedition to the West turned into forty. It always sells well. However, it must be admitted it's centuries out of date."

"Centuries!" Gaunt said. "Are there no more recent accounts?"

Widow Zheng said, "You must understand, most of my customers seek sensations, not facts as such. An old account is full of wonders and hearsay, and can transport you to a different realm. As such it provides amusement for the elite and escape for the commoner. Current facts aren't the province of readers but of traders, who write nothing down but figures. Or of the regional governor, who keeps such facts to himself. Still, I suppose the mountains and the desert are still the mountains and the desert, even after five hundred years."

Gaunt absorbed that figure, then handed over the sum of Widow Zheng's next figure. Gaunt gripped her prize like a dog with a bird. She hoped she'd like the taste.

"I don't suppose," Snow Pine said, "it says anything about a fiery mountain in the West."

Widow Zheng's expression grew distant. "How strange. I thought I was the only person interested in such stories. No, Envoy Da never speaks of such a mountain. But once he describes an abominable roaring whose source he can never confirm, and days of ash-filled skies, and sunsets of a beautiful yet bloody hue."

"As though a mountain had burned," Gaunt mused.

"I do wonder. Ever since I was a girl I have loved a particular story about such a mountain. I will tell it briefly, as you are paying customers."

WIDOW ZHENG'S TALE

Somewhere west of the sun, east of the moon, in the marvelous land of Maldar Khan, there lived a girl named Hui. She was a poor girl who'd appeared out of nowhere one day and was taken in by a kindly widower who eventually adopted her as his daughter. Now, the land of Maldar Khan lay upon mountains so tall the sun passed nearby to warm their peaks every day, and thus snow never formed on the heights, only the lower slopes. Maldar Khan's people fashioned clever bridges of ice down below to connect their peaks and delved tunnels in the rock to serve as cities, while the mountaintops were a paradise of farms and gardens. Hui lived on the remotest peak, where there were only a few farms, but it was also the second tallest, and thus she had a clear view of Maldar Khan's peak.

Only on that one mountaintop was a great construction permitted, and Maldar Khan's temple-palace was a glory of the world, a thousand-windowed fortress covered in gold. The fortress was sometimes mistaken by those far below as the morning or evening star.

The lands of Maldar Khan were lost in haze to the rest of the world, but the khan possessed a fantastic crystal lens with which he could view all the doings of humankind. And at noontime, should wrath ever possess him, he could use the lens to focus the rays of the sun and bring fire and woe to the lands below. But he had only one such moment of wrath, and that was yet to come.

Now Hui possessed one oddity aside from the strangeness of her arrival, and that was her collection of glimmering oval stones, whose origins were as mysterious as her own. She would sing to them and whisper to them and sometimes weep over them.

One day she told her father she must go on a journey to the tallest peak, Maldar Khan's peak, and as she had come into her womanhood, he could not forbid her. It was normal for young people to make pilgrimage to the temple-palace, and sometimes they met their future spouses thereby. Yet Hui's father feared for her, for while he loved her, her origins were mysterious, and she appeared foreign and strange.

Hui filled a pack full of food and her strange rock collection, and journeyed down to the empty tunnels of that peak, crossing its sole ice bridge.

Of her many exciting encounters, with snow serpents and wind sprites, with corrupt townsfolk on the next peak and with shadow-squids in the tunnels, I could talk the whole night. But suffice to say she reached Maldar Khan's peak and joined the throng of young people always milling about the temple-palace.

Now Maldar Khan was the name of the holy ruler—as it was the name of his father and his father's father. For it was not held in that land that a holy man must avoid a woman's touch. And indeed, the young Maldar Khan had a growing interest in women and had announced a bright and beautiful gathering of dancing and merriment, for he thought by this means to discover his future wife. And all the youth were speaking of this event that would come the following month, and by which they too hoped to divine the face of a new beloved.

Thus preoccupied, no one noticed when Hui slipped away. For her object had never been the temple-palace but rather the highest pinnacles of that peak. Hidden by twilight she buried her stones there, for a purpose only she knew.

But while she knelt upon that height, she chanced to look toward the temple-palace. Maldar Khan was polishing his great lens, and for the moment it was reversed in its mounting. By some magic of timing and clear mountain air, she looked through the lens and glimpsed the young man's thoughtful face. She was smitten.

Her thoughts turned for the first time to the glittering gathering a month hence. She could attend, for all were invited. But although no one starved in that wondrous land, she was poorest of the poor, and she didn't believe she could join the others' merriment in her tattered garb. She returned home, hoping with her father's help she could weave a suitable dress.

When she returned, Hui was shocked to learn that in the intervening weeks her father had remarried, for in Hui's absence loneliness had clutched at his heart like a cold mountain wind. He had married a passionate but selfish young woman of a neighboring peak, one who was just discovering that married life involved work. The arrival of a dutiful daughter stirred conflicting feelings in Hui's new stepmother. On the one hand, she was jealous that her husband had affection for anyone else.

On the other hand, she saw in Hui an able servant.

Thus began a time of torment, for her stepmother piled chore after chore upon Hui, and her father seemed too bewitched to defend her. She was forbidden to attend the gathering, and soon there was no time to make the journey, let alone a dress.

Yet there were forces who took pity on Hui.

Strange fairy butterflies came to her. They wove her a dress of magical silk and carried her off to the palace, all in one night. They warned her of one thing, however—at midnight her magical silken dress would turn to iron.

At the temple-palace Hui laughed and sang and danced with the khan himself, and he was dazzled by this vision of beauty. Just as she worried about the time, the khan invited her to his observatory. How could she say no?

He entranced her with talk of strange lands and distant stars; and she entranced him by listening and sharing her own ideas. It turned out she knew far more of distant places than any in his realm, and he marveled at her learning. So taken were they with each other that Hui lost all track of time.

Suddenly her dress turned to iron.

Now, there were guards near the khan everywhere he went, and they were sworn to defend him. Thus when his strange guest's silken dress turned at once to armor, or so they thought, they believed an assassin had snuck past them. In fear and shame they charged the startled Hui, and in that moment of confusion she tumbled off the balcony of the observatory, which rose from a sheer precipice. The khan grabbed at her iron collar, which snapped as Hui plunged. Hui fell to her death upon a snowy peak far below.

Strangely, the collar had turned back to silk. Maldar Khan tied it around his neck and never removed it.

The khan's misery knew no bounds. He believed he'd found the love of his life, only to lose her. The following noon he trained his blazing lens upon the peak that was her grave, making the glaciers weep. Day after day he sent deadly rays upon that mountain, until they awakened an ancient fire within. To this day it belches flame and smoke, so that sometimes all of Maldar Khan's realm, and even lands beyond, can see what darkness he carries in his heart.

Gaunt and Snow Pine shared a look. "That was a sad tale," Snow Pine said, and Gaunt added, "And a strange one."

Bone said, "There are many details that perplex."

"Indeed," said Widow Zheng, "it's often that way with old tales."

"Do any versions give directions to that land?"

"'West' is all they say. But you don't think it's a real place, do you?"

Bone shrugged. "You said traders might have better intelligence," Bone said. "You've seen them come and go. Who would you consult with questions about the Braid?"

"That would depend greatly on what I wanted to do, youngster. And how you are asking."

Bone smiled and bowed. He passed her a coin. Gaunt saw him wince a little. It wasn't a pittance. "Suppose what you wanted to do, Grandmother," he said, "was buy yourself a little something, and what *I* wanted to do was hunt treasure."

Zheng grinned and pocketed the coin. "This old body's impressed by your courtesy, outlander. Treasure hunting, eh? Sounds exciting." She lowered her voice. "Perhaps you're in the market for Living Calligraphy? I'm skilled in the art. I have scrolls that can shed light, and scrolls that can capture wild animals, scrolls that heal wounds, and scrolls that can seek objects."

Bone's mouth twitched at her words, then frowned at the figure she quoted.

"Well, no matter," Widow Zheng said. "Now, as for informants . . . hm. The guy you really want is Katta. Crazy Yi, they call him around here. But he hasn't been seen in these parts in years. They tried to lock him up for attacking an official, but Katta was always slippery. They say he's blind but has a kind of sixth sense. They also say he probably won't be back. Which is too bad, because he knew the sands like a Karvak knows horses. And also because he was a cute fellow. Though word is he has no use for women—"

Gently, Snow Pine said, "Grandmother, are there any others you'd recommend?"

"Hm. Maybe you should look up Geshou Pi and Long Bi."

"'Singer Flint' and 'Dragon Brush?'" said Snow Pine. "Strange names."

"I don't think those are their real names," said Zheng. "They're foreigners like you two. Though they speak the language better, no offense. Treasure hunters too, to hear them talk. Always on the lookout for something shiny. They ply me with wine for stories sometimes." She smiled a little, at some memory. "And a little more in Long Bi's case."

"We don't have a lot of shiny," said Gaunt.

"Widow Zheng's looking out for you, children. Tell them I sent you. They're always badgering me for books, and I've loaned them a few. Remind them I'm expecting a couple back. They're in the Western Market, in a shadowy place between the Inn of Infinite Options and the shrine of the god of literature. It's called the Alley of the Scholars of Life."

Back at the Inn of the Bright Future, chewing on melon, Bone looked across the now bustling Market toward the place Widow Zheng had described. It was the most dilapidated area in sight. He gnawed on a rind.

Gaunt said, "Snow Pine. Friend. I ask that you stay here, with our gear."

"I'll remind you, sister, I'm the only one of us truly competent with a sword. And the only native of Qiangguo."

Bone chewed thoughtfully before sliding his belt so as to conceal a dagger beneath the wedge of watermelon in his lap. Covertly he broke the wax seal. He shifted his belt back to its normal position.

"True," Gaunt conceded. "However, it sounds as though these men are outlanders—not our folk, probably, but not yours either. As for trouble . . . Bone and I are used to playing that particular duet. But we'll want to be unencumbered."

Snow Pine looked for a moment as if she might argue. Instead she sighed. "And, this doesn't seem like a part of town one wants to abandon one's pack. Very well. Take the last melon along, Bone. When conducting business it's good to offer a gift. Given their offices, I doubt they'll be expecting jade."

"Mmph," Bone said agreeably, mouth full of melon.

There were a couple of turbaned people on the bench outside the Inn of Infinite Options, watching the ebbing activity of the Market, and a man in scholar's robes bowing at the shrine of the literature god, but it was otherwise a quiet nook. The alley between these establishments contained a few shadowy offices, marked with intriguing titles: *Jin Huang, knowledgeable about documents and dice games; Shi Lan, fearless soothsayer; Lei Chao, one who can apply sense into the thickest of skulls, and who has many brothers.*

Each was accompanied by an illustration—a pair of dice upon a scroll, a cicada upon a scroll, and a scroll hitting a head in the manner of a truncheon.

At the very end they found a door labeled in questionable calligraphy: *Geshou Pi and Long Bi, Lost Treasures, Lost Cities, Lost Causes.*

The illustration was of a hand clutching a scroll in an upright fashion, its tip blazing like a torch.

The door was slightly ajar, and there was a weak glow from an alchemical fire-gem. Gaunt knocked, and there was no answer. She pushed the door open with her boot. They advanced into the dim.

When Bone's eyes adjusted, he had two surprises.

The first surprise was that Geshou Pi and Long Bi, although dressed in robes mimicking those of scholar-officials, were from the remotest West. Not simply from far down the Braid of Spice, but from Gaunt and Bone's own part of the world. One was a tall man of light-brown visage, like the folk who populated the coast of the Midnight Sea, while the other was a stocky, pale man with a red beard fading to white—a fellow who might have hailed from Gaunt's own Swanisle.

The second surprise was that three strangely costumed figures were waving peculiar serrated swords toward the tall man, while a fourth held a dagger to the bearded man's neck.

CHAPTER 4

ÍNTERLUDE:
CONFESSIONS OF A
MAGÍC CARPET

O great one, you who have no doubt heard tales from Yao'an all the way to Mastodon Mountain, set aside whatever thoughts of treasure and violence fill your mind, and hear my own tale.

We say in Anoka that to fashion a carpet without flaw is to invite the ire of Heaven, for perfection belongs to the All-Now alone. If so, God and I are surely on excellent terms.

For look upon me, O new owner. Does it not appear as if a weaving contest had been conducted simultaneously upon one loom? Half my surface is given over to the geometric gul-patterns at your feet. See how they dazzle with blue like the turquoise of Anoka's domes, red recalling the plumage of birds from Qushkent, and white mimicking milky jade from the rivers washing Madzeu. Your gaze can thus soar through a cloud-streaked sky, captured at the moment afternoon sinks into the blood of sunset.

But look beyond, how the remaining half is a labyrinth of gray and jet and lapis lazuli, recalling not the colors of the bright cities but the countenances of the mountains that rear around the deserts of these lands, their snowmelt giving life to the trading oases or taking it away. Here your eye struggles like a weary caravan master evading war and brigands.

In me is embedded a tale of weavers laboring under the bellowing of contradictory magi. Direct your gaze, O dread master, to my middle, where the mountain-maze culminates in a vortex of white and red, the colors echoing neither jade nor birds but rather snows fringing the blazing caldera of the Bull-Demon Mountain. Behold how this ominous swirl is bisected by the cool sweep of the sky-pattern.

My edges are ragged and tell of a tug-of-war between two willful masters. A bloodstain upon my underside testifies to a resolution. Please do not turn me over to contemplate it, great one, but sit rather, and listen.

For more than one party seeks what you seek. Others hunt the Silk Map.

Now, my initial owners, before they decided out of prudence to soak me in lamp-oil and put me to the torch, argued about my conflicted nature.

"We have awaited its stirring for three days. We wait in vain."

"I spent sixty silver on it, woman. We can wait another day."

"I say we cannot, and that our money is wasted, and worse. It is an evil thing."

"I trust my eyes, not gossip. But very well. Let us sell it to the next caravan master who departs through the gold desert or the red. Mad Katta leaves soon. He will buy anything peculiar—"

"Gossip can save your life. Beside the well they say Mad Katta talks with demons and djinn. And they say the wizard Olob's tower burned because his apprentice Op turned against him. Neither have been seen again."

"What of it? That has allowed us to buy magic goods at fire-sale prices."

"With no magician to tell us what's bad about the goods. Here is what they say: Olob conceived the carpet as a way of awakening the Bull Demon of the great fiery mountain, whose smoke sometimes bloodies the sunset."

"I doubt its existence, as I doubt that of griffins, hydras, honest men, and oceans."

"Op did not doubt! You see upon the carpet his attempt to subvert the weaving into that of a harmless carpet of the sky, such as the wealthy fly in far-away Mirabad."

"Then he failed. The thing lies there by the window like a drugged cat."

"Yes, husband! It does not fly. So its nature must be corrupted by its original, evil intent. Here, I have oil, and the servant approaches with a torch. Let us burn it in the courtyard."

"It stirs! It listens!"

"Burn it now!"

Now evil is, as you know, O great and terrible one, quite a subjective matter, but for my first confession, let me admit I have a deceptive streak. In the dark of the night I'd already tested the limits of my mobility, and my owners hadn't noticed I was several inches nearer the window than when they'd first unrolled me. Interesting as their conversation was, I deemed it prudent to fly.

Yes, I can fly, after a fashion. Have you ever seen a plump chicken frightened by a small child who's thundering up to its coop? That mad skittering skyward to perhaps the height of the child's scolding mother? That undignified plunge into the mud?

I have perhaps half the grace. But I do fly.

Singed and smoking in a way that brought me still further from competition with the divine, I flung myself out the merchant family's window. Luckily they were prosperous and it was a high window. Unluckily that window faced a dilapidated alley. Colliding with refuse I twisted and rolled around a corner, seeking some haven.

Thus did I encounter the city.

Anoka! I have never returned, but I will never forget you, your minarets, your mosques, your sweating bazaars, your view of mirages and mountains, your coffee, your cinnamon, your oxen and your goats. I miss your bustle and braying and your still, quiet breezes. I miss the flutist playing a sad song to celebrate the dawn. It was in your alleyways that I learned myself, your celebration of the senses vibrating into my enchanted loops and knots. It was in your marketplace that I learned to travel, swishing low and bouncing off red stone like a wounded kite, inches away from the hands of urchins.

I would have known more of you, Anoka, but it is the way of a flying carpet, even a bad one, to ever be moving somewhere.

It was in desperation to evade the children that I plunged over a stone bridge crossing that mighty, lazy river that flows from haunted Efritstan to carve the mountains south toward Mirabad. There were scraps of arcane knowledge woven into me by makers, yet none of them whispered of *swimming carpets*. Perhaps I might have persevered, but immersion terrified me. As soon as I could, I squished and dripped exhausted onto a rocky shore innocent of people and rolled myself out beneath the sun.

Oblivion came to me for a time. I dreamt after a fashion, and my dreams concerned fire and incantations and screams.

I woke to rough hands grasping me and two desert-leathered faces squinting down upon me.

"I don't like this," said one face. "It's ill-omened. Do you see the burn marks? The blood stain?"

"Blood can be cleaned," said the other. "The burns are at the edges. This looks like something we could sell the caravans."

Darkness returned. When I woke again it was night.

I felt a great snugness, and it took me some time to recognize that I had been rolled up. In this condition the sensory spells woven into me were somewhat inhibited. I perceived that I stood outdoors, tipped against a stone wall beside many other carpets. The courtyard in which I found myself was filled with men, women, and camels, all illuminated by the flickerings of many cookfires and the steady glow of a gibbous moon. *A caravan staging area*, the thought came to me. These folk were passing to the East or West along what I recalled was fancifully termed the Braid of Spice. The night was chilly, save when a wind fanned the fires and brought me heat, smoke, and the scents of horse meat, beef, lamb, carrots, chickpeas, noodles. I heard a babble of relaxed chattering in half a dozen languages, but I could understand only the tongue of Anoka and that of Qushkent, the next great city along the Braid to the East.

"You are fully conscious?" came a calm voice, cold as the desert night, of a woman hidden beside the carpets. "You have come to your new awareness?"

Almost I answered. Much might now be different if I had.

But a rasping voice gave reply, male most likely, as if from a throat made of sand.

"I hear. I know."

"Listen carefully. I am empowered by ancient pacts with your master. You must obey."

"So you say."

"There is a man here. In this place he is known as Katta, but in your host body's city he is called Surgun. He has many names and many tricks."

"His image is in the meat's mind."

I was by now quite glad I hadn't spoken. I had to urge myself not to quiver.

"This is the hour when he likes to walk alone in the desert, beyond the city's protection. You will find him there, and hail him as a friend. You will take his life. On his person you will find a map painted upon silk. You will bring it to me."

"*The meat thinks it may not be so simple.*"

"You will take this."

"*That is no weapon. It is a rock.*"

"Rocks are not weapons? But look closer. Embedded within is the shape of an ancient nightmare from the days when these deserts were a sea. Throw this at your target, and it will awaken to claim him."

"*As you wish.*"

"Go now."

I heard one pair of footsteps shuffling away directly behind me, and another pair striding swiftly into the firelit dark. For a moment I was able to perceive the second individual, but only enough to glimpse a tall, bulkily robed figure swishing into the gloom.

I reposed there under the moon and stars until I was sure they were out of earshot, wondering. I vibrated myself a voice, just loud enough for the other carpets.

"Ah, hello?" I said in the language of Anoka. "I don't suppose any of you possess sapience and an interest in discussing a magical artifact's relation to the problem of complicity? No?" I repeated myself in the manner of Qushkent. Silence greeted me. Only the moon and stars knew I'd overheard the inception of some awful crime. Who could blame me for inaction? I am a carpet.

Yet dim memories of an explosion and screams still haunted me. Moreover, someone had recently tried to burn me alive. You could say it awakened a sort of compassion in me. Or perhaps it was a misdirected thirst for vengeance, draped in compassion's fabric. I am still not sure.

I shook myself out and skittered after the shambling form.

I didn't see my quarry and thought I'd best look for Katta—the Mad Katta my murderous owners had spoken of, as I realized. Although there were guards at the compound's gates, no one was specifically guarding the carpets. Keeping to the shadows, I hunted flaws in the wall and eventually wiggled through a crack out onto dry, stony ground.

I'm free, I thought. It seemed to me, under all the twinkling treasuries of Heaven, that the desert stretching gray and smooth before me was no barrier to one such as I, who needed no food, no water, not even shelter from the sun. True, I couldn't fly well, but perhaps I would improve. And what had humankind given me but moments of confusion and terror?

But, I thought, as the full desert chill rustled the sands and shivered my frayed and blackened edges, what is a flying carpet without someone to convey upon a quest? Someone to say, *Let's go find the djinn* or *Let's go claim a magic lamp* or *Let's go harass the thieves and earn the love of a sultan's daughter*. A flying carpet alone was like a pair of forgotten shoes. Why, hard-bitten feet were out there! Somewhere out there a hero needed a lift. Even if it would only carry her a handful of cubits.

And somewhere out there a man was about to be murdered.

The idea held a grim fascination for me, who had so recently been granted awareness. What did it mean to deliberately snatch away such a gift?

I was not fashioned to sigh, but I rippled.

My search took me out to slippery dunes, where I could gaze (in my fashion) back toward the staging compound, seeking figures in the moonlight. But I saw no one.

My hunt was cut short when, slithering like a snake, I triggered the collapse of a dune. To escape becoming a self-referential burial shroud I flew. The wind of the upper air whisked me toward the compound, and frightened of discovery I wrapped myself into a ball, thudding to the rocky region at sand's edge.

By the time I unrolled myself I was pinned by a wooden staff.

I tried gently extracting myself, making the motions seem random, as if the wind were responsible. But I couldn't budge.

The staff belonged to a man who seemed lively but for whom old age was surely over the next dune. He was darker than the men of my short experience, putting me in mind of lacquered wood. Outside his white desert robe he wore necklaces bearing peculiar metal charms.

The man said something in a language I did not know, and then, "Intriguing," in the manner of Qushkent. "This seems no ordinary theft; rather it appears someone cast my merchandise over the wall . . ."

At least the man did not have a voice like sand. Nevertheless I did nothing. Silence had been good to me so far.

The man knelt upon me and began behaving in what I considered a peculiar fashion. He patted me, running his hand over my surface as if searching for a lost key. "Hm," he said, and, "Well. I perceived you were a magical thing when I purchased you from those layabouts. Now I'm certain. You have iron-silk embedded in your sinew. But it seems you have a dual nature." He pushed his nose against my fabric and sniffed here and there. "And a violent history."

A strange thought occurred to me, and I was so struck by it, I spoke it aloud. "You are blind."

At once the man tumbled off me onto the ground, whipping up his staff into a defensive posture. He rose slowly, backing away in a measured fashion, his staff tracing a pattern like wings in the air. If not for his behavior earlier I would not have guessed his infirmity. As it was, I feared him, and I skittered skyward in my spasming manner, plummeting onto a low dune.

The man approached, murmuring what sounded like an incantation. I feared him all the more, thinking him a sorcerer.

"Spare me, Mad Katta, and I'll tell you a story!" I'd overheard the bedtime of my initial owners' children and had gotten the impression that was a good ploy.

He halted and lowered his staff. A smile flitted across his lips. "Very well, O magic carpet. Tell me a story."

Layali of the Tales, she who beguiled her sister's would-be executioner for hundreds of nights, would have been disappointed in me. I could have told at least one tale by now—my own—but my mind had gone entirely blank. Instead I found myself considering the nature of that emptiness. I wondered what my nature was. Could magical constructs truly have minds? Did we have souls, cherished of the All-Now? Having been fashioned by followers of the Testifier of God, was his religion mine too? Was it right to worship uncriti-cally in the manner of those you were born among? What would happen to me if the sorcerer destroyed me?

Such dizzied contemplations should have been the end of me indeed, but Mad Katta chuckled. "I perceive your answer, carpet. Unfolded beneath the moonlight, you reveal the tale that is yourself. Alas, while it's gratifying to graduate in Anokan eyes from 'Blind Katta' to 'Mad Katta,' your guess was true. I cannot see the patterns woven into your fabric."

"I can think of no story," I said. "Only fear."

"You needn't fear. Not me, at any rate. I sense nothing of Charstalkers about you."

"You need not fear me either, M . . . Katta."

He chuckled. "This much I'd begun to suspect. There is something marred about you, O carpet. You've seen woe, and more. Your making was botched, was it not? You're as one born maimed."

Something in his words aroused my ire. "It's easy to mock me, isn't it, O man? You who have full use of your limbs!"

Katta was speechless, his smile lost like a city buried under sands. After a moment he lowered himself to his knees. "I beg your pardon. I was inconsiderate."

It occurred to me he surely had frustrations of his own, he who could not perceive the beauty of shining sands beneath the moon. "You have my pardon."

"I am grateful. Yet I would give recompense. You presented the story of yourself, and it's no fault of yours I cannot perceive it. But now expectation crackles the air. Thus it is I who will speak, for something in your crafting hearkens to a tale of long ago and far away."

MAD KATTA'S TALE

Long away and far ago, there lived in the Country of Walls a girl named Xia who made ironsilk.

Now *silk*, you must know, for the cocoon of the bombyx moth, makes a prized cloth, fit for royalty. In Qiangguo they call it "woven wind." Had not a princess once smuggled silkworms in her hair on her way to marry the lord of Madzeu, Qiangguo would guard the secret still. But ever since that time, the cultivation of *ironsilk* has taken place only on a secret island in the heart of Qiangguo, the province of a particular and peculiar clan. There lie the caverns of the Iron Moths.

Xia was daughter of the clan chief by his late senior wife, and together with Jing, her half-sister by the second wife, it was her task to gather the cocoons of the Iron Moths and make of them bolts of ironsilk. Jing was lazy in this task, and Xia did most of the work, uncomplaining. Yet Jing always considered Xia spoiled and cruel, while envying the love her father felt for Xia. While Xia labored, Jing wandered the caverns, pitying herself.

Now, the Iron Moths are sapient beings but are unlike you and me. Legend has it their larvae arrived on this planet by way of a meteorite, and the crater of impact is now the lake guarding the forbidden isle. They worship a many-headed insectoid deity called Purpose, and they say that whatever face of Purpose lays eyes upon you when you eat your first rock, that is the aspect of the god you will follow. The Iron Moths bargained with the rulers of Qiangguo for the delivery of precious minerals with which to enrich their bodies, and in return the Moths offered themselves. The royal family possesses many a shield that was once an Iron Moth wing, many a sword that was once an Iron Moth leg, and even a few lanterns that were once shining blue Iron Moth eyes. Supple and strong, Iron Moth artifacts are gifts to kings.

But the true glory of the isle is ironsilk.

Once a Moth commits to Purpose, its caterpillar form chews upon rocks and minerals until it's ready to spin a cocoon. The silk of this cocoon is as supple as mundane silk, yet it responds to stress with the strength of iron. Its uses are endless. The Iron Moths willingly offered this material up as part of their bargain.

One day in her wanderings, Jing found an Iron Moth caterpillar and, motivated by a cruel impulse, carried the creature to Xia's mother's tomb.

She tossed the immature entity inside and told it, "Eat."

When the defilement was discovered, Xia's mother's sarcophagus and half the tomb carvings had been consumed, and the devourer was enshrouded in its cocoon, presumably dead, for conditions in the tomb weren't benign for the developing pupa. Xia and her father mourned anew. The tomb was sealed off.

Jing said nothing of her act, and from that day there was enmity between the clan chief and the Iron Moths. There came a bitter day when Xia's father argued with the Moth elders in the Cavern of Fire where the arrayed cocoons stayed warm above a bubbling pool of lava. Xia's father demanded more limbs and wings for the emperor's armory. The elders refused.

Enraged, Xia's father kicked a cocoon into the lava. The heat killed the pupa within. The elders responded by rending the man, his guts following the cocoon into the molten rock.

Xia was distraught. But some whispered that Second Wife was not entirely displeased. With no male heir at hand, Second Wife took command. She soothed matters with the Iron Moths but proceeded to terrorize the humans of the isle, Xia chief among them. Only her daughter Jing did she cherish—especially as Jing had discovered a secret.

During the chaos of the clan leader's death, only Jing noticed that when the ironsilk cocoon floated upon the lava, it unraveled without being cut by the emerging pupa. Ordering servants to bring tongs and pots, she fished the ironsilk from the molten rock and splashed it with water. When the steam cleared, she saw unbroken strands of ironsilk stretching on and on. Jing and Second Wife quickly realized that the longer strands of ironsilk would be of immense value.

Negotiations ensued. You and I might be astonished that some Iron Moth caterpillars would accept being boiled in lava. But remember that their god Purpose has many heads. Their elders realized that they could demand ever-richer minerals from all corners of the empire in return for the elongated strands of ironsilk.

Soon more and more caterpillars felt cajoled by the new face of Purpose.

But Xia wept. She loved her work and could not bear that these creatures, alien though they were, should perish for anyone's greed. She unsealed her mother's ravaged tomb, the only private place she knew, and she sobbed all the anguish of her short life.

"Daughter," came a voice from the old cocoon. "Heed me."

"Talking to yourself, old friend?"

Katta rose. "Mazhar?" For a moment Katta's posture was unguarded, as the man stalked out of the night, black robe swishing against sand.

Although younger than Katta, he'd also passed the halfway part of life's journey, and the sword he held, curved like a living thing, suggested he'd cut more than a few others' journeys short.

The newcomer spoke in the manner of Anoka, so it took me an instant longer than it should have to recognize the entity who'd referred to the body it wore as *meat*.

"Katta!" I cried, skittering toward the assassin. "You're in danger!"

The would-be killer was as startled at my approach as I'd been at his. The sword-cut that slashed at my patterns was hasty, and I fluttered backward, unharmed but cursing my awkwardness. Katta's earlier words had stung because they were true. Something about me was botched, and I envied any creature with full command of its body.

Yet it seemed clear Mazhar could not be said to have command of anything. Rather, the entity that now billowed like a cloud of noxious smoke out of his nostrils and mouth and ears, taking up a position above the warrior, was in command.

Tendrils of darkness still linked the black blot to the orifices of Mazhar's head. The cloud itself formed three spectral eyes blazing like bonfires seen through a sandstorm.

"*You're tougher than the meat believed,*" the three-eyed thing spoke through Mazhar's throat. "*But you will still die.*"

Clearly the threat was not directed at me. I felt oddly offended by that. I also wondered just what Katta was up to while I was busy saving his life. Directing my senses his way, I was chagrined to see he'd pulled out what appeared to be a sweetcake. He leaned over it as if preparing to nibble.

"Nourishment later, O living thing?" I shrieked.

Katta smiled. "All things perish. To one who has released attachment and embraced compassion, death holds no fear."

"The middle of a fight's no place for philosophy!" I replied.

Seeing as I'd get no help from Mad Katta, it seemed prudent to flee. Yet I'd gone to some trouble to save the fool, and I was loath to abandon him. And something about the story of Xia and the Iron Moths had tugged at my tassels.

But what could I do against a swordsman, let alone a possessed one? I am a carpet.

Yes, I thought, *I am a carpet*.

As I was slightly upslope from Mazhar, I rolled myself up as if for delivery and tumbled downhill.

Mazhar stumbled. He didn't fall but lost a few moments regaining his footing. I unrolled myself and sprang.

I heard Katta murmuring a prayer, or at least what sounded like a prayer:

Being is as one with Nothing
Nothing is as one with Being
Being is Nothing
And Nothing is Being

This seemed to sum up what help he would be being: nothing.

I engulfed Mazhar, and also the darkness that engulfed him.

At least one of those things would need air.

My strength surprised me, and I wondered uneasily what tasks the wizard Olob had truly envisioned for his carpet. Mazhar fell. He flailed and jabbed, but he lacked the space to make a worthy attack.

The thing of smoke and blazing eyes had other resources, however. I felt a great dry slithering within, and heat blazed upon me in three places. Fresh smoke filled the air, and the spells that gifted me perception now filled me with pain. It seemed fate wanted me fed to fires.

I unraveled, and Mazhar laughed. He had risen, an ornate circular cap tumbling from his shaven head, sword tracing designs in the air. *"Know your place, rag."*

As Katta's laughter had kindled my anger, the insult roused my pride. "I am a carpet of the kilim tradition! My kin were born upon the steppes thousands of years ago. We'll still be woven long after the rains have washed you away!"

Fiery eyes flashed at me. They seemed to truly regard me for the first time. *"Rag! Pus-cloth! How dare you display the image of the fiery mountain?"*

"How should I know!" I replied. "Do you think I wove myself?"

"Who did? Blind Katta?"

"Charstalker!" called Katta. "You rant like someone famished. Eat!"

Something flashed through the moonlight, to pass through the blazing-eyed black cloud.

The sweetcake landed near me, smoldering. I perceived that it had the shape of a discus.

It seemed to mean something to the demonic, smoky thing, however—the Charstalker.

It writhed outward like an inkspill, losing substance as it did. Its eyes smeared, weeping hissing red tears. *"It is imbued!"* it growled in Mazhar's voice. *"You imbued a cake with power?"*

"It might as aptly been a blade," said Katta, a hard cheerfulness in his voice. He pulled from a pouch a second cake. "Flour and metal are both illusions. Yet I'm more a baker than a smith. And I lack sufficient enlightenment to eat steel."

"*We shall see!*" snarled Mazhar and turned toward Katta with weapon raised. At the same moment he lifted an irregularly shaped lump of rock and flung it. It seemed this was to be a battle of strange projectiles.

In the next moment I realized just how strange. For when the rock fell, it shattered, and a blast of frigid air came forth, white wisps whipping toward the stars. The vapors wove together a form out of nightmares. It towered over us, a vaguely conical beast as large as a manse, with man-sized spikes for legs and similar spikes lashing the air above. In silence it bore down upon Katta.

He somehow seemed to perceive it, and he flung his second sweetcake in its direction. He could hardly miss.

One leg of the nightmare unraveled and became as morning mist. The beast hesitated. At that moment Katta was obliged to raise his staff as Mazhar swung his sword. The Charstalker's eyes blazed, and its puppet's voice gloated.

"*Behold a monstrosity of archaic times! Before the desert came, before the time of humanity or the fallen Karthagarians, before even the crimson seas of the Leviathan Imperium, there were nightmares in the Earthe!*"

Clearly the words were meant to intimidate. Yet through ragged breaths, Katta said, "It is but . . . a memory . . . of a dream . . ."

I rallied my tattered self. If Katta's insanity could keep him defiant in the face of such danger, surely I, with no internal organs to stab, could aid him.

Once more I tackled and smothered Mazhar.

This time I was ruthless, rolling tight to give him no room to strike and folding myself so the Charstalker couldn't billow forth. Dimly I perceived Katta flinging cakes at the vast prehistoric ghost, but I could spare no time for that. The Charstalker unleashed its powers, and once more I burned in three places. But this time Mazhar screamed and coughed most wretchedly.

"Enough!" Katta said, his staff striking the sand beside me. "Release him, carpet!"

Now I saw no titan of former times, but I did see Katta looking mad indeed. His face was covered in such frost he might have stepped directly from the arctic.

"He means to kill you," I said.

"It was the Charstalker's doing. I will make reply. Release him. Please."

I unrolled myself. By now Mazhar had ceased flailing. He lay quivering, breath ragged. But the Charstalker, as Katta called it, rose up beside the ordinary billows of smoke. It swirled as a dust devil does, eyes like distorted sunlight.

The Charstalker had no voice now. But soon the fiery light sketched words in the air, using the flowing script the Anokans adopted from the folk of Mirabad. THE MEAT DIES. GIVE ME THE MAP, AND YOU CAN SAVE HIM.

I recalled the Charstalker's counterpart speaking of a silk map, and I wondered how the Charstalker expected to carry it. But the entity had displayed many capabilities I would not have suspected of a smoke cloud.

"Come and get it," Katta said.

The cloud rushed upon him like an oncoming sandstorm, tendrils lashing toward ears and nose and mouth.

At the last moment Katta tossed his sweetcake and swung his cane. The wood connected and spattered crumbs into the space before Katta.

When the Charstalker intercepted them, an agonized keening rent the air. The cloud dispersed like a clutch of snakes, hissing away into the sky. I glimpsed them re-forming, the fiery eyes weak as dying embers, as the whole mass shot off to the east.

Katta chanted, "*Travel on, travel on, cross the river of perception, and know at last the other side.*"

"I think it has indeed traveled on," I said. "But your friend may soon go farther."

Katta might have been mad, but he clearly cared for his friend. I wondered at the contrast between his graceful battle against the Charstalker and his cautious movements now. Though far from helpless, he was careful to use his staff to explore the ground. Yet in battle he might have been a sighted man at noon.

Katta knelt beside Mazhar and placed his hand first upon the warrior's twitching face, then the chest tormented with coughs. "Mazhar! My friend! Can you speak?"

I heard in Katta's voice something of the tone my initial owners had used with each other on the rare occasions when they showed affection. I wondered at the depth of the friendship that might be perishing now.

Mazhar made a valiant effort. "I—" Whatever he meant to say was buried by an avalanche of hacking.

"He requires a healer," said Katta. The equanimity he'd displayed during the fight was now fraying like an old rug. "One dwells just within the city wall, beyond the caravanserai. If you could convey him—"

"Alas," I said, "you were right about my capabilities. I would surely injure him in the attempt."

"Alas indeed."

"I could go myself and bring help," I said, "but I do not know the way."

"And I might go, but I fear every minute lost. Even were I not dog-weary . . . dogs . . ."

"What is it?"

"I have heard of barbaric lands where dogs are trained to guide the blind. I have my own resources and have never sought the truth of it. But you—"

"Yes!" I said, rising up. "Grab a tassel, and I will guide you."

"We will return soon, Mazhar."

Mazhar's weak reply was grateful but incomprehensible. I hoped we would be swift. Yet even through my concern I thrilled at the possibility of being useful, rather than the botched result of one wizardly scheme or another. After a shaky start, Katta and I fell into a pattern. I was able to control my quivering movements enough to avoid toppling him. I led him around boulders and warned him of ditches.

"I dare to hope," Katta said, some of his earlier equanimity returning. "But once Mazhar is safe, we must depart."

"'We?'" I asked.

"The caravan. We'll leave a night early, for I will not further endanger Mazhar. In time we may leave the others as well. If the Charstalkers hunt the map, surely more fragments have come to light. The race is on."

"What?" I said. I was ignorant on many points. I am a carpet. "And again, 'we'?"

"All in good time. But I could use such a guide as you in the shadowed places I must walk. I will pay—once we work out what payment suits a magic carpet. And I sense you might like to leave this place."

And thus I began leading my master through the darkness. There was much darkness to come. Yet the thought of being of value to someone set a light blazing through my mind.

And thus I confess how I set tassels on the road winding through desert and cave and mountain toward the wounding of Persimmon Gaunt and Imago Bone. Aye, and the world. But that is not the worst of it, O dread one.

No, the greatest confession is that I would do it all again.

CHAPTER 5

DOLMA

Bone was still munching on a dripping slice of watermelon while carrying an uncut cousin of the original under his arm. He realized he looked like an idiot, and he played on that realization to buy himself more time. "Whaaaat?" he slowly uttered, while his eyes peered at the mysterious warriors and the treasure hunters they threatened. His mind raced.

The room was bare of useful materials; there was only a desk, behind which stood the threatened bearded man and a chest beside his compatriot. There were four assailants, all dressed in a manner foolish for hot country, for they wore close-fitting black tunics with cowls covering most of their faces. The faces themselves possessed an intriguing variety of hues. The one holding a knife to the throat of the bearded man had the look of a person of Qiangguo or its frontiers. One of the sword-wielders did as well, but a third figure's face was night-dark, and the last looked like another pale journeyer from the remotest West.

Though Bone had spoken in the Tongue of the Tortoise Shell, this last assailant replied in Roil, the polyglot language of Bone and Gaunt's home territory. "Leave now, or their fate will be yours."

"Perhaps you should do as she says," the threatened tall man added. "There comes a time at last, for the dying of the fire." Bone noted the tall man and the bearded fellow were unarmed. He was regretting Snow Pine's absence.

Bone let a black seed fall from his lips. He did not want the treasure hunters killed. On the other hand, he did not want he and his wife to die. He glanced at Gaunt and felt a sinking feeling within his gut; there was a glint in her eyes he'd seen many a time, usually when there was an underdog to protect and death howling close at hand. If she was about to do something poetic and rash, he'd best do something thiefly and rash—and first.

There comes a time at last, for the dying of the fire. That was an odd phrase, wasn't it? Bone squinted at the fire-gem flickering in the maw of a lacquer

Eastern dragon coiling upon Geshou Pi and Long Bi's desk, illuminating many intriguing charts and scrolls, its light erratic as that of the gems Snow Pine had yesterday called *unreliable*.

"Okay," Bone said, making sure his eyes looked wide and spooked.

He drew and threw the dagger whose wax he'd broken.

The steel hit the fire-gem. A small explosion shattered the lacquer dragon and set the documents ablaze.

Many things happened in the sudden wash of freakish firelight, only some of which Bone had anticipated.

Bone *had* expected the knife-wielding foe to try killing the bearded treasure hunter, and he had expected the bearded man to struggle.

He had *not* expected the assailant's dagger to strike sparks from the bearded man's neck before flying through the air and clattering to the floor.

Bone *had* expected the tall treasure hunter to either seek a weapon or flee.

He had *not* expected him to fling open the trunk, grab a dimly glowing saber secured to the lid, and then leap *into* the trunk, disappearing into darkness.

Bone *had* expected Gaunt to draw a weapon of her own.

He had *not* expected it to be a money belt.

He had certainly not expected her to bellow, "Lei Chao and brothers! Lei Chao and brothers! Easy money! Fight some bandits! Easy money!"

She whacked a sword-wielder with her loop of coins and scored a resounding hit against the enemy's forehead. That much showed the value of surprise.

However, the foe's quick recovery showed the danger Gaunt and Bone were in. This was the pale assailant, and she made blade-motions testifying to long training and a willingness to kill.

Bone had already concluded angry guards weren't the worst thing in his life, and he popped the seal on another dagger, holding it ready. "I have good aim," he warned.

"I can see that," said the pale foe.

Another sword-wielder snapped commands in a language Bone did not know. That one, and one other jumped into the improbably deep chest after the tall treasure hunter.

Meanwhile the bearded man proved himself a fellow student of Gaunt's school of tactics, for he snatched up a clutch of burning papers and flung them into his unlucky foe's face. With a power belying his portly frame, he kicked the desk over, jabbing the pale sword-wielder with the desk's legs.

"Run, fools!" the bearded man barked in Roil.

Bone immediately revised his estimation of the bearded man upward. To facilitate this wise suggestion, Bone flung his uncut watermelon at the wobbly sword-wielder's head.

With an angry flourish the sword-wielder ended the fruit's uncut status. Red melon-meat splashed the walls, but Bone and Gaunt were already backing out, the bearded man scrambling toward them.

They passed three burly-looking ruffians, the biggest of which said, "Money?" Under other circumstances, Bone would have considered them a serious threat.

Gaunt tossed him the coin-belt, pointed, turned, and ran. Bone and the bearded man were close on her heels. There was considerable shouting and hooting behind them, and much thudding against walls.

"Name's Quilldrake," the bearded man said as they gasped their way into the Market square. "Much obliged."

"Are you hurt?" exclaimed Gaunt, for Quilldrake was covered in gory-looking red pulp.

Quilldrake licked at his beard, smacked his lips. "Don't think so. Not bad. From Madzeu, I'd reckon."

"I would reckon we should run like hell," Bone said.

"Quite. Have you a hidey-hole? Ours is otherwise engaged."

"Across the Market," Gaunt said, "but only if we can shake them. Let's move!"

Luck was with them in that the boisterous throng accompanying Washing Day was still lively, and as they plunged into the square's heart there were many people to weave among.

Luck was not with them in that two black-clad assailants, as Bone verified with a quick look back, had already emerged from between the literature god's shrine and the Inn of Infinite Options.

He hoped the stains on the leader's sword were all from melon.

Bone had expected anyone dressed head-to-toe in black would be loath to eviscerate them in public, but fresh doubts chilled his neck.

These doubts were confirmed as screams and shouts of outrage erupted behind them.

"They really want you," Bone noted to Quilldrake.

"You too, by now."

"Wonderful. Gaunt, I don't want to lead them to Snow Pine."

"Indeed," she said. "Do we leave a hot trail or cold?"

"Hot, I should think."

"Agreed."

"What do you mean, 'hot trail . . . ?'" said Quilldrake, voice trailing off, as Bone grabbed his arm and dragged him into the midst of a group of entertainers.

They ran between the wooden legs of stilt-walkers and dove past a human pyramid, making those acts suddenly more challenging. Angry stage magicians threw knives, and angry sorcerers threw fire.

"I thought tricksters and true magi hated each other!" Bone protested under his breath as he dodged steel and flame.

The crowd cheered, especially when a swordsman caught up to Gaunt, Bone, and Quilldrake, waving the blade in a triumphant squiggle in the air.

Bone bowed, then shoved his companions beneath the stomach of the monstrously large camel who supported a batch of musicians, still bravely playing overhead.

Alas, the other assailant-in-black, now with sword drawn, was already on the other side.

Bone, Gaunt, and Quilldrake shifted and dodged and jostled beneath the camel, as the pair of flanking enemies jabbed at them. The camel snorted and stomped. The air went out of the flutes and voices, though the fiddlers played on, their tune growing ominously creaky.

Bone saw his chance, though the angle was poor. He threw his dagger at one sword-wielder.

The foe swatted his blade out of the air.

The dagger sank into the camel's flank.

With a bellow the beast abandoned its training, perhaps for good, and charged toward the Market gate.

"Grab on!" Bone's experience with the xiezhi had been instructive. He clutched the straps on the camel's underside, and Gaunt and Quilldrake did the same. Soon they left their foes behind. But while Bone and Gaunt were acrobatic enough to cling tight to the huge beast, Quilldrake was dragging.

"Oof—oof—oof," Quilldrake said, or perhaps something more colorful, until he at last let go, and the camel left him behind on the stones of the square, their foes rushing toward him.

Bone responded first; he let go, dropped, rolled, and threw a dagger at the faster enemy. That one also deflected the attack, but it forced a halt, at least. Bone got Quilldrake to his feet with a yank.

"In here!" came the voice of Snow Pine.

Bone and Quilldrake ran to the doorway she'd peered from, and in his grateful rush Bone did not at first realize this wasn't the Inn of the Bright Future. Rather it was a temple of the Undetermined.

Bone didn't have the background to judge which of the three huge seated statues represented the Undetermined himself, as opposed to the Thresholders, though his bets were on the beatific gold-plated one in the middle. Left was a jolly-looking, big-bellied statue of lacquered wood that had Bone's immediate sympathy; right was a kindly looking figure of bronze, shown pouring out a libation. Candles and basins of water were everywhere. There was a thick smell of candle smoke and incense.

The washers and devotees were shouting at the newcomers, and emerging from amid the hundreds of candles and dozens of basins loomed a man of an ethnicity unknown to Bone. He boasted a wide face and black hair woven into braids sticking out like ox-horns. His clothing was bright blue, but the metal of his raised sword reflected orange in the candlelight. His teeth glinted, as he favored the newcomers with a battle-ready grin.

"A Karvak," Quilldrake muttered. "They had to guard their temple with a Karvak."

"I thought followers of the Undetermined were pacifists," protested Bone.

"Karvaks aren't," Snow Pine said. She sheathed her blade and raised her hands, palms out. "Sanctuary!" she called. "We're fleeing marauders."

Bone sheathed his own blades. "They're coming fast," he said.

"Very well," said an elderly officiant in an orange robe. His body was stooped, but his voice rang through the candlelit temple. "Nine Thunderbolts, stand ready."

At once the Karvak, with a last contemptuous look at the newcomers, strode to the door.

He immediately found himself in combat with one of the swordsmen in black. Metal clashed in the interface of sunlight and candlelight. The Karvak, Nine Thunderbolts, found himself pushed back, knocking over a basin of ceremonial water that smelled of incense and sandalwood.

Sword-swipes chopped candles in twain. Far from looking worried, Bone thought he saw a look of wild joy on Nine Thunderbolts' face. He reminded himself never to tangle with Karvaks. His hand strayed to a sheathed dagger.

"No," Snow Pine cautioned him. "If you draw your weapon again we lose our right of sanctuary."

Nine Thunderbolts heard her. Though he never looked away from his enemy, the Karvak boomed, "This one is mine! Not since I crossed the Desert of Wise Vultures have I had such a worthy foe!"

"He's got a friend," Snow Pine called out.

"Excellent."

Not excellent, Bone thought, looking this way and that. *That is surely translation trouble. Where is he? Or she. . . .* The devotees had cleared out, which suggested another doorway. Bone asked the old priest, "Is there a way out through the roof?"

"I've offered you sanctuary," said the priest, "not the deed to the temple."

Quilldrake broke in. "Do you not recognize me, Yuan Da? Geshou Pi and I have donated to your temple."

"Long Bi," the priest said, eyes narrowing. "Yes, I remember you. You donate to everyone from whom you might need favors."

"But we are very generous about it."

"Come," snapped the priest, not exactly agreeing, but leading them upstairs nonetheless.

The temple was a three-level pagoda, the third level capped with a bell loft. Bone, Snow Pine, and Quilldrake scrambled out onto the third-story roof. From here Bone had a good view of the Market and, because the temple rose beside the Market wall, of the neighboring ward with its peony garden.

He also saw guards on that wall, and guards in the Market square, all shouting and waving weapons. Persimmon Gaunt was with the Market group. *Good idea, that*, he thought, *summoning guards*. He wasn't used to that approach. Her response to his jaunty wave was to aim her bow at the roof.

"Wait!" Bone said, holding up his hands, "wait! It's us!"

Gaunt fired.

A shape Bone had been unaware of leapt from beneath the bell. The arrow hit the bell instead of the shape, raising sparks and a deep hum.

Embarrassed to be caught flat-footed, Bone saluted Gaunt and faced the black-clad foe. The enemy had fallen hard in escaping Gaunt's shot, and a sword lay fallen nearby. Bone tossed it to Snow Pine, who yelped with surprise—but caught it.

"I did it!" she said, drawing her own sword so that now she waved two. "Don't ever do that again," she added.

"Ah, you lack confidence—urk—"

The foe was demonstrating an indifference to disarmament by grabbing Bone's throat with a grip that would shame a blacksmith. The world began turning purple around the edges. He grabbed at the arm, but it was like trying to uproot bamboo. He kicked wickedly between the foe's legs, but the enemy merely grunted.

Snow Pine was suddenly there, threatening Crazy Grip with two swords. Bone found himself dragged around the roof like a potato sack as the maniac-in-black dodged. Snow Pine managed to draw blood from an arm; it was the wrong arm, naturally, but Bone still approved. He would approve even more of air.

Suddenly Snow Pine had other problems. Another black-clad lunatic burst from the bell-loft. It was all Snow Pine could do to maintain her guard against the newcomer. *Where is a Karvak horde when you need one?* Bone imagined nomadic archers on horseback; they were colored purple-black and were filled with shimmering multicolored stars . . .

His opponent shrieked and let go.

The arm in front of Bone now had an arrow stuck through its biceps.

Bless you, Persimmon Gaunt, were the words of his mind; "*Hhhhhggggggllllll-laaaa . . .*" was the word of his mouth. He and air wanted to strike up a passionate new relationship, but at that moment the foe's other fist connected with his nose. "*Gllrrk!*" was the new word of his mouth. It occurred to him Quilldrake had yet to engage, which annoyed Bone, given their efforts to protect the man. And one would think a fellow with a neck that repelled sword-strokes might find ways to be useful.

As if hearing Bone's thoughts, Quilldrake acted. He grabbed a roof-tile loosened in the battle and chucked it at Bone's opponent.

"Hello!" called Quilldrake. "Yes, you! I'm the one you want. Remember? The one with the Silk Map. See you in another century!"

With that Quilldrake leapt off the roof and onto the ward wall. He did not pause to acknowledge the guards but leapt again, landing amongst the peony bushes.

Bone didn't recognize the language in which Snow Pine's opponent spoke, but he knew a curse when he heard it. That one broke off from her and jumped to follow Quilldrake.

Bone's own foe tried to follow, but Snow Pine was in the way.

For the first time, his disarmed enemy had a back turned.

He launched himself onto his opponent and together they sprawled to the tiles. For the second time Crazy Grip's face kissed the temple. Bone was no religious scholar, but he doubted this would produce enlightenment. He knew a thing or two about choking, however, even if he wasn't Crazy Grip. He pressed hard on two arteries.

Crazy Grip proved good at breaking grips too. Bone found himself shoved backwards. His fingers clawed at something and held, and he rose to his feet with Crazy Grip's hood in his hands.

Bone and Snow Pine confronted the assailant and stared.

This was the pale woman from the Alley of the Scholars of Life, as Bone had begun to guess. He had not guessed she would be maimed.

She stood defiantly with a freed tangle of brown hair whipping in the wind, revealing that her right ear had been cut away. The scar was neat, as though she'd subjected herself willingly to the knife. She met their stares of wonder and pity with one of disdain.

"You've unmasked me," the woman said, "but it will avail you nothing. If your fates are tied to the treasure hunters, you will fall. We'll do whatever it takes to protect what we love. Even in the palaces of Riverclaw or Archaeopolis you cannot hide."

Although she spoke of Eldshore's capital she didn't look like most Eldshorens, who tended toward somewhat lighter skin. She had the darker look of the Contrariwise Coast.

Like him.

"Talk is easy," Bone said, in the dialect of that faraway place. "Bring that bone to some other dog."

The woman blinked, as if hearing that lingo for the first time in decades.

"You are far from home," he added more gently.

"Home is in the clouds now," she answered in the Tongue of the Tortoise Shell.

"Fight another day," suggested Snow Pine. "There's only one of you up here."

"You don't know everything," the woman said. She pulled forth an irregularly shaped piece of gray-black pockmarked stone that hung from a silver chain around her neck. "None of us is alone."

As she crushed the stone into smoky pumice, his keen ears heard her whisper, "Not anymore."

The dust erupted into a cloud looming over the rooftop. Dark as a thunderhead, it emitted a gentle rain of ash. Three fiery spheres appeared within its form, and Bone had the sensation of hate-filled eyes staring down at him. It was not the hate, he sensed, which one man might feel for another. It was more the hate with which a man might regard a biting insect.

"The mortals will try to follow me, Charstalker," the one-eared woman said. "Prevent them."

An arrow shot through one of the fiery eyes. Gaunt must have swiftly sized up the situation. Bone felt a swell of pride in his chest.

The smoke quivered and the eye transformed briefly into a blazing squiggle, drawing the character that meant *Burn* in the Tongue of the Tortoise Shell.

Bone felt a quite different emotion in his gut. On instinct he shouted, "Look out!"

Each eye belched forth flame. One bolt lashed at Bone, a second at Snow Pine, a third at Gaunt and the guards in the square.

Bone evaded, and in such a way that he was there to grab Snow Pine's hand when her own dodge threw her off the roof.

As he helped her climb back up, he had a clear view of Gaunt, who'd dived out of the blast's path. Others were not so lucky, and one man rolled to snuff his blazing clothing.

Bone also had a good view of the one-eared woman leaping to the ward wall and then the peony garden. He felt a gaze on his neck as he yelled to both Snow Pine and Gaunt, "Go! Help Quilldrake!"

"But you—" Snow Pine objected, staring at the smoke-thing.

"I've been dealing with magical lunacy since before you were born. Go!"

His wife, accompanied by guards, was already running toward the ward gate. Snow Pine jumped to the ward wall. His companions cared about him, and that pleased Bone; but they trusted his judgment, and that pleased him more.

He ran past the smoke-thing and into the bell loft, as three blazing eyes formed the three characters for the idiom *A clawless tiger*.

"Indeed!" Bone called out, his voice echoing through the loft. "Come inside and say that!"

He checked the pulse of the unconscious priest beside the bell-rope. He was relieved to find the man alive.

Eschewing the stairs, Bone slid down the rope into the shaft as the sky darkened with smoke. Clanging announced his return to the temple.

In the nearly empty room of the statues, candlelight flickered upon basins of water. The Karvak lay against the jolliest-looking statue, a bloody hand pressed against a bloodier stomach. Nevertheless the warrior managed a weak smile. "I suggest you draw a weapon after all," he said.

"Are you a follower of this faith?" Bone asked as he looked around at the chamber's layout.

The Karvak shook his head. "But they are good employers . . . I respect them."

"Do you believe them devout? My question has a practical thrust."

"They are as fervent as any, and kinder than most."

"Then," Bone said, while an ashen cloud flowed downstairs like the stuff of a tipped-over volcano, "I will take a risk."

The triple-eyes of the Charstalker shone with three fiery words. This time they were not in the Tongue of the Tortoise Shell, but in Roil.

TIME TO DIE

"You are wrong," said Bone, snatching up a basin. "It is bath time."

Bone muttered a prayer to the Swan Goddess for insurance and splashed upon the Charstalker what he hoped qualified as holy water.

The smoky entity tried to evade, but there was no missing those fiery eyes.

There was a sound like water dousing a campfire, and a shriek filled the chamber as the Charstalker twisted and coiled. One of its eyes was sputtering.

The two other eyes shot blazing lances at Bone, and he barely managed to take cover behind the bronze statue of the holy being offering a libation. The metal did not melt, but candles did, and bowls of ritual water steamed.

Under other circumstances Bone would have fled such a fight. But he'd been provided a chamber filled with weapons! He ran to the gold-plated statue, grabbed a wooden bucket, and drenched the Charstalker again. Smoke whirled like a cyclone, and a second eye grew erratic. A single blast burned its way toward Bone, but he was running already, a jug in hand. His next shot was wild, but now the Charstalker seemed worried; if smoke clouds could flinch, this one did.

Now a vast splash hit the Charstalker, and one of the eyes went completely out.

It was not Bone's doing; he stared and saw the Karvak on his feet, grinning, bleeding, basin in hands. Bone grinned back, though he worried for the steppe warrior.

Both sought more basins. Both were hit by flames.

Bone's clothes were alight, and once more he was grateful for this arena. He threw himself into a trough that was likely the proximate source for the basins, buckets, bowls, and jugs.

Drenched, he escaped burning. However, it was difficult to extricate himself—and now the Charstalker billowed over him.

Two eyes flared. They displayed the two-part symbol, which in the Tongue of the Tortoise Shell meant *Death.*

The symbol hissed and frayed as water splashed upon it; hot drops hit Bone's face.

There stood the stooped priest, conscious, bearing an empty bowl and a defiant smile.

Bone stumbled out of the trough and reached the priest just in time to embrace him.

Thus when heat erupted around them they did not burn. Bone steamed a little, however.

"Ha!" he said, scooping up the old priest and hauling him around the statue of the laughing figure. "It suddenly occurred to me I'm drenched in holy water. I should have done that in the first place." He stopped laughing as he saw the smoking body of the Karvak. "Ah, hell."

"He was a good man," the priest said. "Let us finish this, you and I."

"Agreed, Grandfather."

They came at the monster from around either side of the statue, a basin in each hand. The priest chanted what sounded like "Om Mani Padme Hum," and Bone shouted, "For the Karvak!"

The Charstalker had but one eye left. It drew, not a word but a rude gesture made of flame, as priest and thief splashed it with its doom.

Its final act was fiery, and as Bone expected the blast sizzled toward the priest, but Bone had already launched himself from the platform of the laughing figure to occupy the air between smoke-thing and holy man.

It hurt. To be sure, it hurt a great deal. But Bone kicked through the fire and jabbed a wet boot in the Charstalker's eye.

Bone's next move was to connect with the outstretched hand of the gold-plated, beatific figure. The result was not enlightenment but unconsciousness.

CHAPTER 6

FLINT AND QUILLDRAKE, LIMITED

Gaunt ran through the peony garden with her bow at the ready, city guards puffing beside her, Snow Pine nearly out of sight up ahead. Under other circumstances, Gaunt would have been alarmed by the presence of a dozen guards. She was not quite used to the notion of being an honest visitor, and yet it was true enough, for her party meant no trouble to Yao'an or its inhabitants.

True, their long-term goal was to find and plunder what Qiangguo would probably consider its rightful property. But no one needed to know that.

As she avoided branches and roots and little streams and miniature temples, she considered it surprising the guards allowed an outlander to accompany them. But they'd seen her shoot. They'd also witnessed astounding swordplay from the foes and a supernatural visitation upon the temple roof. She hoped Bone would be all right. But she trusted his skills.

They needed Quilldrake, she was sure now. Whether this Silk Map was related to their quest or not, with enemies like these he must be the sort of person who could help them.

She'd lost sight of Snow Pine. The group moved more slowly now, as they came up to a line of wooden houses bordering the garden. The guards began bellowing threats to any person who would dare hide from them. She did not think that would be very effective.

Gaunt paused and opened her senses to what was there. As a young poet she'd spent an exorbitant amount of time seeking inspiration in dark grave-yards. Whether her poetry had thereby improved was a matter of taste, but it was a fact that she'd trained her senses to be alert for birdsong, crickets, a twist in the breeze, a swell in the moonlight, and (just in case) the rising dead.

It was daylight, and there were no rising dead, but she did notice Snow Pine crouched at one corner of a house. Her companion's two swords gleamed.

Gaunt kept silent, for if Snow Pine had sensed something, Gaunt didn't want to disturb her. Gaunt crept closer. The house was a two-story affair suggesting modest wealth. More shapes seemed apparent on the upper story. She raised her bow, squinting. She lacked Bone's facility with heights, but that was what arrows were for.

Light flared within an upper window.

It was not firelight, nor reflected sunlight, but a bizarre green radiance that oozed like a liquid. It illuminated an intricate two-piece wooden panel that blew open as if a strong wind had erupted from within. The wind had a voice. Gaunt knew it.

"Who dares disturb the nap of Widow Zheng!"

Within the strange light she saw two figures in black, one hooded, one not. The un-hooded one held its right arm awkwardly.

Gaunt fired at her—for this was surely the one who'd attempted to choke Bone.

The woman reacted by diving into the weirdly lit chamber. Gaunt couldn't be sure if she'd scored a hit. Likewise, she didn't know what had happened to Snow Pine—for her friend had vanished and all sound was obscured by the bellows of the guards. Some of her new associates clutched crossbows and commenced discharging them at the remaining figure.

Gaunt waited no longer but ran toward the house.

She discovered an open door on the ground level, entering a dwelling that seemed made for the comfort of codices and scrolls, with some small provision for a human inhabitant. The way to the stairs was marked by a spill of swirling green light.

At the top Gaunt encountered a workshop that under other circumstances would have fascinated her. Books in various states of mending sat upon one large table. Yarrow sticks for divination lay upon another. A scroll of unfinished calligraphy dried upon a third. The walls were as book-lined as the ones below. All these things Gaunt would later reconstruct in her mind like the fading impressions of a dream. Of more immediate concern were the five figures in the room.

Widow Zheng the bookseller stood beside the table of calligraphy. Quilldrake hid under the table of mending. Snow Pine crouched before the table of divination. The two assailants faced Snow Pine, one wielding a sword, the other raising hands that Gaunt knew were only a little less dangerous. The unarmed foe's right arm was wrapped in a bloody cloth.

Gaunt had already readied an arrow; she aimed. "I trust you remember me."

"Give him up," the one-eared woman said.

"I cannot!" replied Widow Zheng. Gaunt now saw that the eerie light emanated from a blank scroll in the bookseller's hands. "This man owes me a book. Surely you understand."

"At most you delay us," said the other figure in black. The voice sounded male. "No matter where you hide, we will find you and claim what's ours."

"Can't we discuss this?" Snow Pine said, adjusting her swords with every twitch of the warriors in black. "Reach an understanding?"

"No," said the man, pulling forth a flat black stone from around his neck.

"No," said Quilldrake, much more quietly, from under the mending table.

Gaunt shot the stone.

Her action was intuitive, surprising her. It surprised the man in black as well. He staggered backward, an arrow in his chest.

I have become a cold thing, Gaunt thought dimly. But smoke rose from where the man fell. Three blazing eyes were forming within it.

The one-eared woman snarled and kicked at Snow Pine. Snow Pine slashed and cut the woman's leg but nevertheless fell into a tumble of table and yarrow sticks. Gaunt scrambled to draw a fresh arrow. Widow Zheng swore and snatched a new scroll, rapping it upon the table. The calligraphy upon it glowed with purple light and leapt off the page. Gaunt thought she recognized the proverb *One who is snakebit for an instant, dreads a rope for ten years*. The characters twisted like a cable and wrapped themselves around the smoke-thing.

The thing's eyes blazed, and triple gouts of flame lashed at the purple calligraphy. The logograms writhed like grass in a fire and vanished.

Widow Zheng swore more emphatically.

Gaunt now had her arrow, and she fired at the one-eared woman. Wounded, disarmed, and breathing hard, the woman was still formidable; the arrow, aimed at the heart, only grazed her shoulder.

Now crossbow bolts were pummeling the chamber, and heavy boots could be heard upon the stairs. The one-eared woman snarled something in a language unknown to Gaunt, before looking at the smoke-creature and bellowing an incomprehensible command.

The thing swirled into a dark vortex, and the woman leapt into it. It bore her away like a leaf in a storm. Together they roared out over Yao'an.

In the moments before the guards arrived, Widow Zheng gasped to Quilldrake, "You, Arthur, owe me a book . . . two magic scrolls . . . and an explanation."

"It will all be yours, my dear. But that last cannot be spoken within Yao'an."

"Give me the rest, and I'll arrange your departure."

"Done," said Quilldrake.

"What *was* that thing?" Gaunt asked, helping Snow Pine up.

"Hate undying," she thought Quilldrake answered, but anything more was drowned out by the triumphant arrival of the guards.

Clearly this was to become the tale of how brave Gate Captain Sun and his hand-picked men vanquished foreign sorcerers. The way Widow Zheng kept weeping and praising and almost fainting into his arms, Gate Captain Sun probably felt like he'd rescued the whole western half of the city. Zheng also seemed to enjoy being held by the strapping gate captain. Gaunt couldn't entirely blame her. She also preferred Widow Zheng's story to, say, a tale of suspicious foreign treasure hunters bringing trouble upon Yao'an.

For Quilldrake was known to the guards, and it was clearly a mixed notoriety.

"Where is your partner-in-crime?" Captain Sun demanded, when he was finally able to turn his attention from Widow Zheng.

"My colleague is away on business."

"What sort of business?"

"Scouting a new caravan route. I hope he succeeded."

"Are you planning a long trip?"

"I think so."

"Well, we might all be relieved by that. Do you think your trip might commence tomorrow?"

"It's quite possible."

"Good. That assurance may save you a lot of trouble when I talk to my superiors." He turned to Gaunt and Snow Pine. "Now you two—"

Gaunt said, "My husband may still be in danger."

The gate captain shook his head. "The scarred fellow? Just before we entered this house we received word that he and a priest defeated a demon-thing. And possibly a Karvak spy—reports were conflicting. The priest is looking after your man."

Gaunt let out a long breath.

Captain Sun said, "Widow Zheng, you've clearly been through a trial. You may finish your nap, of course. You other three will come back to the Western Market with us, and you will stay within that ward until summoned."

They weren't exactly a group bursting with respect for authority, but their responses this time were silent nods.

In the Inn of the Bright Future they considered their own. Bone lay upon a cot, rubbing his bandaged head, muttering occasionally about pain and enlightenment. Gaunt held his hand, sometimes squeezing it when he ranted. "So," Bone said to Quilldrake. "Your colleague. How will he fare?"

"I'm concerned, to be sure," said Quilldrake, stroking his beard. "But Liron Flint's a resourceful fellow. If he got a good enough head start he'll have collapsed our tunnel upon our murderous friends. It was he who devised our escape route. Or rather our connection to it, for an earlier version once led from the first watchtower to an inn in this very Market. It was made for the convenience of the royal family long ago, and then rediscovered by enterprising soldiers. We've had a delicate but profitable relationship with some of the guards hereabouts."

"Your friend wielded an interesting sword," Gaunt recalled.

"You have an eye for the loot, don't you, now? Yes, it's a relic of some distinction. Well, I can't blame anyone for admiring treasure." Quilldrake leaned against the wall. He had a belly to him and had eagerly taken all food offered. His voice held jollity, but there was a haunted look to his eyes. "I thank you for our rescue. Strange as it sounds, I take our assault by mysterious figures as a good sign! But we'll save that discussion for later."

"I would appreciate hearing more now, Master Quilldrake," said Gaunt.

"Call me Art. One half of the firm of Flint and Quilldrake, Limited. Authorized to trade in Amberhorn, Palmary, the Sublime Sultanate, and Skidtown. And Yao'an, of course."

"One of those places is not like the others," said Gaunt.

"We've indeed been footsore in recent years," said Art. "So have you, my dear."

Gaunt nodded and introduced their little group; she was relieved to see no glimmer of recognition at her and Bone's names. "My husband and I came to Qiangguo via a series of ships. Having had various adventures here, we, with our friend Snow Pine, plan to try our hands at the Braid of Spice."

"You'll be trading, then?" Quilldrake asked. "Or hiring out as cavern guards?"

"I suppose we hadn't thought this through," Gaunt said. "We only just arrived."

"And immediately got into trouble," Quilldrake said. "Welcome to the Braid. But I'm curious. You say you had no plans for the road, yet you looked for *us*. We have a fairly narrow brief. We buy exotic treasures or else hunt them."

"We are chasing a legend," Snow Pine admitted. "A wise . . . person . . . hinted of a source of ironsilk. Not the forbidden island in the warded lake. A source beyond Qiangguo."

Bone said, "Widow Zheng said you might offer advice."

"Did she now," said Quilldrake. "Well, this is interesting timing. Peculiar, even. You see, those people you drove off are likely after the same thing, albeit in a less friendly manner."

"What?" Bone said. "Were they hoping you'd reveal the location?"

"We don't have the location. Not exactly."

"What do you have?" Gaunt demanded.

"I have the Silk Map," said Quilldrake. "Or part of it, rather."

"The what?"

Quilldrake removed his outer robe, revealing a patchwork tunic beneath. It was somewhat in the piecemeal style of the women's dresses Gaunt had seen in the other wards of Yao'an. Her eyebrows rose, but she'd seen all manner of costume in her travels and reflected Quilldrake's garb was his own business. Quilldrake patted the region over his heart. The particular patch here extended to shoulder and collar, and had already caught Gaunt's eye. It had the sheen of silk, yet it lacked the flora or fauna decorating most silken clothing. There were no birds or blossoms. Instead, she saw ridges of mountains, tracks of rivers, little pagodas. An unfamiliar vertical script marked some of the features.

The edges of the patch were irregular, as if torn in a moment of great violence. The other fragments were also haphazard—and yet Gaunt had the sense these were deliberately fashioned so, to draw attention away from the unique shimmer of the piece covering heart and neck.

"The Silk Map," Quilldrake repeated.

"To be more precise," Bone guessed, "it is an *ironsilk* map."

Snow Pine whistled.

"That is why the assassin's thrust didn't kill you," Gaunt said. "You had ironsilk armor."

"Only a fragment," Quilldrake said. "And I like to think I have *some* wherewithal for survival, ironsilk or no ironsilk. But yes, it was quite valuable today."

Gaunt said, "Indeed. Ironsilk is precious. So who would squander it to make a map?"

"And where does the map direct us?" Bone said.

Quilldrake smiled at Bone as though discovering a long-lost cousin. "Where does it direct 'us' indeed? Well, perhaps you have heard the poem? 'In Xembala did Mentor John a lofty lamasery raise . . .'"

Gaunt broke in, "'Where Aleph the holy river flows . . .'"

Quilldrake's eyes twinkled. "'Through labyrinths that no man knows . . .'"

"'To an ocean innocent of days,'" Gaunt concluded.

"I think I may become jealous," Bone said, looking from Gaunt to Quilldrake.

"Nothing is preventing you from learning more poetry," Gaunt told her husband. "Although in this case it's unsurprising you haven't heard it. It's a work of the Mad Mariner, and he's an acquired taste. It's said he wandered up and down the docks of Archaeopolis, clutching at passers-by and reciting fragments of beauty and woe."

"Yes," Quilldrake said with a distant look. "I've heard more than one version of this poem, some you would find quite strange. But this seems the one that matches other legends. Listen."

THE MAD MARINER'S VISION IN A DREAM, A FRAGMENT

In Xembala did Mentor John a lofty lamasery raise
Where Aleph the holy river flows
Through labyrinths that no man knows
To an ocean innocent of days.
And thrice nine miles of alpine hill
Were walled about by his dread will
Where folk of strange countenance strode
And dreamed of ages bronze and gold
By fountains that preserved their youth
And served as mirrors of piercing truth.
And there blossomed groves of fairy fruit
Lofting in one day from seed to root
And rotting in the misty night
To rise anew by dawn's gold light
As our sacrificed Goddess shall one day live
And to us sanctification give
As sworn in the teachings of that Good Swan
Who is likewise loved by Mentor John.
But no! the chill from Aleph's flow which thundered
Down a shadowed gorge with wisteria webbed—
As haunted a scene as any dreamer sick with wonder
Rising slick with sweat from troubled slumber
Might snatch from tides of nightmare lately ebbed—
As fraught as any eve I've tossed
Since first I shot the albatross!
Yet Aleph called from beyond the fields we know
And I followed its flow to the dark below
Whence it brought that scent of golden pear
And snatched the voice from fountains fair

And carried dreams into the dark
Brooding under a mountain gray and stark
Washing a forge of demon-fires
And quenching weapons of living iron.
It was a monument drear and dire
A pitiless summit with caves like pyres!
And from that cacophonous smoking tomb
John heard intimations of his doom.
A maiden in a cheongsam
In delirium I pursued
Her dress a shimmering map
Torn to quiver and flap
As she fled through desert ruins.
I tore not the qipao
Nor drove her thus away
And if I could embrace her now
So with valor cold and brave
I would face that demon on the heights!
I would rise with brave endeavor!
But the albatross will not take flight
And in my dreams it screeches, Never! Never!
Xia's dying breath! John's burning fever!
And we are all as on a darkling river.
So flee the demon of the forge
For he on fairy fruit has gorged
And scorched the fountains of forever.

"An eerie tale," Snow Pine said.

"A flimsy lead," Bone noted.

"Perhaps not," Gaunt said. "That word 'qipao'—I don't think it's current in the West, where such dresses are indeed known as cheongsams. Perhaps the Mad Mariner did indeed glean information from dreams."

"Some details match other tales we've heard," Snow Pine said. Bone grunted.

Quilldrake's expression reminded Gaunt of a bird watching the morning soil. "Whether you believe it or not, Imago Bone, my associate and I do indeed think there's a true Xembala. That within it rises a fiery mountain, home to a colony of Iron Moths long separated from Qiangguo's. That in some manner an ironsilk dress was fashioned there, showing the way. That it was torn into fragments and scattered. And that if the Silk Map could ever be reassembled, one could find the way to that mysterious land—and to its treasure."

"It seems we're pursuing much the same goal," Gaunt said. "Which worries me. It seems too much of a coincidence that you, we, and those charming people in black are all seeking the same thing, at the same time."

"I know little of all of you," Quilldrake said, "but Liron Flint and I have pondered the Silk Map for years. I came upon this fragment far to the west, under circumstances I prefer not to relate. I kept it, for it has its obvious benefits beyond the cartographic. When I teamed up with Flint I came to learn that Xembala's tantalized him since his youth. But despite other successes, Xembala's remained out of reach. Only a few weeks ago did we hear of a discovery in Shahuang that could point the way to a lost fragment."

"And news travels fast," Bone said. "Our friends in black know too, I'd assume."

"We'll be lucky," Quilldrake said, "if they are the only opposition. Across these lands there may be several parties with their own fragments, all hoping that this long-lost piece will grant the information they need. And as we've seen, some may be delighted to eliminate their competitors. We dare waste no time."

Quilldrake patted his ironsilk patch. "So there you have it. The four winds have blown us together. Flint the explorer wants the glory of discovering Xembala. I want the glory of the world's greatest loot. We have lacked only personnel mad enough to join us in this venture. I suggest that whatever your plans, you depart the Jade Gate with me and accompany me until we can find Flint."

"Art," Gaunt said, "make yourself comfortable in our lodgings, as it's unwise for you to return to your own. We'll enjoy the Market and return with dinner and our answer."

"Most generous," Quilldrake said.

"If we're wrong," Snow Pine said once they stood within the babbling ano-
nymity of the Market, "if this is a distraction from our true hunt, then we will
waste weeks wandering the desert."

"We must stick together, Snow Pine," Gaunt said, putting her hand on the
younger woman's shoulder. "That's not fate, but intuition. We chase a legend,
on behalf of a legend. The only thing I trust here, really, is our friendship."

Bone sighed. "I also. I am stirred more than I can say by all this talk of
treasure and lost lands. But we have lost too much, Gaunt and I. We would
not part now with a friend."

Snow Pine looked to the sky. The morning star shone dimly to the northwest, just over the city wall. "Village people," she mused, "have superstitions
that the morning star will kill parents if not properly venerated. I don't ven-
erate anything . . . but I'll take this as an omen. It may be that I should trust
this encounter." She shut her eyes. "We'll go with Quilldrake."

CHAPTER 7

BEYOND THE JADE GATE

"You want a piece of jade? Well, we got 'em! Gift? Luck charm?"

"Luck charm," Snow Pine said, looking at the morning light glinting off the milky green. "I'm going far away."

"Far away, girl? You a princess being married off to some horse-lord?" The merchant laughed at his own joke.

"No, I'm already married. I just want to remember where I'm from. How about the monkey?"

"You're Year of the Monkey?" The merchant chuckled again as he placed it in her hands. "I'm Year of the Dragon. Great match! Too bad you're married." He quoted a price.

She haggled. He reminded her a little of her lost husband, in fact, in his cheerful, unabashed greed. She was inclined to go easy on him, but in the end she said, "Ah, I have to wrap it up quick, my husband will come looking. He's a soldier, and he gets grumpy if I don't meet him on his break."

The merchant quickly reached a fairer price. Business concluded, he said, "Your husband's a soldier, but you're shopping here, not at the Eastern Market? Trying to get to know the West? He getting posted up the road in the Final Fort? Trouble with the Karvaks?" A knowing, calculating look filled his eyes. "There is, isn't there? I've heard tell their fleets are on the move. Big gathering. The kind that leads to wars."

This was how rumors began, Snow Pine thought, with people daydreaming they were better-informed than others. But that wasn't her problem. She thanked the man and moved on.

In the gray light she could see the diversity of temples bordering the Market, rubbing shoulders with the inns, stables, smithies, apothecary shops, scriveners' offices, and the like. The shrines of the Undetermined were dark now, for their devotees had been up late with image-washing. There was a mosque for worship of the All-Now, built in the manner of a pagoda, and the followers of the Testifier were up early for prayers. There was a temple of the Nightkindlers, something she'd heard of but had never seen: a tapering tower of black wood, with a mosaic of bright stones in a semicircle at the top, rays from this symbolic sun, or moon, or star, reaching deep into the night. At this hour the temple was dark, but the door was open, and the dawn was creeping in.

There was a temple to the proliferation of Southern gods known often as the Million or One, for despite their diversity as to numbers of limbs (two, four, a dozen), and manner of heads (beautiful, elephantine, monstrous), and aspect (beatific, sensual, fierce), they were said to all hearken back to one primal source. And here and there stood temples to various personages important to Qiangguo—the Grand Marshal in Charge of Time and the Calendar, the Old Men Who Dispense Longevity and Happiness, the Queen of the Sky, and many others. She saw no temple to the Swan Goddess, and Snow Pine realized anew just how far her friend Persimmon had traveled. Imago Bone was mostly indifferent to gods, though sometimes she saw him toss offerings to anyone in charge of luck.

She touched her new monkey charm; she'd made her own provision for luck and now was looking for something else.

Her feet took her to the temple of the Queen of the Sky. It was not a big structure, more for private observance than for public worship. Snow Pine entered and looked up at a statue of the Queen, who was said to dwell near the polestar. Outside there was a contraption like a stylus upon a pivot, a bed of sand beneath. The lightest touch would allow one to draw a line.

As she inspected the device, two temple officiants in red appeared and bowed. "Do you wish to contact a god?" said the older one. "Or perhaps the dead?"

"The dead," she said, offering a coin.

"Grip the stylus here. The two of us will help summon the correct vibrations."

Snow Pine could imagine Imago Bone rolling his eyes. Perhaps it *was* foolish. It was a temple offering however, so maybe there was merit in it. And sometimes the messages received in this fashion were strangely apt.

She framed a question in her mind. *What would you have me do, Flybait? Do I follow this mad quest?*

The stylus swished. When she removed her hand, a logogram meaning *Acceptance* lay in the sand.

"It seems your departed wishes you to be at peace," said the older officiant.

"Peace?" Snow Pine kicked the sand.

"Hey!" said the younger officiant.

"I have not walked across half of Qiangguo to look for *peace!* Up yours, dead husband! Be useful next time! Don't expect me to talk for a while!"

The officiants looked as if they'd just seen an angry spirit as they retreated into the temple.

"Perhaps you should be forgiving," said a nearby voice. "I've heard that such functionaries sometimes suggest their own messages. And suppose you really have reached the one you seek? Perhaps he merely wishes you well."

Snow Pine was unnerved to find a man beside her. He was strange even by the standards of the Western Market: a white-robed, hulking fellow whose face was concealed by a shroud, as though hiding some disfigurement. He bore a walking stick and many silver charms around his neck. There was something unnerving about his posture. Perhaps he was a hunchback.

His girth troubled her as well; it seemed to shift and quiver at times, although the man's boots and gloves stayed still. It was as though the morning wind had singled him out.

"This is between me and a dead man," Snow Pine said.

The man bowed. "That is fair. Then I ask that you be forgiving of me. I have taken an interest in you since the disturbance of yesterday. I have accosted you in order to give you advice."

"All right, you're here. Go on."

"Quilldrake and Flint are known to me. We are engaged in a similar enterprise, one might say. They are not what I would call honorable people. I warn you not to trust them. And yet, if you must travel with them, they will lead you where you need to go."

Snow Pine snorted. "A cryptic warning from a mysterious stranger! My morning is complete!"

"What is so mysterious? I am merely an old traveler offering advice."

"Ha. Old men of my acquaintance always want to swat youngsters or lecture them."

"I suppose I am lecturing you, at that. You seem like one far from home, cut off from her origins, and thus you remind me of me. You have a contradictory nature. You have lost something dear. Perhaps more than one thing.

It might be better to let go. But you and your companions do not let go of anything easily, do you? Beware of them, too—for I see in your friends the mark of madness."

Snow Pine looked far away to where Gaunt and Bone sat silently at their breakfast. "Give me your name," she said. "I don't trust people without names."

"I could conjure a name out of the illusion we call thin air. Would that make me more trustworthy?"

"Indulge me."

"Dorje. Think of me as Dorje. And think of my advice as a gem to pocket, a cheap one perhaps, but one that will sparkle in the right light. Let its rough edges nag at you until that moment comes. Follow Quilldrake and Flint. Do not trust them. That is all."

Dorje bowed and walked into the crowd. For such a heavy-looking man, she thought, his robe billowed over-much, and his steps were light.

She patted her luck charm. These were not the answers she'd sought. However, they would do.

For now.

"You look guilty," Captain Sun told Imago Bone in the cool morning interlude before the Jade Gate opened. The ward doors of the thoroughfare leading from Market to gate had swung wide with the first direct sunlight, and by now the street was full of camels and horses and wagons, and babbling travelers garbed for the desert sun, and chattering locals trying to sell the travelers one last thing, and boxes of red peppercorns, ginger, salt, and medicinals, and padded bags filled with porcelain cups and jade figures, and clothing embellished with cicadas and dragons—and outnumbered guards trying to rope this snorting, many-headed beast of commerce with the brittle twine of authority.

Bone smiled at Sun, glad he wasn't him. "Being interrogated makes me feel that way."

"If you think this is an interrogation, you're more naive than you look. Well, you may be innocent of wrongdoing in Yao'an. But you're surely guilty of something."

"That describes all men."

"Do you have a problem with authority, outlander?"

"No; I enjoy authority."

Captain Sun grunted. "You are fortunate. All of you. Under other circumstances I might have to detain you. But we've gotten word that the Protector-General's chief assistant has died in mysterious circumstances. Smothered in a locked room! He was accounted a wicked man, but no matter. Magistrates and guards will be busy with this; no one wants to hear about trouble in the Western Market."

"We will leave immediately!" Quilldrake said. "We simply have a few more items to gather . . ."

"I am surprised," Bone said, "given this murder, you are not sealing the gates." He winced as Gaunt stepped on his foot.

Sun shook his head. "They assume it is a city insider, someone who hopes to gain advantage by the death, and thus one who wouldn't announce his guilt by fleeing. The killer also stole an item of art—I know not what, but they say it's bulky and would be difficult to transport. And the Protector-General's not about to lose face by publicly acknowledging the crime. Thus you may leave, but not just yet, for you must wait for . . . ah, she is here."

Widow Zheng must indeed have powerful clients, Bone realized, and have claimed favors. For there was the lady herself, outfitted to travel and leading a shaggy two-humped camel laden with supplies and books and scrolls.

"You are going with us?" Quilldrake sounded both excited and aggrieved.

"Well, you owe me explanations, young man," she told the graying Westerner. "I have consulted the *Book of Jagged Lines* and tossed the yarrow sticks, and it appears this is an important matter." She smiled. "Just as important, this old body perceives the opportunity to taste the wide world one last time."

"I might emphasize the 'last time' aspect," Quilldrake said. "Zheng, you know this will be an arduous journey. And possibly dangerous."

"And thus you should not eschew the company of an adept of Living Calligraphy."

"She has a salient point," Gaunt said.

"We'll keep to established roads for a time," said Quilldrake, sounding resigned but not altogether displeased, "so there's ample opportunity to change your mind—"

"And I expect a full share of the loot," Zheng said.

"A full share?" Resignation was flung off like a wet cloak. "A half-share, perhaps! I cannot accept every last hanger-on . . ."

"A full share for her," Snow Pine said, "or none of us go. Yes?"

"Yes," said Gaunt.

"Eh?" said Bone, who was squinting closely at the scrolls of Living Calligraphy, scratching his chin. "Oh—yes."

"Gah," said Quilldrake. "If it weren't you, Zheng . . ."

"Thank you," Zheng said. "Careful with those," she told Bone, "you might set one off and get trampled by an inked elephant."

Bone backed away, hands raised. "I'm worried enough by your camel."

"Ease your fears, pup, for you must purchase camels of your own . . ."

In the end they bought three more camels, two to carry goods, another to carry a person. The plan was for Zheng to ride always, while one person out of the remaining group could rest during a portion of each march.

Bone, Gaunt, and Snow Pine next watched with growing bewilderment as Quilldrake and Zheng haggled for last-minute trade goods. It seemed to Bone this was hardly an auspicious moment to cobble together a caravan, and that the wares on offer were far from choice. And yet Quilldrake and Zheng cajoled people they evidently knew well, speaking of past favors and difficult circumstances, future promises and hints of blackmail.

Before long they were proud owners of damaged bolts of silk, bottles of doubtful remedies, cracked bricks of dubious tea, and bags of "five-spice blend" that surely held no more than three actual spices.

"We've announced we're off to sell our fine products in Madzeu," said Quilldrake in Roil. "As far as anyone knows, we're simply honest traders. Thus we'll slip our pursuit."

Loading the goods was an operation nearly as delicate as acquiring them. Bone regarded their shaggy, two-humped bearers with trepidation. The feeling did not seem to be mutual. One camel trotted up and licked him.

"Ergg!" he said, struggling not to shout. "Blkk."

"Are these Western curses?" Snow Pine said.

"Only in Bone's native language," Gaunt said. "A most peculiar tongue."

"You have 'peculiar tongue' right," said Bone, mopping himself. He looked up. "Ergg," he said, pointing, referring to a person this time.

Three persons, in fact, if not four. For there, out of breath, was the priest from the Market temple where they'd battled; and there on a pallet dragged by two acolytes was a large oblong bundle shrouded in white cloth.

"There you are, Imago Bone," said the holy man. "You asked me what you might do to compensate us. You vanished before I could give you an answer. Perhaps you did not wish to disturb my meditations."

"I have great respect for the power of silence," Bone said. The camel licked him again. "Blkk."

"Here is your answer. Nine Thunderbolts requested his body be disposed of in the Karvak manner. Preferably abandonment to the animals of the steppe."

"The steppe," put in Quilldrake, "is weeks away from here."

"His instructions indicated he would accept the desert as an alternative. Would you do this thing?"

Bone looked at the pallet. In death the shrouded Karvak seemed even bigger than he had in life. Bone wanted to say no. But Nine Thunderbolts had been a valiant comrade, even if only for a minute or two. And Gaunt would surely step on his foot again. He nodded.

Corpse disposal added one more complication to the business of getting proper papers from a nearby official, one who moonlighted, in broad daylight, as a counterfeiter. Bone found the contrast with parts farther east intriguing. Those provinces had been less regimented, yet their civilian officials were proudly honest. But perhaps he should be grateful; without corruption he, Gaunt, and Snow Pine might not have been allowed in Yao'an at all.

He felt relief like a cool breeze when the travelers grandly waved their papers and set out through the gate.

It was not truly made of jade. That lovely substance did clink through the stone tunnel in great quantities, however, along with the rustle of cloth, the glint of gems, the aroma of spices. The tunnel ran through an exceptionally thick portion of the city wall, with provisions for archers to fire through murder-holes.

"Good-bye, Yao'an," Gaunt said. "I don't know if I love this city or hate it."

"The going consensus," said Quilldrake, "is that the answer is 'yes . . .'"

Verses interrupted him, crooned by a performer on the Yao'an side of the tunnel.

Blossoms of pears, like the white desert moon.
Willow branches green like the steppe.
One day willow fluff will blow west like mountain snow.
Beyond the Jade Gate where spring is forgotten.

Light swallowed them, and they were on the Braid.

The desert did not immediately confront the travelers, for a river lay in their path, bordered by willow trees. Wheels spun, churning up the flow for thirsty irrigation ramps. Rafts bobbed, ready for hire, yet another fee. But it was that or give up the camels and ride on cheap bamboo floats buoyed by goat corpses. They hired two rafts.

"Aiya!" Gaunt said, employing a generalized term of exasperation—for as they poled off she lost her balance, until Bone and Snow Pine caught her. She laughed a little. "That expression . . . you know, I don't know how I got by without it."

Snow Pine said, "Do you not swear, away in the Far West?"

"Of course. But to my ear we do it with less music. I'm glad to have more curses in my quiver."

"You'll have cause," Widow Zheng said, staring out west at the brightness as though reconsidering her choice, "to use them all."

They left the river behind, bells tinkling on their camels, their corpse-pallet dragged behind the last. Beyond was not a road but a track worn smooth by countless hooves and feet. The land soared to their left, dry scrub giving way to lush bushes and trees with increasing altitude, before bowing before rocks and snow, peaks and sky. The land to the right was an empire of tan sands, save for a line of vegetation following the river and the Heavenwall northward, farms and villages tied to it like knots on a green cord. River, wall, and green diminished in stature with remoteness from Yao'an, and not simply because of distance. However, this was hard to judge, for the desert air shimmered with heat. Here on the road it was comfortable enough, as breezes flitted down from the mountains, and occasionally their feet were sloshed by the waters of short-lived, desert-bound streams.

"Perhaps it's time to speak, Quilldrake," Zheng prompted after they'd traveled several li.

"Not yet," Quilldrake said, looking around carefully at the various travelers within a stone's throw.

Several farms, a few villages, and a pair of wayside shrines lay within a day's travel of Yao'an, and as the hours passed, most of the walkers peeled off toward one destination or another. As the day waned, there remained only their own caravan and a more ambitious train of thirty camels, both nominally bound for Madzeu. Quilldrake kept casting anxious looks backward at the larger caravan, though Bone could see nothing worrisome about it.

As the sun reddened, Quilldrake groaned and called for a halt. "Bad melons!" he kept repeating as he lay upon the ground, but he waved off the other caravan's offer of aid as they passed. Once their last camel had disappeared around a bend of the southward hills and the last bell's tinkle had vanished into the whispers of the wind, Quilldrake had an immediate recovery.

He led them at a crawl until they'd passed around the bend and encountered a dome-shaped roadside shrine. Here Quilldrake halted again, made a perfunctory bow before a stone image of the Undetermined, and unsecured the corpse-pallet.

"Um," Gaunt said, "what are you doing?"

"An important observance." Grunting, he dragged the pallet into the shrine.

"I had not heard," Widow Zheng called from her camel, "that the Karvaks had converted to the ways of the Undetermined."

"Truly?" the unseen Quilldrake called. "I could have sworn I heard differently. At any rate, I'm hot and tired enough to convert to anything . . ."

Feeling an inconvenient responsibility to Nine Thunderbolts, Bone followed, but Gaunt was faster.

The structure was cramped but cool. Quilldrake and the pallet were on the other side of a pillar inscribed in languages Bone could not read.

"Quilldrake—" Gaunt began, and then gasped.

The shroud was moving.

CHAPTER 8

THE DESERT OF HUNGRY SHADOWS

It never ceased to astonish Persimmon Gaunt how monster-prone she and her husband's lives had become. "Bone?" she called, her voice giddy. "Everyone? *Walking dead!*" She drew a dagger and prepared to throw. Behind her, unable to see clearly, Bone cursed and found his own weapons.

The body was moving more emphatically now, as if enraged at being found out. Well, good. Gaunt threw. The dagger connected with a *thunk* at a part of the shroud nearest the floor, yet the thing only moved more swiftly.

"Swan's Blood," she said, finding a second dagger, "Quilldrake, you should take burial customs more seriously—"

"My dear—!" Quilldrake began.

But all were silenced by the corpse's next action.

A sword blade transfixed the shroud, and with a sound of rending cloth a figure burst forth, armed with a saber whose metal shone like moonlight.

She heard one of Bone's daggers clatter to the stone floor, but she could not spare time for that. She made to throw.

A hand gripped her wrist. "Gaunt," Bone said, "it's not the Karvak."

"I've been mistaken for many things," gasped the man with the saber, "but never that."

She blinked. It was the second Westerner from Quilldrake's office.

Gaunt relaxed, lowering her dagger and breathing hard. "I do apologize, sir. Mister Flint, I presume."

"Indeed," said Flint, setting his weapon on the stone floor. The saber ceased to glow as it left his trembling grip, though the intricate gem-laden metalwork of the pommel glinted still. Something about its appearance tickled her memory, but there was no time to wonder about that now. "You'll pardon me if I do not immediately shake hands, Persimmon Gaunt, Imago Bone. But I've had a long and bumpy day."

"You are unhurt?" Gaunt asked.

"Yes. Heat and bruises are my trouble. I'm glad it's not yet summer. I fear your dagger hit my companion the dead man."

"Oh." Gaunt retrieved it, whispering fresh apologies to the fallen Karvak. By now Snow Pine and Widow Zheng had entered as well.

"We were traveling with a live corpse the entire time?" Snow Pine exclaimed.

"And a dead corpse," Quilldrake said. "I guessed as much when I saw how big the shroud was. We have contacts in many temples. I'm not sure the priest knew, but others did."

"Indeed," Flint said, snatching a waterskin from Quilldrake and greedily quaffing. He was a head taller than Bone, and even in his disheveled state he had the manner of an immortal looking down upon the world with rue. "I was obliged to collapse our escape route in a way that forced me back into the city, to our access under the House of Tender Breezes. I wished for tenderness indeed but could waste no time. I lurked here and there until overhearing the priest's plan to foist this body upon you, and my path was clear."

"Clear to a madman!" Widow Zheng scoffed.

Flint bowed.

"Well, I do regret assaulting you," Gaunt said.

Flint shrugged. "I prefer to forget what vexed me in the past, that I might focus on what vexes me in the present."

"That's not exactly a path to bliss," Snow Pine said.

"We don't all seek bliss in this life."

"I admire your approach," Bone said. "Do you feel pursuit is close at hand?"

"I don't know. I think we're safe enough from ordinary observers at this moment, but I gather Charstalkers are involved."

"You two owe us explanations," Zheng said, "especially about them."

"Agreed!" Quilldrake said. "But survival comes first. The immediate thing you must know about Charstalkers is that they can fly like smoke upon the breeze, or inhabit animal minds."

"The human animal included," Flint said. "Thus the desert is, ironically, a haven, as it is inimical to animal life. Our demonic foes must make themselves obvious if they're to hunt. Of course the sands present their own dangers, but there's no help for that. Death licks every heel." He retrieved his sword. Gaunt noted that on this occasion it did not glow. "Sunset approaches. I'd prefer to travel by day, but we must get off this track. Let's leave signs that we've camped here, then make our exit."

In that way a companion who'd been utterly silent all day now took the reins of the entire expedition. Though clearly much younger than Quilldrake, Flint gave orders. Gaunt was uncertain what to make of it all, but Flint seemed to know his business. As they returned to the camels, she shared a wary shrug with Bone. They had to follow through on their best guesses, and that meant following Flint into the desert.

They removed the camels' bells and stepped into sands seemingly turned bloody with the sunset. Gaunt reflected that those she trusted numbered three, and they might still overpower Flint and Quilldrake if need be (though that sword was worrisome).

I have become a cold thing, Gaunt thought.

The desert became cold too.

After some ten li they reached a rocky rise jabbing at the stars like a giant's broken blade. There they camped against the northern face, for Flint and Quilldrake wished only to escape sight of the road. For the same reason they sparked no fire.

"I suggest we sleep," Flint said. "Save talk for tomorrow. It will be a hard day."

At dawn Bone and Quilldrake carried the body of Nine Thunderbolts high onto the rocks. "This method of corpse-disposal," Quilldrake said, gasping, "is closer to that of Qushkent than to that of the steppe. But I doubt he'll object. We're close enough to the road to attract scavengers, I'd think."

"He's heavier than I'd have credited," Bone said. "As though he's wrapped with something weightier than this shroud . . ."

"It is not our business," Quilldrake said, letting Nine Thunderbolts drop.

"Farewell, brave warrior," Bone said, feeling that he should say something. "May you ride upon starlit grasslands, fight wondrous opponents, and bed miraculous women."

"So let it be," Quilldrake agreed.

The others were readying the caravan, bells and all. Flint had snapped a desiccated branch from a long-dead tree, and was using it to sketch a map of the known world, all the way from the littoral region of Qiangguo to Swanisle. Gaunt was studying it with great interest, and Bone joined her.

"I'm not going anywhere," said Widow Zheng, hands on hips, "until I have the answers to two questions. Where exactly are we going? And where is the book I loaned you?"

Flint said nothing, as he added finishing touches.

"Xembala," Quilldrake muttered, as he walked up.

"That sounds like a long way to take a book," Snow Pine said.

"I see no Xembala on that map," Bone noted.

"Indeed," Flint said. "One day I hope to add that name."

"You have a slight inaccuracy on the southern coast of Qiangguo," Gaunt noted. "The coast bends inward more near Riverclaw."

"That indentation is obscured by the name of the city," Flint retorted.

"As you wish."

"I think the book was taken by our friends in black," Flint continued. "And as for Xembala? Well, perhaps we will see it. But first—" He jabbed his stick. "We are here, a little west of Yao'an. We go to Shahuang deep within the desert." Another jab.

"You hardly moved the stick at all," said Bone.

"And yet a flick of the stick, on this scale, means many days' travel. I want you all to understand what we undertake, and how much territory it may encompass. The first leg is comparatively easy. We must see the Cave of Ten Thousand Illuminations and consider for ourselves this record of the Silk Map. Then we can decide where we must go."

They began the long journey into the desert.

"'Comparatively easy,' he said," Zheng groused after an hour, fanning herself atop her camel. "Can't we travel by night?"

"There are two bad ways to cross the desert," said Flint over the tinkle of the camels' bells and the soft fall of feet and hooves upon the bright sand. "The first is to travel by day, under the unremitting heat and glare. The second is to travel by night and risk getting lost with no hope of recovery. We'll likely do some of both. The only truly good path, I'm afraid, would be to turn around."

All around them lay mute supporting arguments—thousands of dunes, rocky outcroppings shaped into weird sculptures by the wind, trees dead for decades, the occasional bones of a horse. The mountains behind them had receded into a dark and wavy suggestion of mass, while the horizon ahead was a blur of merged sand and sky that was not so much like the world's edge as an absence of form altogether.

"I like this fellow," Bone muttered to his mount, whom he'd privately named Scoff. (The camel-merchant had called her Fragrant Flower of the West, but he reasoned she deserved better than sarcasm.) "He sees a universe of disaster in a grain of sand." He was grateful for his white robes and hood but still felt as if he were an ant traveling through a very large oven.

Gaunt, just ahead of him and behind Flint, pretended not to hear Bone. "Is there then no good way, Master Flint?"

"Flint will be sufficient. Or Doctor Flint, if you prefer formality. Master Flint was my father. There are indeed good ways. You can fly, if you have access to an aerial mount. You can use tunnels, if you are a sand-goblin. If one dared tame the dragon-horses of the Forbidden Steppe, one might cross the sands in a day. And perhaps, if you are a sorcerer, you can translate yourself magically from one side of the desert to another."

"As I understand it," Quilldrake put in from ahead of Flint, "even the legendary Archmage can't manage such a feat. Even great wizards are forced to walk."

"Indeed," said Flint. "My real answer is that the only good way to travel the desert is by consulting a book about it."

"I agree," said Widow Zheng from behind Bone, as she and he peered warily at a distant skeleton. "I look forward to our camp and perhaps some candlelit reading."

"How far to the first oasis?" called Snow Pine from the tail of their caravan. Bone remembered that she'd grown up beside the Ochre River, and that for all the hardships of her life, insufficient water had never been one of them.

"I believe we're making reasonable time," Flint called back. "But I still anticipate some travel by night. We have been here before, but we'll have to judge at sunset whether we can safely travel the rest of the distance in the dark. Otherwise we must camp in the open."

"Would that be so bad?"

"Possibly!" shouted Quilldrake. "The oases have old warding-stones blessed by priests of the three faiths hereabouts, and sometimes glyphs left by wandering wizards! One hopes at least some are efficacious!"

"And if none are?" asked Gaunt.

Widow Zheng cackled in a way that made Bone a trifle nervous. "That's what Living Calligraphy is for," she said.

They settled into a quiet progression for the next hour. Had this been a forest or a grassy plain, Bone thought, chatter would have cut the silence, but in the desert simply moving was a disciplined endeavor. He recalled the milder desert beside the city he'd once called home, and the words of his mentor in the thieving art. *Beware places of no concealment*, Master Sidewinder had said. *Grand plazas. Open sand. Honest relationships.*

Must I have no honest relationships? Bone had asked.

Of course you may! With me you will never, even in the tiniest degree, ever have cause to think I would deceive you in any matter whatsoever. Rest assured, I am as trustworthy a man as has ever been born.

You are a genius at thieving, Master Sidewinder, but you are a little obvious with your sarcasm.

My work here is done.

Bone smiled at the memory. He missed his long-dead teacher and wished Gaunt could have met him. He missed Palmary and cities in general. He regretted none of his time with Gaunt. Well, maybe certain events. The cannibals. The philosophical torturers. The dragons. But not the whole. Yet it seemed to him that for a city-thief he spent an inordinate amount of time outdoors. Someday, when they'd won back their son, he would take them into an overcrowded, noisy, polyglot enclave where nature was nowhere to be seen, to get away from it all.

Glancing behind, he thought he saw a trail of windborne sand, as though some beast were approaching. It would have to be on the large side, he thought, surprisingly so for this desert. It seemed that he would not be getting away from nature any time soon. "Say—" he began.

He was cut off by a shout up front.

"Sandstorm ahead!" Quilldrake said. "We'd best dig in!"

Bone squinted ahead, possible pursuit forgotten. The haze beyond the dunes seemed as featureless as ever. "I see no storm!"

"Do you not see my camel?"

Quilldrake's mount, the oldest of them, had ascended a low rise crowned by a rock outcropping. It lay down upon the sand and burrowed its head. The other camels lumbered up to follow suit, moaning and bleating.

"I suppose we're stopping," Bone said to Scoff, who joined the others, dropped, and nuzzled her way into the sand.

"The old one senses the approach of the burning wind," said Flint. "The younger camels take its lead. We should too. Lie down, with the camels between you and the approach of the wind. Put your faces in the sand and cover your heads with cloth."

"How long will it last?" Gaunt asked.

"As long as it lasts."

Bone and Gaunt lay beside each other. Bone looked up and saw a wall of dust approaching, its tan shroud billowing halfway up the sky. It approached faster than a galloping horse.

"Hold my hand, Bone," Gaunt said. "If we're fortunate, future scholars may display our skeletons together."

He took her hand. The sandstorm rushed upon them.

It seemed to last hours, though Bone was unsure he could trust his judgment. It certainly grew very hot. He squeezed Gaunt's hand now and then, and she squeezed back.

He began hearing hints of voices on the wind, curious snatches of conversation that could not be real, as they seemed far too relaxed to be the speech of his companions. As time passed, some of the fragments touched his memory and seemed the voices of his past.

The more you fight . . . came the voice of Snow Pine's once-mentor, Lightning Bug.

The more it slips away . . . answered Flybait, Snow Pine's dead husband.

You are one flesh . . . came the voice of Eshe, the priestess who'd performed Gaunt and Bone's marriage . . . *come whatever may* . . .

All things are in your hand . . . came a much rougher voice, much nearer at hand, . . . *You who whirl the days* . . .

The storm had ebbed before Bone was quite aware of the fact. Gaunt was tugging at his hand, her voice conveying a trace of alarm. "Bone! We're free of it . . ." her voice trailed off in wretched hacking.

Bone found himself in a golden world, for though the thick of the sandstorm had passed, the air was full of haze, making a ripe orange of the sun. Everyone had endured, though they announced their safety with a chorus of coughs.

Flint passed around waterskins. "We've lost time. We should move as soon as we're able. I recommend traveling through the night. The oasis will provide shelter."

"No argument," Gaunt said.

Now Flint took the rear, perhaps fearing someone would slump exhausted from their camel and be left behind. The desert treated them with a degree of kindness for the rest of the day, which was to say it passively seared them, rather than actively smothered them. Bone saw no animal life but what they brought with them, and while corpses of old trees thrust here and there from the sand, there was nothing green.

In early evening, cool breezes at last kissed their faces, and a sort of exhausted jollity came to the caravan. Gaunt sang, giving Bone a rare reminder that she'd studied as a bard. Quilldrake quietly conversed with Widow Zheng; Bone suspected he was making sure, from her responses, that she was bearing up. He overheard Snow Pine talking with Flint. There was something in their voices that raised an uncomfortable feeling in Bone, though he could not identify it. He patted Scoff. "You are doing well?"

Scoff grunted.

"I never would have expected you to make friends with a camel, Bone," Gaunt said.

"We have much in common," said Bone. "Perhaps when at last we settle down, we should consider having a pet."

"You and your camel will keep a pet? How interesting. Be sure to write me about it."

When the sun set, there was nothing westward to hide it, no hills, no mountains, no approaching caravan laden with melons. Bone had the impression the land was one vast, luminous scab. Stars appeared as they proceeded into night, and every time Bone was convinced the sky was full, the horizon dimmed further and more glories blazed.

"It's cold," Gaunt said, and this was another thing Bone had not quite noticed, but he shivered as she said it.

"This is among the hottest and coldest of places," Quilldrake called back from where he guided them by the stars. "Still, I prefer the cold to the heat. If landmarks didn't matter, I'd always travel by night."

They reached the first oasis before moonset. It was little more than a large pond with a score of poplar trees escorting it through its days and nights, a guard of four obelisks attending them. Each monument bore an inscription— two in the Tongue of the Tortoise Shell, one in the script of Mirabad, the last in a vertical script unknown to Bone. The ones that looked familiar were for-biddances against evil.

Gaunt said, "I am curious what we need defending from."

Widow Zheng said, "They say there are night-horrors in this desert. They make sounds that lure the traveler from her companions and leave her lost and alone. If she's lucky."

"I suspect the rumors exaggerate, however," Flint said. "You may have heard peculiar sounds already? As temperature changes, masses of sand may shift, their acoustics strange and disturbing. While the world has its dangers, the mind magnifies and multiplies them."

Whether or not the wardings were efficacious, they succeeded in calming the travelers' nerves. Soon they'd tied up camels, filled up waterskins, tossed bedrolls, and collapsed into sleep.

Six days, four oases, and one more sandstorm passed in like fashion. At first they had little energy for talk, but by now Bone was beginning to settle into a routine, and late in the afternoon of the sixth day he walked beside Flint and said, "I'd like to know more about Xembala."

"Wouldn't we all!" Flint shook his head, staring at the blurred horizon. "The lost paradise, spoken of in many legends. Once, Imago Bone, I thought I could locate it by reason, triangulate it. You see, in Qiangguo, the Pure Land is said to be in the west. But in Palmary, the Lost Garden is said to lie to the east. Far, far to the south in Harimaupura, they say the Enlightened Kingdom lies to the far, far north. So you see, I suspected I could trace all these legends to a particular spot in the physical world." He chuckled. "And to a degree I succeeded! Alas, my 'spot' is a region over a thousand miles across. In the great trading cities of Anoka, Qushkent, and Madzeu, and in the oasis towns, paradise is said to rest among the clouds. So I concluded Xembala must lie upon the Plateau of Geam, home of mystics. I climbed the mountains and battled vultures and vertigo to attain it. In Geam, the holy ones told me Xembala was an idea, that paradise was in my head. Very helpful. But there was a twinkle in their eyes as they said it, and I think they knew much they wouldn't convey."

Quilldrake had joined them. There was a worried look in his eyes that his bright tone belied. "And here you see the basis of Flint's and my collaboration! For *I* am interested in mere treasure to rival the wealth of emperors. Flint seeks the sublime revelations of exploration."

"In any event," Flint said, "I think Xembala must lie amid the mountains near to the Braid of Spice. And I feel sure that, before the year is out, I will find it."

"We have a more immediate problem, I fear," Quilldrake said, his voice now in accord with his expression. "We should have reached the next oasis by now."

Hours of backtracking commenced, during which the sun set and the stars emerged, their steady beauty a prickling contrast to the journeyers' increasing worry. Quilldrake at last called a halt, consulting with Flint in low tones. Flint sighed and turned to the others. "I think further searching is counterproductive. We'll seek a rocky spot to camp."

"I don't dispute you," Gaunt said, "but I hope it's defensible."

"I suspect we will be safe." Flint added, "But I do suggest roping ourselves together before sleep."

Thus they and their camels arranged themselves beside lonely boulders. Widow Zheng, now much recovered, told them a bedtime story about how the Great Sage, Equal of Heaven, once tipped over this or that alchemical vessel in the heavens, producing bright nebulae that remained to this day. Quilldrake and Flint were vocal in their appreciation; Bone, Gaunt, and Snow Pine more muted. At last Bone and Gaunt curled up next to each other, and Bone sank into an exhausted slumber.

"He will not be here. Any more than my son is here."

Mama!

At Gaunt's words a tremor crossed Zheng's face. "Your son?"

"He is lost."

"I—I lost a son too. He fought the Karvaks . . ." Zheng looked around at the desert, seeing it anew.

"I am sorry. My son lives. Or so I may hope. But he's trapped in a faraway place."

No, I'm here, Mama.

"Trapped . . . Persimmon Gaunt, in *Lamentations of the Great Historian* we learn of great crystal trees beneath the desert . . . the creations of the Leviathan Minds in the days when this land was a sea. Our great works, like our Heaven-walls, are as nothing before what they wrought."

I'm not a crystal tree, Mama.

Zheng said, "The Minds used the trees as we use libraries. Each flower summoned thoughts as pollen attracts bees. For Leviathans the process was harmless and pleasant. But other creatures found themselves absorbed, crys-tallized, hanging from the branches like fruit."

Mama, don't listen to her.

Gaunt said, "I know it's a trick, Zheng. I know my boy's voice, and this is a good facsimile. But I also know the nature of the place where he is impris-oned. Time flows differently there, and his speech will already be deeper by now."

Mother, came a different, older voice.

"Nice try," said Gaunt, tightening her grip on her bow. "Do you think you're free of the compulsion, Zheng?"

"Perhaps . . . perhaps it's well you spoke of your child. It may be easier for you to resist because you are younger," Zheng said. "You have fewer memo-ries to haunt you. Though I do not know why your young man proved so vulnerable."

"Looks are deceiving. Bone has ample memories. Will you stay with me? I must help him. Whatever comes."

"What of your son? Do you have no hope for him?"

Mother . . .

Gaunt could not reply.

Zheng placed a hand on her shoulder. "I will stay with you."

They followed the voices. Gaunt's son did not appear.

Gaunt saw the crystals before she saw the men. She was put in mind of the mineral formations of deep caves, which may branch in seemingly organic ways. It was as though the crowns of crystallized oaks pierced the sands.

In their midst Imago Bone stood transfixed in the act of stabbing the crystal cocoon that had engulfed him. Quilldrake was nearer, outside the cluster of treelike structures. He could still speak, although crystal formed a hood around his head and imprisoned his body mid-stagger. "Run," he gasped. "Go. Don't weep for us. We'll be immortal after a fashion. Our thoughts will shine within eternal matrices."

"Bone needs no eternal matrices," Gaunt said, raising her bow. "He has me."

She fired at Quilldrake.

"Ah—"

His gasp ended in the shattering of the material covering his chest. A great shriek lashed the desert, as fragments spun through the air. With the pieces came snatches of speech, and even splinters of thought itself, conveyed to her mind as a shard might convey glass to her blood.

I must see everything, came a young man's voice, and it took her a moment to recognize it as Quilldrake's. *With my own eyes! Imagination's not enough . . .*

(Her hand cramped in the narrow study, streaks of sunlight crossing the paper as she copied yet another map . . .)

The sensations receded. There had been many more, but only a couple stuck in her memory.

"That was a memorable arrow you shot," Quilldrake rasped.

"It was not the arrow that was memorable," Gaunt said. "If Zheng is correct, these crystals are memory itself."

"I'm concerned what it may do to me, to have it shattered all around me."

Gaunt nodded. "That is why I will be careful." She did not add, *And that's why I'm shooting at you first.*

More crystal shattered, and again Gaunt's ears and mind were assaulted. She tuned out the impressions and concentrated on freeing the treasure hunter. At last he stumbled up to them, bearing bloody cuts on his face, but basically intact. Zheng assisted him in breaking free of clinging shards.

Gaunt set her sights on Bone, but already the crystal had responded. A translucent curtain now encircled her husband. She fired, and a section shattered, but it began re-forming even as she nocked another arrow.

"Arrows are not enough," Gaunt said. "I must go to him."

"You'll be trapped as well," said Quilldrake.

"We'll see." Gaunt advanced, firing again, and again.

Voices and visions danced around her. Voices male and female, old and young, called out amid surf and snow and the braying of animals and the clash of weapons.

"Gaunt! Persimmon!" Now Snow Pine stood beside her, and Liron Flint too, both shivering.

"They've brought my scrolls," Zheng called from behind them. "There's a chance."

"What can you do?" Gaunt said.

Zheng strode forward, for a moment seeming much younger in gait. "Stand still, Gaunt."

Zheng flung open two scrolls simultaneously. Silvery writing winged forth, proclaiming, *A wise woman heeds the silence in her mind, not the noise of the mob.* At Zheng's whisper, the words fluttered into Gaunt's ear. They tickled. The other formed characters so gray in the approaching dawn light, it was hard to believe anything was there. Yet rather than fade, these words arrayed themselves like a sword blade with a hilt of black ink. *Determination whets the sword of character*, the logograms read.

She took up the sword and bowed to Zheng. "If one must bow," Gaunt told her, "bow low and make it count. So it's said."

In truth, she couldn't hear her own words, for all sound was dimmed. She raised her sword of calligraphy and strode to the crystal barrier. Where she'd fired arrows, there lay ragged cracks. The jeweled archive tried to assault her mind, but she heard nothing, insulated by Zheng's Living Calligraphy.

Meeting the barrier, she swung the sword of words, and bits of the wall shattered. She covered her face with her off-hand, but shards still stung. With them came glimpses of other lives. She beheld a green land and a fur-clad people hunting a mastodon. She witnessed a strange, short folk painting the outlines of their hands onto rocks. She saw peculiar saurian humanoids raising corkscrewing towers beside a narrow sea. A part of her wished to become lost in time, to know all these unwritten histories.

A cold resolution, woven into her thoughts, yanked her back like a tether across the abyss of days. Then she was Gaunt again, striking at the wall.

Now Flint stood beside her, his saber drawn and glowing like a crescent moon, also hacking at the barrier. It seemed to her that with each swing a metallic screeching babbled unintelligible words into the desert air, a new voice for each attack. She had no time to wonder at this, for her own arm ached to destroy what kept her from Bone.

At last they clove a gap.

Bone's eyes blinked at Gaunt through his cocoon of crystal. She imagined him saying, *It was foolish to come back for me.* She imagined responding, *How could I not show you my sword made of words?*

Flint had followed; he frowned at his palely glowing saber. "I fear that Crypttongue will slay Bone as soon as free him."

Gaunt's eyes widened, for she recognized the name. She saw that Bone's did too. But she simply raised her weapon of shining words. "Then stand aside, for I must try."

She swung.

She circled him, hacking, trusting that the sword of her own determination would not harm her lover. Shards flew. She bled upon the sands. The same sands were once rocks beside a disappearing sea. Within that sea strange octopus-like beings, crooning in their emerald majesty, inhabited obsidian citadels in the shape of sailing ships. Lesser beings crewed their vessels, meeping rodent-things, hulking ancestors of the saurian folk, insectoids reminiscent of scarab beetles. Their age was passing, and they would encode their knowledge into the crystal trees beside the shore, that none would forget their majesty. It seemed to Gaunt that her blood was a doorway into time, and through its red medium she beheld onyx eyes regarding her coldly. A wind blew across the ages from their aeon to hers, and with it came the message that she was a nothing, an afterthought; what could she say that would justify refusing their gift of jeweled entombment?

She thought, *I can say, "It's for a reason when the wind gusts from an empty cave." I can say, "It's better to bend in the wind that to break." I can say, "When the wind blows its changes, you may build walls, but I will build windmills."*

All the endless proverbs and idioms that embellished Qiangguo's language, and that had shut her out like a thicket, she now embraced as shelter in the mind-storm. And were such aphorisms, when all was said, not the greatest works of civilization? Whatever, they were human sentiments, and they pulled her back to the human world.

"Gaunt . . ." Bone was rasping. "Gaunt . . . we'd best get out of here. I wrenched my foot escaping the last of that damned crystal . . . don't believe I can carry you . . ."

He was free, save for a dusting of crystal, and his arms were around her.

"Flint is here, so let us both help you."

They fled the keening place of living crystal, trying not to look at the skeletons interred within the branches.

When they were at last near camp Bone said, "Thank you, Gaunt . . . all of you. I thought I was lost in ancient memories. I saw horrors, like things of another iteration of creation. . . . We glimpsed things like this once in a hall of mermaids, Gaunt."

"Yes, I remember. Perhaps their memories reach back farther than humanity's." Gaunt shivered, sharing some of Bone's chill. "It is somewhat frightening to imagine that this world once belonged to things nothing like ourselves."

"That is not what I find somewhat frightening," muttered Quilldrake.

"Then what is?" said Zheng.

"I think our camels have disappeared."

"They will know to look for water," Quilldrake said, after the travelers circled the camp, calling out uselessly. "If they were terrified by night noises, they'll likely have fled to the nearest water source. Unfortunately."

"Why unfortunately?" said Gaunt.

"The nearest water source," Flint said, "is Hvam, the haunted city."

"They won't have the sense to avoid such a place?" Bone asked.

Quilldrake said, "Camels won't be frightened by human ghost stories. Perhaps we shouldn't be either. Though Flint and I have never dared. We've always skirted it in favor of an oasis one day beyond."

"How will we fare without the water?" Gaunt asked.

Neither treasure hunter answered.

"I see," said Bone. "Well, do we make our desperate attempt by night, or by day?"

"Night," said Flint.

"Day," said Quilldrake.

"Wonderful," said Snow Pine.

"I suspect Quilldrake feels the need to recuperate," Bone said. "As do I. My foot still winces. Otherwise I'd concur with Flint."

"Without the waterskins," Flint said, "we won't last long. Night travel will help our chances."

"You haven't experienced the clutch of the crystal," Quilldrake said. "Bone and I won't be good for much travel, not until we rest. I regret wasting the night, but wait we must."

"Is there not another alternative?" Widow Zheng said. "Each of you treasure hunters knows the way to this haunted city. Let Quilldrake stay with Bone, Gaunt, and Snow Pine, and I'll accompany Flint through the night. The rest of you, catch up as you can. If we're successful we'll lead the camels back toward you."

"That could work," Flint admitted. "Though I'm reluctant to split our band. And with the greatest respect, Grandmother, our last stretch will surely be by day, and speed is called for. You'll be better off here."

"I will go," Snow Pine said. "I don't know the desert, but I'm wide awake. And I would rather not separate these two."

"Are you certain?" Gaunt said. "Bone and I have a way of finding each other again."

"I saw you separated from him for much too long. We'll see each other soon."

"All this honor," Quilldrake muttered. "Self-sacrifice. Courage. I think I will be ill."

"It's only contagious after long exposure," Bone said.

"Good luck," Gaunt said.

CHAPTER 9

THE HAUNTED CITY

"I didn't want to ask, before," Snow Pine said to Flint, after they'd ascended and jogged down perhaps ten dunes, "but how far to this place?"

"The rest of the night, I think," Flint said, "and half the day."

"A tiring trip."

"With a haunted city for our reward!"

"I'm glad to be doing something. It's hard for me to sit still when there's trouble."

"I can believe that. You have a restless look."

"You should talk. Most men I've known seek riches, or at least a place in the world. Except the few who abandon the world. But you're in some strange place in between. You want knowledge."

"Indeed. What confuses me is why the compulsion isn't more common. Here we are in a world of wonders, and people are content to stare down at their feet. Look up, Snow Pine! Thousands upon thousands of stars, and if you were to look through a spyglass, you'd see an order of magnitude more. What wonders must be out there. And what past wonders lie in the sands beneath our feet? We weren't made to crawl about in the same hovels age after age, nor numbly chew the same roots. We were made to learn, and record what we learn, so that our descendants may learn even more."

"Well, you are like other men I've known, in one respect. You like to talk."

"My apologies. I do go on."

"I did not say I minded."

That shut him up. She did not mind that either. But he was interesting company, even as a silent presence. She was not above enjoying it.

They passed over a flatter region of sands, and cold breezes stole their voices for a time. They passed a monumental spire of rock, jabbing gashes into the starfield, and the wind ceased for a time. She heard Flint's prayer of thanks. *Thank you for this night,* she thought he murmured, *you who whirl the days.*

"So," Snow Pine said. "You pray to a god?"

Flint looked at her. It was hard to tell in the starlight, but she thought he smiled a little, though his voice was wary. "Why do you ask?"

Snow Pine smiled back. "So you can try to convert me. That's what every devout Westerner wants to do, isn't it?"

"I'm a Westerner if you say I am. We're not the converting type, though. And we don't always fit well with other Westerners."

"Why is that?"

"Ha. My people spend much air, and spill much ink, asking why others keep spilling our blood. The truth is I don't really understand it. It's almost as if the hostility proves we're truly the Painter's chosen."

"Painter?"

"Well. My people account themselves People of the Brush, in the hand of the Painter of Clouds."

"Interesting! So what does the Painter ask of the brush?"

"Everything. Because the Painter paints everything. But most often . . . justice, knowledge, reverence for life and living. Some also say that the Painter demands we be tough-minded. But I think perhaps that part comes from us instead. A survival trait."

"Does this Painter do anything for you in return?"

"My, you are full of questions. What does he do for us indeed! I suppose, if I'm in a kindly mood, I'd say the Painter calls us to appreciate the canvas. Water in the desert. Loyal animals. The craft behind tools and clothing. Each other. . . . And clouds, of course. Though I can't spot any now."

"There are dark shapes in the starfield ahead," she said. "Round shapes. They're moving, I think. They might be clouds. . . ."

"I hadn't thought of that. To see clouds as absences. Perhaps you're right. Well, that is another thing. To see things in new ways. And to regard them, even for a short time, as the Painter sees them, precious and part of a whole. To do that is to rise above pettiness. For a while. From that perspective it is easier to advance knowledge, and work for justice. That might justify some of the trouble it brings down on our heads. Maybe."

"You don't sound too fond of your Painter."

"I'm not!" Flint chuckled. "Self-righteous, changeable bastard, if you ask me. The only times I really get along with him are when I don't believe in him."

"Wait. What?" She could not help laughing. "Do you believe in this Painter or don't you?"

"Well, yes and no. My people's history makes claims about signs and miracles, but we're also supposed to be tough-minded, yes? And all my conversations with the Painter of Clouds have been one-sided."

"Maybe he doesn't like you."

"Maybe I don't like him."

"Maybe he likes you so much, he could listen to you all day."

"Ha! I like that. But how would I ever know?"

"You could ask him."

"Are women of Qiangguo always so practical? Or should I say whimsical?"

"You'll have to go ask them. I'm just the one who's here. What I say is, how can you talk about this maybe-maybe-not deity of yours so roughly? My people think our gods—and demigods, and spirits, and cosmic forces, there are so many—my people think the powers that be are flawed. There's every reason to believe this. And yet we're very careful to honor them and to never annoy them."

"That seems prudent."

"But you, you attribute the shaping of reality itself to your Painter! And yet you mock him, snarl at him. Aren't you at least a little bit afraid?"

"Very."

"And yet you say you don't necessarily believe in him?"

"Usually not."

"Aiya. This seems a perverse thing, to have such an awesomely powerful god to not believe in. In a way it'd be easier to follow the Undetermined and believe that nothing at all is real, that it's all a kind of dream."

"Well, maybe so. But then you wouldn't be real, so I reject that theory."

"You're a very strange person, Liron Flint."

"Well, you're invigorating company, Snow Pine. So I hope you don't mind strange."

"Perhaps I don't."

The night grew ever colder, and the brief shelter of the rocky rise vanished, bringing on the wind. They traveled in increasing physical discomfort and increasing conversational warmth. Snow Pine talked of her life, such as it had been, of her defiance of family and life of crime, of her gangster husband, of her daughter, lost as far away as anyone could be this side of death. Flint spoke of dropping objects from buildings to time their fall, of spending days lost in a world of numbers, of disinterring corpses for clandestine dissection. They were more honest than many married couples, yet remote as enemies, there on the cold sands with only the stars for witness.

Dawn came cloudless, and with it a promise of warmth. They crouched for a meal of dry meat and a shared waterskin.

"I wish I could promise it will be soon," Flint said. "But I think we made good time. We may reach the place before noon."

"I can eat as we walk," Snow Pine said.

There were not even dead trees within the desolation revealed by the morning sun. There were rocks weirdly sculpted by the winds into shapes evocative of chalices, seashells, or billowing curtains. There were endless dunes like the humps of petrified sea monsters. There was a peculiar whistling as the wind meandered amongst its stony or sandy obstacles. There was much to marvel at. But there was nothing alive but them.

After silent hours, they beheld a ridge of golden rock, like a mountain range dragged down to a sandy grave. A few scraggly birds circled that region.

When at last they stood upon stone, Snow Pine's spirit felt like dancing. Her body felt like staggering.

"Soon now," Flint said, and they moved through shadow and light through a dry riverbed toward the ridge's heart.

They entered a stone valley guarded at all sides by rocky hills. There rose a walled, four-sided town smaller than Yao'an but clearly following Qiangguo's model. The wall was a shell, however, and only a pair of towers stood within it. The gate was long gone, and nothing green grew save a grim scattering of bushes. Wind howled through the ruins.

"Is this it?" Snow Pine asked.

"Hvam," Flint said. "Depopulated by the Karvaks."

"Depopulated? I hope you mean the people were driven out."

"Some were driven out," Flint said. "Others are still here. Do you see, at the gates, the towers of skulls?"

"Aiya," Snow Pine said and bowed her head.

"Hvam made the error of refusing surrender," Flint said. "What's more, they slew the Karvak in charge, a son of the Grand Khan. It's said his sister, who was still only a young girl at the time, proved a better commander. She was systematic in her revenge. She dammed the river that gave the city life. Wells remained, but they were not enough. When the citizens were at their most desperate, the Karvaks attacked a second time. Some inhabitants were spared. The bulk were slaughtered, as though these walls were a pen."

"How could human beings treat each other like that?"

"You ask something I don't think even the Painter could answer."

Snow Pine frowned. "I think of my homeland as so powerful, Flint. And I've hated so much about it. But what if Qiangguo fell? Standing here, I feel as though it could."

"I have no answer but this. Cherish your existence. I urge you to marvel at your life as if you were a member of some wondrous lost civilization. After all, from some future perspective, you probably are."

She stared at the grim monuments. "Let's find our camels and get the hell out of here."

They passed beside the piles of skulls, and Snow Pine made herself look at them, even when she realized that many were too small to be adults. There were even skulls of cats and dogs and birds. They also passed between the shadows of the towers that yet stood, broken stone domes with pinnacles in the style of shrines of the Undetermined. Inside they saw rubble, for everything wooden had burned.

There beside a central well stood their camels, snorting, as if to say, *What kept you?*

Relieved, they verified that animals and gear were in reasonable shape. "The well's nearly dry," Flint said, tying a rope onto a small bucket, "but it's worth filling the waterskins."

"Go ahead," Snow Pine said, patting Bone's camel Scoff. "I'll watch for ghosts."

She saw no spirits as the bucket clinked its way against the stone sides of the well. And yet something worried her. It was not the stillness of the place, for she expected quiet. Perhaps it was because the birds were still circling, never landing. Or perhaps—there was something not quite right about certain patches of ground within the city walls. Rubble was everywhere, except for five great patches that lay nearly smooth. She squinted and saw ropes emanating from that nearest smooth spot.

Ropes?

She whirled, and now to her suspicious eyes certain structures no longer resembled shattered buildings. They were sandy-brown tents of circular shape.

"Flint," she said.

"Almost done."

"Flint, leave the bucket. We have to leave now. Trust me."

"Ghosts?" he said, but his tone showed concern.

"Worse."

He left the rope and bucket behind, and they led the camels toward the entrance.

As they reached the shadows of the towers, they saw that it was too late. It had always been too late.

At a shouted order a score of armored men scrambled out from behind rocks. The nearest few held swords or spears, but the majority aimed bows, including a dozen on the city wall. The camels fled, and without consulting each other Snow Pine and Flint let them go, in the thin hope they'd be of use to the rest of their party.

The warriors wore helmets with face and neck guards and tassels at the top. Each had a bow and quiver. Many wore beards; all wore fierce expressions.

A woman, unarmored but likewise aiming a bow, walked toward them. She wore a blue coat, and her black hair was coiffed high above her fiercely glowering face. As two soldiers ran to catch the camels she snapped an order, and at once the men stopped in their tracks.

"You," she said in the Tongue of the Tortoise Shell. "What are you doing here?"

"Our apologies," Flint said with a bow. "We were unaware this area belonged to the Grand Khan."

"You are incorrect," the woman said. "It belongs to the Great Khatun. My mother."

Snow Pine gripped her sword but did not draw. She said, "I think this place belongs to the dead."

Quickly Flint added, "My friend is sun-touched. We are the survivors of a caravan destroyed by the hazards of the desert. We wished only to reclaim our camels."

"I suspected someone would come. Well, you are in luck, as we have provisions to spare." The woman did not lower her bow.

"We thank you for your hospitality," Flint said, "but we have no wish to impose. And we should be recovering our animals."

"Your camels will return of their own accord. There is nowhere else to go, or they would not have come here. And I think you misunderstand me. You will not be leaving, for even if you are what you claim, you must not alert anyone to our presence." She lowered her bow as she nodded for her soldiers to disarm the travelers. Snow Pine realized there was no point in resisting, unless she wanted to become just another ghost of Hvam.

A falcon landed upon the Karvak woman's outstretched arm, and Snow Pine understood, with a feeling like that of an exposed field mouse, where the circling birds had come from. "I am Lady Steelfox, daughter of the late khan and your host. You are guests of the First Aerial Expeditionary Force of the Il-Khanate of the Infinite Sky."

PART TWO

KNOT

What worms will we feed, dear Bone?
In what land or clime?
On the emerald downs of home
Where iron bells still chime?
On the roaring coasts of yours
By wrecks of many wars?
In grim mountains of the East
Where vultures flock and feast?
We walk and sail to far and near
And wonder shines and burns
And I still hear the call, my dear,
Though all will end in worms.
I'll not complain, nor Reaper cheat
One hope alone I dare repeat
Though it seems grim to you—
May there be more than worms.
May there be stones.
May there be more than two.

—Gaunt, untitled,
the Desert of Hungry Shadows

CHAPTER 10

INTERLUDE: TESTIMONY OF A TRAVELER'S ROBE

I am grateful for the dusting, O Great One, and the period of repose. Now, when last we spoke, I had related the circumstances by which I became the guide of Mad Katta and learned he was no ordinary caravaner. In time I would know him for the great enemy of the demonic Charstalkers, the very ones you have bound to your service. But the nature of the conflict was not revealed to me until we arrived in the great city of Qushkent. I felt a knotting of excitement when our road turned into the southern foothills, and the rocky promontory rose before us, birds circling around its towers, and the mists of the CloudScar, that great abyss that borders the city to the south, whirling everywhere.

In the Bazaar of Parrots we sold our wares, and Mad Katta paid our guides and handlers and guards. For a short while one remaining guard, Kilik by name, argued about compensation, and in a most impertinent way. I could hardly comprehend my master's patience.

"I, Kilik, can cut a man's throat by tossing my sword above my head! I, Kilik, can shoot a man's eye when he stands upon the horizon! I, Kilik, am offended by your payment of two feathergold!"

"The world's edge, the inhabitants of other planets, the skills of Kilik. I marvel at all, though I must take all on faith."

"I, Kilik, will not be mocked, nor assuaged by anything less than three feathergold."

At last Mad Katta said, "Enough! Two now, and we will discuss the remainder of your payment tomorrow, after we've sold the last of the goods." He was, I thought, a better man than I.

Indeed, although I do rest, and dream after a fashion, I could not sleep, though my master and his employees snored around me in the market caravanserai. I meditated upon this messy business of respiration, and how easily it could be thwarted.

At last I could bear no more sounds and rolled my way downslope to a place where stone garbage ramps led directly from the market to the CloudScar. I waited until no human was near and unfolded myself. I enjoyed the cool breezes that rippled over me from that fathomless gash in the world. Finally I felt my mind untroubled by Kilik. I thought instead of the delights of air currents, and how they would never be mine.

It is curious how a mind of melancholy bent can travel one intellectual byway after another and yet always find the paths that are darkest. My body wished to echo this mental state by leaping over the nearest barrier, and so it did. There I teetered at city's edge, where only birds, cats, and humans madder than Katta would walk. Sunset's rays speared out from the western deserts, while out in the abyss red vapors swirled and swam, with distant mountaintops rising beyond like islands of bloody ice. I beheld the great towers named for the Crake and the Lark and the Spiderhunter; and the necropolis that occupies a great stone shelf overhanging the CloudScar. Beyond the graves rose a solitary tower. There, Katta had said, lay the great Knot that the Nightkindlers' Fire Saint had left behind when he transcended this world and became a blaze of lightning.

I longed to reach that tower. Were I a true flying carpet, it would be no great trouble, save for whatever defenses the kagan of Qushkent left for such eventualities. But I was merely what I was: a sort of decorative guide dog.

With a swirl of feelings as convoluted as the clouds, I returned to the caravan and, after my fashion, slept.

In the morning Mad Katta discovered that Kilik had departed his service without further payment.

"Curious," my master said.

"Perhaps shame came upon him," I suggested, "for yesterday's behavior."

"Perhaps. In any event I will leave a gratuity with the master of the caravanserai, to be donated to orphans should it not be claimed."

"You are too generous, master."

He grunted. "Even its greatest worshippers understand that coin is, at base, an illusion. And do call me Katta."

"Very well, Lord Katta. Where shall I guide you?"

He sighed. "To the Tower of the Crake. You shall become my robe for a time."

The crake is a bird active in twilight, and thus the tower was gray, and its interior dim and hushed. The priests and clerks of that place wore gray robes, though from time to time we passed scar-faced psychopomps with clothes the color of soot.

We entered a realm of drifting dust, shining in beams of sunlight. Circular book stacks filled the tower's central shaft, rising ten stories to a stained-glass skylight portraying a blazing fire. The shaft descended downward as far as we could see. Moveable ladders granted access to the books at each level, with trapdoors here and there making it possible to rise higher or descend lower. I noticed that all trapdoors above were closed, and all those I could make out below were open. "Do they not wish us to ascend?" I said in the low vibration that was my form of a whisper.

"It is a visual representation of Nightkindler doctrine," my master murmured. "It's easier to descend into darkness than ascend into light."

"Indeed, visitor," said a gray-robed man who stepped clinking toward us through the dust. "The shadows drag us down, like gravity. It takes effort to reach the light . . . Surgun?" He raised his hands. Both wrists were wrapped in chains, one linked to a ring filled with keys, the other connected to a thick codex. "Is that you?"

"Ozan! I am so glad you are on duty. And that you remember me."

"Oh, how could I forget?" The clerk embraced Katta with a clatter. "How do you fare?" He glanced at me, draped around my master's shoulders. "You seem to have prospered."

"Well enough. Though I have my worries."

Ozan's voice became serious. "I know that voice. There is danger." He leaned in to whisper, "Charstalkers?"

"Yes," my master said. "There are things I must research. And if you think the risk is acceptable, I would test the catacombs."

Ozan drew a waving line upon his heart. "I will help you, but I wish you'd alert the pyrarch. It's his function to defy such evil."

"And all evil for a thousand li knows this, and watches him with narrowed eyes. No, I risk much even setting foot in Qushkent. I must be about my research and vanish before day is gone."

Ozan sighed. "You are using the stubborn voice. You are impossible when you're using the stubborn voice."

"I have no 'stubborn voice,'" objected Lord Katta.

"Come along," said Ozan. He shifted a ladder, and we ascended to a trapdoor, which he unlocked with one of the keys upon his chain. He repeated the process on the next level, and the next, until we stopped close to the brightening window. There was but one floor above us. Dust motes swirled like miniature constellations as Ozan pushed the final ladder to a place that did not correspond to a trapdoor but rather to a peculiar pattern of books within the stacks.

Most of the library's codices had covers of leather ranging from black to tan to red; an occasional white color emerging like a rare desert cloud.

Yet in this section books with black covers had been shelved to compose a diamond shape, like a negative star. A single white book, almost dazzling by contrast, lay in its very center.

Ozan said nothing about this strange accident of organization, and it occurred to me that for all my master's skills, he could not perceive the pattern of the books. I wondered if this was a matter of concern, but I dared not speak.

Ozan said, "Shall I list the relevant titles, Surgun?"

"No need," Lord Katta said. "I wish to consult the *Testimony of Sanguine Hong*, the *Geisthammer*, and the *Speculum Tyrannus*."

"A little light reading," muttered Ozan, ascending. Three times he drew upon his keys, and three times unlocked books from chains. All the books were black. Descending, he set the three upon the balcony and sat cross-legged against the stacks. I noticed that he chose a position at one remove from the dark diamond. "What passages do you seek?"

"Shadowy ones, dear friend," said my master and commenced inquiring of Charstalkers until the books were all opened.

"Shall I read for you?" Ozan asked.

My master shook his head. "I have much to consider, and you will have other duties."

"But—"

"I have gained certain advantages since you saw me last," Lord Katta said, and I nearly billowed with pride.

When Ozan had descended once more, Lord Katta bade me drape myself over the first book and read aloud, in a language he'd taught me.

O dread one, I began my testimony yesterday in the manner of a confession, and now I must confess that I lack heart to repeat all that I spoke under the stained glass. You and I, master, are rather in the position of those desert ants which sometimes scurry onto my surface, finding themselves lost amid turquoise and ruby swirls. Having entered into my labyrinths, the insects might reasonably conclude certain things about the world, that it is made up of fibers gathered in knots, that it possesses certain colors, that it lies more or less flat. If I were to fly, even in the spasmodic manner that is my curse, the ants would soon learn how dismayingly limited was their vision.

So it is with us. Humanity and its contemporaries make assumptions based upon narrow perceptions and pass these down as writ. Yet that which we think we understand is but a tiny patch of fabric in the desert of space and time, and even that patch may one day be snatched away.

By the time I heard Ozan throw open the nearest trapdoor, the glow through the image of flame overhead had dimmed and reddened. I went silent and still, but my master nodded to me as if satisfied.

"I have prepared a lantern and provisions," said Ozan.

"You are too good to me."

"That is true. Do you still have a lover at every oasis?"

"You overestimate my charms."

"I do not think so. I should be wiser by now, but I wish you might stay."

"You deserve better."

"Is permanence still an illusion to you?"

"You know the answer."

"I think you don't even believe in your own life," Ozan said. "Luckily for you, as illusions go, you are a pleasant one. Follow me."

We followed the impertinent clerk down many ladders until the window of the fiery image was like a distant candle flame above. Down here in the murk were works of meditative self-improvement. It struck me as intriguing that diabolical works should be kept near Heaven, as it were, and these so far below ground.

Presently we stood before an iron door, which Ozan unlocked with a key that did not belong to the chain on his wrist. He opened the door, and a chill entered the library. A passage darker than anything I'd read of now lay before us. Ozan handed Lord Katta a lantern and a pouch. He raised the book chained to his hand. "I have not recorded you in the ledger."

"Thank you."

Ozan kissed my master then, and despite this impertinence, Lord Katta responded with warmth.

"I expect nothing," Ozan said. "Just keep yourself safe."

"You should expect better than a wandering lunatic. Be wary, Ozan."

"This is the heart of Qushkent," Ozan said as we passed through the portal. "Boredom is our greatest threat."

"May that ever be true. Farewell."

The door closed behind us with a clang. My master sighed and padded into a dusty, rough-hewn passageway.

"You did well keeping quiet," he said. "Thank you for that."

"It was hard not to speak. You allow people to take too many liberties. You are a person of stature."

"Ha! I am a wayward lunatic, is what I am. But fortunately I am a lunatic no longer traveling in the light."

"How far does this tunnel extend?"

"Many li. It links to deep subterranean places. But it also connects to the *karez* system of underground irrigation channels. By this means we can move far into the desert. While hostile eyes watch the caravans, we will be safely away."

We reached a crossroads, and without hesitation he turned left.

"And then where do we go?"

"Into the desert itself. I have other tricks. Beyond that, I think we shall be going to Shahuang, perhaps first with a stop in Yao'an." At another intersection he turned right.

"I thought you were chased out of Yao'an."

"That is mainly because the chief assistant to the Protector-General became jealous I stole a lover from him. Imprudent of me, but we'll be fine if we keep our heads low. Well, my head, your corners."

"I've been keeping my corners low, as you say, and I have been thinking about our reading. So—we seek the Silk Map? To find Xembala?"

"To deny Xembala to exploiters. The world is full of them. Imperialist Qiangguo. Conquering Karvaks. Money-worshipping Westerners . . ." He had paused, touching a section of wall. "There is a hidden door here. It's been touched by evil."

"You can see it?"

"I've a gift, if you could call it that. I perceive entities of great negative karma, and their residue. This power I've possessed since childhood, and even when disease claimed my sight, the Sight remained. Natural light makes little impression on my eyes, but the monsters' essence does, as black dogs might be glimpsed against evening shadows . . ."

There came a click, and a section of stone slid aside.

"I take it we are investigating."

"Yes."

We proceeded down a tunnel with many branchings, and my master confidently took many turns, sure as a hunting hound.

Abruptly he said, "Do you want a name, carpet?"

"What?"

"We have traveled far together, and you have never given me a name. Perhaps I could give you one? I have had so many aliases."

I wondered at this impulse but found the question intriguing. "What is your favorite name?"

"At this moment I'm partial to 'Mad Katta'! But if I ever return to the Plateau of Geam, land of my long-suffering mentors, I will be Dorje, which you might render as 'Gemcut.'"

"And what was your first name?"

"My milk name is forgotten," Katta said. "But when I was cast out by the True People, they called me 'Deadfall.' For I was cut loose from my roots in the northern forests, like a fallen tree. It seems an inauspicious name however—"

"Deadfall," I said, liking the sound, leaving the rest to muse upon later. "I approve."

"Strange . . ."

"What?"

"We are here. The center of the disturbance."

A new door slid open, and we entered an empty chamber lit by alchemical gems. The floor was inlaid with a mosaic portraying an interesting pattern of three hares. The walls were filled with holes, with wind whispering through them. But these were not the most intriguing features of the room.

Placed upon a railing ringing the hare-pattern, lofted by small platforms of honor, were dozens of severed ears.

Lord Katta murmured a sutra. I was rapt by the grisly majesty.

"Master—"

"Sh. Listen."

Now I could hear snatches of voices, laughter, arguments, conspiracy, conveyed through the many holes to the many ears.

"Some magic is at work here, Deadfall," Lord Katta whispered. "The ears are not entirely dead. Their former owners can still listen through them, and by means of these holes hear much of what transpires in Qushkent. And Qushkent is perhaps the hub of the Braid."

"It also occurs to me, master," I replied with low vibrations, "that whoever stands in this chamber can issue orders to a small army—"

He raised his staff. "Something comes. Something tangible. Something that slaps against the corridors, as one wearing rags. We must go."

"I suggest I resume my role as guide."

"Agreed." Soon his staff was in his left hand, while his right clutched my tassels. I flapped my way through many more turns in the darkness. In time he said, "The symbol of the hares reminds me of old rumors. There may be more than one party attempting to guard Xembala. But if so, I am greatly concerned."

"Why? Would they not represent allies?"

"Perhaps. But why would the protectors of paradise invite Charstalkers to their sanctum? For that is the very evil that led me to the room of ears—wait."

"What?"

"That which we heard earlier has crept nearer. Or something very like it. I—"

With a hiss a figure leapt out of the darkness.

It was humanoid, with dry, leathery skin and empty eye-sockets filled with crimson light. Golden jewelry hung around its neck and wrapped its thin fingers. Something else wrapped it too, pale strips of what at first I took to be cloth, inscribed with unfamiliar runes, twisted and jagged. These bands engulfed most of the thing's body.

It clawed at Lord Katta, who swung his staff and connected with the head in a dry *crack!* By then I could throw myself around the creature, immobilizing it. Any hope that I could smother the thing soon faded, however, for it clawed and kicked without pause.

I felt great offense as to the entity's disinterest in air. I constricted myself as much as possible, and when this seemed only to hem it in, I twisted myself into the shape of an arch. I heard a dreadful popping and crunching within me. Dreadful, and yet satisfying. When I unrolled myself, the creature twitched but could no longer move.

"Well done," my master said. "Now let's run."

But even as he spoke, three more entities leapt from the darkness and grabbed his ankles, knocking him over onto the stone. He spoke no more as they dragged him out of sight.

CHAPTER 11

CAVE OF A THOUSAND ILLUMINATIONS

At dawn Bone, Gaunt, Quilldrake, and Widow Zheng all awoke, each trying to outdo the other with complaints.

"I had nightmares . . ."

"Ah! My string arm . . ."

"I am getting too old for this . . ."

"'Getting' too old for this? I passed *that* oasis long ago, youngster . . ."

In this manner they packed their bedraggled camp. Bone stumbled over a beautiful carpet, swirling with colors and patterns, that he'd never noticed before. "Where did this come from?"

"Eh?" said Quilldrake. "Must be Zheng's."

"Not mine. I'd remember a thing like that! It looks expensive. Though it's had rough treatment."

"I agree," said Gaunt, frowning. "I'm certain I did not see it before."

Quilldrake scratched his chin. "Well, perhaps Flint bought it when we were separated. It hasn't been our best-organized expedition."

"We'd best leave it behind," Gaunt said. "It will be hard to carry."

"Not a chance! Have you seen what these sell for? If Flint bought it, he's going to have to dispose of it himself."

Somehow they got the gear, even the carpet, loaded onto packs. They kept Zheng's load light, but even so Bone was concerned for her. Yet nothing for it but to walk.

Hours passed. Bone's wrenched foot was somewhat improved, but he still slowed them down. Slowly, like a drifting ship, a range of bare hills loomed closer. When they arrived they saw no life, not even shrubs or lizards or birds. Bone remembered the thing that had raised dust earlier. He looked behind but saw nothing. He hung his head.

"Are you all right?" Gaunt asked him.

"All this . . . desolation. I feel small, Gaunt." He shook his head. "We may never get him back, Persimmon. If this does not work . . ."

"If it doesn't work," she said, "we'll reach the West, and a whole new range of possibilities."

"If this doesn't work. . . . How can I ask you to start a family with me again?"

"You cannot begin to ask me that."

"I understand."

"Husband, you cannot understand. Time was different in the scroll. I knew our son for as long as I have known you."

There was nothing to say to that. The others were either too respectful to interrupt, or too tired. Bone had the fleeting impression Quilldrake's pack twitched. Nerves and heat, surely.

Wearily they struggled their way to Hvam. They regarded the ruin in silence. No one greeted them.

"I am very worried," Quilldrake said.

They passed the gates and skulls and found the camels clustered around a well. Nothing else stirred.

"Peculiar," Bone said, patting Scoff.

"Suspicious," Gaunt said. "Look around. There are remains of bonfires."

They noted five such, and signs of the passage of large numbers and the impressions of tents. Round tents. Nearby lay caches of dry meat and, hidden in cool shadows, skins full of yoghurt and mare's milk.

"Karvaks," Zheng said, tasting the milk and spitting.

"Karvaks?" said Quilldrake. "No hoofprints? Karvaks without horses?"

"*Miraculous*, not suspicious, may be the watchword," Bone said. "I have no explanation better than ghosts."

"Ghosts do not eat yoghurt," Gaunt said. "These Karvaks have some subtle means of crossing the desert. What, we don't know. But we must assume they captured our friends. And that they're using this ruin as a base. So where are they now?"

"I can guess," Quilldrake sighed. "Shahuang is the closest town."

"We must warn them," Zheng said.

"We're likely too late already," Bone said.

"We must try! You see all around you what the Karvaks do!"

There was silence, before all nodded.

They tossed enough trade goods that all could ride, all night and through the day. (Quilldrake refused to discard the carpet.)

At last they crested a row of dunes and were startled by Shahuang.

"They call it the Butterfly of the Desert," said Zheng. "I can see why."

In the midst of tan sands, small twin lakes of shockingly blue water stretched out like wings. Someone with geomantic training had contrived green fields and a cluster of buildings to complete the illusion that a butterfly of turquoise, emerald, and ruby had landed upon the sands. Like a pin piercing the butterfly, a straight stone road ran from Shahuang eastward, where after many li it would eventually reach Qiangguo's Last Fort.

"I see no trouble," Bone said.

"In a way that worries me more than if we saw them, Bone," Gaunt said. "Let's approach with caution."

"Don't we always?"

Gaunt gave him a look she'd learned from the camels. As they threaded the green fields, children emerged from farmhouses and paced them, yelling various inanities.

Wandering holy folk! Desert madlings! Are you from Madzeu? Qushkent? Are you ghosts?

Gaunt smiled and waved. "They do not seem very invaded."

There was no guard post, but they'd been spotted, and a pair of armored men, their equipment rather less spotless than that displayed in Yao'an, rode up on horseback.

"State your business," said one. The tone sounded harsh to Western ears, but Gaunt sensed there was no true hostility.

"We come—" Zheng began.

"We are dealers in silk and tea, medicine and spice," said Quilldrake, cutting her off with a warning look. "We've come a long way across the desert."

"Three of you indeed look as if you'd come a long way. The fourth looks as if she might have been kidnapped."

"Do not insult your elders, boy!" said Widow Zheng in her haggler's voice, though she scowled at Quilldrake. "I go where I wish, with whom I wish."

The guard grunted and nodded to his partner, who dismounted and poked about the camels. "Interesting carpet," the second guard said. "Otherwise the wares look much like what you'd find in Yao'an."

"In the barbarous West," Quilldrake said, "my people struggle to imitate the treasures of the East. You do me honor by saying we have approached that ideal."

"There is no dishonor in saying you got lost in the desert," the mounted guard said.

"Sir!" Quilldrake said with reproach.

"Ha. You can go in. I am less interested in your wares than in your news. Did you happen to notice strange flying creatures in the desert?"

"No," Gaunt broke in. "In fact, I would find it strange if anything at all lived in that desert."

"Even so. Yet during the night some stargazers claimed they saw vast shadows in the sky. A couple of us went to check it out and haven't returned. We're not worried—yet. There's an abandoned temple out that way, with a bunch of paintings in caves. They may just be exploring a little."

"Temple?" Quilldrake said innocently. "Caves?"

"About a half day's ride northwest. There's an old madman who's appointed himself curator, if you want to check it out. Nothing much to interest a trader, though."

With a recommendation for an inn, they entered town. Gaunt looked around her, even as the curious townsfolk, many winding down their labor, looked back at them. The style of buildings, with their iron gates and lacquer lattices and sweeping roofs, recalled Qiangguo's cities, but the oasis town had a different air. Perhaps, Gaunt thought, there was something to the local attempt at geomancy, for there was an aeolian spirit to the place, with more towers and spires, more lanterns and statues, than she'd seen in Yao'an. Strange, she thought, that Yao'an should appear more blunt and militaristic than this exposed, independent settlement.

The Inn of the Water Sprite shared Shahuang's soaring atmosphere. Its pagoda rose from the southern end of the strip between the two wing-shaped lakes. Stone butterflies adorned various corners.

Soon the travelers conspired in a room with a view of the stables. "So, Art," Zheng said, once Bone had checked for eavesdroppers. "Why didn't we shout 'Karvaks! Karvaks!' at the tops of our lungs?"

Quilldrake said, "I think Shahuang's in no danger. And the strange sightings prove it. The Karvaks have gone to the old temple."

"You think we're dealing with *flying* Karvaks?" Zheng scoffed. "They've tamed dragons?"

"It can be done," Gaunt said. "Whatever the truth, the sighting can't be coincidence. The old temple is where we originally planned to go, no?"

"Yes," Quilldrake said.

"The Karvaks have gotten wind of the Silk Map, then," Bone said.

"If they didn't before," said Quilldrake, "now they have Flint and Snow Pine to give away the game."

"Something is nagging at me," Bone said. "Something I've seen in the past . . ." He frowned and shook his head. "It's not coming clear. Age is catching up with me."

Zheng and Quilldrake gave him doubtful looks. Gaunt said, "Perhaps it will return, my love, like a thief to a rich house. In any event, I am thinking that I should pay a visit to the old temple."

"Agreed!" said Bone, looking as excited as a boy given a chance to play beside a cliff.

"I said 'I,' Bone. You are still limping. And we will need someone to watch the camels."

"Watch the *camels?*"

"Not merely that," Quilldrake said. "Someone to play the part of a merchant!"

"*Merchant?*"

"Not only that." Quilldrake frowned, as though forcing himself toward a difficult decision. At last he said, "I'd like you to guard the fragment of the Silk Map."

Bone scratched his chin. "I am not sure . . ."

"We may be going into danger."

"Danger may find me here as well. No, I have a different idea. I want Gaunt to wear it. She is more likely to enter combat than you, and it can help protect her."

"Why, thank you, Bone," she said. "I can't recall you ever giving me clothing before. It's sweet."

"There was the escapade outfit . . ."

"I'm sure that was my idea. You've simply stared at it so much you think it was your idea."

"Truly?"

Quilldrake coughed. "If it has to stay with me, I'd rather it be guarding *my* neck . . . but I see your point. And I trust you not to run off with it. You are among the most honorable ne'er-do-wells I've ever known."

"Don't make us blush."

Under cover of night, Gaunt, Quilldrake, and Zheng (who'd insisted she was refreshed and ready for adventure) ascended the dunes to the northwest. This time they were beyond Quilldrake's knowledge and had to make their best guesses.

Hours passed. Gaunt was getting more comfortable with Quilldrake's patchwork dress, and it helped keep her warm beneath her travel clothes.

Quilldrake slowed, squinting.

"Now . . ." he began.

"Halt!" came a voice behind them.

"We must be cautious . . ." Quilldrake concluded mournfully.

They turned in the moonlight to discover the two guards who'd greeted them in Shahuang. "You!" said the leader. "What are you doing out here?"

"Evening constitutional," Quilldrake said.

"Don't insult them with lies," Zheng said. "Sonny, we misrepresented ourselves. We're traders, sure, but we're also treasure hunters. We think there's a treasure in that old temple. We also think there may be Karvaks after it."

"Now I'm starting to believe you, Grandmother," said the guard. "The treasure, now, you can work that out with the crazy hermit—"

"Captain Yang? Sir? Isn't a cut our due?"

"You've spent too much time in Yao'an, Jia. Shahuang's an honest town. Now, if there are Karvaks around, that is our business. We don't necessarily mind, but there's history there."

"Indeed," Zheng said.

"We were already on our way to investigate, so we'd be glad to join you. Shall we?"

They reached the temple at moonset, Yang and Jia guiding them to a vantage where they might glimpse it unseen. A rocky promontory rose pale and shadowed against the stars, and upon its face were carved two great humanoid figures, each with one hand upraised. Between them opened a wide tunnel.

There were also two small figures, torchlit, bearing spears. These were more lightly armored than Yang and Jia, wearing breastplates, shields, and tasseled helmets.

"Karvaks," said Yang.

"Let's attack," said Jia. "There are only two."

Gaunt said, "There may be many others in the shadows."

Yang said, "The outlander speaks true, Jia. Now we've verified there are armed Karvaks, we should return and sound an alarm."

Quilldrake said, "And then we have battle. Perhaps a siege. Protracted and messy. What about your poor mad hermit?"

"Looking this over? Sadly, he's probably dead. And it's not the hermit you're really concerned about, is it?"

"I confess to some urgency in exploring these caves," Quilldrake said.

Yang sighed. "You're lucky I found you. And you're lucky I have some fondness for Old Crazy Wei. Jia, I'm going to lead these worthies into the back entrance in hopes we can extricate the hermit. You will proceed back to town and sound the alarm."

"The women can return too," Quilldrake said.

"You're trying to cheat me already, aren't you?" Zheng said. "I'm coming. Gaunt?"

Gaunt almost felt she was a schoolgirl again, egged into exploring the Abbess's private library. "I've promised Bone to be careful."

"And so we will!" said Widow Zheng.

Gaunt thought Zheng's definition of *careful* must be an interesting one, but she found herself nodding. She must trust her own instincts now. She had to admit, it was satisfying not to consult Bone on everything related to sneaking and thieving.

"It has been an honor serving with you, Captain Yang," Jia said with a bow.

"You are such the pessimist! Did we not play in these ruins as boys? I will be fine. Off with you!"

Shaking his head, Jia trudged away into the sands.

"Let us be about this nonsense before I change my mind," said Yang.

He led them far around the rocky promontory and up a narrow, snaking gorge. It terminated against a blank face in the sandstone mass. Yang crawled out of sight beneath a boulder. Gaunt followed and found herself sliding into a cold carven passage. The others scraped and thudded behind her.

"You are all right?" Quilldrake asked Zheng.

"Haven't had this much fun in years."

"I do not suppose any of us brought a light source?" Yang asked, and was answered by silence. "Excellent. It is good to know only seasoned professionals are on this mission."

"I do have a means," Widow Zheng said. "I'm down to but four scrolls of Living Calligraphy, but perhaps it's time to make it three."

She opened a scroll, and the characters upon it glowed like candle flames: *Better to light one candle than curse the dark.* They spilled off the suddenly blank paper and fell to the floor, where they commenced roaming around like a caterpillar composed of fire. Zheng gestured and clicked, and the illuminated proverb flickered ahead of them.

"Marvelous," said Yang.

"Thank you," purred Zheng. "You are a man of courtesy, handsome one."

"How long does it last?" Quilldrake asked.

"You are a man of business," groused Zheng. "An hour, perhaps two."

"Let's be about it then," said Quilldrake, and Gaunt saw sweat upon his brow, shimmering with the magical firelight.

A hundred feet down the passage, Gaunt glimpsed a figure. Her hand went to her dagger before Yang said, "It is but a statue, an image of the Undetermined."

"What is that around his forehead?" Gaunt asked. "A mirror?" The cross-legged figure was the tan of sandstone, with faded remnants of red, yellow, and black paint clinging to it after centuries. Yet the sculpted headgear of the Undetermined still retained the shiny look of cloisonné.

"That is the symbol of the Dust on the Mirror," Zheng said, the usual growl departing her voice. "It's an offshoot sect, more popular on the roads West than in Qiangguo. They believe in enlightenment but seek it by way of wanderlust and adventure."

"Thus has Crazy Wei expressed it," Yang said with surprise. "Are you a nun?"

The growl returned. "Ha!"

"Very well, we've seen a statue," snapped Quilldrake. "What of the hermit?"

"I confess to a gamble here," Yang said. "This area's hard to locate by entering from the front, and I'm hoping Old Wei made it here when the Karvaks arrived. Otherwise I doubt we'll find him."

"Are these secret hiding places?" Gaunt asked.

"'Secret' may be too strong a term. But Wei said there were little-known sections for esoteric teaching. You see how the statue gestures with one hand toward an upward-sloping path and with the other to a downward-sloping path? Upward lies the grand galleries, downward the chambers of deepest meditation."

"Fine, fine!" said Quilldrake. "Which way will Old Wei be?"

Yang frowned at him. "I think he'd go downward if he could."

"Let's go," Gaunt said gently, to forestall Quilldrake saying it rudely.

They descended through a passage that wound this way and that, snake chasing tail. From time to time they peered into cells painted with strange beings, angelic, demonic, beatific, ferocious. At last they entered a remote chamber with a vaulted ceiling, whose walls swirled with color. At the far end sat a statue of an enlightened and haloed human, flanked by painted holy folk in saffron robes. Spreading out from there was a panoply of earthly life—deserts, mountains, valleys, cities, even oceans and islands. Above soared winged entities sublime or monstrous, circling a mandala of crimson energy. In Widow Zheng's flickering light, the whole tableau took on an illusion of depth and motion. Gaunt had to reassure herself that rock remained beneath her boot.

"Wei?" called Yang in a hoarse voice, struggling along the path between audibility and concealment.

There was no answer.

Yang cursed. "They must have caught him. We'll have to ascend."

"Wait . . ." Quilldrake murmured, stepping closer to a painted stretch of desert. "Zheng, perhaps you could send your light this way?"

"What do you see?" Zheng asked, crooking a finger toward her living calligraphy. The room brightened near Quilldrake.

"These look distinctly like Shahuang's butterfly-wing lakes. Now look at these nearby hills."

Gaunt leaned closer. Beyond Quilldrake's extended finger lay an illustration of poplar trees clustered around a lake beside a rocky hill. Under the trees were a few pagodas representing a settlement. "A different village," she said, "next to a vanished lake. In the same area as this temple?"

"It's said that lakes come and go in the desert," Zheng added. "Streams and aquifers are fickle . . . is that a flag?"

It did indeed appear that a flag flew from the tallest building of the lost settlement. Zheng picked up her glowing handiwork as though cradling a kitten, and the light swelled. Now Gaunt could see that the flag had a peculiar shape. It was a long tube, gently crooked, like the lower part of a cheongsam.

"A fragment of the map?" Gaunt said.

"I intend to find out," said Quilldrake.

"I too . . ." murmured Zheng. "Perhaps those ruins are nearby . . ."

"Soon we may find the path," Quilldrake said, "to treasure incalculable."

"You people sicken me," Yang said. "A man's in danger—an entire village—and you can only think of treasure."

"If you only knew what treasure—" Quilldrake began, but Zheng shushed him.

Yang's words stung. "I will help you, Yang," Gaunt said. "The Karvaks may have captured friends of ours too."

Quilldrake said, "A moment! A moment! I must commit this painting to memory."

"Come along, Art," said Zheng. "I'm taking the light with me."

"Very well, very well. I have it. Fortunately my memory is excellent."

They returned to the statue with outstretched hands, following the upward path this time. Gaunt wondered why she felt shame. She'd never represented herself as a hero of any sort, for all that Bone accused her of it now and again. Yet her cheeks burned. Perhaps that was why she told Yang, "Your armor clinks as you walk. Let me move ahead of the light and alert us to trouble."

"That is brave of you."

"It's nothing."

She padded forward into the darkness, imagining Bone by her side, whispering things his old teacher Sidewinder might have said. *Exploring ruins is a marginal occupation, for rarely will you be first on the scene. Better to plunder those warm in their mansions than those cold in their crypts. But if you must go, tread lightly, for the dead have no need to walk their own halls. Pits and spikes and collapsing walls cannot disrupt their morning routine. And the mighty of old may have banes untold!*

She began to hear a harmonious-sounding language somewhere in the halls ahead. The speech had a musical quality to it, and it was hard to ascribe it to brutal barbarians; yet it was surely the Karvak tongue. She motioned to her companions to proceed more slowly, and drew a dagger.

Three steps later, and an attacker was upon her.

Gaunt had only a glimpse of a side passage and the sound of a scuffle upon the stone to alert her; the man came seemingly out of nowhere, grabbing her by the neck and mouth. She knew that her reaction must be swift, or her life might be over.

She twisted and plunged her dagger into the man's chest.

He screamed and released her, tumbling to the floor.

Much happened at once. Gaunt shifted, the dark wetness upon her blade shining in the magical firelight. The man gasped upon the floor, a dark pool spreading beside him.

The musicality of the distant voices ceased; what she now heard was barked commands.

Yang was on his knees, saying, "Wei! Wei!"

"What?" Gaunt said.

"Foreign devil!" the guard captain snarled. "Why did I trust you? You've killed an innocent man."

For indeed the assailant was no Karvak but an old man of Qiangguo, hair pale and wispy upon his agonized face.

"He attacked—"

The man was not yet dead, saying, "Old Wei . . . he wanted to stop you . . . ahead lie Karvaks . . . their eyes so bright . . . one day they must gain enlightenment, but until . . . you must hurry . . . flee to the lowest chamber

. . . look behind the mirror . . . Old Wei will no more dream of taking the caterpillar to First Wife's tomb . . . has he been reborn enough? He has lived among the beautiful images . . . he goes to the reality . . ."

"Wei?" Yang said. "Wei?" There was no answer. Yang hit the wall with an armored fist. "He was always mad, but a good friend to us children who braved the sands. He deserved a better fate than this."

"I am sorry," Gaunt said.

"I too," said Zheng, her voice distant.

"But the Karvaks come," Quilldrake said.

"I will not leave him to them," Yang said and lifted up the body. Gaunt sheathed her bloody dagger, hands shaking.

They returned to the statue of the outstretched hands. Yang said, "I will take him out to the sands, that he may escape them."

"But he said, 'the lowest chamber,'" said Quilldrake.

"Mad babbling at the end," Yang said. "Would you risk your life for it?"

"I will," said Quilldrake.

"If he's going, I am," Zheng said.

Gaunt hesitated. In the end she could not say it was courage that led her on, but a hunch, and perhaps a desire to honor the man she'd inadvertently slain. And maybe a desire to escape Yang's eyes. "I will go to the lowest chamber."

"As you wish," Yang said, voice thick with contempt. He disappeared through the passage out.

The three who remained raced to the lowest chamber. It was no different than before, except in this respect: now they had the certainty the Karvaks would find them.

"Mirror, mirror . . ." Quilldrake said. "What could it mean?"

"There's no mirror," Zheng said, "not even like the one on the signpost statue."

"Well, is this it?" Quilldrake said. "Doomed at last?"

"'The dust on the mirror,'" Gaunt said, trying to shake free the dust of guilt, though it darkened her sight. She stared at the statue of the enlightened figure. "What would a mirror *see*?"

She spun.

The doorway into this chamber was off-center, and thus directly opposite the statue was a wall. On it was a painting that closely resembled the enlightened image. It was more faded-looking than anything else in the chamber.

Gaunt approached it, as the sounds of Karvaks neared. It was a near-perfect match for the statue, except that one hand pointed toward a star high up the wall.

"Quilldrake, boost me up!"

They heard sounds at the crossroads overhead as Gaunt teetered on Quill-drake's shoulders and pressed the painted star. At once the ragged image of the holy figure rumbled sideways and a door stood revealed.

Quilldrake knelt, letting Gaunt off. "Hurry," he said.

Gaunt, Quilldrake, and Zheng slipped into the hidden corridor as the door ground shut. Soon after they heard a beautiful language twisted by angry throats. Weapons pounded upon walls.

The hidden corridor slanted both upward and down. By unspoken agreement, the three slowly moved up. At last they could no longer hear the Karvaks.

"Well," Zheng said, "it seems we're entombed alive. At least the end was exciting."

"Perhaps it's what I deserve," Gaunt said.

"Nonsense, both of you," Quilldrake said. "Persimmon Gaunt, you were in the dark, facing hostile invaders, when someone attacked you. You responded in fear. Such incidents happen whenever soldiers march."

"He meant only to stop me. And to keep me from crying out."

"Even so, no blame attaches to you."

"I am not so sure. I think perhaps the blame began when I took up a life that required the blade and the bow."

"I'm not your confessor, but this old treasure hunter would absolve you if he could. Meanwhile—Zheng, be glad of my occupation! I've heard of ancient temples of the Dusters, with their negative spaces."

"Negative what?" Zheng asked.

"Captain Yang spoke of special spaces for esoteric teachings. Well, secret areas such as this are just such spaces. They were also fine places for temple treasure. Perhaps here we'll find the map—"

"That's the first thing you think of?" Gaunt said. "When your friend Flint is probably a prisoner here?"

"Not at all, not at all. For the negative spaces were also good for spying on the less enlightened. Follow me."

They ascended to the level of the upper corridors and found that Quilldrake was right. While these regions were largely unadorned, here and there they possessed paintings that resembled scrolls of religious instruction. On this side it was easy to perceive the doorways such images marked. There were also many peculiar concavities, inversions of the statues of the Undetermined and the Thresholders. Thin eye-slits allowed one to peer into the public chambers.

Gaunt peered through one such mask and beheld Karvaks moving through the corridors. Zheng clicked softly at her Living Calligraphy, and it went out like a snuffed candle. Now they proceeded through the dark.

Quilldrake was disappointed in his treasure hunting, for the secret chambers seemed devoid of goods. He could not help swearing now and then under his breath. Gaunt allowed herself a grim satisfaction at that. Something about the treasure hunter angered her this night.

Perhaps, she thought, it was the anger of recognition.

At one point Zheng looked through spy-eyes and gasped excitedly. She tugged Gaunt over and pointed. Through the slits Gaunt could see a chamber filled with faded paintings of a peacock-crowded, fountain-filled paradise, but that was not the cause of the gasp. Many objects were collected here, including Snow Pine's dao sword and Liron Flint's magical saber, the sword Crypttongue. No guards were in evidence.

"There is a doorway not far from here," Quilldrake said. "We can recover the weapons."

Gaunt said, "We'd best find the wielders first."

"Of course."

Three reverse-statues later, Quilldrake's thirst for treasure was still unquenched, but they found their companions. In a chamber lit by a torch-bearing Karvak guard, Snow Pine and Flint lay asleep. The walls were painted with myriad and contradictory visions of hells, and Gaunt imagined she saw demons gawking and souls writhing. A second guard bore not a torch but a spear.

The companions conspired in a dark antechamber. "Zheng," Gaunt said, "you said you have only three more scrolls of Living Calligraphy. Do any of them shed light?"

"Yes, but I have just one more of those."

"That is all we will need. Now here's my plan . . ."

CHAPTER 12

DAUGHTER OF THE SKY

From the beginning of Snow Pine's sojourn with the Karvaks, she contemplated fighting. She'd clutched the dao-sword tight when the Karvak princess, a young woman roughly her own age, began her pronouncement about *guests*. Snow Pine had no desire to be such a guest, but she'd doubted her ability to defeat so many Karvaks. Flint, however . . .

"You have a magic sword," she'd whispered in the critical moment.

"Crypttongue *is* formidable . . ." Flint had begun.

"But not that formidable?"

"I'm an explorer, not some warrior-mage of old. To give the blade what it requires, to fight off so many . . . no."

"I don't understand you," Snow Pine said, "but I trust you."

"I'm honored."

"Don't make me regret it."

They had set down their weapons.

The Karvaks had proven kindly captors. Their offers of horse milk and dried meat stood in livid contrast to the pyramids of skulls. Likewise, their preparations of five great blue canvases, at the direction of a tall, sprightly fellow in a white robe and turban, did not seem at all like the business of a marauding horde.

A person almost as out of place as the man in the turban had approached the "guests," an individual whose gender Snow Pine could not initially guess, a bow-wielder of the northern taiga, sweating in a blue Karvak robe with silver charms hanging over it. This individual had stared and pointed at Snow Pine and Flint in a disconcerting fashion, before walking away.

"What in the world?"

"Show no fear, Snow Pine. That is the Official Starer. People think everyone surrenders to the Karvaks because of military might, but the true power is in the Starers. Whole cities have capitulated to avoid being looked at in that way."

Snow Pine had glimpsed their visitor across the ruin studying their weapons and staring back once more. Snow Pine broke into laughter. "I am glad to have your company."

"Likewise."

"The Official Starer seems interested in your magic sword."

"It does get attention."

"Gaunt and Bone seemed to know it by reputation."

"It's an uncomfortable thing, carrying a sword more famous than yourself." He had said no more.

Soon they'd beheld five blue gasbags swelling above five Karvak gers. Flame shot from openings at the tops of the tents to heat the air within the blue envelopes. Miraculously, nothing ignited. Or perhaps miracles had nothing to do with it; Snow Pine glimpsed hints of blazing triple-eyes within the fires.

"Yes," said a voice beside them in the Tongue of the Tortoise Shell. "I have harnessed demonic powers for my balloons. And I have enlisted Karvak Wind-Tamers—and one taiga shaman—to guide them. In this way do I compromise my natural philosophy. But I must fly."

The speaker was a spindly man wearing a long white tunic and an orange two-wrap turban. His brown, mustachioed face was animated by an energetic, youthful bearing, though Snow Pine noted crow's feet and dark circles around his eyes.

"My name is Haytham ibn Zakwan ibn Rihab, though you may call me Haytham."

Snow Pine was in no mood to pretend this was a teahouse, but Flint spoke first, introducing them and adding, "Pleasant to meet you here in a lifeless desert, surrounded by Karvak warriors."

"Likewise," said Haytham. He smiled at Snow Pine. "And charmed, beautiful one."

"Save it for the Charstalkers," Snow Pine said.

"My companion hasn't had one of her best days," Flint said.

"I quite understand, Master Flint."

"Just Flint. You say you're a natural philosopher? You seek the world's secrets, without recourse to magic?"

"Yes!" Years seemed to blow away from Haytham like sand. "I am used to blank looks all around. Are you an empiricist as well?"

"Not precisely." Snow Pine saw Flint struggle for modesty. "I am an explorer. I can't claim to be a pure researcher, as fame and fortune do factor into my calculations."

"You don't say, Liron," Snow Pine put in.

Haytham studied her anew. "Your companion . . . even her mockery is music."

"I enjoy that music regularly," Flint said.

"I'm right here," Snow Pine said.

"And I do deserve her mockery," Flint continued, "for I am perhaps just a greedy treasure hunter with pretensions."

"Ah, that might describe me as well," Haytham said. "One must make concessions in terms of patronage and methods. But the essence—the advancement of human knowledge—that remains pure. You are clearly willing to employ magic as well, Flint. Is that not the very sword of Younus that our delightful shaman is poking at?"

"If you know the sword's history, Haytham, then you will respect why I'd rather not discuss it."

Snow Pine said, "Maybe *I'd* like to discuss it—"

"Perhaps," said Haytham, "we should wait for a time less full of eavesdroppers. . . . Ah, at last we have lift! Behold!" Haytham beamed and strode toward the swelling balloons.

"Look at them, Snow Pine. Flying craft . . . genuine flying craft. . . ."

"With Karvaks in them, Flint."

The aerial fleet floated northeast, over desert that became increasingly rocky but no less lifeless. While one of the blue balloons was marked with Lady Steelfox's standard—not a fox, as it happened, but a falcon—the Lady herself rode in an unmarked craft, her "guests" beside her. Haytham was elsewhere, but the staring shaman was aboard the cramped ger, along with several warriors.

Within a rune-inscribed central brazier, a Charstalker writhed. From time to time triple glares focused on the travelers.

"They are loathsome company," Lady Steelfox said, "but we had difficulty creating a portable method of lift. Haytham calls such magical impositions 'shortcuts.' I tolerate them, as I tolerate these 'portholes' he carved into good Karvak felt."

"The Charstalker is a somewhat dramatic shortcut," Flint observed.

"Well, I suppose I am a dramatic person."

"What are you doing out here, Lady Steelfox?" Snow Pine said. "This can't be a pleasure trip."

"Because we Karvaks are simply monsters, with no idea of pleasure? Don't bother answering, it is on your face. I don't expect anything else from a daughter of Qiangguo. But I'll answer. I seek a lost treasure. The clues to the treasure may lie in a fragmented map, painted on silk . . . ah, I see in your eyes you've heard of this. Perhaps it's not an accident that you're out in the desert, so near to the Cave of a Thousand Illuminations. No? No matter. We will see what we will see."

"You go to the cave now?" Flint asked.

"Indeed. If we time matters correctly we'll arrive in the night and secure the ancient temple. We'll learn all there is to learn and be gone before anyone is wiser."

"Leaving our dead bodies behind, no doubt," Snow Pine said.

"You insult me. If it's the bloodthirsty face of the Karvaks you want, I'll show you the door. It's ever thus with your kind. You provoke us for ninety-nine years, and if we finally chastise you in the hundredth, you call it a century of Karvak terror."

"Provoke, nothing! You invade and steal, because you're too lazy to make something of your lands."

"Bah! We never wanted to steal, not at first. We wanted safe havens for trade. It's Qiangguo that keeps trying to choke us off."

"So if people refuse to trade with you, you have the right to murder them?"

"Perhaps," Flint said, "these are historical matters which have no bearing—"

"Enough," said Steelfox. "My sister keeps saying I'm too soft, and perhaps she's right. Men, bind and gag these people who insult hospitality, and set them beside the Charstalker. So much for 'civilized' folk."

Snow Pine spent the rest of the journey furious at Flint for not employing his sword's powers to the fullest, at the Charstalker for singeing her shoulders, and at Steelfox for being a Karvak. As night fell her temper cooled with the air. What she'd said was true, of course, but it had been impolitic to throw it in their captors' faces. She must restrain herself, if their restraints were ever removed.

Such a development seemed far off, however; for even once they'd landed they remained bound, carried by Karvak soldiers into a tunnel framed by two enormous statues. Inside, torchlight revealed a shimmering, swirling fantasia of painted beings, from the enlightened to the striving to the benighted to the diabolic. Snow Pine felt thoroughly disoriented, as if she were swimming between worlds.

She'd had time to think, however. She had no weapons, but no one had noticed the needle inserted into her robe above her heart, what Lady Monkey had called *a needle for weaving events*. She did not know how to call upon it, or what would happen if she did. It would have to be a last resort. But the time of its use might soon be at hand.

At last they were deposited in a chamber with what seemed a hellfire motif, a snarling demon-statue glaring at them under a headdress of skulls. Only then did the Karvaks free them. She and Flint groaned and stretched. The guard by the door, and the torchbearer beside him, said nothing. She supposed they did not speak any of their languages. But she could assume nothing, and thus couldn't confer with Flint about the fates of their companions.

Soon a third Karvak appeared with food, and Lady Steelfox with him.

"We haven't found any caretakers to question," she said without preamble. "Despite our efforts, we must have been spotted. Our search has turned up a secret corridor near the entrance, however. There seems to be a set of hidden chambers, perhaps more extensive than the public ones. If there's anything to find, we will find it. If you have anything to share, it would please me to hear."

"Or you'll torture us?" Snow Pine said.

"Your question reveals more about you than it does about us. I can be a grateful patron, but my patience is not infinite."

The shaman appeared in the corridor, stared at the prisoners, and spoke in the musical-sounding Karvak tongue.

Steelfox said, "We may have found what we seek. A passage leading to a village buried beneath the sands. It's surely very old, for the temple inhabitants must have been excavating it before their own end came. We will investigate."

The door closed behind her. The guards stood impassively.

"It is not actually necessary," Flint said, "to argue at every turn with the woman who could kill us."

"Oh! It is all *my* fault!"

"I did not say that."

"You implied it. Well, I'm *sorry* that magic mind-sucking crystals scared off our camels and made us go to a haunted city where we were captured by a horde of flying Karvaks."

"Apology accepted."

"You are impossible! You have never been married, no doubt."

"No, and I am finding myself in no hurry to change that."

"Ah, such calm detachment. Would it kill you, Liron, to show a little emotion?"

"You mean, you would like me to yell and argue uselessly, instead of calmly analyzing uselessly."

"Yes!"

"All right, then! We are completely doomed! And it's all your fault!"

"Thank you!"

"You're welcome! Now, I suggest, since all our behavior is useless, we get some rest. We may need it soon."

"Fine!"

"Fine."

She did not quite know why she was so angry at him. Or perhaps she did know, and that made her angry too.

To hell with your 'acceptance,' dead husband. It's too soon. Whatever my body may think. And yes, I'm still mad at you.

Mad or not, the thought of him cooled her somewhat, and soon she slept.

Judging by the heat, they had slept well into the day. She woke ahead of Flint, and she gratefully accepted water from the torchbearer. She couldn't help thanking him, though he merely smiled back.

"Flint, wake up."

Flint was a fast riser. After a disoriented look around, he said, "All is well?"

"We are still doomed, and it is still my fault."

"Ah." He rubbed his eyes. "Perhaps it can be my fault today."

"You have a deal."

"Snow Pine." He took her hand. She stared at his hand taking hers. "I—"

The door opened, and Lady Steelfox returned. There were cuts on her face, and she looked as though she hadn't slept. "I would discuss . . . oh. I am an unkind host, I see. It is not too much to grant you two privacy, if you—"

"No."

"No."

Snow Pine wasn't sure who broke whose grip first. Steelfox blinked. "Very well. I would like your opinions on a certain matter. Below the desert is a lost village, and I am certain it holds what we seek. That's because five of my men have been killed by the walking dead who inhabit it."

"If you want my professional opinion," Flint said, "some treasures are simply not meant to be found."

In my opinion five fewer Karvaks is a good start, Snow Pine thought. But she remembered the torchbearer's smile. "The world is full of things that shouldn't be disturbed."

Steelfox nodded. "I might be persuaded to leave it at that. But in my shaman's opinion, Flint, you carry one such thing. Your sword."

"Lady Steelfox, I won't be coy with you," Flint said. "Crypttongue is a dangerous weapon. It was forged by the legendary King Younus for the slaying of demons."

"Then it would seem an ideal tool for the matter at hand."

"We are not all King Younus material, Lady. And tools that involve demons are invariably tainted by demons."

"I will take your advice to this extent. I will not wield the sword. But if you will do so on my behalf, freedom is only the first of your rewards."

"And Snow Pine too?"

"Of course."

Snow Pine said, "Free us first. As a matter of good faith. And then let us discuss."

"That is somewhat more trust than I'm willing to extend toward someone who's called me a murderer."

"Then the two of us are in a similar place," Snow Pine said.

"I think it is Flint's decision." Steelfox's voice turned a trifle mocking. "Or do you have a special claim on him?"

Snow Pine found nothing to say that would not make things worse.

"How many walking dead are we talking about?" Flint asked.

Steelfox paused. "Hundreds."

Flint nodded. "I don't think you are lying. Thank you. I will have to think about it."

"There are still hidden areas to explore, so I can wait. But I intend to leave before dawn tomorrow, map or no map. We've lingered too long as it is. Sadly I've already had to kill two people who stumbled upon the temple."

"People from Shahuang?" Snow Pine asked quickly.

"I believe so." Steelfox studied Snow Pine for a moment before returning her gaze to Flint. "If you don't answer by midnight, or answer no, I must choose another champion to wield your sword, risk or no risk."

When Steelfox had gone, they commenced a strange afternoon. The yelling was done, and all that was left was the impassive warriors, and the unnervingly beautiful paintings, and talk. They shared worries about their comrades. They talked of lands they'd seen. Snow Pine spoke of Qiangguo and a girlhood of defiance and danger. Flint spoke of the distant city of Amberhorn and a boyhood on the docks. Neither was a stranger to rough company. Each had somehow managed to encounter scholarship and learning, less as a trophy and more as a prize thrown at their heads to keep them quiet.

Only as the air cooled did she broach the subject. "Will you fight the walking dead?"

"I still don't know. I may not know until midnight."

"I'll fight beside you."

"Snow Pine, the only comfort in that battle would be knowing you weren't in it."

"I may have my own surprises."

"What—"

"No, I can't speak of it. I'm not even sure what I would say."

"I know the feeling."

"What?"

"No matter. I think we should sleep. Unless there is more arguing to do?"

"Ha. Later."

"Later, then."

They were awakened when the demon-statue started glowing and screaming.

Even with all she'd been through, Snow Pine was startled to see fiery pin-pricks in the demon's eyes and an unearthly howling that nonetheless seemed dimly familiar.

She put her hand upon Lady Monkey's needle and nearly called upon it (with what result, who could say), but suddenly the bloodcurdling screeches echoed in her memory.

It was Widow Zheng's sales voice.

She put her hand on Flint's shoulder and hissed into his ear, "Friends!" To his credit he simply accepted this and followed her lead. "Aiya! Save us!" she cried, backing toward the door, and Flint did similarly.

The Karvaks, she had to admit, were courageous. They charged the demon-statue to protect their charges, with only the slightest hesitation. She and Flint, likewise, did not hesitate to depart.

Unfortunately, there were two more Karvaks outside.

Fortunately, so were Gaunt and Quilldrake.

Quilldrake was wielding a dao-sword so adroitly, it took Snow Pine a moment to realize that it was her own.

That meant the sword in Gaunt's hands . . .

"Crypttongue—" Flint said.

"I know!" Gaunt said. "Bar that door!"

The door was surely not of the same vintage as the rest of the temple; perhaps it was the work of the caretaker. The Karvaks had hauled a boulder to block it at need, and Snow Pine and Flint rolled it into place. A pounding commenced on the far side, but the courageous demon-fighters were stuck.

Gaunt wielded the strange, silvery-glowing sword with skill Snow Pine would not have credited. Nonetheless the poet was no swordswoman. The Karvak slashed at her, slicing her travel robe and exposing the shining section of the Silk Map. He froze.

"Surprise," Gaunt said, and whacked his head with the flat of the blade. Her foe fell, groaning.

"Help, please?" Quilldrake said.

Snow Pine kicked the Karvak in the side, Quilldrake tripped him, and Gaunt hit him with Crypttongue's jeweled pommel.

Gaunt, panting, knelt and leaned on the sword as if upon a staff.

"Yes," Flint said, leaning beside her. "It is disorienting. Have you slain . . ."

"No," Gaunt murmured. "I restrained it."

"Good."

"You should have this back, Flint."

"Wait a moment. Letting it go can be disruptive."

"How did you come by such a thing?"

Quilldrake said, "That's not a question for now. Our plan was effective, but noisy. We must be moving."

"Art," Flint said. "There's an underground village accessible from the temple. I think the map's down there. There's an access near the entrance."

"I think there's also one back whence we came," Quilldrake said. "No time to explain. I suggest you come with us—"

There came a sudden *whump* of a dagger-hilt connecting with a skull, and Quilldrake toppled like a log.

Behind him, unhooded, stood the one-eared woman from Yao'an.

Snow Pine grabbed the dao-sword and slashed; One-Ear leapt smoothly over the blow. Flint tried to tackle her and slammed into the wall.

Gaunt rose and jabbed at One-Ear as though some invisible puppeteer yanked her exhausted limbs. But even with Crypttongue on her side, the poet was overmatched. One-Ear advanced and slashed. More of the Silk Map was revealed, dotted with Gaunt's blood. Gaunt stepped backward.

"It goes with me," One-Ear said. "And you will never leave—"

A Karvak arrow hit the mysterious woman from behind. She staggered, with a shaft in her shoulder. A second arrow flitted to Gaunt, and jerkily Gaunt knocked it out of the air.

As Flint recovered and approached, a third arrow struck him in the leg. He toppled onto Snow Pine as a group of Karvaks, led by Lady Steelfox, advanced.

"The map!" Steelfox said.

"Gaunt!" Snow Pine called. "Run! Don't forget! Innocence! Joy!"

Gaunt hesitated.

"Go!"

The poet turned and ran.

Snow Pine managed to rise, sword in hand, to confront Lady Steelfox.

Before either could speak, One-Ear snarled and threw herself into a flying kick at the Karvak princess. Without thinking the matter through, Snow Pine got in her way. The impact slammed her against the same wall that Flint had involuntarily kissed a moment earlier.

When she recovered, she saw One-Ear in the grip of three Karvaks, and Steelfox staring at Snow Pine as though at a two-headed falcon.

Snow Pine put her hand upon Lady Monkey's needle.

I call upon your power!

"Why—" the princess began.

Do something, needle!

"Why would you help me?"

Stupid needle!

"Just—help my friends," Snow Pine managed to say, before sliding down the wall.

CHAPTER 13

THE QUESTION OF FLIGHT

Bone spent a fitful night at the inn, for he worried about Gaunt and about the little noises that haunted the night. Many times he leapt out of bed, dagger drawn, thinking an intruder had entered, but he saw nothing more sinister than the rolled-up Anokan carpet.

In the morning he set himself up in the town square between the two wing-shaped lakes and began selling their goods.

"Sabretooth powder!" he called. "Good for one's nocturnal energy! Silk, from a distant land, my weary feet hope to tell you! Tea, of the same variety that emperors have sipped! Five-spice blend, whose ingredients are a well-guarded mystery!"

"Can you verify the truth of your claims?" asked a skeptical townswoman.

"Do I look like a dishonest person?"

"Yes."

"I have never done anything dishonest as a businessman."

"Twenty silver for the carpet."

"Honestly I tell you, that is not enough."

In all honesty, he was reluctant to sell the carpet, which was to his eye worth all their other goods plus the camels. He did manage to sell some bricks of tea. Knowing that he only needed to cover expenses allowed him to bargain harder than he might have. As the morning progressed he was beginning to have a little fun, though the ire of the townsfolk cut at his pride, and worry for Gaunt nipped at his heart.

The town's children were more willing to engage him, though rather less able to buy anything. "Roll out the carpet!" they pleaded, and he did so, cautioning them not to get it dusty. Its appearance, fully spread out under the sun, struck his eye as beautiful and jarring all at once. The clash of motifs, one cool, one hot, seemed the work of an argumentative partnership or one highly conflicted mind. The children perceived the dichotomy immediately and began hopping from one side to the other. Bone watched them and scratched his chin. The carpet rippled in the wind (perhaps a little more than he would have expected). Bone peered at a dark stain in the midst of the design, where a swirling vortex of red and black dominated. He began to suspect the stain had some violent origin.

The children eventually tired of this business, and of asking him about his homeland, and older siblings distracted them with paper tricks. Bone was somewhat relieved, as he'd already explained how his house had perched upon the head of an absent-minded giant, how his first occupation had been to polish the setting sun at day's end, and how only the male Westerners really hatched from eggs. He was running out of tall tales and missing Gaunt all the more.

When the children left the carpet he flipped it over. He watched the older siblings fold paper animals and craft paper darts that soared upon the desert wind. Once again the carpet seemed to ripple. It almost seemed a companion, it had such personality. "It would be quite something to fly," Bone said out loud. "I mean, deliberately. Clinging terrified to a dragon's leg is something else altogether."

He could not feel the breeze, but one corner of the carpet slapped the dust.

Now a girl lit a candle and held a tube of paper over it; the paper rose into the air. It kindled a vision in his memory.

"Haytham ibn Zakwan," he murmured. "Whatever became of him. . . . Shapes in the sky . . . oh, no."

He looked this way and that, but of course nothing in the great bright blue confirmed his suspicions. He bowed to the children, packed his remaining wares, threw the carpet onto a camel, and returned to the inn. From there he marched to the tower of the magistrate.

There was at least one advantage to being a bizarre outlander: people were interested in talking to him. In short order he was in the magistrate's presence.

"You mean to tell me," the man said, frowning beneath white whiskers, drops of perspiration gleaming upon a spotted bald head, "that we are menaced by paper balloons?"

"Not paper, eminence. These will be spheres of cloth, filled with hot air, suspending baskets. Such contrivances are at the mercy of the wind, but Karvaks have Wind-Tamers, I'm told."

"I do not think this is the hot air we must worry about."

"Eminence, hear me out. I have heard of such things from . . . a friend."

THE TALE OF THE THIEF,
HA, I MEAN MERCHANT, OF COURSE

Far away, beyond Anoka, beyond Efritstan and the Sandboil, there stands beside the sea the city of Palmary, a city in the shape of a hand.

(A sea is more than a vast lake. Imagine those moments in the desert heat when we see a mirage of water shining in the distance. Imagine that water becoming real and filling everything, that the vastness of the sands becomes the vastness of the waves, that an oasis is now an island, that mountains are mainlands. I do not lie in this.)

Even as your town is shaped as a butterfly, giving your people, I suspect, a free spirit, so my Palmary is a place of trading, of building, and grasping. By ancient edict the city cannot grow beyond the outline of the five fingers and palm, save for a ragged dockland we call the Sleeve. And as our city thrives, so its inhabitants build upward rather than out. A thousand towers spear the skies over Palmary. Knowledge and learning thrive in the looming shadows. A steady stream of iconoclasts, philosophers, heretics, and madmen come to this place. And likewise inventors.

Haytham ibn Zakwan was one such. A striking figure, he was garbed in the gilded robes of a Mirabad noble. Rumor had it he'd been chased away from his family's haunts for unorthodox ideas and raucous living; he certainly lived up to the reputation. Haytham rented the upper two floors of a six-story tower on Lifeline Road. It had to be the upper floors because of the nature of his research. From time to time observers saw smoke rise from that place by day and dark shadowy orbs by night.

Certain whispers reached a man I knew. Let's call him Osteon. A gentleman thief, you might say. The sort of person who had stolen a fortune many times over, yet always managed to spend it in free living and reinvestment in his schemes. You frown, that I would know such a person? I've heard it said that a holy man might know all manner of persons without shame or defilement, for the light travels with him. And I have also heard it said we should imitate holy men. There you have it.

Truth to tell there was a certain zest to Osteon's criminality, and his reputation grew. He liked a challenge. Certain individuals professed curiosity about Haytham's activities and offered Osteon payment for the intelligence. In good confidence, he commenced the work.

The tower of Haytham's residence was in the respectable middle of Lifeline Road, not the rowdy or decrepit ends, and greenery surrounded it, affording Osteon an arboreal ascent to the third story. An ironsilk strand tied to a hook dipped in ur-glue facilitated his progress.

He reached the fifth floor and discovered a window ajar. He coated the hinges with olive oil (a fine variety from a grove down the Sleeve) and widened the gap with great patience. An odor of soot greeted his nose, and Osteon understood why the inhabitant would want fresh air. The inventor was about his work, whatever that was. This also meant the man was on hand.

Had this assignment been of Osteon's own choosing, the expedition would have ended there. An empty dwelling was a puzzle to be solved at leisure; an inhabited one was a gauntlet. Osteon far preferred puzzles. He'd never killed a householder, though there were guards in their graves who had cause to curse him. To triumph over enemies was never his joy. To revel in storied objects snatched from the chambers of the mighty—that was glory.

Still, although the inventor's presence was unwelcome, the mission was one of intelligence, and Osteon would honor his contract.

The thief believed in preparation, and in his lair hung cloaks fashioned to match the stonework of every tower in the city. He raised his sleeve, hoping the inventor's eye would overlook the sudden widening of the sill. He peered around the cuff. Firelight spread fluttering illumination around the shadowed room like the caressing fingers of a collector. Its source was another chamber, and from time to time the muttering shadow of a turbaned man sliced the light.

Osteon had hoped to glimpse a treasure-chamber out of desert tales, like a cave crammed with pearls and sapphires, golden goblets, bejeweled scimitars, bags of dirhams and dinars, magic lamps awaiting a rub. What slowly came clear was another class of treasures—telescopes from Kpalamaa, sextants from Swanisle, mechanical clocks from Loomsberg, mathematical treatises from Mirabad, even abaci from Qiangguo. Vials of crystal bearing varicolored powders stood near candles like soldiers at their liege's camp. A slender glass tube held an attenuated clump of quicksilver. Charts and notes were strewn over every flat surface, covered with diagrams and notes in the flowing script of Mirabad. And upon an easel stood a sketch of a basket with a man aboard, suspended by ropes from a flying sphere. Thus did Osteon see his first balloon.

A curious sensation came over Osteon as his eyes swam with wonders. Even the most wholesome sorcery aroused an itch of unease within him, for the suspension of the world's usual rules seemed to deny the worth of stealth and wit. Yet this was a form of learning equally baffling yet somehow bracing. If sorcery was a dank but glittering cave, the inventor's craft was a windy peak revealing the lands all around.

Thus dizzied, he stepped silently into the room.

Immediately there came the itch of unease.

It was far from reliable, but a long association with magic had given Osteon some sense for its presence. It served him that evening, for he rolled to one side even as a shape descended from the ceiling like some cocooned snack dangled by a giant spider. The shape was humanoid and hulking, yet touched the floor with a gentle, dry creaking. Wrapped in what resembled rune-inscribed bandages, the thing tugged at the white strip still connecting it to the ceiling; it came loose, and the entity whirled the arcane wrapping through the air like a whip. Ancient writings glowed with a green phosphorescence, a match for the radiance that spilled from the sockets where a living man's eyes might have been. Haytham ibn Zakwan might have been a natural philosopher, but he guarded his work with the unnatural.

I had already come too far.

"I must interrupt your story," said the magistrate in a regretful tone.

Bone sighed. "I neglected to maintain the pretense of 'Osteon,' didn't I?"

"That is true, but it is not the problem. Rather, the nature of your supposed inventor's defense indicates you may have knowledge of the Leviathan Imperium."

"Eh, the what?"

"The aeons-old inhuman realm of cephalopods whose eldritch ruins yet underlie our sands."

"Ah, that Leviathan Imperium."

"As such, I wish to question you more closely. Knowledge of such things is prized." The magistrate clapped, and two guards entered. "Show this gentleman to the Room of Great Understanding. I will speak to him later." To Bone he added, "Do not fear! Knowledge is the root of wisdom, and questions are the seeds of enlightenment."

As the guards grasped his arms, Bone asked, "Is truth like a tree of crystal?"

"I apprehend by your question that you do indeed belong in the Room of Great Understanding."

"And I perceive that you have little true interest in your people's welfare. I come to warn you about Karvaks borne through the air!"

"Amusing. I will in turn tell you of sentiences who swim through the sand, and whose works still direct our fates. Take him."

"Sir?" asked one of the guards. "Will you not now sound the alarm against the Karvaks? This is the second report we've had—"

"I won't have the peace of Shahuang troubled by such matters. Our friends beneath the sands will protect us from all things. Put this man beside Lieutenant Jia in the Room of Great Understanding."

As the guards marched Bone down the stairs, a strange hulking man intercepted them, a fellow who seemed of great bulk yet light step, with his face shrouded by a turban. "I will take him the rest of the way," said the man in a dry, rustling sort of voice.

"We have orders," said one of the guards. "Who are you?"

"A friend."

"Well, go away, friend, unless the magistrate himself orders us differently."

Bone had an intimation about this person. Almost an itchy feeling. He groaned and feigned a swoon. "Oh, the heat . . ."

The bulky man unraveled.

That was the only word for it. The clothes scattered, the turban fell, and the carpet within opened up to engulf one of the guards.

With the second guard unbalanced, Bone heaved and knocked him from the staircase. The man groaned and struggled to rise. Meanwhile his companion twitched in the midst of being smothered.

Bone recognized the carpet he and his companions had brought out of the desert.

"Uh—carpet? Thank you, but that is enough! Let's . . . make haste?"

The carpet hesitated, even as shouts rose from elsewhere in the pagoda. At last it billowed up from the gasping guard, following Bone down the stairs in a staggering, drunken way, something like a rag savaged by a playful dog.

"Very well, O thief," said the carpet. How it spoke was a matter of some consternation, but Bone had the impression that the carpet was vibrating the air along its whole breadth. The voice was deep. "Yet you do not command me, not until I know for certain my true owner is dead."

Bone nodded, looked this way and that, and beckoned the carpet toward a window. He climbed out, offering his hand. The carpet squeezed through, clutching the sill with a corner. They were three stories up.

"I do not claim to own you," Bone said. "I would never claim a sentient being. Merely a sentient being's possessions."

"In my case, O rogue, being and possession are identical."

"I am not your owner, carpet, though I confess to great curiosity as to who is. My more immediate question is, however, can you fly?"

"In a manner of speaking."

"Your tone is not entirely encouraging."

"I am improving, but still my flight is problematic. We could soar for a time, but the landing would be hard."

"Do you see yonder wing-shaped lake? Perhaps you could aim that way."

"Hold on."

The journey was seven seconds of gyrating terror, and one of slapping, watery impact. Drenched, man and carpet scrambled out of the lake.

Bone looked over his shoulder. "I am limping. I fear we'll be caught. But I thank you for your efforts. Do you have a name?"

"I am Deadfall. I, too, limp after my fashion. The dunes are high, but they are softer than rock or sword. If you think you can hold on, Imago Bone, I will convey you into the desert."

"Know you the way to the ruins?"

"I observed your companions' departure as surely as you. Do you have your essential possessions?"

"I lack my travel pack, but I have weapons and a little water. I always assume the necessity of a quick escape." Bone knelt and grabbed the carpet's edge. "I am prepared."

"So you believe."

The carpet lashed the air, whipped the ground, scaled the sands. Bone winced and whimpered and coughed but never let go. He heard the sounds of pursuit but never looked back. Suddenly they crested a dune and glided downslope, raising a small sandstorm as they sledded sand. Then up they went like a dry leaf over the heat of a fire.

From time to time Bone felt nothingness beneath them and dared to glimpse the desert from the air. The dunes seemed endless, arrayed in chaotic yet gentle contours like diaphanous ripples in a tan silk dress, dropped at the arrival of a lover.

After each such glimpse Deadfall would slam into the sands, a rude awakening from such fancies.

At last, after what seemed an hour, Bone could hold on no longer and tumbled to a shadowy valley between masses of sand. He retched, chugged some water, retched again.

From somewhere nearby, Deadfall said, "You are tougher than you appear, O meat."

"You are likewise not what I would have guessed . . . cloth. Who sent you? How did you come to be among us?"

"I serve my maker Lord Katta, he who wanders the Braid of Spice battling the schemes of Charstalkers."

"Charstalkers . . . I know that name . . . I feel as though I've heard the name Katta as well . . ."

"Lord Katta is a prince and lama of the Plateau of Geam. An enlightened being. He charged me to assist him in his quest."

"Something must have gone wrong . . . if you will pardon my impudence. I thank you for my escape, Deadfall . . . but you are surely an unusual flying carpet."

Something cold entered Deadfall's voice. "Indeed, O cargo. I have been marred by many things."

"And your maker?"

"Lost. Not dead, I hope, but lost. I carry on his fight. The Charstalkers seek what you seek. The Silk Map."

"What are they, truly?"

"Agents of an ancient malice. Reborn to lives of hate, and reborn again, until their human and even animal forms have given way to a pure fire of wrath. Their knowledge of many incarnations allows them to possess other forms, for a time, but always they revert to the savagery that defines them. More to the point, they will soon find your companions."

Bone rose, painfully. "If we are still hunted, we will lead the magistrate's soldiers after us."

"That may be to the good."

"Do they not serve the Charstalkers?"

"I do not think so. I believe they represent another power—wait. Someone approaches."

"A guard?"

"Perhaps. Stay here."

"I can fight—" Bone began, but when Deadfall rustled off, he did not protest, feeling dozens of aches and scrapes.

Presently there came a muffled shout and the sound of something heavy flapping upon the sands.

Bone stumbled over two dunes to discover Deadfall swishing beside the body of the senior guard who'd greeted the group on arrival at Shahuang. His dead face was ghastly.

"I had thought him a decent man . . ." Bone said.

"We know those guards serve an evil. Evil must be smothered."

"Alas."

"Shall we be off then?"

After another long, careening flight Bone staggered through the sunset in time to see a balloon rising from the ancient temple.

Just as when he'd beheld the work of Haytham ibn Zakwan, Bone marveled at the inverted-teardrop shape climbing the sky. This one was larger than the balloon at Palmary years before; it bore a peculiar round structure of timber and hide, big as a Western peasant's house. The balloon itself lacked the intricate patterning and calligraphy of Haytham's design, but rather bore a simple hue of deep blue, a white raptor upon it, rising toward a crescent moon with its horns aimed skyward.

He squinted and spied figures peering out an opening in the great basket. He had the impression of a flash of auburn hair.

"Gaunt!"

"We are too late," said Deadfall.

"Can you reach them?"

"I have not the skill."

Bone's gaze looked to the rocky hill of the ruins. Titanic statues, portraying the Undetermined and one of his Thresholders, looked back at him. "What if you had a flying start?"

"That will be a painful ascent for you. It might break you."

"Let that be my concern. Drag me up there. I will cling to your corner as to a rope."

"Be it on your head, O fool."

The climb was much easier decided than endured. Despite a long career involving contusions, constrictions, and collisions, Bone discovered several new places to ache. At last he moaned atop the citadel of enlightenment, the sunset painting the world the color of hurt.

"Are you mobile, Imago Bone?"

Bone got shakily to his knees. "You . . . did not spare me at all . . . did you?"

"I reasoned you would prefer speed."

"Alas, true."

The balloon, a little below their altitude, was turning due west as a high easterly wind cut the desert air. Four other balloons were rising, each an undecorated blue. The three highest followed the falcon-balloon westward, while the last drifted southwest—possibly toward Hvam. The behavior of the sand below told Bone the lower-altitude wind came from the northeast. "Wizards," Bone said. "Weatherworkers. Wind-Tamers. Whatever the Karvaks call them, they are guiding the balloons. If we can reach that high easterly wind . . ."

"Yes. A good leap and we might glide all the way to the craft bearing your Gaunt. We dare not delay."

Bone backed up as far as he dared before running pell-mell toward the cliff. If this was all some elaborate trap, Bone thought as his feet left the stone, he had to concede defeat.

Defeated or not, he flew.

It was among the more terrifying moments of his life, yet he would always treasure it afterward, the time he soared, more or less, on a magic carpet. That it was more of a whirling dive than true flight, and that he was hanging from

Deadfall rather than standing atop it—these were quibbles. Earthy, dusty heat rose from below. Sunset dunes twisted with jabbing shadows, like persimmons spattered with ink.

I am coming, love.

A falcon whipped past him, claws extended.

He dodged, but he was in the raptor's element. Blood trailed from his face to join the sands. The bird shrieked and whirled around again, its grace a mockery of Deadfall's jagged path.

He did not dare draw a dagger, but when the falcon passed again, he kicked. This accomplished nothing but to prevent another raking, but that was enough.

Or perhaps not—"You have thrown us off target, O thief"—for they collided with the balloon's envelope.

Whether by impact or Deadfall's decision, Bone lost hold of the magic carpet and dangled from one of the ropes that connected the envelope with the suspended ger. Quick looks right and left revealed no sign of Deadfall. He considered ending the flight with a dagger right then, but another look at the desert below convinced him to save the blade for another target. He shimmied down the rope and looked down upon the peculiar gondola. It had a hole in the roof, and a glowing cauldron of embers revealed the source of heat. Entry would be difficult . . .

The falcon returned, screeching. Bone thought he glimpsed something more than animal in the bird's enraged eyes. Now he thrust his left arm between rope and canvas and drew a dagger with his right. Mad jabs prevented his losing more blood to the talons. The wound he'd already sustained dripped onto the roof of the ger. He worked his way closer to the hole; the falcon shrieked, and he yelped, shifted, and whirled as the cauldron inside belched flames.

This falcon is guided by someone within, he guessed. *Very well . . .*

"I want only the redheaded barbarian!" Bone bellowed at the bird when next it attacked. His kicks and jabs kept the raking to his arm only. He wheezed in pain. "Her, and any woman of Qiangguo you've taken. You can have the Silk Map if you want it so badly. Just give me my friends!"

The falcon gave no sign of response, but it broke off its assault, its path spiraling out over the sands. Still there was no sign of Deadfall.

The voice that answered through the gap was not one of his companions'. Yet it was familiar all the same.

"Imago Bone! Imago ought-to-be-dead-a-thousand-times-over Bone! You are the last person I thought to meet in this desolate place! And yet did not an antique poet say,

> *We're nothing more than shadowed stones*
> *Upon the board the All-Now owns*
> *Dark or bright squares our nights and days—*
> *Who can guess the ploys He lays?*

In any event, well met! It's good to hear a civilized voice."

Bone called out, "I thought this might be your handiwork, Haytham ibn Zakwan ibn Rihab! Are the Karvaks your patrons now?"

"Indeed! Reports of their barbarity are somewhat exaggerated!"

"You didn't have a look at Hvam?"

"All civilizations have their crimes! But these Karvaks are of a different mettle! Now, won't you toss your weapons inside and join us?"

"That looks like an excellent opportunity to roast me. I prefer the air. Invigorating! Here's my offer—land this craft and let my friends go!"

"This matter," said a disconcerting voice at Bone's elbow, "must be forced."

Deadfall rushed past him into the opening of the gondola. Smoke belched through the hole.

"Aiya," Bone muttered, and followed.

He landed upon Deadfall and rolled into the commotion of the flying tent. Someone had decided that breathable air was of more immediate concern than gravity and had flung open the tent flap. The ground rose closer, red closing off blue. "Gaunt!" Bone called.

"Fool," said a woman's voice, and it was not Gaunt's.

Out of the smoke, a cut rope tied upon her wrist, came the assailant he'd fought upon a rooftop in Yao'an. "Your Gaunt is not here." Fear and longing and the hues of sunset had confused Bone. "The mummies below the temple have claimed her now and the fragment of the map she bears. Neither you treasure hunters, nor the Karvaks, will find what you seek!"

She proceeded to kick at Bone, aiming to add crimson to the desert.

Another woman hit the assailant with an iron skillet.

The one-eared woman fell backward into the smoke. Bone thought he glimpsed three glowing eyes in the haze, but that was perhaps his imagination.

"Bone!" came the rasping voice of Snow Pine, as she dropped the skillet. "I don't know how you found me! Flint and Quilldrake are on another balloon with Lady Steelfox."

"Who?"

"Never mind!" Snow Pine looked out at the careening landscape. "Can we get out of here?"

"Yes," said Deadfall, and a billowing, smoldering shape rushed toward them.

"Grab hold!" Bone told Snow Pine, and together they commenced a gut-wrenching journey out the opening and into the sunset.

"Bone!" called Haytham from the gondola. "You are making a mistake! Our goals are not disharmonious . . ." The voice was lost in the rushing of wind and the shouts of Snow Pine and Bone's own voice.

"Eee—"

"Gah—"

"Cease your whining," said the carpet. "I am doing all I can."

Their impact sent Bone and Snow Pine tumbling into the sand. For several moments Bone lay there as Snow Pine coughed and Deadfall flapped itself upon the ground to slay any remaining embers.

The Karvak balloon was meandering southward, smoke trailing it, in a wind that no longer seemed so directed. The falcon whirled around it as though bound by an invisible tether. A column of fire rose from the gondola in a manner that seemed eerily directed, never endangering the hide of the craft. The balloon rose.

Bone thought he glimpsed within the fire a new suggestion of three blazing eyes. He blinked, and it was gone.

Snow Pine offered her hand. "We'd best get into the temple. There may be a chance to find Gaunt and Zheng."

"What," Bone said, rising, "did our one-eared friend mean about mummies?"

"It's a long story. Come on!"

"I will aid you," Deadfall said, "for Lord Katta vanished in battle with walking mummies, and I would learn more of such creatures."

"Ah," Bone said, gesturing to the carpet, "Snow Pine, this is Deadfall."

"I believe we've already met," Snow Pine said. "At Yao'an. Did you go by the name of Dorje?"

Deadfall managed a bow.

CHAPTER 14

THE GIFT OF THE GREAT SAGE

As they ran between the great stone statues and into the temple, Snow Pine wondered at her changing emotions. Once she'd scorned her homeland and hated its enemies. Now she felt love for Qiangguo and grudging respect for the Karvaks. Likewise, she considered her companions her friends and Deadfall a mystery—but she recalled Deadfall's warnings in Yao'an, and trusted Flint and Quilldrake, at least, a little less.

Flint. No, she had no time for her new feelings there.

There was an old conflict in Qiangguo, between the philosophy of the Forest, which saw all things in flux, and that of the Garden, which emphasized social order. Now, here beyond the Jade Gate, Snow Pine could see the two as complementary. With her feelings churning like the wind, it was good to have the solid stone of loyalty to remember—loyalty to her daughter.

"I will get you back," she whispered.

"What is that you say?" rustled the carpet.

"I am promising to find," Snow Pine said, wondering how Deadfall might respond, "my friend Flint."

"He is still alive?" Bone said, locating one of the many torches abandoned in the Karvaks' quick departure.

"Yes," she said. "They took us at Hvam and brought us along on their expedition. They never meant to threaten Shahuang. They only wanted the clue to the map."

"Yet they've given it up?" Bone got the torch lit. Deadfall said nothing but shifted farther away, always looming in the darkness behind.

"The clue seems to point to a lost underground village," she said, leading them into a side tunnel the Karvaks had marked with stakes and a banner. Within the hidden catacombs they beheld open-palmed images of the Undetermined, nimbus-crowned Thresholders, swirling mythical creatures, and vortices of pure color. "I . . . don't know how to find the path downward."

"Allow me to guide you," said Deadfall, rustling ahead of Snow Pine. "My senses are different from yours."

As they followed the carpet, Snow Pine said, "The Karvak leader thinks she doesn't need the fragment down here. She thinks she knows enough, having glimpsed the one Gaunt bore. She claims to have the eyes of a falcon and the memory of a mastodon."

"Then you're sure Gaunt's alive?"

"She was, and Zheng too . . . but we may already be too late, for them and for our children."

"We have blood in our veins. There's hope."

They made many turnings, always descending. Snow Pine suspected they'd left the temple behind and had passed under the dunes.

"Pardon my question," she said, "but were you damaged in some way, Deadfall?"

"There is more than one answer to that question, O traveler. I was damaged in my making, for more than one hand had a role in my creation. It is a difficult thing, having more than one loyalty."

"That I can appreciate."

"Further, in our battle in the balloon, I struggled with a Charstalker. It attempted to conquer my mind, to escape its imprisonment. I am not flesh, however, and foiled it. But the experience was unsettling, even more than the harm to my substance. It has awakened me to the presence of negative karma around me . . ."

A strange, hazy illumination filled a chamber ahead, as if moonlight had been captured and chained.

"I believe we are here."

They entered a cavern that should not have existed, for its circular walls and domed ceiling were formed not of stone but of packed sand. A modest chamber Snow Pine might credit, but this one was the size of a small village.

And like a village it had its structures. Scores of gently bent timber posts rose beside oblong wooden shapes too small for houses, each guarded by a marker resembling the end of a paddle.

"Are they . . . boats?" Bone said.

"I do not think so, O thief," said the carpet. "Perhaps they are places of storage."

"I think that's true," Snow Pine said. "I think they're graves."

They approached the wooden graveyard beneath the sands, and there was utter silence save for their own breaths, and footfalls, and scufflings. And then a gasp from Bone—"Gaunt!"

Persimmon Gaunt and Widow Zheng stood near graveyard's center, eyes shut. Beside them, two of the wooden posts were rising without visible cause.

As the posts escaped the sand, pointed tips emerged.

The shafts tilted backward, gentle as monks doing morning exercises. So elegant were the motions, Snow Pine was slow to understand their purpose.

The posts, in whatever giant invisible hands gripped them, had become giant spears.

"No!" Bone cried, running forward. Snow Pine did not know if this was the wisest course, but she followed. She lost track of Deadfall in the dark.

Still gripping his torch, Bone leaped onto a levitating post, knocking its point into the sand. Snow Pine did likewise with the other. Bone lowered his torch; dry ancient wood ignited. A vast angry hissing filled the air, and it was not merely the sound of popping and blazing wood.

Spectral figures swirled into view, a mob apiece for each of the spear-posts.

They were human, though of a folk unfamiliar to Snow Pine, wearing russet robes and, in some cases, feathered caps. Their expressions were those of murderous outrage, as though the intruders had broken some essential taboo simply by the act of living.

Snow Pine should have backed away from them; she'd lost her sword to the Karvaks. Yet *should* was a word that applied increasingly little to her life.

She ran along the fallen post toward the ghosts, screaming insults she'd learned among the thieves of Qiangguo's capital. They surely had no idea what it all meant, but her tone was universal. Ghosts began flowing up the post. She saw that each had an indistinct silvery cord swirling through the air, linking it to one of the wooden ovals in the sand.

As she reached the nearest ghost, a transparent, bearded man with a misty spear, she kicked. Her foot went through the ghost's face, feeling suddenly icewater-cold. She hopped backward as the spirit silently snarled and jabbed. The ghost-spear grazed her shoulder, and although it passed through her flesh without wounding, she felt a lancing cold. It was all she could do to keep her balance and retreat.

One of Bone's daggers flashed through the ghost's face; this seemed only to confuse the specter.

"I don't like these odds!" he said, applying his torch to her post.

"At least they dislike fire . . . the coffins! Or whatever they are. Threaten the coffins."

"These?" Bone waved the torch near one, then another. The ghosts ceased their advance. "Interesting."

"Keep threatening them. I'll try to free Gaunt and Zheng from their trance." Snow Pine reached her companions and snapped her fingers before their faces. "Gaunt! Zheng!"

They remained transfixed. "Hey!" Snow Pine called. "Your poetry is pap and your calligraphy is sloppy! Wake up!" No result.

Snow Pine wondered about the coffin over which they stood. This was surely not a spot an experienced traveler would meditate if given a choice. Snow Pine kicked at the coffin, jumped on it, uprooted the nearby marker and whacked it. "I'm desecrating a grave!" she said in a sing-song voice. "I'm desecrating a grave!"

Gaunt and Zheng began trembling. *Something* was responding.

She saw Crypttongue in its scabbard, secured to Gaunt by its belt. Snow Pine considered taking the weapon, but Flint's words about it left her uneasy. She hoped Gaunt wouldn't mind if she borrowed a dagger. . . . Snow Pine jabbed the blade into the ancient wood. It splintered, and she coughed as dust filled the chamber.

She set the dagger down, grabbed, tore, widened the gap. There was something in there, a humanoid shape . . .

A hand reached up to grab hers. The fingers were desiccated, dry flesh peeling from bone. The rest of the hand was hidden by strange wrappings resembling snakeskin leather strips, covered with eerie glyphs.

"*Naut! Yok Ysar!*" sang a voice in a long-dead language, and Snow Pine was sure she'd have found the message terrifying if she could have understood it. As it was she reached for Gaunt's dagger and began sawing at the dead hand.

A screech went up. Gaunt and Zheng fell to the shadowed sand. The weird illumination of the chamber brightened in Snow Pine's vicinity. A ghost stood before her, a man in white robes covered in glyphs similar to those on the mummy's wrappings. He had wild, dark-red hair, a silver octopus pendant upon his neck, and the expression of a prophet. A thin silver filament, twisting like a cord underwater, connected the ghost to the dead thing tugging at Snow Pine.

"Bone!" Snow Pine called out. "If you're not busy—"

"Define 'busy'!" But she heard his voice moving closer.

All at once something heavy *thumped* into the sand—the magic carpet had returned, slamming itself over the ghost.

The ghost passed without agitation through the carpet, smiling in a most condescending way.

"This strikes me, O spirit," said Deadfall, "as perverse and unfair." The carpet rolled itself into the grave.

There were sounds of struggle and snapping bone. The ghost shuddered and screeched. The dead hand released Snow Pine.

But the ghost compensated, grabbing her around the throat. It was as though frost surrounded her windpipe and ice crystallized within.

Her vision swam with colors. This might be It, the moment every gangster wondered about, the time every follower of the Forest hoped to meet, if not with equanimity, then acceptance. She felt heavy, ready to slump; strangely, she felt heaviest in her heart, as though a great weight there was pulling her down . . .

Choked by a ghost, it seemed to her that a ghost spoke to her. *Wondrous*, someone was saying. *Wondrous Lady Monkey . . .*

Flybait? she tried to croak. *Husband?*

Gift of the Great Sage . . .

She put a hand to her heart and felt a coldness there.

"The needle," a voice was saying. "The needle from Lady Monkey! Try using it!"

It was Persimmon Gaunt. She'd snapped out of her trance and was vainly jabbing the ghost with a dagger. Widow Zheng was behind her trying to open a scroll.

Snow Pine reached up and found the needle that had once rested behind the Great Sage's ear. She freed it. Once again she felt as though the weight of worlds lay within that tiny metal length.

She still had no idea how to invoke it. But with a great effort she raised it the few inches necessary to plunge it into the ghostly hand.

"*Kwyall?*" screamed the ghost, and released her. It staggered backward, its silver cord thrashing like a fishing line.

Snow Pine forced herself to rise, to raise the needle. It seemed longer now, but she had no time to consider this. She jabbed at the silver cord.

It parted.

The ghost vanished with a scream that was, all at once, cut off. It was as though a candle had been kicked over.

The carpet Deadfall emerged from the coffin, covered in dust.

"May I inquire what happened?" it said in its low-toned voice. "And what is that weapon you're holding?"

Snow Pine stared at the unadorned metal rod she held. It paradoxically felt lighter than it had as a needle. "I truly do not know," she said.

"Look out!" Gaunt said, as something grabbed Snow Pine's ankles.

She looked down and saw that many of the inscribed wrappings from the dead man had snaked around her feet. They tugged her with unnatural strength toward the grave.

She whacked and jabbed. At each motion the rod grew longer, as though the bulk of its material had been tucked away in some unseen dimension. It felt lighter yet, and she felt more comfortable wielding it, yet she could not manage the leverage to injure the wrappings.

Gaunt was jabbing at the snakelike strips with her dagger, with little better effect. Widow Zheng's scroll spilled out, and the words, including the character for *wind*, blurred and became a howling squall. Snow Pine fell, and the wrappings still coiled beneath her. Deadfall threw itself upon her, hopefully in an effort to crush the things.

"Off!" Snow Pine yelled. "Everyone, back off!"

There was such a thing as one's companions being too helpful.

The carpet rolled away, Gaunt pulled back, and Zheng's winds subsided. As the widow plucked out another scroll, Snow Pine clubbed the ground.

A concussion ripped the air, and the wrappings danced a bit from the vibrations in the sand. Snow Pine pulled herself free.

Now Bone was there, shoving a torch into the coffin. Fire licked up from the mass of wrappings, and, as though all were linked, the ones threatening Snow Pine retreated.

Crackling, hissing, and burning, they wriggled away through the far coffins.

Zheng unveiled her next scroll, and Snow Pine could read the whole proverb this time: *Rein your anger for a moment, and you may ride contentment for a hundred days.*

The words became a set of dancing lights, like fireflies. They spun about the chamber, and the ghosts beholding them ceased to advance but rather marveled at the Living Calligraphy.

"It will not last long," Zheng said. "It can soothe one angry man for a day, but crowds dissipate the effect swiftly. Usually that's enough to disperse a mob. But a mob of ghosts? We'd better get the hell out of here."

"No," said Snow Pine, and it was as if the strength of worlds flowed through her weapon arm. "No. For we are here to find a fragment of the Silk Map. And I have the weapon of Wondrous Lady Monkey in my hand."

"That was the needle?" Gaunt asked.

"It affects ghosts?" Bone asked.

"Yes and yes."

"It is the only thing we have that can affect the spirits," Zheng said, "for that was the last of my scrolls."

"I think there's one more thing," Snow Pine said, looking at Gaunt.

"I'd prefer to draw Crypttongue as a last resort," Gaunt said.

"I don't blame you—"

"Quickly, kids!" said Zheng. "If we're doing this, we're doing this. That map fragment must be buried here."

"We can't possibly break into all these coffins," Bone said.

"I have a feeling, Bone," Zheng said, a wondering tone to her voice. "I have a feeling we're close."

"How can that be?"

"We don't need a feeling, Bone," Gaunt said, peering at the ghosts. "We just need to see which ghost's wearing the fragment."

"Are you sure anyone is?"

"A beautiful item of clothing? Immensely valuable? I think yes."

They advanced among the transfixed ghosts. Snow Pine peered here and there, rapping her staff against her left palm. It felt right and proper to wield the iron from the stars—

She saw it.

A female ghost, a proud-looking woman with a piercing gaze, wore a simple brown robe, but beneath it Snow Pine glimpsed a hem of shimmering silk. Upon it Snow Pine could see images of snow-capped mountains.

"I found her," Snow Pine said in a hush, pointing with the staff. For a moment she imagined the hem must be real, so beautiful was the ironsilk. She stepped closer, squinting, finding that the fabric was in fact translucent.

Snow Pine searched for, and found, the twisting silver cord.

She followed it toward a distant coffin.

The light of the calligraphy dimmed. Zheng called out, "The spell is fading!"

A great hissing filled the chamber, and the light from the ghosts wavered as they shifted and began awakening from their reverie. "Stay close!" Snow Pine yelled, running up to the coffin. She slammed the staff against the wood. It shattered.

Screeching filled the chamber, and the light of the Living Calligraphy was gone. The ghosts whirled as one and flowed toward Snow Pine.

She looked into the gap, and there was enough crazy illumination to reveal the body within. The dead woman retained a grim beauty and dignity even after centuries, for all that her face appeared much as charred bark, and her hair as strips of dry cloth.

This body did not stir, and Snow Pine had a moment's regret at disturbing its resting place.

But only a moment. In the next, the ghosts were upon her.

It was all she could do to defend herself. One after another, she struck charging spirits with Monkey's staff. One after another they burst into flares of light, and with a blast of cold air they were gone. Yet there were always more.

Suddenly her companions were there, along with the magic carpet. Bone taunted and dodged and threw fragments of coffin-wood to distract the spirits. Deadfall threw itself against them, doing no damage but attracting much attention. Zheng cursed and prayed and reached into the coffin.

Persimmon Gaunt drew Crypttongue.

A strange whispering arose, audible even through the screeching of the ghosts. It seemed no louder than the spirits' cries; rather it had the timbre of dozens of voices whispering into Snow Pine's ears.

Gaunt struck.

Her target did not ignore the blade. Nor did it vanish in a burst of light. It rippled, distorted, and flowed into a gem upon the saber's pommel, like a reflection upon draining water.

Gaunt trembled and nearly dropped the sword. "It is . . . still with me . . . its knowledge is mine . . ."

"Watch out!" Snow Pine called and destroyed a ghost that reached out for Gaunt.

Gaunt's jaw was set as she slashed at a fresh target.

The two women—with a bit of assistance from man and carpet—kept the ghosts at bay. Yet the specters kept coming, and soon their guards would fall.

"I have it!" Zheng cried at last. "It's beautiful!"

"Let's go!" Snow Pine replied.

It was easier said than done. Luckily the coffin of the map fragment was on the side closest the entrance. Even so, they were too hard-pressed to move.

"Deadfall!" Bone said. "Gaunt and Snow Pine can fight their way out! But you'll have to haul me and Zheng, one at a time."

"I do not have to do anything, O thief," replied the carpet.

"Please, O wondrous and clever carpet."

"Ah, very well."

"Zheng first."

"I can face danger as well as anyone, boy."

"You have the map fragment. We need you safe."

Zheng cursed. "Very well."

"I will convey her to the entrance," Deadfall said.

"Wait," said Gaunt, frowning as though hearing a distant voice. "There is a better way out. *To the dark ship* . . ."

"Say again?" Bone said.

"The dark ship that sails under sands. Its magic is the reason this area stays clear." Between sword strokes she nodded through the gloom, away from the entrance. "That way."

"Intelligence from the ghosts?" Bone asked. "By way of the sword?"

"Yes."

"Can you trust it?"

"I think so. Deadfall, do you sense a passage that way?"

"I do, O poet."

"Take Zheng that way. If you are willing, Zheng."

"Well . . . I've lived a full life," Zheng said. "Let's see what we'll see."

"Keep her safe!" Gaunt told the carpet.

As Deadfall carried Zheng through the dark, her cursing redoubled.

"I'm not certain travel with Deadfall qualifies as 'safe,'" Bone muttered.

Gaunt and Snow Pine were too busy fighting to speak. In truth, despite all the danger, Snow Pine exulted in the power of the staff. It grew warm in her hands, and a crazy grin lit her face. Only dimly did she become aware of Bone's shout.

Snow Pine looked through the darkness and saw three wrapped, shambling figures moving through the ghosts toward her.

"We have to move!" Snow Pine said.

The three of them advanced along the wall after Zheng, but the ghosts kept them from making much progress. Bone threw a dagger at one of the wrapped mummies. It stuck between glowing red eye-sockets. The mummy kept coming.

"Almost there," Bone began after a time. Then: "No . . ."

A fourth mummy blocked their path, standing within the passage Zheng and Deadfall had traveled.

"Very well," Bone said, "I'll distract him. Run!"

"You're not allowed to die here!" Gaunt said, dispatching a ghost.

"No one stays behind," Snow Pine agreed. "We stay together and trust to luck."

As she spoke, the fourth mummy chuckled and reached into a pack at its feet. It pulled out some manner of discus and flung it at a nearby ghost.

The spirit sighed and crumpled, and its substance dispersed like a flock of doves.

Snow Pine heard the fourth mummy chant, in her native language, "'Travel on, travel on, cross the river of perception, and know at last the other side.'"

The mummy—whom she was beginning to doubt really was a mummy—

threw another discus, and another ghost dissipated. The group reached the thrower's side, and the stranger pulled the wrappings from its head. Snow Pine saw now that the wrappings were simply paper.

"Ah, this is enjoyable," said the mummy, clearly a living man, "but we must be escaping. Deadfall and Widow Zheng await us."

"Who are you?" Gaunt demanded.

"I've had many names. Dorje. Surgun. Yi. Perhaps you know me as Mad Katta."

"Deadfall's master?" Bone said.

"Let's compare karma later, eh?" Snow Pine said.

"Follow me," Katta said.

They retreated down the tunnel. Snow Pine struck its side, and collapsing sand sealed off the graveyard. Now they were alone.

"Unwise," Katta said, though he kept walking.

"It buys us a moment. Who are you, really?"

"A friend. You need friends, if you are to escape the realm of the Engulfed. Come, our companions are already aboard the ship of glass."

They reached a remnant of the buried village where timber posts formed the suggestion of a pier. Beyond it was a twisted monument of black crystal.

Snow Pine had seen many vessels during her time in Qiangguo's capital. She had seen great voyaging junks, sleek dhows, crowded galleons from places as far away as Mirabad and Kpalamaa. But she had never seen any craft like this. It was as though a three-masted ship had been assembled from leaves and thorns and branches of some brambly growth—and then transmuted to black glass. She felt lacerated just looking at it.

"Who made this?" she asked.

"Leviathan Minds," Katta said. "Beings of nearly forgotten aeons, whose realm lies buried beneath the sands."

"I remember," Bone whispered. "When I was imprisoned in the crystal forest, I saw them. They were minds unlike ours, wise in magic, beyond human notions of good or evil."

"The dwellers of the lost town remember them," Gaunt said, raising Crypttongue and frowning at its pommel. "I hear them murmuring to me, warning me of the Leviathans' power."

Snow Pine looked at her friends. "You two make me nervous."

"Says the woman with Monkey's staff," Gaunt said.

Snow Pine shrugged.

"You are an intriguing group," said Katta. "Alas, we must postpone conversation." He pointed down the way they'd come.

Howling ghosts were shimmering their way through the wall of sand.

He gestured toward a boarding ramp that lay before them like a giant obsidian sword. Striding up, he added, "I suggest the armed women stand ready. No offense, sir."

"None taken!" Bone said.

As they reached the deck, Snow Pine saw Zheng kneeling before a blank scroll, ink block out, pen at the ready. Deadfall was swishing beside a ship's wheel that seemed fashioned of ruby, its eight jabbing points reminiscent of an oversized shuriken from the Five Islands.

"All is in readiness, Lord Katta," the carpet said.

"I told you not to call me that, old friend." Katta gripped the ruby wheel, hands landing upon two of the points. Snow Pine winced. Katta seemed unperturbed as his blood dripped upon the wheel.

Strange light, as of trapped fireflies, glowed within the red crystal.

"Intriguing," said Gaunt.

"You've not seen the half of it."

"Are you all right, Grandmother?" Bone said to Zheng with unexpected politeness, bowing in the manner of Qiangguo.

"Shut up and let me work, boy," said Zheng.

"You said it takes weeks to make a scroll of Living Calligraphy."

"And so you're preventing me from getting started?"

Bone raised his hands and backed away. Snow Pine turned away herself and stood at the top of the ramp . . . except that it wasn't a ramp anymore. Somehow it had silently been drawn up onto the deck, the jagged railing swinging shut against the opening. There being no obvious point to guard, she simply stood, waiting. Gaunt stepped beside her.

"I had not expected us to become like a pair of doomed warriors in some ballad," Gaunt said.

"Nor I," Snow Pine said. "You know, our stories about magical weapons usually end badly."

"Ours too."

"Well, however it ends, I'm glad to stand beside you, my friend."

Gaunt squeezed her shoulder.

The ship shuddered, and crimson light flared behind them. Snow Pine would have turned to look, but at that moment the screaming ghosts arrived. The mummies weren't far behind.

Like a howling wave the spirits flowed up the side of the craft.

A proud-looking, transparent man loomed over Snow Pine. She bowed to him and disintegrated him. Beside her Gaunt stabbed a misty woman, whose form flowed into the gray sword.

"Sir!" Snow Pine heard Katta say. "You possess good aim! Employ the weapons in yonder pouch."

Snow Pine swung the meteoritic staff, and ghosts erupted into light. But it seemed to her that some of the ghosts beyond her and Gaunt's reach began shattering like old ice.

All at once the ship lurched forward, and she and Gaunt tumbled. The ghosts wailed in sudden panic as the glass vessel surged toward a wall of sand. The spirits fled just as impact came.

Yet there was no impact as such, for the sand flowed around them like the dust of a sandstorm. In a moment the ship was entirely encircled by darkness; the feeling of movement did not abate but actually increased.

"A ship that sails beneath the sands," Snow Pine breathed.

"A relic of lost aeons," Gaunt murmured.

"Cakes!" Bone said.

The women turned and saw Bone scowling at an orange sweetcake. "They are cakes, and yet they destroy ghosts."

"It is truth, not baking, that dispatches things of evil," said Katta at the wheel. Now it glowed like a molten thing, yet the man still displayed no hint of pain. "The greater the ill-will, the greater the inner torment. I seek to reveal that reality to those who haunt the land. On the Plateau of Geam I learned the art of imbuing offering-cakes with blessings. Although," Katta added with a hint of pride, "the discus shape is my own innovation."

"All hail Great Katta," said Deadfall.

Zheng dipped a bit of ink upon her scroll. "I thank you, Great Katta, for keeping the ship mostly steady. I will also thank you to explain what the hell is going on."

"My name is not Great Katta," said the man at the wheel. "Nor is Lord Katta or Mighty Katta or Holy Katta or any such elaboration. I will accept Mad Katta, because it has a certain charm, in a way that Blind Katta never did."

"You are blind?" Bone asked. "That is surely not true."

"It is. I am blessed, or cursed, with a form of second Sight, allowing me to perceive things awash in negative karma. In situations such as this, I am hampered very little! And yet, were I to throw myself endlessly against the monsters of this world, filling my Sight with horrors, I should in time fully earn the title 'Mad.'"

"You are not mad," Deadfall said. "You challenge evil, and I am forever in your debt. But how came you to survive the mummies near Qushkent?"

"I might have the same question for you, friend carpet. I was dragged deep into the desert, where the Leviathan Minds yet hold sway, feeble in comparison to their ancient powers, yet still dangerous. I am not entirely unfamiliar with those realms. When I was younger and more reckless I explored many a vile catacomb, where evil thoughts left their residue upon the passageways, allowing me to dimly 'see.' Dangerous roads, but knowledge of them has made me greatest of travelers along the Braid of Spice. And on rare occasions I have managed to take one of these—a ship of the Leviathan Imperium."

"I have more questions than there are grains of sand swirling about us," Gaunt said.

"You are not alone in that," said Katta.

"Perhaps a trade," Bone said, "one for one?"

"Very well. What do you seek, and why?"

"That's two," Snow Pine said, feeling a trust in Mad Katta that surprised her, "so answer two in return. We seek the Silk Map, so we can bear a treasure of ironsilk to Lady Monkey whose staff I bear."

"Indeed?" Widow Zheng said, looking up from her scroll.

Katta's eyebrows raised. "That is an ample answer, and I will be accordingly generous."

"Then who are you, anyway? And why do you seek the map?"

"He is a holy man," said Deadfall. "He gave me purpose and friendship when I lacked everything."

"Deadfall," said Katta, "I am many things, but I am not holy. Nevertheless I seek the holy. I am an itinerant of the Dust on the Mirror."

"You serve the Undetermined, then," Bone said.

"I follow in his footsteps, in my own meandering way. I was once an apprentice shaman of they the Karvaks call the Reindeer People. But I heard the teachings of the Undetermined and all that changed. I have had . . . many false starts, and perhaps even now I am not on precisely the correct path. Yet the Undetermined remains my polestar."

"What, then, is your interest in the map?" Gaunt asked.

"You repeat an earlier question, so I will not count that. The map points the way to a land of enlightenment."

"Xembala," said Zheng.

"Yes. I have never reached that place, but I am sure it exists. I do not want it tormented by outsiders. I know that the vile beings called the Charstalkers have been seeking Xembala for too long. I must oppose them. I believe that this is the purpose that the Thresholders intend for me. Now, a question for you—why do you serve Monkey?"

"She has an answer," Snow Pine said, "for the question that haunts Gaunt, Bone, and me. How do we find a particular magic scroll lost beneath the eastern sea? The scroll that contains our children."

"Wait a minute!" Zheng said. "I travel with you for weeks, share battle with you, risk everything, and you never say this? But this fellow comes along and you blab all your secrets?"

"I apologize, Zheng. I just feel time is short and that we can trust him." The answer sounded inadequate, even to her. Yet what she'd said was true. It was as though all her self-understanding was like the sunlit opening of a cave, with strange depths unlit behind her. Every friendship she had ever had—even her marriage—was like lighting a campfire near that entrance. Her relationships had thrown flickering light upon the deepest parts of her, but nothing had come clear.

But the eyes of this not-holy man were like bright lanterns, as though they reached the deepest parts of her and did not turn away. She found the sensation uncomfortable, but she could not turn away either. "We have been seeking a way to it, and to them, in vain, and only the Great Sage, Equal of Heaven, the Wondrous Lady Monkey, seems confident of helping us. But her price is the Iron Moths of Xembala."

"I know legends of Monkey," Zheng said. "She was not trustworthy."

"I have heard of her also," said Katta, "and while it is often said she was impetuous and foolish and destructive, it was never said that she was a liar."

"This is what we are reduced to, however," Gaunt said, "dealings with untrustworthy demigods."

"We will not give up," Bone said.

"Do you know of a way, Mad Katta?" Snow Pine asked. "A means of reaching our children?"

"Not as such," said the wanderer. "But I will say this: the masters of Xembala are said to possess great wisdom. It may be that in following Monkey's quest you will find another answer to your own. And now I know my next question. Will you share your pieces of the Silk Map?"

Even Zheng left off her scroll work to see the bright, shimmering pieces of the dress set down upon the black deck. The patch that Quilldrake had worn lay above the lower portion retrieved from the grave. There was a thin strip from the second piece that ascended to near Quilldrake's fragment. They touched in just one point, a place representing a mountain at the edge of a mist-filled chasm.

Katta kept one hand on the ship's wheel as he tossed a rolled-up third fragment to Gaunt. This was a fragment that would have covered chest and belly. It fit snugly with the other two.

Bone squinted. "Do you see it, Gaunt? The dress, the map, is oriented so head would be north, and feet south. The upper parts look like the deserts along the Braid, but the lower . . ."

"It shows a great mountain range," Gaunt agreed. "And a huge plateau. Yet . . . I have never seen a map that presented that jagged valley cutting through the peaks."

"I haven't either," said Snow Pine. "Hey, at one end of the valley, do you see the characters for 'iron' and 'silk'? As tiny as can be?"

"Yes," Zheng said with the air of someone hearing far-off music. "That is where we're going."

"To a chasm?" Bone said.

"To Xembala," Katta said. "I've been certain of its existence for a long while, since the day I first found my section of the map."

"Strange," Snow Pine said, staring at the dress. "I'd never quite visualized it as both map and clothing before now. It's almost as if the wearer—Xia, was it?—almost as if she were here with us."

"Yes," Zheng murmured, staring at the fabric. "Strange . . . there. Do you see?" She pointed at the interface of the three fragments. "That mountain at the edge of the chasm, the one that vaguely resembles a bird. That is the site of Qushkent."

Gaunt ran his finger along the ironsilk. "That's the direction most of the Karvaks were flying."

Katta chuckled to himself. "Flying Karvaks! The wonders of phenomena never cease to amaze."

"And look more closely," Zheng continued. "If you peer here, you see a line drawn from the beak of the bird, down to the valley floor."

"A secret passage?" Bone said.

"The implication of one, at any rate," Gaunt agreed. "Without all these pieces there, it would be easy to dismiss any segment of the line as a flaw in the artwork. But with all together the intention is clear."

"Lady Steelfox," Snow Pine said. "She saw only the upper two fragments, not Katta's. She can't be as certain as we are that this is the way to proceed."

"I think she has a fairly good guess," Bone said. "And she may not even need the hidden path, not with her—"

He was cut off by the mummified hands that grabbed his throat.

One of the arcane mummies, shrouded in its pale leathery wrappings, must have gotten aboard back at the lost village. Snow Pine was angry with herself. Like it or not, fate had made a warrior of her, and she should have been more watchful. She raised the meteoritic staff as Gaunt drew Crypttongue. Zheng grabbed Katta's sackful of enchanted cakes. The mummy backed away, careful to hold the gasping and flailing Bone before it like a shield.

Katta said, never moving from his post, "I advise no sudden moves, my friends. This entity can snap a neck as easily as snapping its fingers. Begone, creature! There is nothing for you here."

The mummy did not respond, except to point with its right hand, aiming at a direction to Katta's left. Its left hand was still sufficient to immobilize Bone.

"You wish me to turn the ship in that direction?"

The mummy nodded.

"Do your masters await us there?"

Another nod.

Bone was by now shaking his head as much as possible, which was only an inch or so to either side.

"Are its masters the Leviathan Minds?" Gaunt said.

"They surely mean us no good," Snow Pine said.

"Life is ultimately an illusion," Katta said, turning the ship to match the mummy's chosen heading. "As are physical threats. But there is no merit in allowing this creature to kill an innocent."

Bone gasped something.

"Don't be pedantic, Bone!" snapped Gaunt. "Of course you're innocent. Relatively speaking. Let him go, thing."

The mummy rasped words unknown, in a language unspoken for centuries. It relaxed its hold on Bone, but the thief stayed put.

They traveled for hours, at a speed Snow Pine could not estimate but which she suspected was swift indeed. She wondered about the people of Shahuang, and about the camels, which she would surely never see again. She wondered about Quilldrake and Flint, traveling with the strange, proud Karvak leader. Likely she'd never see them either. She found herself wishing Flint could comfort her in the matter of Flint's loss, which was a peculiar daydream to be having, on many levels.

Stop daydreaming! she told herself. *Look for a way out!*

It occurred to her she could not see Deadfall anywhere. She shifted a little, seeking the carpet. The mummy edged backward at her motion. Peering in that direction, she saw a dark rectangular shape against the black crystal deck, almost impossible to see in the dim light. How long had it been there?

If it was Deadfall . . . she could not explain to the others. That might give things away. She moved a little forward, a little sideways, and the mummy retreated, back, a little left, back again—

It stepped into the dark rectangle.

At once the four edges of the carpet snapped upward like the petals of some carnivorous plant. Bone had appeared entirely quiescent, but he instantly seized his opportunity. He kicked his legs into the air. Deadfall pinned the mummy's legs, and all three fell to the deck. Bone wiggled enough to escape the neck-hold, though the mummy still trapped one arm.

Now, however, Snow Pine, Gaunt, and Zheng were ready. They whacked, stabbed, and threw cakes. The mummy's middle collapsed, its head was severed from its body, and the arm that held Bone burst into dust.

Snakelike bandages writhed to the edges of the deck and slithered off, leaving only a pile of dust behind.

"Gah!" said Bone, holding his neck. Gaunt put one arm around him. The other held Crypttongue, at which she stared wonderingly.

"What is it?" he managed to say.

"This sword," Gaunt answered. "It did not absorb the mummy's essence. As though there was truly nothing to take."

"Is that a good thing?"

"For me, just now, yes. I do not want the sensation of escorting more trapped minds. But I wonder at the nature of the entity—"

"Hold tight," Katta said. "I will attempt to escape whatever fate was intended for us."

Snow Pine had previously been unaware that the ship's wheel could be *raised*. Katta did so, and the ship ascended through the darkness.

Light blazed across the deck as the dark vessel burst above the dunes. They reached a place where sand gave way to dry grass and shrub, strange rock formations twisting on the desert's edge like the headlands of a coast. Farther south lay an indistinct haze of brown; farther north slashed the green of true grassland.

A herd of horses in every hue moved among the drab shrubs, nuzzling for the ragged clumps of pale grass rising from the russet earth. They were powerful-looking beasts, and Snow Pine had the sense she'd seen them before. When some looked up at the magical ship and snorted their disinterest, she noted they possessed more ribs than the norm and realized what they were. "Dragon horses," she whispered.

Katta heard her. "The fastest beasts on land, Snow Pine. Each one is worth a fortune. I tried to find a herd of them."

"How did you manage to sense them?" Bone asked.

"All senses are enhanced when steering this vessel, including ones that are damaged." Katta closed his eyes for a moment. "It is a disorienting pleasure, like strong drink."

"By the way, the herd's not the only thing I see bearing the word 'Dragon,'" Gaunt said. "Look there."

Snow Pine followed Gaunt's gesture and looked into the west. Far away there swirled a fiery conflagration, rising far into the sky, red lightning flashing in its midst.

"The Dragonheat," Bone said. "Where the dragons go to mate, bound in some fashion by the influence of the Heavenwalls."

Snow Pine found the meteoritic staff had grown hotter in her grasp.

"Then Qushkent's a whole desert away," Zheng said. "We're on the north side, not the south. How—"

Something new erupted from the sands.

Vast pale tentacles whipped around the crystal ship. They possessed suckers and smaller, branching tentillia. Both tentacles and tentillia were covered in arcane inscriptions that Snow Pine had seen before.

Mad Katta released the wheel and leapt, just as a tentacle tried to squash him. "Depart the craft!" he yelled.

"I believe the phrase is 'abandon ship,'" Gaunt said, following his order regardless.

"I have never even been on an ocean!" Katta said.

"Deadfall!" Bone said. "Help Zheng get down!"

"Are you quite sure . . ." said Zheng.

"Better that than leaping the rail, Grandmother."

The carpet skittered up to Zheng, saying, "You do not command me, O thief, but I will help her nonetheless."

"Thank you," Bone said.

"Well, let's be on with it," Zheng said. "Gahhhh—"

As Zheng and Deadfall fled the ship, Gaunt look Snow Pine's arm, and they joined Bone and Katta at the railing. The starboard side was now leaning toward the sand. It was a long drop but a survivable one. Not for the first time, Snow Pine wished she had learned the esoteric secrets of her mentor Lightning Bug, who could make her body so light as to nearly fly. *Once a sturdy peasant,* she thought, *always a sturdy peasant, I suppose.*

She jumped.

As she lay face-down in the sand, she felt someone trying to lift her up.

"I'm okay," she said, a trifle annoyed at her companion's pushiness.

She felt a sucker attach itself to her back.

"Shit!" she yelled and tried to roll away. A tentacle loomed over her, its arcane markings twisting as its muscles flexed, its suckers puckering like pale, squinting eyes.

Snow Pine whacked her staff against the tentacle, and it severed with an immense sound like tearing paper. Dry innards spilled onto Snow Pine's face like hay after a heat wave. She spat the stuff away and swung again. The tentacle released her, and she scrambled away. The rod was hot now. There was a sound of distant thunder.

Terrified, she ran for the rocky region between the sands and the horses, and did not stop until she'd climbed to the highest spot. Only then did she see that Katta had made it here too, while a little ways below Gaunt and Bone were assisting Zheng onto the rocks. She searched for Deadfall and was startled to find it curled up like a dog near her feet.

The tentacles dragged the crystal ship beneath the sands. Snow Pine could see no body to the Leviathan Mind, no eyes, no proof that the tentacles had any central connection at all. It was as if the desert itself had reached out its hand.

Yet she heard a voice, and she could not be certain if it came to her upon the wind, or through the pathways of her mind, or if she was dreaming while awake.

Your kind transgresses, said the voice, a dry thing suggesting experience beyond all hope or bitterness. If a sand hourglass had a voice, it would be like this. *You play with relics that are not yours to toy with. You imitate our great works, with your Heavenwalls, and your Chain of Unbeing, and your city shaped like a hand. But you lack the wisdom to know when to stop. Slowly but inexorably you ruin the Earthe, as we nearly did.*

Mad Katta heard the voice too. "Yet you are not done with the world, either, eh? You watch and wait, and you are not indifferent to the Silk Map."

There is a great evil that dwells in the hidden valley. Greater than we. It has long hungered for our relics. You know this, wanderer. If you allow outsiders in, what will get out?

"No one can foresee all events. What I do know is that the people I travel with have good motivations. I believe I can help them without causing larger harm."

Let it be on your cranium then. The Dragonheat will finish you in any event.

Ship and tentacles vanished into a pit in the sands, and the pit filled itself in, leaving only a cloud of dust to mark its passage.

"Well," Bone said, stretching and cracking his knuckles. "That was terrifying."

"I'm not certain the terror is over," Gaunt said, studying the fire and lightning that curdled on the horizon. "What did it mean about the Dragonheat?"

"I do not know," Katta said. "There are times when the storm moves away from its usual location, with predictably disastrous effect. Yet I know of no reason why it would threaten us."

"I do," Snow Pine said, staring at her glowing staff. "Monkey told me the needle—this staff—was a gift from a dragon queen. It must have a connection to them."

Zheng said, "The dragons may be responding. Or the Dragonheat, the storm itself."

"Either way," Gaunt said, "we may be in danger."

"Without wishing to panic anybody," Bone said, "I must weigh in with my opinion that the storm is getting closer."

"We could be lucky," Gaunt said. "Perhaps the dragons mean to help us."

Snow Pine studied the storm. "I do not feel particularly lucky."

"I will be ready to panic," Zheng said, her voice calm and matter-of-fact, "when the storm is twice its apparent size."

They all watched the storm swell. To Snow Pine's eyes it was already an eighth or so larger.

"So!" Bone said brightly. "Horses, you say!"

"Allow me!" said Katta. "I have had dealings with dragon horses before. Deadfall, I would be most grateful if you would guide me."

Snow Pine saw the magic carpet flow over to Katta and offer one corner of itself to the wanderer. Staff in one hand, carpet in the other, Katta descended.

The horses turned their heads toward the travelers. Their eyes, so Snow Pine thought, were wary but not frightened. The animals continued to eat. From time to time they looked toward the oncoming storm with somewhat more attention.

Katta hummed a mantra to himself as he approached a stallion brown as a desert stream, mane and tail black as Zheng's ink. The horse's eyes seemed to Snow Pine to hold a vast patience that was also a grim imperiousness. There was within them a compassion humans could never comprehend, and a wrath unimaginable, should that compassion be mocked.

Katta released Deadfall (who coiled about in the sparse grass like a snake) and spread his hands. "Great one. That which has given rise to this form and this name pleads to that which gave rise to you. Something in the karma of both phenomena has brought us to this place. We are drawn together in this moment. Thus I ask to incur a debt that may endure a hundred lifetimes."

The stallion snorted and swished his tail.

"Indeed, and yet you know me, and you know I keep my oaths."

The stallion whinnied, and his hoof tore the earth.

"Yes, there are many disturbances, and I understand why you would come here to better sense them. I am fortunate that you did so."

The stallion tugged its ears back and sneezed.

"Qushkent."

The stallion nickered.

Katta turned to the others. "We are in great luck. Our friend here—his name is not truly repeatable without the equine vocal apparatus, but might be rendered as Firstsnorter Proudneck Earjab Hightail—our friend is willing to bear us to Qushkent, along with two others of his herd."

Staring at the huge beasts, Bone said, "You know, historically horses and I have not gotten along well. I prefer friendlier beasts. Like camels. Or dragons—"

"Do you want to tell that to the Dragonheat?" Gaunt said. "I think it's just now reached the apparent size where Zheng said—"

"There is always time to start a new friendship!" Bone said.

"Agreed," Zheng said.

At Katta's recommendation, Snow Pine and Zheng mounted Dawnracer Windneigh Maneshake Laughswish, a dappled roan female with a teasing manner, and Gaunt and Bone climbed onto Springjumper Wildgroan Head-toss Backkick, a gray male with a look of coiled energy ready to whip into motion. Deadfall consented to becoming a horse-blanket upon the stallion. Snow Pine got a sense of sullenness from the magic carpet.

CHRIS WILLRICH   237

The atmosphere had changed. There was a wind moving toward the storm, as though the Dragonheat was calling the air toward it. Now it filled half the sky. Flame and smoke, clouds and rain, lightning and lava tormented the air. Now and again Snow Pine thought she glimpsed a shadowy suggestion of sinewy winged shapes, tiny within the conflagration, but it might have been her imagination. The Dragonheat, created by the mating energies of the dragons, seemed a living thing of its own. A thing that sought their death.

Monkey's rod nearly burned her hand; on intuition she cleared her mind and pushed it from two directions.

It shrunk swiftly back into the form of a needle, still hot to the touch but manageable. She threaded it into her robe, hoping the fabric would not burn.

"Impressive trick," said Zheng.

She nodded. "Time to go."

"I agree," said Katta, "but it is not our decision. The stallion and his herd communicate as to when and how they will meet again."

"At this rate," Bone muttered, "the answers will be never and by no means—"

His voice was cut off by the movement of horses scattering in all directions but west-southwest, whence the blue lightning danced amid a crimson veil.

CHAPTER 15

THE GASH IN THE EARTHE

When Bone first scrambled onto the dragon horse, he found his perch even higher off the ground than he'd believed. He wondered if perhaps Gaunt shouldn't be the one in front but was reluctant to admit it. He was comfortable with high rooftops, to be sure, but rooftops did not gallop, shake, or attempt to buck off their occupants. And just as he was making peace with his distance from the ground, the ground began to move. Swiftly, to a drumbeat of hoof-falls, the russet borderland became the rocky desert edge and then the expanse of sandy waste, the shadow of the dragon horse outlined in fiery red.

"Are you all right?" called Gaunt.

"Just getting used to the gallop!"

"This is a trot! Will you be all right?"

"I can hold on to the mane, yes—whoa!"

Whoa did not seem to be an instruction that Springjumper Wildgroan Headtoss Backkick recognized. In fact, Bone decided—after the ground became an orange-red blur and his companions shadowy suggestions of motion, so that only the Dragonheat itself seemed a constant presence in an indistinct world of sand and sun—the dragon horse did not seem much aware of his or Gaunt's presence at all, let alone their words.

This at least allowed him to curse as colorfully as he wished.

From time to time he looked over his shoulder, and each time he wished he hadn't. He still saw no dragons, only the chaotic madness of the Dragonheat. He was sure now it had an independent life, quite apart from the wishes of the dragons who had given rise to it. How else to explain why a thing of blood-red fire, icy-blue lightning, and tomb-gray cloud, the confluence of these things filling two-thirds of the sky, would deign to pursue them.

But pursue it did.

At first it seemed the storm would catch them, for it approached sidelong, and twice the horses were slowed in leaping over two inexplicable fortifications the height of houses. (Only later did Bone realize these must be the far western extensions of the Heavenwalls.) Yet gradually the conflagration shifted until it was at their backs.

For hours it followed them past bizarre wind-sculpted rocks twisting like squids and staircases and crowned heads. It followed them over endless dunes, each trough a new gut-plunging sensation for Imago Bone. The sun set, and still the dragon horses galloped, and still the storm followed, bright enough that its illumination cast rushing horse-shadows upon the sands.

At one point the stallion came near to them, and Katta shouted to see if they were all right.

"Never better!" Gaunt said. "Alas! I think the storm is doing well too!"

"Is there no place to hide?" Bone called out.

"We may find a karez!" Katta said.

"The what?" Gaunt said.

"The irrigation system Qushkent spreads far into the desert! Its tunnels lie under the ground!"

"Under the ground sounds good!"

"Are we near?" Bone asked.

"Yes! Another hour, perhaps!"

"I'm not certain we have another hour!"

"We will either see a karez," Katta said, "or our next incarnations!"

"I'm not sure we Westerners get multiple incarnations!" Gaunt objected.

"I will gladly loan you two of mine!" Katta laughed, and Bone was uncertain if he was serious.

Bone might have napped, in the half-awake, half-alert manner he'd learned hiding upon balconies in Palmary, waiting for his moment to strike. It was so long past, that time before Gaunt, so many cities and mountains and oceans and deserts ago. Like another incarnation. He stirred and gripped her hand. It was dark but hot, and the horse's shadow stretched like a narrowing road into what seemed unending shadowy sands. The stars were bright above them, but the storm was almost upon them, threads of fire and smoke making increasingly daring incursions upon the Heavens. It was unfair. Innocence Gaunt was lost to the waters, and Persimmon Gaunt would be lost to the fires. A-Girl-Is-A-Joy would never know her mother's world.

Rage snapped and growled inside him. The followers of the Undetermined might say that his anguish was the result of undue attachment to the illusory things of this life. Yet if there was a difference between these particular attachments and he, himself, Imago Bone could not unravel it.

Still, consideration of such matters at least put a thread of distance between himself and his anger. Bone realized his rage arose in part from having his and Gaunt's life in the hooves of one Springjumper Wildgroan Headtoss Back-kick. He was used to the threat of death, but there was always some ploy remaining even unto the end, a dagger to toss, a wall to scale. Now there was nothing he could do.

No, not nothing, he realized.

He could admire the stars, and he did.

"Thank you," he told the horse.

"I love you," he told Gaunt.

"What?" she murmured.

The horse snorted and the stars disappeared.

Only from the blue-streaked crimson glare behind them could Bone discern what had happened. They were galloping down a narrow stone passage with a watery channel beneath. The footing looked terrible, and the path winding, and Bone couldn't understand how the dragon horse managed to maintain such speed. From time to time moonlight flashed down upon them, as the openings of wells passed overhead.

The Dragonheat hit.

Fire blazed into the karez, but only at the entrance far behind or below the openings of the wells. Once, lightning blazed into the passage, but it claimed the bucket-rope and the bucket, never hitting the water. A crumpled, seared lump of metal flopped into the channel.

Without warning the dragon horse halted, finally giving in to its weariness. Bone embraced Gaunt, as a man should hold his wife at the end of days, or at the end of an argument, or simply when a manifestation of titanic energies rolls past overhead. The horse snorted and stomped the water.

At last there was silence and stars.

By a unanimity that stretched across species, Bone, Gaunt, and the dragon horse slept.

Gaunt awoke from a peculiar dream, and it struck her so strongly that before any other action she played a memory trick so she could transcribe it later, coiling a clump of her hair and muttering to herself, "Tongues of fire." Then she remembered the fires of last night and stood.

Daylight entered the cramped gallery of beige bedrock, by way of a well-shaft nearby. Bone and the dragon horse continued to sleep; the man upon a thin shelf, the steed poised upright over the channel flowing through the passage's middle.

"A narrow escape," Gaunt murmured.

The day was already growing warm, but the water of the karez was cold enough to sting. Had she or Bone rolled over in their sleep, they would not have drowned, but the plunge into cold water, suffered in the desert night, might have slain them from the chill, here in one of the hottest regions of the world.

Bone rose abruptly. "Gaunt! Are we dead?"

"We are not dead, Bone. This is no paradise, no hell, no rebirth. This is ordinary discomfort. No breakfast and no easy place to pee. Life."

"I'm glad to join you in it. Is the horse sleeping?"

"I think so. I think, after all he has done, we must let him rest. There's been no sign of the others."

He stood and stretched, stepped into the cold water, cursed. "That makes sense. If there are more structures like this in the area, the odds of survival would be better with one horse to a karez. I hope we can find each other." He walked carefully to the well-shaft and looked up. "That must go up twenty or thirty feet. I wouldn't want to try climbing it with its rope destroyed."

"We'll wait for the horse. Bone . . . I had a dream."

He was suddenly all attention. "Tell me."

"I had a comfortable house, filled with all the trophies of our adventures, even the artifacts we've lost. You were sleeping, as were our two children. I was up and about and startled to discover that a fire was yet blazing in the fireplace, and that sparks had landed upon the scrolls I'd piled unwisely nearby. So far all that billowed from the paper was smoke—a narrow escape. I poured water onto the ruined scrolls, all the while imagining you, me, the children, all going up in flames. And yet rather than fear, I felt a calm gratitude that no such thing had occurred. It seemed to me that rather than put out the fire, I should mend it, stand vigil." Bone said nothing, and she uncoiled the tangle in her hair. "I looked out a glass window and saw a temperate clime filled with trees, and nearby all was . . . deadfall, with new green shoots rising through a chaotic lattice of dead branches and trunks." She lay back against the bedrock wall, watching Bone across the channel. "That is all. I don't know the meaning of this dream. But it has left me with a quiet determination. I will see it through. All of it. This is not a battle cry but a statement of fact."

"We had visions of children before. Before we had to flee to the East."

She nodded. "And our real son resembled the boy of my vision. I do not claim special powers, but I have seen what I have seen. I sense we will get him back, and that he will have a sister."

"The girl of my vision," Bone murmured, "the one riding joyfully along a beach." He frowned. "We haven't spoken of it since, but in your vision, our son had a cruel visage."

"It's true. He was older than when I knew him, borne upon a litter, commanding men in cowls who bore serrated swords."

"Gaunt . . . the one-eared stalker and her crew."

"Swan's blood. Yes."

Bone pounded the wall.

"Ow," he said.

"Bone. Have hope! That was the sense of my dream. If One-Ear—let's call her that—is fated to be tangled with Innocence, then at least it's a threat that's entering the light. I don't know if we will ever be granted the haven in the woods. And the image of the burning scrolls makes me think we'll lose much. But we will all be together—even she who has yet to arrive. I am sure of this."

At her words, Springjumper Wildgroan Headtoss Backkick gave a snort and his hooves clomped the passage.

"I do not speak dragon horse," Gaunt said, "but I think he is ready to go. Thank you, mighty one."

The horse surprised her by nickering.

All three of them seemed in accord on turning away from the darkness ahead, though rotating the dragon horse was an awkward process, quite a contrast from the majesty of the night before. He walked steadily enough once aimed toward the distant light, but it was clear escaping the Dragonheat had been an ordeal, and that progress today would be slow. Gaunt and Bone did not even consider riding.

The Dragonheat was nowhere to be seen, only the ordinary heat of mid-morning, as they emerged from the karez and beheld a cultivated region like a green shawl stretched over the desert's brown. There were grape orchards and mulberry trees, wheat fields and rows of cotton. Field workers in plain robes of white, gray, blue, or tan, most also wearing round hats with elaborate weaving, were busy clearing debris from the passage of the storm. Gaunt had the impression they'd had a long night.

The thought of grapes made her stomach groan. But she suspected that answering questions now would be uncomfortable. She steered stallion and man around the passage's opening and up the sandy slope.

Here was a borderland, a last gasp of the desert between the irrigated land and the alpine high country to the south. Thus it surprised Gaunt to discover, after some twenty minutes, a small community of tents. Each was inhabited by a wizened human being. Most of these old dwellers were accompanied by one or two younger helpers, or else by an occupied birdcage. Some of the ancients sat on chairs, some on rugs. All had their feet buried in the sand.

They passed two such people without attracting comment, but a third hailed them, and it seemed best to stop. The travelers and the horse regarded the sand-bather and his parrot. The old man possessed a long beard, a white robe, and a hat that reminded Gaunt of the plumage of tropical birds. He sat cross-legged upon a carpet that recalled, in decoration at least, the elaborate patterns upon Deadfall. He spooned pieces from a melon slice cut like a wide smile. He himself was expressionless, but his voice was cheerful as he greeted them. Unfortunately, Gaunt and Bone did not recognize the language, and if Springjumper Wildgroan Headtoss Backkick knew it, he wasn't talking.

"Do you speak the tongue of Qiangguo?" Gaunt asked, demonstrating that she at least did.

"Why yes!" said the old man. "Long ago, though it seems like last week, I was a caravaner who went as far as Yao'an. Those were the days!"

"Those were the days!" said the parrot in the cage.

"You weren't there, Hakan," said the man with a smile. "Honestly, what a braggart. I don't know why I put up with him. But only the man who has nothing has no problems."

"Do you and the parrot live here?" Bone said, bemused.

"Light in the darkness, no! My sons and daughters and their families take turns helping me out here, twice a week." He nodded toward his unseen feet. "Hot sand is good for aching joints. But it's not very conversational out here. Care to join us?"

"Care to join us?" squawked Hakan.

The man's name was Aydin, and he had melon to share, and this was enough for Gaunt to consider the name Aydin a good fit for sainthood. Bone and the dragon horse seemed pleased as well. The equine demolished an entire melon, and then another, until Gaunt felt compelled to leave some coin behind. Aydin would have none of it.

"Don't insult my hospitality, young lady! Besides, this is the best story I've had in a year. Is this truly a dragon horse?"

"We will tell you half of everything," Gaunt said, "if you keep it to yourself for half a week."

"Done," said man and parrot, almost simultaneously.

Bone fidgeted as Gaunt wove a tale of their travels that excised all mention of magic scrolls, demons, demigods, Leviathan Minds, sand-ships, or iron-silk maps. This still left caravans, swordfights, sandstorms, secret passages, mummies, Karvaks in balloons, and dragon horses. She was a little circumspect about the geography. Aydin did not pry.

"I confess," he said, "I am not at all certain I believe your story, though the horse is surely impressive. But it is marvelous nonetheless."

"I have not told you half of what I have seen," Gaunt said.

"In a way," Aydin said, rubbing his beard, "that thought is more satisfying than believing I've heard it all. The grandchildren have ransacked my brain for every story from the tales of Layali who stayed the executioner's blade, every account of the Undetermined's prior incarnations, every marvel of Qiangguo's Rivers-and-Lakes, every wonder-story of the Fire Saint, may his words light the future, and every perplexing true anecdote of my days along the Braid. I have reached the bottom of my memory's cask, and even scraped beyond the wood into the muck below."

"Muck below!" said the parrot.

"There is a feeling of being wholly spent of stories," Aydin said, "which is perhaps appropriate for an old man who sees death on the horizon like a beautiful storm. And yet, it is good to have a little wine in the cask, at the end, and the belief that there is still an untapped vineyard, out there in the world."

"Last night's storm," Bone said. "Did you see it?"

"We had reports from the watchtowers when we descended this morning. It is lucky the Dragonheat did not rise beyond the sands, or the alpine forest might have caught fire, and with it Qushkent. Do you know why the energies of the dragons might have chased you?"

"We have a talent for annoyance," Bone said.

Aydin chuckled. "As you wish. Do you go to the city?"

"I think so," Gaunt said.

"Your horse would fetch a fantastic price in the Market. But be alert. Ours is a city of honest folk, but we attract some rough sorts as well. Watch your step in the Bazaar of Parrots, but it is the best place for commerce."

"Commerce!" said the parrot, sounding proud.

"Avoid the Street of Peafowls, for though you may fetch higher prices from the grandees there, they are treacherous and wield private armies. Exotics such as yourselves are safest staying in the Alley of Babblers, where strange ideas are the norm. Avoid the District of Doves, which is named ironically, and the Avenue of Spiderhunters, who are twilight folk. Learn the chirps of each street and be ready to take wing. We have a saying, 'Before entering a place, consider your exit.'"

"It is one of my principles as well," Bone said.

They thanked Aydin and proceeded south, and up.

From the realm of the sand-bathers the land rose like a petrified tidal wave. Desert swiftly gave way to dry grassland, broken by granite slabs. Solitary bushes and poplars were the heralds for an army of trees, with gnarled undergrowth crunching underhoof. Where at first the stones seemed interlopers in the soil, rock and dirt became equal partners in an ancient dance, and at last the rock predominated as the dance ended at a precipice kissed by clouds.

The dragon horse snorted and stamped, excited for the first time since he'd awakened. The late morning was still cold up here, and his breath was visible. He rippled his back in a way that finally convinced Gaunt and Bone that he wanted to be ridden.

They trotted west along the precipice. Gaunt reflected that Bone's love of heights must be facing its ultimate test.

Soon there came whinnies from the west, and beyond a stand of pine trees they encountered the other dragon horses, with Snow Pine, Zheng, Katta, and Deadfall beside them. The humans and horses looked weary but safe. The carpet looked like a carpet.

The horses reared and stamped and snorted, facing the edge of their desert world.

The others had halted beside an egg-shaped boulder vast as an Eldshoren cottage, perched as though awaiting some mountainous bird to warm it. Gaunt imagined that a sneeze could topple the stone, but the snorts of the horses merely sent vapor coiling past to descend into the whirling cloud mass rushing past the cliff face. Had the rock actually fallen, it would have plunged but a few feet before the white swallowed it whole.

Snow Pine and Gaunt hugged, and Katta said, "I am pleased you did not perish."

"It would be wasteful," added the magic carpet, "if you were deprived of breath."

"Behold the CloudScar," said Zheng, perhaps wishing to change the subject. "Before today, I never thought to see it."

"How far does it extend?" Bone asked, in a tone he usually reserved for jewels.

"No one knows," Katta said, "for its eastward and westward extents lie deep amid mountains, where none go, but rumors say it's half as long as the Braid itself. As for its width, accounts agree the far wall is rarely more than a few miles off. If my sources are true, then by peering out there you might glimpse rocky ramparts rising above the white and the pearly helms of the Heavenwalk Mountains. Beyond, to the southeast, lies the Plateau of Geam, where the lamas taught me baking and the lore of the true and the transitory."

"Which has proven more useful?" Gaunt asked. "Baking or lore?"

"They are reciprocal skills. When a cake fails to rise it is helpful to recognize the rising and falling of the cake as illusions. When contemplating reality it is helpful to see illusion as the sugar on a pastry. The bread would nourish without the sugar, but the sugar would be meaningless without the bread."

"You may not be making me a follower of the Undetermined," Gaunt said, "but you are making me miss pastries. And cities. Where lies Qushkent?"

"You can see it from atop Egg Rock, here." Barely had Katta's words joined the hushed sound of the wind than Bone had ascended the great stone. Gaunt dismounted and followed; she was pleased to note she was only a trifle slower.

"I see a stone mountain to the east," Bone said, "one resembling the head of a bird. But no city."

"Look again," Gaunt told him, guiding his hand. "The bird is the city."

And indeed, the snowless peak that lofted blue-gray above the CloudScar had been shaped by artisans of courage and subtlety, coaxing a roughly avian shape into the head of a raptor. The neck was a sheer cliff dropping perhaps two thousand feet into the whirling white, but at the flat crown it narrowed into a beak-like projection jutting into emptiness.

"Ah, Qushkent," Katta said as he assisted Zheng up the boulder. "At most times I am detached about my blindness, but alas this isn't one of them. Enjoy the sight. This is among my favorite places . . . but one must watch one's step, even as the thin air makes one watch one's breath. Here we will find the way to Xembala."

"Ah," Zheng said, minding her footing. "It puts me in mind of a poem." She said:

> *Why argue?*
> *Win your robe and bowl*
> *While I walk the clouds and rivers*
> *Where I will carry water and chop wood*
> *And wipe the dust from the mirror*
> *Dust that is as true as we.*

Katta looked startled. "That was written by a follower of the Undetermined, in Qiangguo, a long time ago. He lost a sort of . . . contest. The poem has vanished in the mists of time."

"I don't really understand it," Zheng admitted. "I don't even remember where I heard it."

"The author . . . thought he'd been unfairly criticized on an esoteric point. So he went to walk the Earthe." Katta smiled, his look distant. "Perhaps he was just a sore loser. We try to see beyond worldly illusion, but pride is always there, and with it attachment, and suffering."

"'Life is suffering,'" Bone said. "That's your creed in a nutshell, isn't it? There are days I would agree. Many of them recent."

"Outsiders often fixate on that phrase, and I'm afraid it misleads them a bit. You could just as easily say, 'Life is bliss.'"

"Well, I *would* rather say that . . ."

"But that is not it either. Life is also boredom. And lust. And sleep. And pain. And that funny feeling immediately after burping when you feel obscurely proud of yourself."

"You get that too?"

"The point is, life will give you all these things, unpredictably. But we keep wanting to control it all, to get what we want, when we want. *That* leads to suffering."

"So life *is* suffering."

Katta rubbed his temples. "I am starting to think so . . ."

"Perhaps you should burp."

"These are intriguing questions, to be sure," Gaunt broke in, "but I'm afraid I have one even more intriguing."

"Oh?" Bone said.

"What are our opponents up to?"

Snow Pine followed where she was pointing, squinted, and sucked in her breath.

"I would be grateful if you told me what you saw," Katta said.

"The Karvaks have reached Qushkent," she said.

As they neared the gates, they argued. Bone would always wonder later if he'd been on the right side. There was expedience, and there was knavery. He had always believed he'd had honor, for a thief; afterward he would question that.

It began with Katta saying, "I do not understand how they could have beaten us here. How could their balloons have outrun the dragon horses?"

"Never underestimate a scholar of Mirabad," Bone said.

"Nor a Karvak," Zheng said.

"I suspect," Gaunt said, "the Dragonheat had a salutary effect on the air currents. They might have had as rough a ride as we. I notice only one balloon over the city, when three went south."

"Then Liron—" Snow Pine said. "Flint. And Quilldrake. They may have been lost."

"We know only what we see," Bone said. "But what we see worries me greatly. They may have had a whole day to seek the secret path to the valley below." A cold, clever idea occurred to him. "I think we should sell the horses."

"Bone!" Gaunt said, sounding shocked.

"Hear me out. Our funds are low, and we may need to grease many palms to find the path. Indeed, we may need more money simply to survive. What harm can the dragon horses suffer? We have witnessed their power. They can surely escape when they wish, mighty as they are."

"I am with Bone," Zheng said. "Let's fleece the locals. It's for a good cause."

Snow Pine said, "I can't tolerate these creatures being imprisoned."

"Nor I, Bone," Gaunt said, as if he'd sprouted a third eye. "And there may be magics that can bind even such as they."

"We can be careful whom we sell the horses to," Bone said.

Katta looked into the eyes of Firstsnorter Proudneck Earjab Hightail and into those of the stallion's companions. Katta snorted, shifted, moved his arms. He sighed. "Springjumper Wildgroan Headtoss Backkick is willing. He is willing to trust Imago Bone in this matter. The others are not, but the leader gives his consent."

"I still don't like it," Snow Pine said.

"Are you mad?" Zheng said. "We are going up against Karvaks. And if you expect me to craft more scrolls of Living Calligraphy than one, I am going to need to buy materials."

Gaunt stared at the horses, then at Bone. "I agree with Snow Pine. This is not simply sentiment. I am the wife of a thief. But some things I can't tolerate, expedient or no."

Bone studied her. He knew how much of a treasure that truly was: to have a wife who accepted him, all of him, with all his past, his compromised present, his likely future. Would he endanger that by becoming an even worse man than he was today?

Yet Innocence Gaunt still lay beneath the sea.

"That is two to two," Bone told Katta. "Yours is the deciding vote."

Katta shook his head. "I do not accept your rationale, nor your invitation to vote. You four have been companions for some time now, while I am an outsider. You must decide."

"There is one other who might speak," Gaunt said. "The magic carpet, Deadfall."

"Deadfall is a tool," Bone said, "a contrivance."

"It thinks. It chooses. It can choose now. Will you accept its vote? It is that, or we are deadlocked, Imago."

"Very well. What is your opinion, Deadfall?"

"My opinion, O thief," came the strange, dry voice of the carpet, "is that I would not have this steed treated as a tool or a contrivance. Even if he himself is willing."

"Three to two," Snow Pine said.

Widow Zheng made a disgusted sound, but Bone bowed. "So be it. We will find another way."

"We thank you," Katta told the horses. "One day I will grant the boon you ask, stallion, and find your lost mate, taken beyond the sea."

They watched the horses depart. Slowly the three majestic beasts gained speed as they passed among the trees, then they slipped behind a particularly thick stand of pines, and what emerged on the far side were three blurs that it took imagination to resolve into horses.

Gaunt did not hold his hand as they approached the City of Birds.

CHAPTER 16

ĪNTERLUDE: OBSERVATIONS OF AN OVERCOAT

Earlier, O marvelous owner, I related some of my difficulties after becoming separated from Lord Katta. As you will recall I fluttered, dispirited, through the catacombs beneath Qushkent. At last I emerged into an arm of the karez irrigation system and returned to sunlight. I had lost my friend but not my conviction to continue his mission. If Lord Katta sought to prevent evildoers from claiming the Silk Map, then, I, too, would stalk those who would stalk it. To that end I journeyed to Yao'an, learning how to impersonate a human so as to get close to humans. And finding the company led by Quilldrake, I inserted myself into their midst, after first arranging a small commotion among Yao'an's elite.

I could elaborate on what I have already related—how I rescued the travelers time and again, doing single combat with Karvaks and Charstalkers and ghosts and mummies, and even driving a Leviathan Mind single-tasseled back into the sands—all the while studying my companions and their motives. They did not seem to me to be the tools of evil but rather a mixed band of beings with a similarly mixed bundle of motives. I could not judge them as yet, so I traveled with them, learning. For the sake of Lord Katta's memory, I would absorb all I could, so as to judge whether, in the end, they should be allowed to journey to Xembala.

And then—astonishment—Lord Katta returned!

Yet could I trust him? He seemed less certain of himself than when we parted and more apt to take me for granted than to take me into his confidence. Had the Charstalkers influenced him? Their insinuations into a mind might be more subtle than those manifestations that produced fire and peril.

They might lurk deep within a mind, subtly turning it toward evils of which an individual might not be consciously aware.

I kept such councils to myself, even as I returned to Qushkent.

I will not insult you by giving you a verbal tour of the city, for who could ever forget the winding road up the mountain slope, nor the vast statue-towers of the Gate of the Falcon and the Hawk, nor the Bazaar of Parrots with its hundreds of tents and its eponymous birds upon golden pillars relaying news and prices? Who could not marvel at the mix of architecture in a city with echoes of both Mirabad's minarets and Yao'an's pagodas? Or the towers of day, twilight, and night, known better as the towers of the Blackbird, the Crake, and the Owl? Or at the House of the Pigeons, whose winged messengers flutter in and out through all daylight hours? Or the thousand shining windows of the Palace of Larks?

Not you, who forget nothing.

So I will restrict myself to what could not be glimpsed from the heights. We made our way to the Alley of Babblers. I was carried between Persimmon Gaunt and Imago Bone, who though somewhat at odds at that moment, cooperated in playing the role of exotic servants. Lord Katta was the traveling merchant, Snow Pine his bride, Widow Zheng his mother-in-law. There were those who recognized and hailed Katta, but he kept his pleasantries brief so that we might install ourselves within the Caravanserai of the Dancing Flame. By now it was twilight, and the evening ceremonies of the Nightkindlers had begun, in which offerings are burned to combat the coils of Lightrender, the evil one. Even in this intellectual district of a cosmopolitan city, the call of the local religion left the common room quiet. In the courtyard where the camels and horses and herd animals stayed, prayers began, addressed to a vast brazier. Our party had the much smaller flame of a firepit to ourselves, our nearest companions a solitary, turbaned man from Anoka reading from the holy book of the Testifier, a fur-capped mercenary from Madzeu sharing drinks with his own memories, and a pair of romantically inclined young women of Qushkent holding hands in a far corner. No one even asked why my companions shared space with a carpet, perhaps assuming Katta was simply cautious with his merchandise. Nevertheless I was careful not to speak.

Thus, I could only listen as Katta said, "I am told the balloon has descended only to the garden within the Palace of Larks, there to consult with the ruler, whose title is kagan. No Karvaks have been seen. Nor anyone else from the balloon."

"They must be seeking the way into the CloudScar," Zheng said. "If the kagan knows of a way, and the Karvaks can bargain the secret out of him. Karvaks are said to be very persuasive."

"It is easy enough to enter the CloudScar," Katta mused. "Simply leap the outer wall, or plunge into one of the many civic garbage chutes. Surviving the plunge is another matter. No one has ever heard of a person returning from that journey."

"They don't need to take it," Snow Pine said. "They have their flying gers. I don't understand why they are bothering talking to the kagan when they could simply descend."

"Perhaps they've tried," Bone said. "Perhaps that's why there is only one balloon now and not three."

"The winds whip fiercely within the CloudScar," Zheng said, "or so it's claimed. And none knows what the terrain is like beneath."

"I would consider stealing the balloon," Bone said. "But I too would rather know that the journey was survivable first. A tunnel through the mountain sounds more appealing."

"The Silk Map showed a line running from the beak of the mountain down into the valley," Gaunt said. "So what could it be?"

"I would assume it is a passage of some sort," Bone said. "A tunnel leading from the beak deep through the rock, emerging at last below the clouds."

"What is at the beak, in any case?" Snow Pine asked.

"A shrine," Katta said, "said to be a holy site, blessed by the Flame Saint himself. Within it lies a post and an ox-cart."

"Excuse me?" Bone said.

"Legend has it that Qushkent was long a trading city, its defensible location making it a good stopping point for caravans. Many tribes contested the location, often in bloody ways. At last the Flame Saint prophesied that the next person to arrive aboard an ox-cart should be the kagan of the city. Soon after there came a trader named Timur and his family aboard such a cart. Timur was bemused and pleased to become ruler of a city. The cart he gave to the priests, who placed it in the shrine. The Flame Saint did a peculiar thing, however; he tied the cart's rope to a post, weaving a most intricate knot. There is a legend that whoever can untie the knot will soon reach paradise."

CHRIS WILLRICH   255

"That sounds suggestive," said Gaunt.

"But ominous," said Bone.

"The knot must have a connection to Xembala," said Zheng. "Something about it must be linked to the path."

"How do we get there?" Bone asked.

Katta said, "The region leading to the shrine, the part of the mountain that overhangs the void, is named the Necropolis of Nine Years. Its only access is from the Palace of Larks, reserved for the kagan's family, and the Tower of the Crake, commanded by Nightkindler priests."

"Necropolis of Nine Years?" Gaunt asked, her interest in graveyards of all sorts apparently piqued.

"Each tomb in that place," Katta said, "is built above a shaft, and each shaft has a trapdoor. An intricate ledger is kept of each body, and after nine years to the day of interment, the lever is pulled, and the corpse departs this mountain for the clouds. Another legend has it that one day the mountain of bones beneath the clouds will rise to touch the city, and Qushkent's days will be at an end."

Bone scratched his chin. "This suggests a means of getting to the secret tower. I don't suppose the officiants who operate these levers have nicely concealing full-body robes. Could we possibly be that lucky?"

"Yes," Katta said. "The Nightjar Psychopomps, a specialized order of Flame Priests, wear robes the color of charcoal, only a shade brighter than night."

"Aha," Bone said.

"However," Katta said, "only women are allowed within that order."

"I see."

"They also wear a ball and chain, the silver chain representing the River of Stars, the iron ball embodying the Pit Where Light Screams, the dark heart of the universe."

"Hm."

"And their faces are covered with intricate scars representing the hidden motions of unseen planets."

"Um."

"And they are required to sever their right arms, for the evil one, Light-render, was once named the right arm of Stargrace, the creator spirit."

"Er."

"That all said, you may have a good idea."

"You think so?" Gaunt asked.

"Only three sorts of folk may enter the Necropolis of Nine Years without suspicion—the kagan's people, the Nightjar Psychopomps, and families of the recently departed."

"Well," Bone said, "I suspect it's safer to pretend to be a bunch of robed priests than anything else. So, let's say we steal or mimic the right costuming. We tuck our right arms inside and wear makeup for scarring. We go to the tower—"

"And there our journey probably ends," Katta said. "Very few even among the priests are allowed to venture within. I think I should call upon an old friend knowledgeable about the priesthood. This I will have to do alone."

"Not alone, O master," I said, startling the others, for they had convinced themselves I would not speak.

"Deadfall," said Katta. "I return to the Tower of the Crake. It is safest for me to proceed alone."

"I can be inconspicuous," I said. "You may need protection."

Katta sighed. "Very well. I cannot deny you are useful, as a guide and as a combatant."

"Thank you," I said, and meant it.

"Can the rest of us be of use?" Gaunt asked.

Katta said, "I think resting and gathering your strength would be the best use of your time."

"I must be working on Living Calligraphy," Zheng said.

"I recommend you wait until we know more about our plans," Katta said. "You stated you could only prepare one scroll in a week's time."

"So are you our leader now, Katta?"

"I surrendered the need to lead people long ago. If anyone chooses to follow me now, it is because I follow footprints that greater beings than I laid down. Follow, or not, as you would."

With that Katta carried me out of the caravanserai as though I were a mere thing of cloth. I might have questioned whether he truly dodged leadership as he claimed, but I needed to be quiet. Already I feared the reader, the drinker, or the lovers might have overheard more than they should.

For the most part trading was done in the Bazaar of Parrots, and the soldiers slept in the Citadel of Helmetshrikes, yet the Alley of Babblers was lively until late, and we attracted no special attention, even though I billowed about Katta's shoulders in a fashion unusual for a cloak. At last we reached the Tower of the Crake, which borders several districts and marks a divide between the lower-class neighborhoods and the upper-class areas collectively called the Perch. The tower had many hidden ways and subtle doors, and I helped Katta reach one such, an access concealed in plain sight behind a cluster of rose bushes. Katta used a key given him by his friend Ozan, and with a click and a shove we were once again inside the tower.

The shadowy passage wound up the tower and contained the isolated cells of Nightkindler priests. Without need of sight, Katta ascended to the proper cell and knocked.

"What? Surgun!"

"Ozan. It is good to see you."

"I thought you might be dead. When the Karvaks arrived yesterday, I thought, 'This is surely a Surgun moment.' Yet you did not appear."

"I have indeed been close to death," Katta said, embracing the clerk, "and that is one of many reasons I desire your company now."

I was soon thrown over a chair that swiftly became strewn with other clothing. I have by now observed much human romance, and I confess it holds little fascination for me; meanwhile it seemed I was free to conduct my real business of the night.

Soon I was flowing under the space beneath the door and exploring the tower. Before long I found myself within the great space of the library, seeking the upper range where Ozan had showed Katta certain ominous books. From time to time Nightkindlers passed by, either on guard duty or hastening to one late errand or another, for a sect that so emphasizes light within darkness has more than the usual number of evening rituals. I was careful to time my eccentric flights to moments when the library was empty of humanity.

At one point I found a cart full of unshelved books, and chanced to find one whose binding was white in color. I clutched it, curling one corner about it, for I saw a use for it elsewhere.

At last I reached the range of dark volumes arranged in a diamond shape, and found my target: the bright volume in its midst.

Pulling it out was no difficulty. Reading it was, however; while I possess analogs of human sensory apparatus, these magical senses do not allow me to see in the dark. In any event, I intended to put the book to use elsewhere.

I shoved in its place the book from the cart. It was not a perfect fit, and did require some squeezing; but I can exert a great deal of force if needed.

And now, speed was of the essence. I retraced my path and returned to the exterior door. Luckily it was easy to open. I left the door ajar and furtively slipped back to the caravanserai. There, my companions were still in conversation.

"In Abundant Bamboo," Snow Pine was saying, "I told people I was mourning my husband, and that it was hard, but that I would be all right. I told them in a particular way, heartbroken but strong and brave-looking, so that they would leave me alone. If I said I did not mourn, they would not trust me with myself. If I appeared to mourn too much, they would not trust me with myself. How could I explain that it was different every day? There were days when it was like a mountain on top of me, and days when I barely remembered him at all. Mostly I felt an ache, but one that kept me wanting to live. But what I did not want to do was be food for people's need to prove themselves good."

"To say 'flawed people,'" said Bone, "is merely to say 'people' with an extra syllable."

"How are you now?" Widow Zheng asked.

"I feel alive. I feel I might be able to hold A-Girl-Is-A-Joy again. Knowing that I am trying my best, I am sometimes able to enjoy what I see around me." She giggled. "I fought mummies! And a giant sand-squid-thing! I sailed beneath the sands, and rode a dragon horse above them! No one can know what wonders tomorrow has up its sleeve."

"We had best turn in," Gaunt said with a note of regret. "Tomorrow's wonders may be exciting indeed."

I shuffled up the wall to the sleeping rooms, as my business was elsewhere. I was fortunate that an open window allowed me access to Gaunt and Bone's room. There I took the book and shoved it under what I guessed to be Persimmon Gaunt's pillow, for her writing implements were placed nearby. Then swiftly as I dared, I returned to the Tower of the Crake.

Had I been capable of whistling I would have done so as I shuffled into

Ozan's chamber and made myself an innocent carpet again. I was just in time, but Katta and Ozan were busy dressing, and neither seemed to notice.

"Remember that I did not see you, Surgun. Dalliances are one thing, but disloyalty is another."

"I know that you are loyal to your pyrarch in spirit, Ozan. But I was never here."

Katta threw me over his shoulders.

"An odd overcoat, that," mused Ozan.

"It has proven a good friend. Farewell. I look forward to being not-here again someday."

"I will count the days to the non-event. Be careful, Surgun."

"Be well, Ozan."

Katta walked the way I had lately taken. When we returned to the caravanserai we found that the others had turned in and were all quietly in their rooms. And by this silence I knew Gaunt and Bone to indeed be thieves at heart.

CHAPTER 17

THE NECROPOLIS OF NINE YEARS

"The *Chart of Tomorrows*," Gaunt whispered, reading by candlelight from the title page of the book that had mysteriously appeared in their room.

"A little light reading," said Bone.

"This is an infamous book," Gaunt said.

"I know. And we did not even have to risk dismemberment to get it."

Gaunt frowned. "Who would conceive such a maneuver? Books left beside a pillow. Are they assassins turned librarians?"

"That sounds plausible to me."

"Who could have done this, really?"

"At a guess—and it is simply a guess—Flint and Quilldrake are still active and are perhaps helping us with a clue."

"Yet they did not alert us."

"Perhaps there was no opportunity."

Gaunt fingered the book, flipped it open to reveal pages of intricate island maps with crabbed notes beside. "I won't discount your theory—indeed, I like it, for it means our companions yet live—but it does not feel right. For one thing, this lost book describes pathways through time that exist far to the West, in the Bladed Isles. We have no means of employing it, even if we wanted to. Indeed, I suspect that's why it was taken to the East." She stopped flipping pages, frowning at the image of a hand marked with a rune resembling three lengths of chain intertwined. She was shaky with the language of the Northmen, but she could make out the note *The Mark of the Runethane*.

"Let's keep this to ourselves," Bone was saying. "If someone's brought us this so discreetly, let's remain discreet."

"Agreed." She shut the book so that her mind wouldn't wander new labyrinths. She sighed. "It's good to talk again in this way, Imago. To consider mysterious books and strange cities and upcoming capers. After the desert, and the storm, and the business with the dragon horses . . ." She added, more quietly, "And blood on my hands . . ."

"Let's let dragon horses lie for now. Remember whom we do this for."

"I remember."

The night, even at this altitude, felt warm, and Bone wanted to take her in his arms. But their truce was fragile still, and as he watched her take up *Lamentations of the Great Historian*, he could see that her passion was elsewhere just now.

Bone slept, for one of them had to. Gaunt stayed awake, because no force in the universe could prevent her from reading just then. Yet it was companionable.

At last he dreamed he sailed a misty sea. Ahead were three islands, one bearing their son, one a group of weavers, one a statue of a monkey. He was in a panic, unsure which to steer for, when a strong wind capsized him and he plunged through a realm of clouds toward a death upon a landscape that contained fields, farms, rivers, lakes, and towers, but that all somehow resembled silk.

"Our target, if you choose to accept my thinking," Mad Katta said, "is a Nightkindler priest called Ildus of the Tower, or Ildus the Scolding, by many who work with him." Katta clasped his hands together. "He is Keeper of the Keys, an officer not much inferior to the pyrarch. He is a strict rule-minder— not of the sort who loves law and justice but of the kind who loves catching others out in error. He will do this with scripture, pouncing on anyone who misquotes the Fire Saint, and with procedure, disdaining all dust and all improperly clad clerks. As such, he is little loved."

"And he carries the key we need?" Bone asked, his curiosity fully engaged.

"He does! Getting to him is a matter of some difficulty, as he dwells in the Palace of Larks, and works in the Tower of the Crake, and hardly ever mingles with such common folk, let alone disreputables such as we."

"You said 'hardly ever,'" Gaunt put in, rubbing her eyes. "What is the exception?"

"He has one vice, if you want to call it that. Once a week in the late afternoon he visits the House of Spiraling Veils."

Snow Pine snorted. "A place of fine art, no doubt."

"Indeed. It is a spot where gentlemen sit and drink and discuss whichever matters of business, philosophy, or governance stir their fancy. All while watching diverting dances performed by fancifully garbed women."

"Ah," Gaunt said, shaking her head, "that sort of place."

"You may misunderstand, Persimmon Gaunt. Most folk of Qushkent do indeed consider this sort of dancing an art, although admittedly many are uncomfortable with the idea of professional performances. Both genders may dance, but this particular establishment focuses on women, and men being men, there is a large male audience. But I do not speak of a place of prostitution. There are such establishments elsewhere, though they are *not* considered places of art. There is no trade for greater favors at the House of Spiraling Veils."

"No doubt a disappointment to you," Snow Pine said.

"The dancers are the wrong gender to disappoint," Katta said with a smile. "Are you having trouble with that melon juice, Imago Bone?"

"Quite all right," coughed Bone.

"Indeed?" Gaunt said.

"Could none of you kids tell?" Zheng said. "Ah, the younger generation. So straight-laced."

"In any event," said Katta, "my romantic life is not our trouble. Indeed, it is no one's trouble! No, the trouble is that key."

"Now," Gaunt said, "how are we going to get close to a man who frequents a dance hall? Whom might we know who has an acrobatic flair and an escapade outfit?"

Bone choked on his melon juice again. "You cannot be serious."

"I haven't worn that outfit in a performance since I recited poems from *Crypt Lyrics* back in Palmary," Gaunt said. "It will have nostalgia value."

"You must be careful," Bone said.

"That is a strange sentiment," Gaunt said, "coming from you. But yes, I will."

The bad news, Gaunt reflected after she and Snow Pine were hired by one Kelebek, mistress of the House of Spiraling Veils, was that Ildus was coming that very day. After a heated discussion on the matter, the band chose to observe and strike in a week. So the good news was, they would have several days to hone their plan.

Ildus was a stern-visaged, white-bearded, bronze-skinned man who would not only arrogantly display the keys in his gray robe's pocket but would sometimes finger them absently as he watched the dancers. Gaunt, Snow Pine, Bone, and Katta all got a good look. (Zheng had gone off to scrape up materials for her scrolls. She said, "Unlike you I have no time for play.") Deadfall remained in the caravanserai, dreaming whatever dreams a carpet might have.

The four of them dispersed so as not to seem parts of a group—Gaunt and Snow Pine applying for jobs, Bone and Katta becoming customers.

The escapade outfit did its work, as did the heavy coating of makeup that hid the tattoo on Gaunt's face. She wore her dark-haired wig so at least reports of an exotic redhead would not reach the Karvaks. She did not wish to be parted from Crypttongue in such a situation, so she presented herself as a sword-dancer. The gems upon the pommel she covered with a veil.

Snow Pine had no outfit appropriate for this art and had scoffed at the idea of such employment, but Gaunt had pleaded for the support. Mistress Kelebek was impressed by Snow Pine and fronted the money to buy costuming. Snow Pine seemed shocked.

When they rendezvoused at the caravanserai, Bone commenced sketching the keys, and Gaunt said, "I can help you locate a dress, Snow Pine."

"I can't believe she hired me," Snow Pine said. "I am not a dainty little flower."

"No, you are a ferocious tiger," Mad Katta said. "That does not mean you are not beautiful."

"I don't like this discussion," Snow Pine said. "I will wear the foolish clothes and distract the foolish men, but I don't like it."

"You do not have to," Gaunt said. "I will act alone if need be. You can stay with Bone and be ready to fight."

"No," Snow Pine said. "This is the way to ensure one of us gets close to this Ildus, and two are safer than one. But, all of you, stop pretending that every woman likes this sort of display."

"I am sorry," Gaunt said.

"And I," said Katta.

"Bone?" Gaunt said.

He looked up from his rapid sketching. "I didn't say anything!"

"You didn't have to," Gaunt said.

The day of the caper, all was in readiness, when fate dealt them a pair of unexpected cards.

The two missing Karvak balloons drifted over the city.

"Well, this is interesting," Bone said that morning, craning his head out a window.

"Bone, get in here," Gaunt said. "It's a safe bet they have spyglasses."

The balloons anchored beside their companion over the Palace of Larks.

"This complicates matters," Katta said, "but I think we must proceed. We've heard nothing of Karvaks approaching the Tower of the Beak, so I suspect they have been waiting to see if their expeditions into the valley would succeed."

"What if they did?" Zheng said.

Katta sighed. "Then they may have already secured their Iron Moth larvae. But I suspect if the two balloons managed a landing, then they will try again with all three. If we see all three depart soon, then our own efforts may be complicated."

"Complicated!" Zheng said. "These are Karvaks. If they find the Iron Moths they will take everything they can get, leaving nothing for us."

"I agree it's possible," Snow Pine said. "But we must continue. Now is our best chance."

And so Gaunt and Snow Pine made their way to the House of Spiraling Veils by different paths, for they were not supposed to have known of each other before their hiring. Gaunt kept to the sides of streets and moved quickly when in the open, so as to stay out of view of anybody aboard those balloons. As she passed by one of the parrots upon its pillars, she heard it say, "Pale woman! Dragon horses! Mummies!"

She turned her head. There was but one parrot she'd ever confided in, and this one was much too green to be Hakan.

We will tell you half of everything, she'd told Hakan and his owner, *if you keep it to yourself for half a week.*

Stupid, she thought, turning away. *Never underestimate the gossip skills of birds.* They could not assume the Karvaks were unaware of them. And while they had taken a few precautions as regards the House of Spiraling Veils, they were not exactly lying low.

Still, no turning back now.

Luck was with them, for Ildus appeared, and there was no sign of Karvaks. More, Ildus called for Snow Pine to dance. "She is the loveliest dancer to ever appear here!" he called out.

Snow Pine proceeded to perform moves that seemed more in line with esoteric breathing exercises than with dancing, for all that she spun upon the stage, clinking her finger cymbals.

Dancers could earn an additional fee by serving the customers, and Mad Katta had long since perched himself at Ildus's table, buying rounds. Gaunt came forward in response to his hail and poured.

Luck broke her way a second time, as a tipsy Ildus said, "You—pale one— you started the same day as that girl from Qiangguo. What do you know about her?"

Gaunt came over and poured him wine, leaning close. "Only rumor, my lord. They say she is a princess sent out to marry the lord of Madzeu, but she abandoned him and her title and struck out west."

Ildus stared at the dancer.

Gaunt's hands moved, years of practice behind them. She slipped Ildus's keys from his pocket and replaced them with Bone's replicas.

They would not be functional keys; Bone would have needed the originals for that. But they were the correct heft and appearance, and this was Ildus's day of rest. With luck, they would have hours before he discovered the exchange. And luck seemed to be with them today. Even as she turned away from the table, Ildus got out his keys to finger them as he watched the dance.

Seconds passed, and no word of mistrust escaped Ildus's lips. Bone had done his job well.

Now Gaunt moved among the tables, planning their exit—and her luck turned.

Suddenly she was face to face with Liron Flint.

A shocked look on his face, Flint said, "I sensed my sword was hereabouts . . . Gaunt? Is that . . . Snow Pine?"

She heard whispering from the sword. "Flint . . . not now."

"I'm sorry," Flint said. "The situation has changed."

Into the House of Spiraling Veils strode the Karvak princess, Steelfox, a falcon upon her wrist. Beside her was a person whose visage reminded Gaunt of Katta, and who wore silver charms much like the wanderer's; yet the costuming was unfamiliar to her: a heavy gray coat and pants, with a bow and quiver.

"You cannot leave this place," Steelfox said to Gaunt. "Nor can your friend on the stage. My soldiers are surrounding this building. Flint and Quilldrake work with me now. We will have your pieces of the map."

Snow Pine heard Steelfox, and she leapt from the stage, drawing gasps and boos from the audience and an angry cry from Mistress Kelebek. Snow Pine ignored them all. She landed upon a table, launched herself from it as she tugged something from her hair. When she landed upon the floor, it was with an iron staff ready to help her vault. The next moment she was face to face with Flint.

"You," she said. "After we—"

"I am sorry," he said. "I felt something too. But this is glory."

Snow Pine bowed. "Have some more glory."

She swung Monkey's staff, and Gaunt, before quite thinking about it, blocked the swing with Crypttongue.

There was a concussion of force that knocked both of them backward and that made Flint, Steelfox, and the mysterious archer stagger as well. There came a whispering in Gaunt's mind, like that of the captured souls but thinner, dimmer: *I am not of this world, sword, and you shall not claim me.* She felt also a cold anger that was not hers. Gaunt found herself wanting to strike again, and Snow Pine was on her feet, fury in her gaze. They edged closer to each other.

"The sword," Flint said. "It has bonded with you now. I am sorry."

Before Gaunt could react to his words, Katta was there, putting a hand upon Gaunt's and Snow Pine's shoulders. "No! No, if you fight now, they win . . ." He looked up and saw the strange person beside Lady Steelfox. "You . . ."

"Yes," said the archer, and the voice sounded female to Gaunt, though she was not certain. "I know who you must be. He who gave up the chance to be the greatest of shamans." The archer continued in a language utterly unfamiliar to Gaunt.

"Speak so they can hear," Katta said, "if you please."

"You are he who gave himself to alien gods. You are Deadfall."

"You do not understand the nature of the Undetermined, sister," said Katta. "And that name belongs to another now. Please demonstrate, my friend."

A dark shape fell from the ceiling upon Flint, Steelfox, and Katta's countrywoman. "Run!" Katta said to Gaunt and Snow Pine. "Stay together if you can, but remember the rendezvous."

They ran.

But out in the marketplace, with its hundreds of babbling voices and scores of squawking parrots on pillars, Gaunt saw that Steelfox hadn't lied. More than two dozen Karvak soldiers in full armor stood with drawn swords, the gasbags of two balloons dominating the market square beyond. Gaunt did not understand the orders given, but she knew she was the target. The soldiers advanced cautiously, as though briefed on the powers of her saber. No doubt Flint had told them all he knew. She wished she had that advantage.

There was no sign of Bone. Well, that was as it was.

Snow Pine caught up and stood at her side, their backs to the wall of the House of Spiraling Veils. "Sorry about almost clubbing your head in."

"I am almost sorry I prevented you from doing the same to Flint," Gaunt said. "After everything—"

"I'm not talking about him," Snow Pine said. "You have to get to the meeting point, and Zheng."

"This is not a mission of war," Gaunt said. "I'm not abandoning you."

"You are not abandoning the children," Snow Pine said. "If you have a chance to reach Xembala, even alone, Gaunt, you must take it. I will worry about me. I am a monkey after all." She grinned. "I will clear a path."

"Snow Pine—"

"Save your talk, poet. Just act."

Snow Pine waited no longer but charged the Karvaks, swinging the iron staff as she did. Men fell like barrels. Gaunt whispered a prayer for her friend and a curse for fate, and ran through the gap. A single warrior was in her way, and at a glance she could imagine his story—young, eager, scared but self-mastered, shocked by such an exotic foe as herself, but ready to make a name for himself in the game of war. The poet in her wanted his story to go on. The thief in her wanted to run the way she came. The mother in her would do what she had to do.

She jabbed with Crypttongue, and the sword spent its fury at the staff of iron upon the young Karvak. He screamed as the sword slipped between the panels of his armor and found his heart. Crypttongue slipped smoothly free of him as Gaunt ran past, and nearly as swiftly the Karvak's spirit entered the last free gem upon the pommel.

Swan Goddess, Gaunt thought, *what have I become?*

My name is Luckfire, came a youth's voice into her mind. *Where am I? Have I failed? Am I dishonored?*

Welcome, came a chorus of other voices, and Gaunt felt sick at heart. She was grateful that she could push the babble aside, but she never forgot it was there.

Her wig had come loose in the struggle, and it was impeding her sight. She tore it off, wincing, and almost wished she could shroud her gaze again.

The Karvaks were surprised by Gaunt's ferocity, and especially Snow Pine's, but they seemed determined to live up to their ancestors' deeds, and were not giving up. Several warriors had run to intercept Gaunt.

There were too many. She was becoming weary, and the sword's gems were full of spirits and could steal no more. The babbling of the trapped minds filled her head until it was as though she swung and jabbed and parried within a dark room filled with voices, the external world just a blaze of light through a cracked doorway.

Voices. Acting on a mad impulse Gaunt spun Crypttongue and shoved the pommel into a Karvak's face.

Luckfire, she silently commanded, *I release you!*

Light burst in the warrior's face, light and more than light, a red glow that twisted and swirled and revealed a youth's face wrenched with exaltation and fear as the spirit blazed through the living warrior's head and rose toward Father Sky. Dazed and blinking, the Karvak in front of Gaunt staggered backward, letting her advance to one of the great arches bordering the Bazaar of Parrots.

It was not enough. More foes came, blocking her escape. She jumped onto a fruit cart and ignored the invectives of the vendor as she attempted to release another spirit, but she had not learned any other names, and this seemed to be a requirement. "Tell me who you are!" she demanded and was rewarded by an incomprehensible hubbub as all the spirits spoke at once.

"I think you'd know me by now!" came a voice, and the warriors looked up as a crazy thief swung by a rope into the market. His arrival snapped an awning, toppled a fruit cart and sent apples and peaches careening everywhere, left merchants swearing, and broke the Karvaks' line.

Bone came to a stop by tumbling onto the ground, rolling to his feet, and offering her his hand. She jumped to join him.

He nodded to the arch and winked. She pointed toward it with Crypttongue.

As they ran into the District of Doves, Bone said, "Handy thing, that blade."

"I thought you hated magic swords."

"Well, I am not the one carrying it."

Every city had its own architectural language for saying *rough neighborhood.* In Qushkent the sigils of that language included termite-ravaged shacks and tottering towers of cracked brick, fire-charred ruins never rebuilt, and habitations fashioned like nomadic tents, nestled amongst the rest. Other signifiers included knots of young men staring from behind crumbled walls, older men standing nonchalantly streetside with daggers in hand, faces that peered from windows and darted away just as Gaunt noticed them.

Bone took a coin purse from his belt and tossed it to one of the largest and oldest loiterers, one who had several lieutenants close by.

"What are you doing?" Gaunt demanded as they ran down one narrow lane, then another.

"Spreading goodwill!"

"They won't help us, Bone. After all that talk about the horses—"

"I concede! But do not forget who's chasing us! Qushkent and the Karvaks have history!"

As they ran, trying to seek one of the spots chosen by Katta—whom she hoped was safe—she began to suspect Bone was not crazy, not in this one respect. Out the corners of her eyes she caught sight of tents shoved into streets, laundry stretched across alleys, spontaneous gatherings clogging intersections. The Qushkent city guard was noticeably absent in the District of Doves, and there was no one to command the citizens to make way for the troop of armored foreigners. Angry shouts followed flights of scattered birds into the air, but she saw no Karvaks for now.

They reached a low wall, and Bone leapt atop it, froze, teetered, took a deep breath, and held up his hand.

"I had not expected the outskirts of town to be so near," he managed to say.

Gaunt looked over the wall.

Sheer granite cliff greeted her and an ocean of cloud perhaps a hundred feet below. Cold wind ruffled her hair. "Come down from there," she said.

"It is exhilarating."

"Come down."

He huffed, spun, jumped, bowed.

"I swear, if you fall to your death from this city," Gaunt said, "I will compose a poem so savagely mocking that all your other exploits will be as dust, and the name 'Imago Bone' will be a synonym for 'dolt' for the next thousand years."

"You would not."

She folded her arms.

He sighed. "You have my promise not to die in that manner. I may keep it very soon." He peered over the wall. "Aha, I think that is it."

Gaunt noticed a man upon a tiled rooftop near at hand, and he noticed her. He commenced whistling and gesturing.

A shout went up, and though she still did not know the language, she recognized the beautiful tones of Karvak. The lovely sound probably said, *Our quarry is this way.*

She nudged Bone. "I don't think everyone here hates the Karvaks."

"Ah, human nature," he said, leading her down a single-file path alongside the wall. "Let nine hundred and ninety-nine people agree on the value of breathing, and the next will extoll strangulation."

Gaunt saw one of the Karvak balloons rising from the Bazaar of Parrots. "We'd best hurry."

"I agree! I am not contrary! Ah, here—" He slipped through an old fissure between two great stones in the wall. It took either confidence or blind faith to do this with the void so close at hand, but Gaunt followed.

She emerged onto a stairway so narrow as to make the paths up Five-Toe Peak look like highways. The wind made mischief with her footing, and carrion birds circled through the white.

"Why was this even built?" she asked.

"I have speculated, and now I am sure." He sniffed deeply. "Ah! The dank ripeness of flowing sewage."

Indeed, a trickle of foul water emerged from a tunnel in the side of the mountain, for inevitably Qushkent must drop its waste upon whatever mysteries dwelled below the clouds.

"I already miss the desert," Gaunt said.

They reached the sewer-tunnel, and it was as rank as Gaunt had imagined, as well as low-ceilinged and uncomfortably warm. At least there was a faint glow from Crypttongue, a radiance of many pale hues emanating from all the gems save the one that had imprisoned Luckfire.

"I must say again," Bone said, "a useful sword."

"It harvests spirits," Gaunt said.

"How is your own?"

"That is not a good question for now." They stumbled and splashed into the darkness. At least the slope was gentle. "I don't suppose," Gaunt said after the light behind them was like a coin shining in a sunlit well, "the steppe warriors will refuse to enter such an enclosed space?"

"I do enjoy your poetic fancies," Bone said, "but let's not slow down."

They passed many side passages, but Katta had said they needed to reach nearly the heart of the city. Now they heard sounds of metal and voices of frustration far behind them, and the pinprick of sunlight wavered. Gaunt wished their own light could dim, but this seemed beyond her control.

At last they reached the place Katta had spoken of, where steps led up from the sewer channel and into a steeply sloped tunnel connecting to the karez system far below. They ascended and came to a closed door, and then another. At the third they stopped, listened, and knocked with a distinctive pattern.

Two knocks sounded in return. Gaunt rapped exactly once more. There came the sound of a bolt being thrown, and the door creaked open.

Zheng's face was ghastly, dark paint mimicking intricate scars.

"Quick," Gaunt said to Zheng. "Let us in."

"Only the two of you?"

As Gaunt entered the torchlit room she saw Katta beside Zheng and the rippling shape of Deadfall beyond. The two humans wore soot-colored one-armed cloaks in the manner of the Nightjar Psychopomps. Each had a silver-colored chain around one ankle, and each was attached to a dark sphere. These were made of painted wood, of course. Similar attire awaited Gaunt and Bone. Katta had false scarring applied over three-quarters of his face.

Bone shut and bolted the door behind them. They were in a small alcove possessing three other doors and a spiral staircase leading up. The fire illuminated scenes of a cosmic war, angelic beings representing the stars battling demons of darkness.

Gaunt said, "I'd hoped Snow Pine had gotten here through another path."

Katta shook his head. He continued painting himself as he spoke. "She ran in the direction of the District of Doves."

Bone swore. "We have the Karvaks behind us. I don't think she could have come that way." He scratched his chin. "Gaunt—all of you—you continue. I will search for Snow Pine. We will either join you at the Tower of the Beak, or we will find another way below the clouds."

"Bone, no," Gaunt said.

"I will not lose . . . anyone else."

"Bone. I understand." The torment in his gaze was almost more than she could watch, but she forced herself to look into his eyes. "But Snow Pine's life does not matter to her as much as her Joy's freedom. You must trust me. We are both mothers. You are needed here, now."

He lowered his head. "Very well."

"Karvaks are behind you?" Katta asked, pulling Deadfall (who was itself covered with dark cloth) over his shoulders. "Then we will have to forgo the face paint for you two and trust the costumes are enough."

They snuffed the torch and proceeded through one of the doors.

A long tunnel, blessedly free of sewer-stench, led to an iron door. In the light from Crypttongue's jewels, they could see swirling figures in the metal, shaped like spirits rising toward embedded silver stars or falling toward a spherical darkness. A keyhole filled a gold-plated circle, with the rays of a stylized sun.

Katta tested the door. "I believe the keys are now needed."

Gaunt sheathed the sword and retrieved Ildus's keys, a tricky proposition with only one arm available. The cloaks did have a right armhole, with a flap covering the hole. The right arm could be used, but only if one was willing to abandon the disguise.

She tried four keys before one worked.

The door opened upon a sunlit stairway.

The ascent took long enough that their eyes had mostly adjusted when they emerged into the great graveyard.

"To seem believable," Katta said as they reached the top of the stair, "we must separate, and shamble. Gaunt and Bone, your faces are unpainted, so do not look back. In this manner we will move toward the Tower of the Beak. Sooner or later our odd behavior will be noted."

"Hopefully later," Bone said.

"Yes. If a shout goes up, or if one of us runs, we must all run. The tower will be locked, so Gaunt more than anyone must reach it. Let us hope we all do."

Gaunt squeezed Bone's hand and walked alone among graves.

From an early age this had been an activity she'd loved. She had strolled the green grass under the clouds, and the headstones of her ancestors and those of friends had surrounded her, some simple slabs, some in the form of the Swan ascending, some in the shape of circles representing a procession from birth to death. It had been peaceful here, in a way that her family's bustling manor had never been.

Only years later had she realized that few in her village had dared visit the graveyard when one of her family visited it, and that in a sense she was depriving others of the pleasure. She had never thought of her family as wealthy, for indeed, they were much diminished, and her parents and older sisters' eyes were fixated upon the petty gentry of other villages and their relative wealth. Anxiety over money squeezed the life out of the house; no wonder Persimmon had been more comfortable among the dead.

All that worry and strife, the girl had thought, when the ground eventually claims anything. Make peace with death or not, the most stupid thing in the world was to pretend it wasn't there.

The people of Qushkent didn't pretend it wasn't there. Perhaps here on the edge of a white eternity, oblivion was easier to grasp. She dragged her ball and chain through a paradoxical realm of black slabs. Each was as perfectly shaped as the human hand could craft it, yet there seemed no order to their placement. It was as if a god of night had dropped a deck of cards.

There were no markers, though many slabs bore flowers. Beside each slab was an iron lever, massive enough to surely require great effort for the one-armed psychopomps to pull.

Her path took her near the abyss, and here there was no wall. There was something strangely attractive about descending just a little more, just a little more, seeking a place where one could dangle one's feet into the clouds as if they were a river.

But no, there was shuffling to do.

She heard the shuffling of her companions as well, and no shouts as yet. The sounds of the city were muted; she could not tell if anything was amiss, or if the odd yell or peal of laughter was unusual.

A sudden sound almost made her halt. It was a creaking, slow and labored. The door to the graveyard? But that had not possessed the same timbre. And this noise was closer at hand . . .

Yes. Just up ahead. It was coming from one of the grave slabs.

From inside.

She heard other such sounds, farther away.

Her mind raced, and while none of the possibilities she considered seemed plausible, none made the noises go away. She increased her pace.

Just behind her a slab burst open with a thunderous crash.

She could not help spinning around and thus beheld the corpse slowly rising from the grave. It was a woman dressed in a pleasant robe of rosy colors. Otherwise she rather resembled the desiccated corpses near Shahuang. A disturbing hiss emerged from between yellowed teeth.

Gaunt ran. Another crashing sound filled the graveyard, and another.

"Speed over stealth!" she heard Bone shouting, and indeed even during this sentence his voice moved noticeably closer.

"Interesting!" Katta was saying. "A defensive enchantment perhaps—"

"Shut up, Katta!" Widow Zheng said. "I'm using the scroll now."

"We have not reached the tower!"

"Not sure we will at this rate. Hey, Deadfall, listen! *'The cautious foot can brave any ground!'*"

"Why do you give this magic to Deadfall?" Katta demanded.

"I do not have feet," the carpet said.

"You have problems moving around," Zheng said. "But this seems like a good time for a magic carpet that can soar."

"Ah!" the carpet sighed, as though some old pain had lifted.

Gaunt could pay no more attention to this, however, for the Tower of the Beak rose ahead, with only one slab between her and it.

The slab burst open.

Gaunt swore.

"*Gaunt,*" came a voice rasping from within the grave.

She ran pell-mell for the lever beside the slab, throwing her full weight upon it.

It clicked and dropped, and an unseen slab flew open below the corpse.

"*Gaaaaunnnt . . .*" she heard it say as it plunged into the clouds below.

"Make an appointment," she said.

A scuffling alerted her, and she rolled away from the assault of the dead woman who stalked her.

As the thing clawed at her, Gaunt struggled to free her arm from the damnable psychopomp cloak. She succeeded as the entity's eyes lit up with a fiery glow. "*You have come far, meat,*" gasped the body, "*but the journey ends here.*"

CHAPTER 18

ĪNTERLŪDE: SŪSPĪCĪONS OF A STRANGLĪNG CLOTH

Just as I sleep and dream after a fashion, so I have insomnia after a fashion. The night before the Qushkent caper I found myself restless, rustling here and there like a mundane carpet in a strong wind. Thus I made my way to the refuse chute I'd encountered back when Katta had become rid of his odious employee. From there I risked an excursion.

I found that thinking of the human garbage of that earlier encounter left me angry, and anger gave me unexpected strength. My short flights were a little longer, my balance a little better, my stamina somewhat enhanced. Emboldened, I left the city.

I did not dare explore the CloudScar and its treacherous-looking air currents. But I leapt between pine trees of the edge, enjoying the freedom of the night. I listened to the songs of living night birds. Later, I poked at the corpses of dead birds. Then I returned to the heights to start the process all over.

It was from that vantage that I beheld the darkness in the sky. It was a round gap in the stars, which made me suspicious of its origins. I was even more suspicious when I saw it cover the moon.

To reach it seemed unlikely, and I found myself cursing my poor luck to be hampered by the divided nature bequeathed me by Olob and Op.

Anger made me soar.

With one mighty effort I leapt to the clouds and attached myself to the gondola of a balloon.

I shifted myself up and listened to an intriguing conversation.

"The ultimate goal is of great interest," a regal-looking woman was saying in the language of Anoka, speaking to dancing images in a glowing brass mirror, "and the secondary goals are of some value as well."

"You are certain," another woman's voice emanated from the mirror, "your sister is interested only in the secondary goals?"

277

"She is insufficiently informed to have any other desire. The story of her life, in a sense."

"Your rivalries are of no interest to us," said a man's gruff voice. "Only results."

"I will report—wait. We are overheard. I will speak later."

She waved a hand and the mirror grew dark. She looked this way and that.

"You," she said and clapped. Karvak warriors approached her. "I give you credit, whoever you are. It took the nerve of a baatar to spy upon me here. Show yourself. Perhaps you can be of service."

And thus did I reveal myself to you, great Jewelwolf.

Of our meeting and our arrangement I of course do not need to inform you, only that *anger*, I have now concluded, fuels my power. I suspect in your own way you understand that lesson very well.

I look forward to our dealings tomorrow.

CHAPTER 19

DEADFALL

"Charstalker," Gaunt said.

"That is one name. It will do."

The thing advanced. It grabbed Gaunt's ball and chain; Gaunt kicked and struggled to draw Crypttongue, which lay sheathed and concealed under her robe. *Am I to be laid low by clothing?* she thought. *This is one irony I do not mind missing.*

As if summoned, Bone jumped past her, kicked at the possessed corpse, and sent it plunging through the grave-pit. His momentum nearly sent him after it, but he righted himself, standing on the edge. He wore a smirk she almost wanted to slice off with a nick of the sword she'd just freed.

"I did promise not to die that way," he said.

"You're late," she said and turned to the others.

There were two more corpses stalking Zheng, who was running toward the Tower of the Beak as fast as an iron ball rolling downhill.

There were also two Karvak balloons approaching. From the doorway to the Palace of Larks ran perhaps twenty of Qushkent's guardsmen, lightly armored and clad in cloth of brown and white, with helmets suggesting the beaks of raptors.

Under these circumstances, Gaunt felt no compunction at unsheathing Crypttongue and chopping off her ball and chain. She did likewise for Bone.

"We'd best help Zheng—" Bone began and suddenly stiffened.

A nimbus of red had risen from the grave and flowed into his ears. His eyes burned red.

"No," he continued, his voice gravelly and mocking. *"Nothing can help the meat."*

A second red glow rose up behind Bone. Three burning eyes appeared within its form. As Gaunt watched, hand gripping Crypttongue until it ached, the eyes traced the characters in the Tongue of the Tortoise Shell, which indicated the idiom "An unskilled cobbler."

"That's all you've got?" Gaunt sneered, though sweat dripped down her face. "Calling me a mediocrity? You're going to have to dig up better *chengyu*. Too bad for you most of them have four characters."

"*You are about to eat the bread a devil baked,*" Bone's mouth said. "*That is a saying from your husband's country.*"

"Eat this!" called a voice, and a sweetcake flew through the air and connected with Bone's face.

Gaunt leapt onto the edge of the grave and grabbed Bone, forcing crumbs into his mouth, even as Mad Katta swooped by, riding Deadfall and laughing, flames from the second Charstalker chasing them.

The first Charstalker flowed out of Bone's body, fixing the lovers with a triple glare.

"He didn't quite," Bone coughed, "get the saying right . . ."

"Shut up, Bone. Hey, Charstalker! Meet Crypttongue!"

It was mostly bravado, for she could not know what would happen when the enchanted blade stabbed the hateful nimbus that had just fled Bone.

Luck was with her. A shriek entered her mind as the Charstalker twisted and shrank and flowed into the gem that had once borne Luckfire. That stone blazed brighter than the others, like the eye of sunset seen through a socket of mountains.

They were alone, then, as much as two people in a battleground can be alone. The second Charstalker was in flight, pursuing Katta and Deadfall.

"This is cozy," Bone said.

"We need to help Zheng."

Bone eyed the swirling white beneath the fissure at their feet. "It would be ironic if we accidentally plunged to our deaths right now."

"On a count of three . . ."

They escaped the grave and ran after Zheng. Bellows from the guardsmen echoed among the slabs, but Gaunt did not know the words. The shadows of balloons crossed them, but they did not halt.

By unspoken accord Bone raced ahead to tackle the undead foe nearest to Zheng, while Gaunt attacked the one trailing.

"Hey!" she called. "You! Dead person! A word!"

The dead man spun. Between the nine-year limit and the high altitude, the corpses here were well preserved, making this a perfect playground for possessing spirits. This shambling fellow was clad in princely robes, making Gaunt hope she wasn't about to mutilate a royal body. *Ah, well, they can only execute me once.*

She swung, jabbed, blocked, swung again. The corpse kept coming at her, and the Charstalker refused to give up the body. Of course—all the gems were full. It quickly proved evident that Crypttongue's great power was snatching spirits, not severing heads or limbs.

"Can we not come to some accommodation?" Gaunt asked, backing away.

"Yes," the dead noble said. "*I will agree to eat your heart. You will agree to die.*"

"Your evil reputation is entirely your own fault!" Gaunt declared. "I just want you to know that!" Silently she asked the spirits in the gems, *Please, please, give me a name.* Again a babble ensued, with the laughter of the trapped Charstalker howling above it all.

A whistling creased the air, and suddenly an arrow pierced the dead man's eye. Another took him in the heart, and a third in the throat. The damage to his vitals was irrelevant, but the impacts themselves staggered him backward.

Gaunt looked up to see Karvak archers leaning from one of the balloons, Lady Steelfox among them.

She dared not question this help. Seizing the opportunity she tripped the foe, raised Crypttongue in two hands, and decapitated him.

This did not finish him, for the body tried to rise, and the head mocked, "*Nothing can truly kill us, Persimmon Gaunt! Accept your destiny as meat—*" until she kicked it across the necropolis.

The head kept babbling from where it lay, but the body sagged, evidently too far away from its puppetmaster. Gaunt ran toward Bone, who struggled with his own foe, no magic weapon to aid him.

A name, a name—

"Persimmon Gaunt!" called Lady Steelfox from above. "You have my respect! And these demons have my spite! We would make good allies!"

"Don't listen to her!" came Snow Pine's voice from somewhere within the flying ger. "She wants the ironsilk for conquest!" There came the sounds of a scuffle within.

"And why not?" answered Steelfox. "We bring peace to lands that have never known it! Trade! Freedom to worship as you wish! The Karvak yoke is light!"

Gaunt reached Bone, raised her blade, looked for an opening. To the balloon she yelled, "Let her go if you want to talk!" This said, she continued asking her captured entities for their names. *I can't free you if I can't name you.*

A distant voice, young and male, whispered in her mind, *My name was—*

An arrow hit the stone beside Bone and the undead woman he wrestled. Sparks flew. Gaunt lost the voice.

"Stop!" Gaunt told the Karvaks.

"Gaunt!" called Zheng, who stood beside the black door of the tower. "The keys!"

Gaunt hurled the keys toward Zheng, who began trying one after the other.

They had little time. The Karvaks might hold off, but the soldiers of Qushkent were almost here. Even now they battled the Charstalker who'd inhabited the decapitated corpse. *Please*, she thought, *your name . . .*

Swarnatep, came the voice. *When the fields were green around the shore, before the lake dried up and the sands consumed my home, my name was Swarnatep.*

"Swarnatep, I release you!"

Green light, like sunlight upon grass, blazed from Crypttongue.

Gaunt imagined that the spirit of Swarnatep would depart as had Luckfire's. Instead, the green radiance flowed into the corpse battling Bone, writhing and twisting together with the red behind the dead woman's eyes. For a moment it was as though the eye sockets were filled with red-and-green braids. Then the green dominated, red specks swirling angrily within like flies trapped in honey.

Bone stepped back. "Are we . . . done?"

With a cackle, Zheng got the tower door open. "Hurry!" she called.

The corpse spoke again, this time in no language Gaunt knew. Perhaps only by means of the sword could she understand Swarnatep's speech.

Yet at the sound of it, Zheng gasped. "What? What did she say? It sounds . . ."

Gaunt took Bone's shoulder. "Come!"

Bone followed. So did the corpse.

"That language," Zheng said as they reached the threshold. "From the lost village. It sounds so familiar."

An arrow sang, punctuating its music by sinking into the corpse's back. The dead woman spun and hissed, the red flecks growing brighter in its eyes.

"Do not go any further!" called Lady Steelfox, leaning from her balloon with bow at the ready.

In the silence that followed, Mad Katta and Deadfall returned.

They swooped out around the tower and buffeted Steelfox, who dropped her bow. Other archers fired. Arrows pierced Deadfall, who laughed. Katta did not share the mirth, but he was unharmed.

"Lady Steelfox!" Deadfall boomed. "Let them go! Your sister commands it!"

"What?" Steelfox said.

"They will find the treasure—and with my new powers, I can follow them anywhere! Together the daughters of the Grand Khan will seize the ironsilk!"

"What?" Katta said.

In the dead woman's eyes, the red grew dominant again. *"Carpet! You think you are free of your curse, thanks to your growing skill and Widow Zheng's magic! But we guess now what you are, and your empowerment only makes this easier!"*

A red glow rose from the corpse, whose eyes now burned wholly green.

The Charstalker rose and intercepted Deadfall.

Then came a second, a third, and a fourth.

Deadfall glowed red.

"No," came the carpet's voice. "No! You cannot have me! I am mine. I AM MINE!"

But the carpet shuddered, and it was all Mad Katta could do to hold on. The black cloth with which they'd disguised Deadfall's appearance burned away. Katta screamed, though he held on still.

The carpet's patterns seemed to flow with eldritch flame. The image of the volcano that dominated the middle of one side now swirled with crimson energies.

"I . . ." came Deadfall's voice. "I know now. I see it all. Petty crimes. The theft of the book from the Tower of the Crake, to surprise and test you, Gaunt and Bone. But more, the murders I could not admit even to myself. The innocent Shahuang guardsman. The Protector-General's assistant. The caravaner Kilik. Evil has been within me all along. It is what I was made for."

Deadfall swooped low and hovered just above the door. "I will not harm you now. But this is farewell. I go to meet my destiny. And Katta—you must come too. For the Bull Demon will want a gift."

There was perhaps one moment in which Katta might have saved himself, or another might have intervened. But Gaunt was too shocked to act, as it seemed were they all.

Her inaction would haunt her.

Deadfall shot off into the clouds east of Qushkent and was gone.

CHAPTER 20

TOWER OF THE BEAK

Bone pulled Gaunt through the doorway, and after a moment's hesitation he also let through the green-eyed undead whom he'd battled just moments before. As soon as it staggered through, Bone slammed shut the door and slapped in place its three locks.

Not a moment too soon, for arrows hit the door, and soon afterward guards banged upon it.

"Ours are surely not the only keys," Bone said, "but hopefully they'll have to send to the palace."

"Why did you let that thing in here?" Widow Zheng said.

"It helped us," Bone said. "I think. And you said you found its speech familiar."

"I did," Zheng said wonderingly. "Yet I cannot tell you why."

"*Because it was once yours,*" said the dead woman.

"Aiya!" Zheng said.

"You have the Tongue of the Tortoise Shell now?" Gaunt asked. "Do we speak to Swarnatep?"

"*Yes, and yes,*" said the corpse. "*I know nothing of the woman I inhabit, and it grieves me to disturb her peace in this way, but things are as they are. I took this language from the thing called a Charstalker with whom I shared being, for a short and eternal while. Yet I am Swarnatep, long dead, who should have fled this world long ago.*"

"How," Zheng said, "how could I have known your language? Is it not as dead as your people?"

"*There are those who die, and yet for whom the wheel of existence continues to turn. Your spirit has a familiar radiance. Once you dwelled among us. Of this I am sure.*"

"This is all fascinating," Bone said, "but those of us currently in living bodies have much to lose, should those outside get inside this tower. Let's find this hidden way to Xembala, if it exists."

"And if it does not?" Gaunt said.

"Let's hope the Karvaks are in a generous mood."

The tower was a small place, no bigger than a border watch-post, with one windowless chamber. Magical light gems glowed like stars upon the ceiling, illuminating a dusty cart roped to an iron post by means of an intricate knot. Bone, ever fond of traps and puzzles, could have stared at its ins and outs for hours.

Beside the cart, post, and rope was a black slab, identical with the ones outside except for lacking a lever.

"I suspect this is our way onward," Gaunt said, echoing his own thoughts.

"The lack of a lever is almost a provocation," Bone muttered, looking around. The walls were filled with inscriptions, but there was no clue here for him. The script of Qushkent resembled the flowing calligraphy of Mirabad, but even if he knew that writing system, he lacked the language. "Gaunt, I don't suppose . . . ?"

She shook her head. "I can't make sense of it."

"Nor I," Zheng said, and turned her gaze to the green-eyed undead, who was silent.

Bone searched the chamber and tugged at the slab. Nothing. He stepped onto the cart. He gestured dramatically. "Onward," he said. Nothing happened. He kicked at the iron post with no result other than an aching foot. He sat dejectedly upon the slab. "Greatest second-story man of the Spiral Sea," he sighed. "I am out of my depth on the Braid of Spice."

"The knot," Zheng said. "Surely it has to do with the knot."

"*I remember,*" said Swarnatep, making the others jump. "*I remember a story of a conqueror from the exotic West, red-haired like this woman here, who came to this city and found the knot.*"

"That sounds like Nayne of the Eldshore," Gaunt said. "She is said to have invaded many lands unfamiliar to us, before her army perished in the desert."

"*In the story, the conqueror tries but fails to unravel the knot. She raises her sword in frustration. Yet some glimmer of enlightenment comes to her, and she says, 'To destroy is not to surpass. I want no victory that is unearned.' And alone among cities, she declined to conquer Qushkent.*"

"I am not certain Nayne could have cut this cord," Gaunt mused, studying it. "It looks to contain strands of ironsilk."

Bone scratched his chin. "This implies to me we are on the right track." He turned around. "If only we could read that writing."

There came more pounding on the door.

"We could ask them," Zheng said.

"No, thank you," said Bone.

"I will attempt something," Gaunt said, closing her eyes and gripping her saber.

Her saber. Strange that Bone thought of it that way, and not as Flint's saber. Flint, who, it seemed, had betrayed them. He knew that greed tore apart alliances and knit new ones like a drunken seamstress, and this was one reason in his thieving career he'd worked alone. He did not trust the particular alliance of Gaunt and Crypttongue. It would bear watching.

Meanwhile he crouched beside the knot. Any solution, his instincts told him, must involve this rope in some way. He ran his hands along it, seeking to divine its full shape.

"Are you in love, Imago Bone?" Widow Zheng asked.

"Hush, if you please. I am working."

The pounding resumed.

"Is silence too much to ask of you people?" Bone exclaimed.

"I have it," Gaunt said. "One of the spirits already in the sword was a mercenary of Qushkent. He will translate in return for release." She began studying the walls afresh, murmuring to herself.

One wonders at the ethics of making a trapped soul's release conditional, Bone mused. Then he thought, *I'm dwelling upon ethics? I've been in the East too long . . .*

Zheng and the dead woman had begun talking in low tones. Bone wanted to shush them, but that seemed unfair. He continued to explore the tangles of the knot.

"If I dwelled in your town long ago," Zheng said, "did you know me?"

"*I think perhaps I did. If you are who I believe you to be, then I knew you as a boy, and loved you from afar.*"

"I suppose it is strange for you, being a woman now."

"*One dead body is much like another.*"

"Do you not wish to depart, to whatever paradise or reincarnation awaits you?"

"*That departure is inevitable enough. I find I want to linger near you. Is this acceptable?*"

"It is strange! Flattering, sure. But unsettling. If you knew me, why did your people attack me, beneath the sands?"

"We have long been under the mental sway of the Leviathan Minds. They dislike surface dwellers digging too far beneath the sands. More, there was a relic that they preferred not come to light."

"The fragment of the map."

"Yes."

"Bone," Gaunt said. "Zheng . . . Swarnatep. Listen.

"'Hear now the secret sayings of the Fire Saint, whose resting place is beneath the slab.

"'I have taught that Stargrace is in mortal danger from Lightrender, and needs human help to survive. This is not precisely true. But it is the way of humankind to be flattered by a plea for aid. What Stargrace desires, but does not require, is the joy of all beings who are willing to endure the joy of others. Do not sever or destroy that which can become your lifeline.

"'It is true that one day the wicked will face damnation, and the angels will ask for human help in throwing the evil ones into the fire. But those who volunteer to damn their fellows, they themselves shall be cast in. Do not fall.

"'The ways of Stargrace are strange, and even the Nightkindlers have glimpsed only a reflection of a mote of dust upon Stargrace's smallest fingernail. Much remains hidden, like the valley below. What damnation and salvation truly are, I cannot say, only that union with Stargrace is greatly to be desired. I believe that some in the valley below may have achieved that state, though my words are not theirs. Perhaps you will go there one day. If you do, remember that the pillar of my wisdom is that within this fallen world, all who rise must also descend.

"'Though mysteries abound like mist, you must at times trust to faith, though it seems a slender cord.

"'I wish you joy.'"

Gaunt nodded to the sword. "Thank you. I release you, warrior." Blue light filled the air, rising through the ceiling.

"Was that supposed to mean something?" snapped Zheng.

Bone snapped his fingers. "I think it was! Faith like a slender cord . . . do not sever what can be your lifeline."

"The rope," Gaunt said.

"Yes! We will need it for something."

"Can you unravel it?"

"No!"

"Ah."

"But," Bone said, holding up his index finger, "there is something I did not try with this post."

He gripped it and pulled upward with all his strength. It gave a little, and somewhere a mechanism groaned. "Something about the pillar of wisdom? How to descend, something must rise? Could anyone help?"

Gaunt, Zheng, and Swarnatep assisted him. The post ascended into the hole in the ceiling, and its base rose from a depression in the floor.

Simultaneously, the slab opened with a tremendous thud. The sound startled the four sufficiently—even the dead body—that they let go.

The pillar stayed up.

"My," Gaunt said, looking down through some twenty feet of rock at a swirl of mist beneath the great beak of the mountain.

Bone removed the loop of the knot that wrapped around the iron. This done, unraveling the rope was simple enough.

It was hard to be certain, but it looked to him to be long enough to reach into the mists.

"A test of faith," he said. "Faith in whomever set this up or at least in the strength of ironsilk. The path to Xembala must lie just beneath the clouds."

"And if it does not?" Zheng said.

"Then they'll have rope to hang us with."

"That was not funny, Bone," Gaunt said.

"Zheng had best go first," Bone mused. "You and I can climb down, Gaunt, but we'll secure Zheng and lower her first."

"You are so sure there is something down there?" Zheng asked.

"When have cryptic religious figures lied to anybody?" Bone asked. "Very well, do not answer that. But we must be on the correct path."

"*I know how I can be of use to you, my old friend,*" Swarnatep said to Zheng. "*Tie the rope to me, and I will leap through the grave. Thus we will learn what is down there.*"

"What if you are destroyed by impact?" Bone said.

"Or by the shock if the rope goes taut?" Gaunt said.

"*I do not have so much to lose. I will try to maintain my grip on this body, but if I fail, what of it? I am destined for someplace else, and this body was always meant to fall. If there is an impact, you will know this is the path. If there is not, perhaps I will see something useful. If I wish to be drawn up, I will tug twice upon the rope. You must let me do this.*"

"Thank you," Zheng said.

They secured the dead woman, and without ceremony Swarnatep directed his borrowed body to jump.

Bone rushed to the grave. Down plunged Swarnatep, until his doll-like shape entered the endless clouds. A glance told Bone there was almost no rope left.

At the last possible moment, the rope went slack.

Bone released the breath he hadn't realized he'd been holding. "They did not waste any material, did they?"

"Well," Gaunt said, "we are speaking of ironsilk."

"Imago Bone!" called a familiar voice. "Persimmon Gaunt! Widow Zheng! I am Lady Steelfox, ruler of the Il-Khanate of the Infinite Sky. I can offer you sanctuary. But you must agree soon. Swiftly now, a runner will arrive with the keys to this tower, and then you will be at the mercy of the kagan of Qushkent."

"We will never have time to lower me," Zheng said.

"Trust me," Bone said. "Gaunt, would you mind severing this wooden ball-and-chain, as close to my ankle as you dare?"

"I do not know, husband," Gaunt murmured, sizing up the swing, "I have been rather irritated with you of late . . ."

"You think my jokes are inappropriate—"

She swung, and Crypttongue split the wood like a child snaps breadsticks. Bone could almost feel his soul tugged toward the blade. Imagination, surely. "Now remove the ball?"

"I have another joke in mind," Gaunt said with a smirk.

"Time? Of the essence? Like a river? With a waterfall?"

She swung.

Lady Steelfox was saying, "It is said we Karvaks are brutal, but is it ever said we break our word? Snow Pine will not cooperate with me, but if she speaks true, then your goals and ours need not be at odds!"

Bone snatched the sash from his psychopomp robe. Twisting the wooden chain around the ironsilk line, he tied the rope to its ends. "Widow Zheng," he said, "let me secure this to you." She allowed him to tie her wrists to his arrangement. Then he used her own sash to tie a loose safety line from her to the ironsilk rope.

"What is all this?" she asked.

"You will slide down the rope," Bone said. "I can't promise your safety, but you can control your rate of descent. It is like falling, but with a rope always at hand."

Lady Steelfox said, "Come with us! My balloonists have descended into the canyon, but they cannot land with confidence. Yet we are Karvaks, and we are willing to dare this! We will be stronger together! Be wise and consider your children!"

"She is not entirely unconvincing," Gaunt said.

"She is a Karvak," Zheng spat. "Am I ready?"

"Yes," Bone said.

"So long, kids."

Zheng slid in starts and stops, down toward the clouds.

"Are you ready, my dear—" Bone began, when a shadow fell upon the clouds. A Karvak balloon was out there, and its archers were firing at Zheng.

Once again, Bone could hardly breathe. He saw one arrow, a second, a third, find their target.

Each one bounced off and spun into the void.

He gasped. "I am glad now, we decided to have her wear all the pieces of the map."

"Yes." As they watched Zheng slide into the clouds with a jaunty wave, Gaunt added, "*We* do not have magical armor, Bone."

"That is a problem. Nor do we have sufficient material for rappelling." He watched the round shadow drifting upon the white. "Even if they don't find the keys they need, I expect we'll have Karvaks in here soon."

"Pull up the rope."

They found the rope was slack. Either Swarnatep had removed itself, or Zheng had done the job. They pulled as quickly as they could and at last had all the rope within the tower.

"Now what?" Gaunt asked.

"A certain mad idea has occurred to me."

"Surrender? A bloody last stand? A plunge into the void?"

"So many options! But consider: I have noticed that in addition to its extreme strength and lightness, ironsilk has great elasticity. I also noted the moment when Swarnatep hit something solid. If I judge exactly how much shorter to tie off the rope, we could secure ourselves to the far end . . ."

"And we would fall, reach the end of the rope, and be drawn back by its elastic response! In the end we would dangle just above whatever solid object is down there."

"Yes! Is it not glorious?"

"Unless you misjudge. In which case it is fatal. In fact, if the shock of snapback is sufficient, it might be fatal regardless."

"It is a stark choice. Surrender or a mad plunge."

"You already know my answer."

As Bone tied off the ironsilk rope, Gaunt spoke to the entities within her sword.

Our time is desperate, she thought. *If any of you wish release—but not you, Charstalker—tell me your names. And if you are grateful, use whatever power a spirit possesses to disrupt the activities of those beyond that door.*

Several voices assented.

Soon, many nimbuses of light rushed through the door, and the sounds of agitated soldiers and guards made her smile.

Now there is only you and I, said the trapped Charstalker. Her smile faded.

"I'm ready," Bone said.

"So am I."

They heard clicking at the door as he finished tying her off. She could see the tension in his face, as he forced himself not to rush the job, ready until the last moment to accept surrender, if he could not secure her properly.

He finished.

The door burst open. Warriors of city and steppe competed with each other to see who would reach the rogues first.

Gaunt and Bone shared a look and a smile.

They jumped.

PART THREE

TANGLE

We thought it was about time
Your personal demons and mine
Got a room.
We splurged.
You only get so many personal demons in this life.
The room was up in Riverclaw—
We packed our personal demons onto the Golden Epoch Ferry
In one of those big family cabins that isn't really so big
With the fold-out beds and bunks and the concealed weiqi board
And told them to be good
And remember to write
And not to miss the whistle for the Foreign District
(Our personal demons were foreign devils after all)
And we waved goodbye, arm-in-arm, from the docks at Abundant Bamboo.
I like to imagine
Your personal demons and mine
Jockeying for the best view out the windows
Upsetting the top-heavy boat a little
And the neighbors a lot.
I like to envision
Our personal demons
Drinking cheap wine
The kind we're embarrassed by
Even when we're stone drunk
And somehow turning weiqi
Into a game of chance.
We found a room for ourselves too
We did not splurge

It was our usual one
At the Inn of the Five Bats
Which may take its name a trifle seriously
But nocturnal rustlings
Made agreeable counterpoint
To our own.
I like to envision
Your personal demons and mine
Having a good time too
Even though they cast alarming shadows
And made weird screechings
And scratched the furniture
And had a lot to say to each other
Of an incendiary nature
I'm sure I don't want to know.
We said a lot of things too
Things you only say
On a quiet morning
When you know youth's left for summer lands
And death's sailed from the winter port we'll visit last
And we're a continent away from both
With just each other
And it hasn't all been said
But maybe it doesn't have to be.
I suppose
Your personal demons and mine
May feel they've been tricked
And may take it out on strangers
They may speak loudly
And act condescending
And make fools of themselves in nice restaurants
And kick doors and break windows
And wonder why nobody loves them
And weep steaming tears
Claw in claw

And refreshed, look for a gambling den.
We should bring them back, we agree
Sipping tea.
Any day now.
But they worked so hard
And needed their rest.
All our personal demons
Need a break from us
Once in a while.

—Gaunt, untitled, Xembala

CHAPTER 21

XEMBALA

As Bone fell, his first thought was, *Whatever possessed me to think this was a good idea? I cannot even blame the Charstalkers.*

At least the approach of death was beautiful. In a surprising cold silence the shelf of the mountain seemed to fall upward like a thrown stone, blaze of blue above it, birds prickly dark specks tracing strange messages he'd never understand. Three Karvak balloons bobbed like children's balls, while a fourth swelled beside him like an ocean wave. Spears of darkness swished near them without hitting them, and he blinked his relief at the missed arrows even as he thought, *Four balloons?*

White engulfed them. Misty light made him think of various visions of the afterlife. Perhaps he could compare it with the real thing very soon.

He reviewed everything he'd done with the rope up above. It seemed to him he might have paid more attention to his work, enemy warriors notwithstanding.

What was Gaunt saying? *I love you? How could you?* Hard to say.

They reached the end of their rope.

The preternatural elasticity saved them from death upon whatever unseen rock lay below and propelled them back up above the cloud layer, where the Karvaks were waiting.

Bone saw the balloon looming above, the gondola-ger attached and soldiers looking down with what was surely a mirror of his own expression.

We're going to hit—

Somehow Gaunt had freed Crypttongue. As they shot close she slashed the balloon. Impact ripped the sword from her grasp, but they were safely past.

Safely . . . the mountain shelf rushed toward them like a giant gray hand. It suddenly occurred to Bone he hadn't allowed for the possibility of impact at the upper end. He shut his eyes.

Luckily, they were slowing down. Would they hit?

They hit.

They were fortunate, however. It was like falling hard from a ten-foot drop, but no worse.

Bone and Gaunt swore imaginatively, their curses trailing off as they fell once more.

When next they emerged, the Karvak balloon was plunging into the mists northward like a daylight moon disappearing behind clouds. As they rose they saw more balloons emerging from behind the avian scowl of Qushkent. Their ascents and descents were slowing, and Bone did not think fresh archers would have trouble shooting them now.

Down again, up again . . . yes, the pace was slowing, and the balloons descending.

"Cut us loose?" he managed to say. "Lowest point?"

"Why—the hell—not—" he thought she might have said.

He worked out a dagger and began cutting at their ropes. He did not tell her that he could only be sure of freeing one of them at a time, and that she was going to be first. This meant he was perhaps sending his love to her doom. Yet a brutal logic had been inculcated in him on the streets of Palmary, working from his feet up to his brain. You picked *possible* death over *probable* death, and having reached that conclusion, sending your friends to possible death was a kindness.

He timed it well. "I love you," he said on a downward plunge and cut her loose.

She was entitled to a scream. She did not make one. Gaunt was gone.

And Bone was rushing up and away from her, into the presence of three Karvak balloons. He was surprised to find they were firing no arrows. Then he saw the peregrine falcon winging toward him. *I hate that bird*, he thought. He still had a dagger in his hand, and as he rose he waved it at the falcon, in between slicing at his lines. At the uppermost point of his ascent, it came rushing at him, pausing long enough for Bone to see the message tied to its foot.

The bird shrieked menacingly, but Bone knew that was for show. He responded by waving his dagger and cursing.

It followed him down, for no natural creature can match a peregrine falcon in its stoop.

At the bottom of the plunge he finished the job and cut himself free. He tumbled like a sack of potatoes for perhaps five feet before hitting a rocky surface.

He screamed, as Gaunt had not.

Yet he remained conscious enough to know the bird had alighted beside him. Unable to see the falcon, Bone said, "You have earned a stringy thief as your meal, if you wish it." Or perhaps he said it. Perhaps he simply groaned.

It did not peck at him. Bone reached out for the bird.

"Bone!" Gaunt was calling out of the mist. "Imago Bone! What are you going on about? And are you in one piece?"

"We have a messenger," Bone said, unravelling the note from the falcon's foot.

"He's lost his wits," came the voice of Widow Zheng.

"*No*," followed the rasp of the dead woman, whose form was claimed by the spirit of Swarnatep. *"There is a living thing beside him."*

"Bone!" Gaunt called more urgently, stepping closer.

"It is all right," he said. Upon his claiming the message, the bird soared once more, so completely gone it was as though he'd imagined it. Yet the paper remained with him. It was impossible to read, here in the sunlit mists, so he pocketed it.

"Bone."

"Gaunt."

Fumbling, they found each other, embraced in the cold, bright whiteness. "You are unhurt?" Bone asked.

"Bruises. Abrasions. Terror. You?"

"Much the same. Swan's blood! Painter's tears! We really survived that."

"Don't be too sure. This could be the afterlife."

"*No*," put in Swarnatep.

"So," Zheng said in the silence that followed. "There is still an ironsilk rope."

"Hanging like a sword over our heads," Gaunt said. "We must go."

"But go where?" Bone said.

"*I have senses you do not*," Swarnatep said. "*I will guide you. Will you take my hand, Widow Zheng?*"

"I—yes."

Gaunt took Zheng's hand and Bone hers. He wished they'd had enough rope to make a proper line. Still, being alive at all was something of a shock. Everything from this moment might fairly be seen as the cream on the milk.

The surroundings did indeed resemble cream. Shivering, they crept onto a series of rocky slabs that a kindly or imaginative observer might have considered steps. Stone rose on either side, dark suggestions of form. In such an environment it was easier to credit the teachings of the Undetermined, that all observed reality was emptiness decked out for the ball, and all willful creatures the dancers. He might have asked Katta about that, and it occurred to Bone that Katta also would have made a good guide in a situation where sight was untrustworthy. He hoped Katta would escape Deadfall—and that Deadfall would escape whatever madness had possessed it.

Widow Zheng interrupted his thoughts. "Swarnatep . . . how long ago did you know—me?"

"*I do not know how much time has passed,*" said the dead voice. "*A short while from the Leviathans' perspective. A long while from ours. The Heavenwalls were still being built.*"

"Did I hurt you in some way?"

Silence.

"Speak, if you would. I've loved many men. I've even tumbled with Art Quilldrake once or twice. A woman once too, if truth be told. I've also loved with no hope of response. I can sense such a thing in others. Did I hurt you?"

"*You did not mean any harm. If a man is blinded by the sun, is the sun at fault? Can the sun choose not to dazzle? No one who inspires love from afar can be said to cause hurt.*"

"Some, upon knowing they are admired, use the admiration cruelly. Some who are beautiful privately see themselves as wretches and admirers as fools worthy of contempt. I may have behaved in this way, in my youth."

"*We can guess at karma, but we can glimpse it only as shadows in the mist. Whatever the errors of this life, you were blameless in that one. And perhaps the youth of Widow Zheng was less cruel than you believe.*"

"You cannot judge that, Swarnatep. But I thank you."

"Zheng, Swarnatep," Gaunt said in her most gentle voice. "I don't wish to silence you, but I must. Foes may be pursuing us even now, and our voices may lead them to us."

"Of course," Zheng said, and Swarnatep said, "*Yes.*"

Bone listened, thinking he should have thought of this matter before Gaunt. Yet, although he'd trained himself to consider carefully every dispatch from his ears, he heard nothing but a sigh of winds and the crunch and scuffle of their footsteps upon the rocks.

Down they went, into perceived emptiness. Into Xembala.

It was a difficult passage for Imago Bone. There was a daydreamy quality to his mind, which returned to reality only in the presence of danger. There was the risk of a plunge into some abyss, perhaps inches distant, but the setting was so peaceful and featureless, Bone's mind began winging away, unable to convince itself to focus. His will had to drag his fancy back to his side, like a messenger bird eager to be gone. He had to struggle not to think, not to plan, not to muse, not to imagine how it would be to fly a Karvak balloon to steal fire from the sun. He had to be entirely open to the sensation of descending the fog-shrouded mountain path. The difficulty of it made him feel like a rat gnawing at the mesh of a cage. It would be absurd to slip now, to perish after all that came before, simply because he could not calm his mind. He tried to accept the absurdity, perceive it as he might perceive a peculiarly gnarled lump of rock, hanging over the void. In a similar way he perceived his own imagination, and his weariness, and his bruises, and the motion. He heard his heartbeat and his breath, and the breathing of his companions, or two of them at least.

This way of thinking, this acceptance of his own mind, remained difficult. Yet it was no longer excruciating.

Without warning they broke into sunlight.

The living stopped and stared. Their companion sat its desiccated body upon a boulder and looked with dead eyes upon a paradise.

Down below the endless mists, the cloud cover had a look of liquid gold, sunlight fashioned into a river in the sky. Below lay sheer variegated granite walls many thousands of feet tall. Veins of red crystal twisted here and there within the cliffs, catching the sunlight with ruby reflections recalling blood upon sand. Elsewhere, waterfalls streamed in white threads down the gray, visible for miles in either direction, dozens upon dozens, until the great canyon twisted out of sight to west and east. There were many more waterfalls upon the south cliffs, but the north had a large share. Here and there extensions of the canyon walls jutted out like fortresses, green valley-floor forests like besieging armies. A blue river, like a mirror of the cloudy one in the sky, wound through the woods.

Bone glimpsed upon one of the outcroppings, far to the east, a palace seemingly formed of chalcedony and beryl and jade—a kingly treasure in a glance. He saw no balloon.

"Do you see the palace?" he said, pointing.

"I cannot make it out," Gaunt said after a time. "But do you glimpse the pagoda across the canyon, on the rocky hill? It looks perfect for writing poetry."

"Hm. Can't see it."

"It's somewhat obscured by the trees."

"Hey," Zheng said, "I see something. It's a cottage, maybe a hermit's house. Little bit of chimney smoke. Over in that arm of the valley there."

Squinting, Bone said, "I don't see it." Gaunt shook her head.

"What about you, Swarnatep?" Zheng said, turning. Then: "Swarnatep!"

The body had slumped, unable to maintain its posture.

"*It seems . . .*" Swarnatep gasped, "*the danger past, I cannot compel my spirit to remain any longer.*" The body fell to the ground. "*Farewell, Xia.*"

It said no more.

Bone thought he heard shouts far above in the mist. He could have been mistaken, but the sight of death renewed, revived his worries. "Not so certain it's over."

"It seems wrong to leave this body here," Gaunt said. "But the lady of Qushkent had always expected to arrive down here. Just not so gently."

Zheng looked distant, staring at the bright river of clouds. "Vultures, earth, fire—it is all one. We come, and we return. What did he say . . . she say?"

Bone helped her up. "Come."

The descent through the light was more obviously terrifying than the descent through the clouds, and with precipitous and obvious death looming at either hand, Bone returned to himself.

Thus his mind churned as his feet sought the treacherous stones. *Xia,*

Swarnatep had said. The implications of the name swirled around his brains like clouds around the promontory, and with as little clarity. But if Zheng had somehow once been Xia . . .

Like a storm upon a mountain a thought returned to him. The message from the falcon still remained within his pocket. What he read was a series of characters in the Tongue of the Tortoise Shell.

When the wolf prowls
The haven of silkworms
Trust a fox.

Gaunt descended past alpine flowers and pines, which gave way to cypress and willow and at last to palm and eucalyptus. Where once she'd felt chilly, by the time their path became horizontal, a stretch of red earth meandering through emerald grass into forest shadows, she was covered in sweat.

She'd had some small hope of finding Crypttongue in the valley, but these hopes had drowned as the sweat pooled. There was simply too much green, too much territory. Crypttongue might have impaled a tree trunk and remained there for a generation. And why should that worry her? Surely it was a wicked thing, slaying lives and capturing souls.

"Are you all right?" Bone asked her.

"I've slain others," Gaunt said. "It weighs on me."

"I'm not sure dispatching possessed corpses counts as slaying."

"Before that. The Karvaks in the city." She recalled Crypttongue in her hands, the power it lent her. "A man at the Cave of a Thousand Illuminations. Even in our line of work, it should not feel good to kill."

"I am not certain I know, anymore, what our line of work is."

"You are evading the point."

"Evasion used to be our line of work. Or at least the part that followed the claiming of objects."

"Then we really are in a new realm. I have lost an object and long for it."

"We will find Innocence again, Persimmon."

"Yes. Of course."

She made a point of stepping toward the trees and studying their foliage. Bright-plumed birds squawked to announce their presence. Gaunt wondered if these woods were the source of some of Qushkent's colorful avians.

"We'd best keep moving," said Widow Zheng.

"Zheng," Gaunt said. "What Swarnatep said—"

"I know what Swarnatep said. I also know Karvaks are after us. We must move."

"Where are we even going?" Gaunt asked. "We lack time to consult our pieces of the map."

"Into the woods!" Bone yelled and pushed them along the path to make the point. "I will explain later!"

Beneath twisting branches and the wingbeats of startled avians, they saw another winged form far above.

"A falcon," Bone said. "I think it's Steelfox's. It gave me this." He showed them a note.

"'Trust a fox'?" Zheng said once they'd read it. "To the chickens, the fox and the wolf are interchangeable."

"I am not claiming we should trust Steelfox," Bone said. "But her falcon might have killed me up there, instead of telling me this."

"What, then, is the wolf?" Gaunt asked.

"Too many questions," Zheng said. "Not enough li between us and trouble."

They proceeded into the woods with the vague notion of finding the river. What had seemed a simple matter upon the heights now appeared a ferocious trial. The path faded into the undergrowth, and the three had to contend with vines, bramble, ditches, and a sky full of green. This was the mirror image of desert travel—life all around, but the horizon impossible to see. The green-tinged cloud-light began to ebb, with as yet no sign of the river. Gaunt began considering dubious campsites when Zheng called out, "I see the hermit's hut!"

A vine-shrouded gray ruin rose here, a half-crumbled stone dome reminiscent of the wayside stupas of the Braid of Spice. It was no haven, but it was shelter.

"I could have sworn . . ." Zheng began, before shaking her head. She sat and stared overhead at the green canopy, leaves whispering in the breeze.

"We might as well stop here," Bone said. "I advise every caution, however. Let's search the area, keep to our own food and water, and set no fire."

"We won't last long on our own provisions, Bone," Gaunt said.

"You two do as you wish," Zheng said, rising. "I know mangoes when I see them."

Bone proceeded to search the clearing, while Gaunt investigated the stupa's interior. There was no evidence of hermits. She cut away vines and leveled the earth to make it a more pleasant shelter. She discovered a fallen statue—of the Undetermined, perhaps? The posture was seated, but the face was worn away. It was like the shadow of a man or a woman, turned to stone.

Zheng offered them mangoes, but Gaunt and Bone regretfully declined, even though the orange fruit looked delicious. Soon the pulp spattered Zheng's eager face. For all that the widow was Gaunt's elder, she seemed in that moment like a mischievous little girl. It was hard not to follow suit. But something in Persimmon Gaunt did not trust paradises. *Give me an honest graveyard every time.*

"I'll take first watch," Bone said. "Rest."

Gaunt felt a swelling of gratitude at her husband as she curled up within the stupa. Then, mercifully, she felt nothing for a time.

In the shadowed dawn, heralded by a chorus of squawks and cheeps, Gaunt discovered that Bone had fallen asleep on watch. Fortunately nothing had found them.

"I am chagrined," Bone said when she roused him. "I must be getting old."

"You had a long day yesterday. Zheng?"

She prodded the widow.

"Eh? Is that you, old Bison. Or no, you must be young Aurochs . . ."

Gaunt felt Zheng's forehead. "She is feverish, Bone."

"The mangoes?"

"Impossible to say. She had a long day too."

"The hermit," Zheng said, sitting up. "The hermit has returned."

Gaunt and Bone looked at the forest, at each other, and at Zheng. One thing they did not look at was any hermit.

"Don't be rude, kids," Zheng said, offering her unseen friend a bow.

Gaunt and Bone also bowed, in the apparent direction of the unseen apparition. Zheng snorted at their clumsiness and spoke rapidly. The language was the Tongue of the Tortoise Shell, but Gaunt did not understand it. She suspected it was a northern dialect; she and Bone had learned the Imperial version, a southern dialect, used in the capital, along the Walls and down the Braid.

After her exchange with the "hermit," Zheng said, "His name is Jamyang. He was once a man of Daojing, the emperor's seat of power in the north. He had another name then, of which he does not speak. His new name is in the language of the Plateau of Geam, because Xembala takes many of its beliefs from there."

She sounded lucid, which worried Gaunt more than mad rambling would have. Gaunt asked, "Does he have advice for us?"

"He says this valley is the metaphysical body of the Mother Goddess of the world, whose head is a great volcano to the east, and whose feet break into an underworld to the west. In between lie seven vortices of power, corresponding to seven similar vortices in the human body. Each lies along the river. Once in a lifetime, inhabitants of the valley travel the vortices, seeking harmony within themselves, and perhaps true enlightenment. He has made the journey and can take us to the river."

Gaunt and Bone shared a look. Gaunt said, "Zheng . . . I must confess something. This man . . ."

"Jamyang."

"We cannot see Jamyang at all, nor hear him."

"Nor are there footprints," Bone said, "or disturbed foliage."

"I get the point," Zheng said. She began using the northern dialect again. She stood still afterward, nodding. "Jamyang says the illusion of reality is thinner in the valley. People may see things that are unreal, or they themselves may be perceived by others as unreal."

"In which category," Gaunt asked, "would he place himself?"

After a pause: "He says he is perhaps not the best person to answer your question, for as a follower of the Undetermined, he is accustomed to seeing nothing as real. Indeed, he cannot perceive you and Bone, but he is willing to accept that you exist for me, as he does. He sees no reason to privilege his own reality above yours."

Bone rubbed his forehead. "Maybe I should give up and eat a mango, no liquor being available."

"You may be right," Gaunt said. "Perhaps eating the food here brings us more in tune with the processes of the valley."

"The way you said that, it's almost as if you really understand what is happening."

"I know! Isn't language fun?"

"I'm glad he can't hear you," Zheng said. "You are being a little rude."

"Zheng, you have a fever," Gaunt said.

"I admit," Zheng said, "I don't feel all that well . . . but I do think we should follow Jamyang."

"Where is the fabled practicality of Qiangguo?" Bone asked.

"It's not gone, foreign devil," Zheng snapped. "Let's suppose I made Jamyang up. He's just an aspect of my thoughts. We're no worse off, then. We're still stuck in the woods, trying to find a river. Maybe this is how my mind is trying to help itself. If Jamyang takes us anywhere crazy, you can say so. It's not like I'm asking you to trust a Karvak."

"Who said anything about trusting Karvaks?" Bone objected.

"You did!"

"Did not!"

"Enough, you two," Gaunt said. "Zheng, would you kindly ask your provisionally real friend the way to the river?"

Soon they were following Zheng through unexpected pathways, animal tracks with an occasional stone marker of great antiquity. At last they reached the shore of a wide blue river. The waters looked still and deep and hundreds of feet wide. On the far shore was a better-tended pathway, with a raft moored to a post beside it and a canoe sitting on the riverside mud. No one was visible.

"Could we swim this?" Gaunt said doubtfully.

"Jamyang does not advise it. The currents can destroy the unwary."

"I don't suppose you or he see anyone on the far side?"

After a time Zheng shook her head. "Jamyang says that while it's possible to make one's own versions of the larger or smaller craft, it's best to rely on what the followers of the Undetermined have left us. But we have no guide."

"We lack the equipment to make a worthy boat," Bone said. "A simple raft, perhaps."

Gaunt remembered the river crossing at Yao'an and the bargain-rate rafts of goat carcasses. "Perhaps all we need is something we can hold onto, something that will keep our heads above water."

Bone rubbed his chin. "Steelfox wants ironsilk for her balloons, doesn't she? Maybe we can make air sacs. Wrap the ironsilk into bladders, seal them with sap . . ."

"Yes," Zheng said. "That is interesting . . ."

With great effort they spent the morning and afternoon building a bamboo frame and attaching their makeshift bladders to it. A test proved it sufficiently buoyant to support one swimmer. They decided Zheng must go first, and Jamyang, who believed himself a sufficiently good swimmer to tag along with occasional grabs of the frame, would come along.

Into the water Zheng went. Gaunt feared for her, and once or twice Zheng struggled with a current but spun right again. The widow was surprisingly spry in the water. Eventually she was nearly at the far shore, when the strongest current yet tugged her downstream.

"Zheng!" Gaunt yelled helplessly.

Zheng, appearing almost dragged, cast away the frame and the ironsilk dress with it. She kicked and stroked her way to shore, clutching reeds.

The Silk Map, all they had of it, drifted out of sight.

Zheng poled her way back to them on the raft. Nothing untoward occurred, and soon Gaunt and Bone took up poles of their own. This trip was gentle, but the bamboo frame was long gone.

Zheng looked different, Bone thought, less careworn somehow. She told them, "Jamyang thought you'd do best with the larger craft."

"I am glad you made it," he said.

"So am I. It's easier to see the sunlight on the far side. I don't even regret losing the map. I think it will be all right. I am remembering . . . well, it's like recalling a dream. I do not quite believe it. But this land seems familiar."

In the waters of the river, Gaunt saw her reflection and did not recognize herself. There before her was a hard-traveled desert wanderer, sun-bronzed, near to matching her name, and beside her was Bone, similarly road-worn, at the limits of his strength. She poled the water again, and the reflections changed. Now she and Bone fought Karvaks in Qushkent, but it was an idealized scene. It seemed she truly was the elegant dancer she'd pretended to be, hair lustrous as a courtesan's, tattoo gone, skin pale as if she'd never left rainy

Swanisle. More ripples, and she and Bone climbed the Red Heavenwall far inland in Qiangguo, only there she'd been pregnant with Innocence, here she was clearly not, and able to simply enjoy an escapade with her lover in a far land. When the waters next whorled, she unaccountably saw herself as a tiny figure beside a diminutive Bone, volcanic fury blazing against a night horizon, the sky above painted with the colors of the aurora. All these scenes of her past selves, her dream selves, like and unlike the Gaunt she was. But could she know what she truly was, after all?

"Zheng," she said. "This river is unnatural."

"You don't say," muttered Bone, and Gaunt wondered if he saw what she saw.

"My friend tells me the visions are a gift of the land," Zheng said. "A sign that our identities are dreams, in a river of bubbling, transitory phenomena."

"You haven't disagreed with me," Gaunt said.

"I guess not," Zheng said, chuckling, and for a moment Gaunt's companion seemed like her old self.

They reached the far side. Curiously, no sudden currents had afflicted them, as they had Zheng. As she tied the rope, Gaunt looked downstream, seeing no hint of the fragments of the Silk Map.

What she did see was the wreckage of a Karvak balloon, on the treetops perhaps a mile west. "Let's get away from here." The three—or four—of them strode to the path.

"I . . ." said Zheng, "I am not sure . . . I can make it . . . I feel . . ."

"You can do it," Gaunt encouraged her. "It's not far."

"Should we investigate?" Bone said when they were once again under a green canopy. "Our friends may have been prisoners on that balloon."

"I do not know if Flint and Quilldrake are really our friends anymore, Bone. And is that inventor Haytham a friend?"

"Ha! I'll have to tell you about him later. But what of Snow Pine?"

"She urged me to complete Monkey's task, with or without her. I gave my word."

"What do you say, Zheng?"

Gaunt saw no one.

"Zheng?" Bone called out. "Zheng!"

"Zheng!" said Gaunt, returning to the riverbank. Bone peered into the underbrush. They continued hunting in this matter for several minutes.

Bone swore and kicked the red ground. "There are swift monsters in the world. But I cannot accept that something dragged Zheng off with us standing there."

"Agreed. Something stranger has happened."

"Perhaps we could ask our friend Jamyang."

"That was not funny, Bone."

"But it may be true. Zheng may have blended into the deeper reality of this place, to coin a phrase."

"Hm. Perhaps we should indeed be eating mangoes."

"I see what you mean, Gaunt, but I'm leery."

"What if we pick a couple, the next tree we pass? We will keep them handy, in case we find ourselves at an impasse. Or starving."

"You are wise, O wife."

"Do not forget it, O husband."

They followed the path. Although rough and interrupted with stones, fallen logs, and ditches, it was an improvement on the verdant maze of the other shore. Gaunt told Bone she hoped the temple she'd spotted was no apparition. Bone spoke similarly about the bejeweled palace.

In time they reached a rocky hill, seemingly identical to the one bearing Gaunt's pagoda. They saw no structure, but a winding path led up through the rocks.

"The altitude may provide a good view," Gaunt said.

Bone sighed. "If I do have another incarnation, I may ask to return as a mountain goat."

At the top they knelt from exhaustion; the gesture was perhaps not out of place. For a cluster of tents, akin to the ones suspended from the Karvak balloons, were arrayed in a loose crescent beside a stone statue of the Undetermined. This seated figure was missing a nose and both hands, but a gentle countenance remained.

In its lap sat the sword Crypttongue.

"The tents look old, abandoned," Bone said.

"Time to eat the mangoes," Gaunt said. "But just one of us for now. When that one fades, the other can eat."

"I concur. I'll do it."

"I was going to recommend myself."

"I am—slightly—more adroit at skulking."

"I think quickly. I have good intuitions."

"You've used that sword successfully and can claim it without shifting realities. And if the mangoes bring madness, what of your intuitions?"

"I do not want to lose you, too."

"You won't. Whatever is happening in Xembala, I believe it is not intentionally harmful."

"Much harm can be done unintentionally."

"I have survived much that was truly hostile."

"Very well, Bone. Eat your mango if you're so hungry for danger."

"Thank you."

"Don't thank me. Just eat."

He did this with a degree of gusto.

"Do you feel any differently?"

"Aside from slightly more sated, no." He wiped his chin, peered around. "Nor do I perceive anything differently."

Gaunt frowned. "Zheng slept before she was truly seeing the unreal." She looked uneasily at the sky. "I do not think we'll have the same luxury."

"Karvak balloons?"

"They will surely try to descend, and we are quite exposed."

"Then, do we leave your sword, or claim it?"

"It is not my sword, Bone."

"Then there is your answer."

He gestured as if to go.

She hesitated.

"Ah," he said.

Gaunt gazed upon the sword. "Imago, I have always shunned violence except at great need."

"A wise policy."

"Yet armed with Crypttongue I've been a more effective combatant."

"So I've seen."

"And were we to leave this behind, it might be used against us."

"I confess, I cannot see a Karvak turning away from such a prize."

"So. I am torn."

"I do not think this is something I can decide for you, my love."

"You will respect me? If I employ such a dread thing?"

"I would respect anyone who wielded such a weapon. Probably from a distance. Yes, be assured I will always respect you."

"At times, I've felt ours an unequal partnership. You have skills honed over an unnaturally extended lifetime."

"I would have been lost, many times over, without your wits. If you want this sword, take it. But you need no crutch to be an equal in my eyes."

"I cannot trust my judgment in this."

"Cannot, or will not?"

"You accuse me of cowardice? After everything? Have mercy. I am lost in contradictions. Every step seems to lead toward a precipice."

"Very well."

As if unwilling to consider for more than a breath, he raced toward the statue of the Undetermined, tumbled, and kicked the sword out of the holy one's lap.

It arced into the air and impaled the rocky ground like a spade cutting mud.

Bone reached out—and flinched backward as if struck. Blood dripped from his nose.

"Imago!" Gaunt called, approaching him with drawn dagger. "Is the sword—"

"Not the sword! I never touched it. There's someone here! Many some-ones." He had a dagger out as well and was shifting backward, looking left and right. "I perceive them but dimly, like sputtery ghosts. . . . They are women, dressed in robes of bright colors. . . . They seem most determined, though I see no hatred in their eyes. . . . Back, I say! I do not wish to harm you!"

Gaunt ran forward, waving her dagger.

"You're not intersecting them, Gaunt! They seem to notice you but dis-regard you."

"Let them disregard this!"

She grabbed Crypttongue, pulled it from the rocky ground.

It appeared to her that something knocked Bone's dagger from his hand, and another something pummeled his face, both somethings invisible. She ran forward and jabbed at the air in front of him. Bone ceased flinching.

"You have hit one!" he said. "Now, to the right!"

She lunged right.

"No, sorry, I mean your left!"

She thrust left. "Keep your wits about you, man!"

"A hit! But they are attempting to surround you and kick your legs out from under you."

She swung Crypttongue in wide arcs.

Bone said, "You are driving them off! They cannot lay a hand on you; you're like a ghost to them. Yet they are substantial to the sword! An impressive advantage—ow!"

Bone, surprised, found his arms pinned behind him. If he were not insane, of course, if this weren't a perverse delirium wrought of poisonous fruit. Perhaps Bone was crazy, and Zheng had scampered into the woods . . .

"Can you hear them, Gaunt?" Bone asked, perspiration showing on his face. "A couple of them know the dialect of southern Qiangguo. They order you to stand down, or they may inflict injury."

"Oh?" Gaunt said, stepping forward with the blade raised. In the Tongue of the Tortoise Shell she said, "Do you follow the Undetermined and his Thresholders? Then how can you employ violence?"

"They hear you," Bone said, cocking his head. "One, their leader, I think, says, 'The great work of life is to combat suffering with understanding. But it is sometimes correct to employ lesser means of combating suffering.' I may be getting the sense of it wrong, Gaunt, but I think she's sincere. She says, 'You have harmed some of us already—is this truly what you wish?'"

Gaunt shouted, "How can I be responsible for hurting people I can neither see nor hear?"

Bone said, "She says, 'We can never fully end the suffering we cause, but we can be mindful of it. In a similar way we regret any insect we may have crushed, unknowing, as we walk. And we step lightly when we can.'"

Gaunt hesitated. She did not necessarily agree. She did not necessarily disagree. But somehow considering such matters quenched her fury. She lowered her sword.

Her sword, she realized. That was how she thought of it. She was not about to set Crypttongue down.

Bone's arms appeared to become free. He sighed and stretched, wheeling them in circles. "They've stopped, Gaunt. They are looking at you. With sad eyes, I'd say. They are tending to their wounds." Bone slowly retrieved his weapon and sheathed it. Raising his arms, he said in the Tongue of the Tortoise Shell, "I mean no harm. We wish to reclaim this sword . . . Zheng! I see Zheng, coming up the path! And that man must be Jamyang."

"I do not see anyone."

"She says she's been pulled into the grasp of the goddess of the valley. As I will be."

"That sounds ominous."

"I concede this is a great deal of excitement for one mango. The leader says, 'If you are owner of the blade, we do not contest it. But it is a wicked thing to enslave the mind it contains. We have offered it sanctuary.'"

"In what way can it be offered sanctuary?"

"'Here in Xembala, the land can offer a dwelling place for the wayward spirit. If released, it may pass on to new incarnations, or other realms, or oblivion. But it may also linger, and live among us as an inhabitant of the valley.'"

"There is much here I do not understand," Gaunt said. "But know this: We are on a quest that may rescue more than one lost child. I am willing to keep the entity in this sword chained for as long as that takes. For I suspect such captives empower the weapon."

Bone looked uneasy. "She says, 'I urge you to consider the karmic burden you take upon yourself, compounding your suffering on behalf of these children with the suffering of those you bind. Together they form a weight upon you. Release them.'"

"And give up my son?"

"'You need not give up your quest. A quest can be a good thing. Love of a child can be a good thing. But your choices speak of desperation, of craving. An unhealthy frame of mind.'"

"And does this wise woman know what it is like to be a mother?"

"She concedes she does not."

"Let her walk in my shoes, before she speaks! Let her nurse, and clean, and sing to sleep an infant before she judges my loss! Let her kiss scraped knees and hug away nightmares before she talks about my *craving*, as if I were some disciple of opium! I will not be some good little wife who can just serenely make another baby, and let it all flow by me like a river."

"Gaunt . . ." Bone said. "I do not know what she really thinks. But I never . . . I never . . ."

"Don't talk now," she said, shaking her head, as her body shook as well. "Just interpret."

Bone lowered his head. After a time he said, "Ah. Zheng's friend proposes we journey to the palace—the seat of Maldar Khan! The closest thing this strange land has to a ruler. Let Maldar Khan decide, Jamyang says."

"That is acceptable to me, Bone," Gaunt said, her fury spent. If nothing else, the journey would delay the reckoning.

"And to me," said Bone. "Jamyang is considering . . . oh, no."

"What?"

"Zheng's spotted something. Turn around."

She did. At first Gaunt could not understand what she was seeing. Just over the edge, a vast shape curved into view. Some deep part of her brain feared a monster. But it was no beast.

A Karvak balloon, the same that Gaunt had punctured earlier, rose above the cliff.

The gash in the gasbag had been patched by sections of an ironsilk dress, painted with cartographic symbols.

"Gaunt!" Bone was shouting. "Run!"

She ran. They descended the path, for there was only one safe route of descent.

Yet it was not safe at all, for soon they saw Karvaks in armor advancing up the switchbacks. The warriors halted and unsheathed bows. Gaunt and Bone flattened themselves against the rocky wall as arrows careened off the stone. They were momentarily safe, but the balloonist Karvaks would soon descend the path.

"Just like old times," said Bone. "Why, I remember—"

"Focus, Bone," said Gaunt. "I have a strategy."

"Desperate and dangerous, I suppose?"

Gaunt set Crypttongue against the rocks and pulled out her saved mango. She cut it with the tip of the blade.

"I suppose," Bone said, "desperate plans work best on a full stomach . . ."

"Shut up, Bone." Gaunt stuffed as much mango as she could into her mouth and gulped it down. She threw the rest over the edge. "Now I will eventually become attuned to Xembala or whatever the hell is happening. But you are farther along, Bone. You must run."

"Run where?"

"Over the edge. I've learned much from you, Imago, but you are still the one with a lifetime of acrobatic thieving behind you. Use it all." She lifted Crypttongue.

"Not without you."

"Stupid man, don't be noble." She smiled, for she could feel strength enter her sword-arm from the blade. "There's too much at stake. Innocence and A-Girl-Is-A-Joy. We've tangled with Karvaks. They're not your common warrior. We won't win, but I can hold them off while you escape."

"I—I was offered this choice before. Stay with the boy, or . . ."

"I've tried to forgive your choice." Her voice grew hard. "But I won't forgive you this time. If this is the end, we have had our adventure, Imago, my husband. I cherish it. Now listen to your wife. Save our son. *Go!*"

She ran, howling, up the path.

She did not pause to see which path he took to escape. That was his business. But somehow she sensed he'd gone.

A group of Karvaks ran up to her. Armored as they were, these men did not seem quite human, and her mind painted shadows over them, these sons of unknown women, made them symbols of everything that stood between her and her boy.

Crypttongue empowering her blows, she felled five before the arrow struck her in the leg.

She tumbled, and the sword fell from her hand.

Someone kicked Crypttongue away; the foot's next target was Gaunt's face.

It seemed she dwelled with the aurora for a moment before the world returned to her and she stared up into a female Karvak face. The woman who knelt beside Gaunt was like and yet unlike Lady Steelfox, only a little younger and yet somehow with a gaze like that of a greedy child.

"You fought well," the Karvak said in the language of the Eldshore, "and I respect that. You've earned your life. Your companion's death is inevitable, of course. He has chosen to run like an animal, and we know what to do with prey. Be assured the kill will be swift and clean."

"So generous."

"I know enough about your lands to know you are raised in corrupt ways. Nevertheless, you are a poet as well as a brigand, and you can give my husband, the new Grand Khan, helpful intelligence. Serve me well now, and you will have a place in our empire, yes, you, and even your sons and daughters."

Gaunt considered spitting in the Karvak's face, but with Crypttongue gone the battle-fury had withdrawn. Words were what she needed now.

"You are the wolf," Gaunt guessed.

"You are correct."

CHAPTER 22

TRUST A FOX

Bone fled.

He slid down a nearly sheer slope of scree, earning cuts and raising clouds of dust. He shifted himself down a chimney of rock, descended a cliff until it was just safe to jump, ran down a mossy slope where a twitch of imbalance might send him careening into fissures at either hand.

For a while he had the feeling the apparitional Xembalans, Zheng among them, were calling to him, but he had no ears for them, only for Gaunt.

I won't forgive you this time.

In his gut he wasn't really fleeing a rocky hill that held his wife but was desperately swimming in a collapsing underground island, the Scroll of Years leaving his hands and carrying his son with it. The green canopy under golden clouds was, in his mind's eye, the fragmenting substance of the Eastern dragon who had encompassed that island. His son was trapped in another world, and now his wife was captured—not dead, don't think dead—in a strange, otherworldly place.

He had no notion of direction, only a vague sense of where the palace had gleamed beneath the clouds. From time to time he thought he might have glimpsed a balloon drifting above the branches. He kept running. The undergrowth was not so thick on this side of the river, and Bone was able to make progress, until at last he collapsed.

He must have passed out for a time. The light was as diffuse as always but more concentrated now to the west. He felt a chill. Golden mists writhed around the trees, perhaps an aspect of Xembala he was now permitted to see. From time to time he saw shadowy shapes walking in the same direction, with his gait. Something told him not to hail them, but he could not resist looking.

There stood other versions of himself—haggard-looking in a gray traveling cloak, sans mustache, as he'd appeared in the danker parts of the West; brash and barbaric in a jerkin meant for hot weather, his pale, exposed limbs earning sunburns now that they'd left the shadows of Palmary of the Towers. It was hard to say how accurate these visions were, as he'd only glimpsed himself behind his own eyes. Younger versions of Gaunt walked beside him, laughing, chiding, grasping his hand, pointing ahead. Sun to his moon. She saw herself as grim and gravestuck and he as full of life, but it was he whose heart was shadowed, and hers who blazed.

He had to look away, though he knew the mists shadowed him.

The mists were not the only surprise. When he reached the edge of this forest, he looked out upon cultivated fields.

He saw rectangular stone houses amid terraces of green. Strewn between houses and boulders were ropes bearing hundreds of colorful square flags. He saw goats and cows and yaks. There were no people, however.

The ground was rugged enough that he could run from boulder to terrace to isolated tree, keeping himself mostly hidden. At last he reached a house, its flags rustling upon the ropes leading to its neighbor.

"Good evening!" he called in the Tongue of the Tortoise Shell, for day was fading. "You good?" He tried again in his best rendition of a northern dialect. "Peace be upon you," he tried in the language of Mirabad, and "Hello!" in his own. There was no response. He leaned through an open window and saw no inhabitants, though there was a table set with flatbread, vegetables, and noodles, with a few oranges shining in his sight. His mouth watered.

He'd done much worse than steal food from invisible people, but he restrained himself. He suspected he was not alone. He crept around the house and observed the flags upon the ropes. Many were unmarked, but some bore a vertical script that was somehow familiar. Upon one he saw an illustration of a horse racing through clouds.

Bone shrugged and peeked into the window again.

There was one less orange, and fewer noodles.

Bone waved his arms, jumped on one foot, sang a sea shanty. No one manifested.

He tried to recall one of Mad Katta's sutras.

He said, "'Being is as Being does, Nothing is as Nothing was, Being Nothing's what we do, Nothing Being really true.' All right, I'm fairly sure that wasn't it . . ."

There was a strange tremor in the air, and the flags flapped more violently. He felt a pressure and looked down to see an orange in his hand.

He ran.

In the fading light he looked behind himself to see not one but three dark inverted-teardrop shapes in the western sky. His feet took him into high country, past another village much like the last.

For a time it seemed to him that he was paced on one side by a younger version of himself, swishing and jabbing at illusory foes with a stick, and on the other side by Innocence, as he'd seen the boy on their once and only meeting, running with a fighting staff of Qiangguo much too big for him.

You are cruel, spirit of Xembala, he thought, and yet he mourned when the children vanished.

At last he collapsed beside a boulder and ate the orange.

His attempt to sleep was futile. He counted sheep, but they kept swirling around like cloudy mandalas. He rose and stumbled southeast. Luckily there was a pale glow to the sky for much of the night. Eventually he found a road and wandered along it.

A rumbling startled him, and he leapt off the side of the road.

A horse-drawn cart rolled into view, but he saw no driver. Bone stepped onto the road. The horse whinnied and clomped its hooves.

"Being is nothing!" Bone called out. "You good?"

The horse calmed itself. After a moment, Bone felt someone unseen touch him lightly upon the shoulder. He was led toward the wagon and felt much like someone entering a haunted house when he climbed aboard. But surely he was the ghost here.

He saw no reins as the horse continued, but there must be an unseen driver.

They traveled in silence for hours. The pale light faded, but Bone let the driver continue until he judged they were moving off his course. "I must be going," he tried to say, and the wagon stopped.

"Thank you," he said and, moved by all this inaudible generosity, he left behind one of his daggers, which could surely prove a valuable tool, even in a peaceful place. He leapt off the cart before the apparition could refuse.

Into the cold night he went, trusting to his ears and his footing. He stumbled more than once. Yet he felt a certain freedom, here on the verge of losing everything, his awareness focused only on the journey.

In the gray, cloudy dawn he beheld, almost directly ahead, the wreckage of a balloon floundered against the southern cliffs. A raptor soared above it.

"Trust a fox," Bone murmured.

Vultures rustled upon a nearby hill as Bone approached the fallen craft. He glimpsed a pair of human bodies up there in a state that surely pleased the birds. He looked away.

The once-flying ger was trapped between large boulders flush to the cliff face, like a bit of food stuck in a titan's teeth.

He saw Liron Flint watching the valley, eyes shadowed as one who has not slept in days. Haytham ibn Zakwan was looking over gear recovered from the balloon, cursing to himself. A woman in gray who reminded Bone of Mad Katta was sitting cross-legged, eyes shut. Snow Pine stood beside the one Bone believed to be Lady Steelfox. They were regarding the collapsed envelope and arguing. There was no sign of Quilldrake.

Bone crept closer to overhear the dispute.

"You dismiss all my suggestions out of hand," Snow Pine said, "but consider them seriously when Flint makes them. You reject me because of my background. Am I a person to you, or an emblem?"

The Karvak princess answered, "You were an emblem, woman of Qiangguo, the moment you stepped through the Jade Gate. Of course you embody your Empire, out here—what was that?"

Bone heard it too. There was a scuffling sound amid the rocks, and although the crash survivors looked his way, the sounds did not belong to him. He turned just in time to avoid a blade-thrust.

Facing him was a cloaked warrior with a serrated blade.

He rolled between two rocks and emerged into the crash site. His opponent followed.

A curious thing occurred or, rather, did not occur. The survivors did not see the fight. As Bone and his foe circled each other, looking for the moment to lunge, the others said:

"A dust devil?"

"An earthquake?"

"Ghosts?"

"It is I, Bone!" he called to them.

But the enemy answered, "They cannot hear you. You have been brought into the reality of the valley, as I once again have, at long last."

"You! I know your voice. You're the one from my homeland."

"That is not who I truly am," she said, "any more than you, thief. We are now only what we are."

She jabbed; he evaded. He thrust; she rolled backward. On her feet in an eyeblink she said, "You are the man who serves Lady Monkey, in hopes she will restore your child. I am the woman who serves the valley, though the inhabitants think me mad."

"And you oppose my finding my child?"

"You cannot. You threaten the valley. Even if you take but one Iron Moth from this place, you will inspire others to come."

He dropped low and kicked; she leapt and pounced. Again, the dance.

He said, "You would seem to be too late."

"The Karvaks can be defeated, or assimilated. And this time, less of the Silk Map will remain Outside."

"I swear we have no interest in returning to Xembala."

"What of your son? He is linked to the vital breath of Qiangguo itself."

"How can you know this?"

"The Fraternity of the Hare hears many things, in many places. We've learned how to sever ears and let their owners still hear through them. We've explored deep places of the world and learned to raise up monstrosities long dead. We've made pacts with Charstalkers and Leviathan Minds. We know much. And we've learned there are those who would wish your son to become an emperor."

"They can wish all they want," Bone said, "but to me, palaces are merely more elaborate jails. Innocence will be far away and free of such obligations."

"If he will not serve them, they will kill him, to release the vital breath for another."

"They must go through us first."

She flung sand at his eyes. He shut them just in time, leaping upon a boulder.

The others present looked this way and that, trying to understand the source of the disturbance, all except the shaman, who began to chant in a low voice.

"You are two people," the one-eared warrior said. "In the end, you will acquiesce. And the new emperor of Qiangguo will know of this land. I know what emperors do."

"You claim to know us all so well. I do not even know your name."

She hesitated. "I am called Dolma."

"Did you have a name in the old country?"

"It has been so long that even Xembala seems to me 'the old country.' But as a girl in the West, I was Violante."

"They are both lovely names."

"They are names, and thus merely convenient illusions."

"How did you come to be in Xembala?"

"What is the point of your questions? We are enemies."

"Life is illusion in transition, so what is the point of anything? Was yours a merchant family?"

"Yes!" she snapped. "They journeyed along the Braid when I was a girl. Brigands happened upon us, driving us over a cliff. Yet fate singled me out, for one of the Fraternity snatched me from doom at the last moment. They took me to Xembala for my education, and came to me again when I was twelve, that I might take up arms."

"You did not return in all that time?"

"What of it! I saw paradise, thief! I will die to protect it."

"And kill."

"And kill."

"You'll do neither, you hot-country lunatics!" came a croaking voice.

A vulture settled down upon Bone's rock, glaring directly at him.

"It took me a damnably long time to pierce the veils of this sneaky semi-dimension. And I'm not going to put up with you fools killing each other the moment I do." The bird squawked down at Dolma. "Put down that rock, you! I, Northwing, command it! Spirits of sea and sky, is everyone south of the taiga a homicidal nitwit?"

"You," Bone said, "you're that shaman over there."

The vulture that called itself Northwing studied Bone sidelong. "Why do you ask that?"

"Mad Katta—one of your countrymen, I believe? During our sojourn in Qushkent, he said something about shamans entering the spirit world by riding within the minds of animals."

"Katta!" Northwing squawked. "In my language we called him Deadfall, for he's long dead to us."

"'Deadfall?' You are serious?"

"I am not always sober, you son-of-a-corpse, but I am always serious. You!" The bird spun its head. "Sheathe that sword, pale beauty, or you can fight all the vultures in this area. Don't think I can't do it, or that they'll balk at living flesh this one time."

Dolma stopped climbing the stone.

"What do you want?" Bone asked, sheathing his own blade.

"Ah, sense! Lady Steelfox will be interested in speaking with you. It's for her to decide what happens next."

Shortly, the cross-legged shaman was speaking in Karvak to Steelfox, with Snow Pine and Liron Flint leaning close. Sometimes Steelfox gave her companions a clipped explanation of what Bone and Dolma said. Haytham ignored them, tinkering as he was with his cauldron inscribed with magical writings. Thus commenced a most peculiar interview.

"She told me 'trust a fox.' Didn't she? Who is the wolf?"

"The wolf is her younger sister. Lady Jewelwolf is wife of the newly elected Grand Khan. In my mistress's opinion, Jewelwolf's will is stronger than her husband's, and I concur. Don't delude yourself that he's therefore a kindly person. It's Jewelwolf who was responsible for the carnage of Hvam, and the khan is eager for more such victories."

"That sounds bad for the region, I admit," Bone said. "But I do not see the immediate concern for my companions and me."

"For one thing, she has your friend Quilldrake, whether as ally or prisoner, it isn't clear. For another, Jewelwolf is more than the wife of the new khan. She has formed an arcane alliance with a number of strange individuals. The kleptomancer Koel. The troll-jarl Skrymir. Mythul, mad prince of the Eldshore. And at the center of the group, the Archmage Sarcopia. Jewelwolf craves magical power; her link with these persons is stronger than her loyalty to the Karvaks. They call themselves the Cardinals of the Compass Rose, which I gather means something like 'priest-kings of the four directions.' They mean to divide the whole world between them."

Some of those names were known to Bone, and even he shivered a bit. Just a little. "Nice work if you can get it."

"Thus," the shaman Northwing continued, "the Karvak realm is becoming one arm of a foul alliance. Jewelwolf already sees Steelfox as a rival. There are

Karvak politics involved—I will not try to explain them. But understand that there are men who hate to see women wielding power openly."

"Such men are everywhere," Dolma murmured, "except Xembala."

"Jewelwolf can manipulate such men," said Northwing, "while snatching power from female rivals. Lady Steelfox, husbandless, will be forced into irrelevance. This is a great wrong. My employer was meant for greatness."

"Again, my sympathies, but what has this to do with me?"

A long interruption began, filled with sonorous exchanges in Karvak.

The not-so-sonorous vulture said, "Steelfox is going to defy her sister. Her great advantages are friendship with my people and her experiments with flight. With the ironsilk and its many uses, including the making of armored balloons, Steelfox has a chance."

Bone imagined it: a vast balloon impervious to arrows and crossbows, bringing invaders to Qiangguo. Or Swanisle.

Haytham swore and backed away from his cauldron.

A Charstalker erupted from the device. Immediately Dolma leapt into the flames.

"Dolma!" Bone cried. He'd been too shocked to act.

But she was not consumed; rather, she appeared to absorb the flames, until the red light shone from her eyes. When next she spoke her voice was like a churning of rocks.

"*I now speak to the meat occupying two planes of Xembala, and one who walks between. This Dolma has severed my connection to your imprisonment device. Your balloon will no longer soar.*"

"Let her go," Bone said, though he was not sure why.

"*The Fraternity of the Hare are good allies, Imago Bone. They have realized only we of Bull-Demon Mountain have the strength to repel invaders from Xembala. The world is changing, and lost lands will not stay lost.*"

"What are you, anyway?" Northwing asked. "I've been wanting to question you ever since I stepped aboard one of these blasted balloons. You're like no other spirit I've encountered."

"*Shaman. You are the one form of meat I can respect. I will answer. We derive from the red veins of rock that line the northern slope. They lead to the crystalline forest that underlies the great desert.*"

"The Leviathan Minds' archive," Bone heard Snow Pine say.

"The record of souls," Liron Flint said.

"For thousands upon thousands of years, the meat within reach of the desert has lived and died and been recorded within the crystals. Whether or not true reincarnation occurs for your kind, I cannot say. But under the influence of the Leviathan Minds' creation, a form of transmigration exists. Records of your minds flow within the great archive. Some minds find peace thereby, and some escape to be reborn. Others of us meditate upon the great cruelties of life and afterlife and shed the shackles of morality. We find our way through the veins of crystal that lead to the greatest of us, he who is chained within Bull-Demon Mountain, and who awaits the day of his escape."

"Why do I have the feeling," Bone said, "the day of his escape will be a bad day for everyone else?"

"Know this, meat. You will never leave Xembala in this life. Whether your stay ends in peace or in fire is your choice."

With that, Dolma leapt into the rocky stream. It seemed to Bone that the rocks would surely kill her, but the fiery nimbus blazed even in the waters' midst, regardless of the host body's fate. Soon the Charstalker was out of sight.

"Are you going to follow her, shaman?" Bone asked.

"The vulture in me wants to, but I think it might be unwise."

"I think you're right. Yet I also think she will be back to haunt us."

"'Us.' Then you will join my employer?"

"For now."

"Good. I will relay this."

Bone swished his hand experimentally through Liron Flint's head. He mimed choking the treasure hunter, then kicking him. "Hm," he said. "Northwing?"

"Yes."

"Have any of you eaten the local food?"

"Not yet. I've advised against it. I'm guessing that to partake is to align one's self with the goddess of the valley."

"You've guessed right. Which suggests I'll have some difficulty being your ally."

"Nonsense. You'll be a perfect scout. You can encounter all the mysteries of the valley. Its people. Its magic. Its monsters. Meanwhile we will sip yak's milk and evaluate your performance."

"You must be a valuable servant, shaman. Because I have a feeling Steelfox doesn't keep you around for your charm."

The vulture's laughter was all the confirmation he needed.

One perquisite of being a ghost-scout, Bone reflected, was that they couldn't load him with extra gear. He could affect only a small amount of matter with origins outside the valley. He wondered if in time the expedition's possessions would shift into "his" reality, having absorbed sufficient dust, mist, pollen, and so on. He made a mental note not to inquire.

He led the group east along the southern cliffs. More and more often he caught glimpses of what seemed the very image of the lamasery spoken of by the Mad Mariner.

Steelfox agreed the sight was worth investigating. And moreover, Bone hoped Gaunt had escaped and was traveling there as well.

Outside of his conversations with Northwing, who followed him variously as vulture, hawk, panther, and bull, Bone was in company and yet alone. He could tell the others were uncomfortable with his present non-presence, yet in time they ignored the ignorable and began talking amongst themselves. He drifted close enough to hear Snow Pine and Flint.

"Perhaps you and I should speak," Snow Pine said.

"What is there to speak about?" Flint said. "I am a traitor and a coward. That seems quite final."

"I was angry."

"You are not now?"

"No . . . I am still angry. Furious even. Yet I can see you had your reasons. You have wanted this journey for a very long time."

"Since I was a boy."

"Children forge iron chains for their grownup selves."

"Is that what you think? I've walked in the light of Xembala for so long. It does not feel like a chain but like a lantern carried with me."

"What does it point you to? Not loyalty, apparently. Not . . . friendship."

"Part of the thrill of such a quest is not knowing just where it leads. Perhaps Xembala is paradise. Perhaps it is a trap. Perhaps it is, under the skin, much like any country, with good and bad mingled in endless hues. I am excited that I may soon know."

"That's what it is for you, then. The knowledge. You're different from Quilldrake."

"Quilldrake. Arthur is acting on a dream too, I believe, but it is not the wonderment of a child. It is the fancy of an aging man. He is not lit up from within but rather guided by a gleam from without."

"The gleam of gold."

"I think it is more than that. It's triumph. Accomplishment. A feeling that one's passage left a mark."

"Is that what Bone feels, I wonder?"

"I would not know," Flint said. "Do you not?"

"I do not truly understand him. His wife makes more sense to me. She loves her lost child, as I love mine. I think Bone loves his son too, but it is an abstracted thing. What he truly dotes upon is Gaunt. What she wants, he wants."

Flint chuckled. "That, and gold."

"Maybe for Quilldrake, people are a close second to gold, while to Bone it is the other way around."

"Perhaps." Flint paused. "I fear that for me, neither gold nor people are truly important. Only knowledge."

"And that's why you sided with Steelfox?"

"That . . . and that this alliance seemed the most likely way of keeping you safe."

"Oh."

"I am fond of you. Surely you have seen this."

"Fond of me? I thought people were of no matter to you."

He chuckled. "I place you in a category different from 'people.'"

She snorted. "There's never been anyone more 'people' than me. I'm as common as mud."

"I do not really believe that."

"The followers of the Forest let everything wash over them, Liron. We call nature transitory, but we don't call it illusory. Sometimes, in all these well-meaning traditions—the Swan with her self-sacrifice, the Undetermined with his enlightenment, your Painter with its justice—I see little room for ordinary folk. With their ordinary itches and laughs and farts and songs. Everything must be high-minded and shining amongst the clouds. Only the Forest, in my experience, really acknowledges darkness and pain and shit and blood as things to understand, rather than things to abhor."

"On behalf of all the world's other religions, I would gently suggest you are oversimplifying."

"Heh. Probably. If you weren't a traitor I'd teach you about some dark simple things right now."

Flint coughed. His gait slowed. The two fell behind the others a bit. Bone did as well.

A squirrel bit Bone's leg.

"Ow!"

"That's for eavesdropping."

"That's uncalled for! I was just curious."

"Said the duck who nested on the polar bear. Keep walking."

Bone grumbled, but he did as instructed. The way remained rough. He'd seen no balloons except once, in the distance, two days before, but he remained cautious.

"I hope Snow Pine can find some solace," Bone said. "Not sure about Flint, of course, but the alternative is Haytham—"

"Or you?" said the squirrel.

"I'm a married man!"

"I know all about 'married men.'"

"You don't know me," Bone said. "Haytham, now, he's not so bad, but regarding women he's rather shallow."

"You know him well?"

"Not well. But once I became entangled in his schemes."

"Do tell."

"I think the terrain ahead becomes very challenging soon. I will abridge my telling. So, once, far away, I was paid to investigate Haytham's lodgings."

"Steal from him, you mean."

"No, and who is telling this story? But things went very wrong. A mummy grabbed me, one I realize now was akin to those beneath the desert. It smothered me into unconsciousness—"

"And you died."

"Are you four years old, Northwing? Let me finish . . ."

THE TALE OF THE THIEF (TRULY), CONTINUED

I awoke within a brass prison smelling of old oil. Something about the working seemed sloppy to me, for while the chamber was oval in shape the actual contours were somewhat off. There was a straw mat and a chamber pot resembling an oversized thimble, and a drinking cup resembling a somewhat less oversized thimble.

A booming voice resonated within the chamber. "Aha! I knew it! You carry a bit of enchantment upon you, thus you can be sealed inside the lamp." I recognized the voice as that of my target.

"Hello!" I called out. "Do I have the honor of speaking with the illustrious Haytham ibn Zakwan ibn Rihab, mighty among sorcerers?" I added the last because, mighty or not, it never hurts to butter up a magic-worker. (Of course, I know you would never be susceptible to such transparent flattery.)

"Indeed!" said the echoing voice. "Though you do not know me so well. I am no sorcerer, nor wizard, nor shaman, or whatever bizarre practitioner you might mistake me for. I am a natural philosopher."

"I am afraid you have lost me."

"On the contrary, sir, I have you thoroughly found. But as to natural philosophy. I study the ordinary workings of the world, such as any person of keen observation might glean. I lack any magical gift."

"You could have fooled me."

"Permit me to make a fine distinction, for it seems to me you might be among the few with wit to comprehend. This world has pockets of unbridled, ferocious creativity that are difficult to reproduce. Magic, we say. However, it primarily contains phenomena that are, given sufficient study, predictable. I investigate both matters, with an eye to improving human knowledge. What makes me different from a sorcerer is not just my lack of arcane gifts but my unwillingness to record transitory results. Instead I study processes that anyone with intelligence and the proper equipment might duplicate. Among these is the capture of magical beings."

"So you make monster traps?"

"The process still eludes me. This is one of many vessels—bottles, urns, jars—prepared by the ancient king Younus, whom having once been devoured by a djinn in the shape of a whale, decided to return the favor. The vessels of Younus can trap a magical being upon the utterance of a command phrase. A given entity could only be pulled in thrice, however. This lamp was the abode of a djinn many years ago but was vacant until recently."

"Do you not run a risk, telling me the lamp's limitations?"

"Not really, since keeping you is not a primary goal. I have caught you for a purpose, Imago Bone."

"Oh?" In some ways it was less alarming to be a mere collector's piece. "I thought it was an accident."

"No. Through a proxy I hired you to come here."

"You could have sent an invitation."

"You might have declined. Also, this way, you cannot appeal to the authorities."

"What do you want with me?"

"I have been observing you for some time. In so doing I recognized that, while human, you are protected from mortal harm by a strong enchantment."

"I do not deny it."

"I have also noticed that you do fairly well in an area where my experiments tend to go awry."

"Oh?"

The confident voice became shy. "You have a way with women."

"Ah. Well. One does what one can . . ."

"As do we all. We do not all have your self-assured swagger, however."

"It comes of long experience, Haytham ibn Zakwan . . ."

"Please, just Haytham, or Doctor Haytham, if you prefer formality."

"Haytham, the enchantment you spoke of is the source of my swagger, as you term it . . ."

"Of that I have no doubt."

"For it has allowed me to live a long time in an attractive, or at least healthy, young body. I have had time to learn self-assurance. Beyond that, I've learned to be entertaining company."

"You do have charm and self-assurance, but I do not think it is truly the product of study."

"Oh?" I found myself surprisingly miffed by the suggestion.

"You are inured against fear. You need not fear death, and this self-confidence bleeds over into other areas of your life. It is a contingent aspect of your enchantment, if you will."

"I'm not sure I do will."

"Irrelevant. I intend to make use of your self-confidence for my own purposes. There is in this city a tower owned by the wealthy Arkoyda family."

"I am familiar with it."

"And with its defenses, I know."

"So you know I would be reluctant to return there."

"This time you will have my help. You see, the Arkoydas are patrons of the arts, and within their tower dwell many artists. I have developed a liking for one of these, but I have been unable to obtain her affection. You will help me in this task."

"Confined within a lamp, I am uncertain how to grant your wish."

"Ha ha. I have developed a technique which I call *gharbal* or, alternatively, *siniazo*. You might translate this as "sifting" or perhaps "garbling." I connect filaments of the Cytherean Heliodrosia, with its properties of luring humans to their doom with uncanny illusions, from the lamp to an electrum circlet around my head. Certain other elixirs and ointments are required, none of which need concern you."

"And as a result of this connection, you will appear to be me?"

"Heh, no. I will be me, you will be you. But I will have your swagger, Imago Bone, and you will have my fear. I shall see what affect this has on a certain female."

"And after this you will let me go?"

"That I will have to consider. As this is a foggy night, I see no reason to delay."

"What does fog have to do with it?"

Ah, my foolish questions! This was soon enough answered by a sense of drifting into the air aboard one of Haytham's earlier flying contraptions, this one a balloon utilizing a highly flammable gas. Aboard this vessel we drifted through the city until reaching the tower of the Arkoydas. The tower, I knew from experience, was of dark stone, inset with white marble representing the stars of the Greater Bear.

CHRIS WILLRICH   333

I knocked on the side of the lamp. "When do we begin?"

"Now," said Haytham.

The procedure worked its strange effect. I found myself looking through Haytham's eyes and was aware he was looking through mine. Yet each of us also simultaneously peered through the eyes we were born with.

"I think this will conjure headaches," I said, finding I needed only whisper.

"Perhaps," he murmured back. "However in ordinary life each eye has a slightly different visual field. This is a harder problem but not an unprecedented one."

"What now?"

"We must bypass the guard dogs of the upper levels."

"Do we not need to avoid the guard humans of the lower levels first?"

"Not at all."

He was lowering us down a rope from the gondola of his balloon so that we would end up on a balcony that circled the whole tower at a slant, coiling for three stories. This was a popular area during parties. There was currently none such, although doors to the balcony were open.

He'd not judged the rope quite correctly, and we found ourselves nose-first on the balcony stones but still suspended from the balloon.

"We need to get untied," I observed, "quick."

He twisted himself up to untie his feet. He was not in quite as good shape as he'd imagined; while he could twist himself to reach the knots, he could only stay up for a few moments before uncoiling. Thus escape was proving to be a wrenching process.

I heard pattering feet. "Rats?" I wondered aloud.

His heart pounded. "Dogs."

Three white lapdogs, smelling of rich perfume, bellowed onto the balcony. I think I would have feared rats less.

I was grateful it was not my own face that was about to be gnawed off. Still, as the lamp was stowed on a pack Haytham carried, I was somewhat concerned with his success. "Close your eyes," I suggested.

"Why?"

"The suffering may be less that way."

"I am so glad I recruited you."

"But also, perhaps my fingers can guide yours . . ."

We tried it. He redoubled his efforts to stretch upward, and I undid a set of knots.

We pirouetted on one foot. We had more sway this way and were better able to avoid the dogs.

"Best stretch again," I said.

"Wait." He grabbed a wad of plant material, crushed it into a ball, and tossed it through a door.

The dogs all followed.

"Leftover material from the Cytherean Heliodrosia. They may think they are chasing a cat, or a steak, or an appropriate mate."

"Or your head."

"Or yours, in point of fact. All right, heave—"

With a crash that must have been painful, we were soon free. Haytham swaggered. I shivered. We closed the nearest door and headed up.

There were no festivities, but the upper stories were frequently used as an informal salon, and I was thus unsurprised to see artistic types I'd encountered now and then in the city. In Palmary the elite artist and the elite thief will sometimes share circles, because in our own ways we all owe our livings to the rich. Thus I and Haytham were able to chat our way through a few encounters, on our way to the poet we really wished to talk to.

And there she was. Previously I had only seen her from afar, reading her work aloud, or else crossing paths in ways that left us both in worse moods than before. I felt Haytham's heart race. That at least I could help with. I wished him calm thoughts, chief among them that there were many days ahead, and many women inhabiting them, and that to a greater or lesser degree everything would be All Right.

Thus calmed, Haytham was able to talk of this or that, avoiding any of the crudities I had previously brought to bear when encountering this poet.

Thus the three of us had a conversation better than any we'd had before. I found the poet quite approachable and unaffected (previously I'd thought her vain) and was quite enjoying being Haytham's auxiliary confidence.

Then it all went wrong. Enrapt by the poet's eyes, we did not quite understand the clicking hand gesture she suddenly made and the cooing sound that accompanied it.

Not until the white, perfumed beast jumped into her lap.

"Oh, dear—" we began, as it started yipping, attracting its companions.

We rose, making excuses, when the thing lunged out and snapped at us, tearing at the delicate threads of Haytham's "sifting" apparatus. In retrospect, I believe the beast wanted another taste of the same material Haytham's distraction ball was made of, and smelled it on us. It would not be the first time a human scheme was undone by canine scent.

Regardless, the damage had a peculiar effect. The specific illusion Haytham had arranged was undone, and a new one replaced it.

"You!" said the poet.

"Me?" said Haytham.

"You went to all this trouble—to see me?"

"Of course—"

"And not to steal?"

"Only a heart," Haytham said, the kind of line I could never deliver with alacrity, and he could never deliver without stammering. Together we pulled it off.

Then we ran for it.

On the way out we bumped into one of the guests, a charming young woman, though hardly the poet's equal. Her physical charms were somewhat more expansive than my poet's, and I was a trifle embarrassed for Haytham that he became tongue-tied with her in the doorway, wishing (he was loud about it) that he might become tongue-tied with her in reality. Had he no loyalty to his imaginary girlfriends?

In the contact, the rippling of the illusion was undone, and he again appeared as himself.

"Who," she gasped, "who are you?"

"I am the thief Imago Bone," he said, "disguised as the inventor Haytham. Would you like to ride in my flying machine?"

She was actually thinking about it, when I hissed to Haytham, "You will release me now."

"I can't possibly do that."

"You forget we are linked. I can make you whistle and click and summon those dogs."

"You wouldn't."

I exerted my will; he found himself making the hand gesture.

"Are you acting like I'm a dog?" the woman said, her voice a whole season colder.

"Not at all," he said smoothly, still enjoying my swagger. "This is how I remotely command my vessel. Now it is ready to hear a command phrase. By the ring of King Younus, you are released!"

As he said this he bundled up the plant fibers and the lamp and tossed them over the balcony.

I landed in my natural size with a number of lumps but free of inventors and dogs. I was not free of the memory of the poet.

The lamp never worked for me, so I left it on a museum doorstep. I did not encounter Haytham again, though of course I heard about him. He left a string of broken hearts behind, several attached to wealthy heiresses. He fled the city some months later. Now I know where he ended up.

As for the poet, well, maybe when I saw her again I had a bit more of that Mirabad smoothness about my speech. And maybe she liked me just a little better. For that, I am grateful to . . . Doctor Haytham.

"Thus," Bone concluded, "much though I admire Haytham's inventiveness, I dislike his use of women."

"I lack the context to quite understand this city-story, though I do recognize the antics of men and women. And I also think I know who your poet is."

"I hope I'll see her again."

"I wish that for you, corpse-man. Such a separation must be hard."

"Yes. Have you anyone, Northwing?"

"Now and again. Neither Steelfox nor Snow Pine's interest seems to lie in my direction, and the locals are somewhat . . . veiled."

"My sympathies."

"Bah. . . . You were right about the terrain."

Before them lay a chasm. Far below roared a river, its waters a swirling mix of green from minerals and white from rapids.

"Aiya," Bone said.

"You know, Bone, you can swear like them, but you'll never belong to Qiangguo."

"Who says I want to? Hm. The chasm's too wide to jump or bridge. Farther up we might manage, but it's rough climbing. Further down, we could eventually ford. But we'd be in the open."

"It's natural enough. A barbarian like you, awestruck by the fabled cities, that culture stretching back through time like an endless river. Now, following this river back could get us killed on the rocks. On the other hand, this would be a much earlier descent than we'd planned. Tough decision."

"We have cities, you know. Feh. Much as I long to descend, closer to where Gaunt must be, the heights beckon."

"I'll go have a look. And your cities are smelly villages beside the great places of Qiangguo."

"You're just trying to goad me! You don't even like cities! You've never been to ours!"

"So you think. A spirit-body gets around."

With that she was off, leaping among the boulders, ascending toward the nearest of the great waterfalls. Bone was glad none of the gleaming, crimson veins of rock occupied this southern side of the valley. He looked across Xembala, spotting some of those veins, tiny from this vantage, like the red in bloodshot eyes. He looked for a glimpse of the lamasery and thought once again he saw a golden flash upon a grand plateau at the valley's heart.

When he looked again across the chasm, he swore and dropped low. He crawled to a hidden nook between two boulders.

He saw three huge wooden constructions, flag-draped ropes between them. Each machine possessed a large arm and a dangling counterweight.

"What are you doing down here?" the squirrel said in his ear.

"Look over there."

"My. Not Karvak devices. They look like catapults from Qiangguo."

Bone nodded. "Or Kpalamaa, or the Eldshore. But the construction's a little odd." He squinted. "I see people in colorful garb moving between them. They're loading sacks onto the weapons."

"Interesting. When I try to see with the mind of a human, I do not witness catapults or figures."

"They're going to fire! How close are the others?"

"I've warned Steelfox already, Bone. They're taking cover. Nothing will—"

The strange catapults fired. Ammunition of what looked like flour sacks spun through the air and collided harmlessly with the rocky landscape.

"Ha," said Northwing.

"Wait," said Bone. "Look."

From the shattered sacks rose a cloud of green dust that encompassed the area, tendrils extending to the chasm.

"It's some sort of sleeping potion!" said Northwing. "Get out of here, Bone, we're already caught."

"But you can escape with me."

"No, you've forgotten . . . my body . . . back there . . ."

The squirrel twitched, looked this way and that, and its subsequent vocalizations were purely animal. It fled up the slope.

Bone ran after it. The terrain was too rough—and time too short—to let him crawl. He hopped along the boulder-tops, green dust chasing him. All his experience lived in his feet now. The catapults fired again.

Bone ducked under a sack that exploded in the rubble beside him. Green vapor filled half his vision.

There was only one, mad chance. He scrambled down the boulder on the wrong side, the chasm side.

He dropped.

Hanging there along the edge, he felt icy winds blasting through the fissure from the direction of the falls. As the green dust reached him, the wind whipped it away. He turned his head toward the cold slap of the air, breathed it in, taking as little of the green as possible.

More sacks burst nearby, in the rocks, on the cliff.

But in the end, he knew, they had him. His vision swam with color. Would the valley goddess protect him if he plunged into the water? Would she save him from drowning if he fell asleep on the way down?

His choices were few. As the catapults creaked back into firing position, he hauled himself up the edge, curled up beside a boulder, and pretended to sleep.

Soon illusion was truth.

He found himself dragged upon a litter, and he'd the presence of mind to keep his eyes shut. It was warmer, and he heard an unfamiliar language and also a continuous roar. He parted his lips and tasted waterfall spray. Motion, now. They were ascending. The light beyond his eyelids darkened, the air warmed further, the roar became muffled.

Fight? No. Wait.

Light and sound, fresh waterfall roar.

Darkness and a dimming of sound.

And again light and noise.

This repeated many times, until there was bright light with a sense of openness, the songs of many birds, the chatter of many people, including piping voices of children.

Bone opened his eyes.

He and his companions had been conveyed by many figures in bright robes. They'd entered the vast courtyard of a lamasery filled with fruit trees and fountains, a whole village within the walls. A rocky promontory on the far side sheltered a fortress with three sweeping levels, split in twain by the rush of water descending a canal cut from a vast extension of the southern cliffs.

The water flowed through this gigantic park until plunging into a great pit near at hand.

A number of individuals in orange robes were approaching—wizened, bald, of both genders. Bone knew an opportunity for a dramatic entrance when he saw it.

It was surely the antithesis of a thiefly approach. He leapt up from his litter, bowed before the elders, and said to none of them in particular, "Mentor John, I presume."

CHAPTER 23

MALDAR KHAN

If one was traveling to the palace of enlightenment, Gaunt reflected, a balloon was hardly the worst way to go. Even surrounded by guards ready to push you out.

In the company of Lady Jewelwolf, her Wind-Tamer, six warriors, and Arthur Quilldrake, the flying ger took Gaunt over the great river and its flanking emerald forests, bright-plumed birds and rainbow-hued butterflies rising as they approached.

She turned away from the porthole to look beyond her two minders at the fiery cauldron tended by the Wind-Tamer. Charstalker eyes glared back. In the flickering light, Crypttongue hung from the bamboo rafters on the opposite side. Another strange artifact hung nearby, a disc of bronze big as a dinner plate. It spun with the pitching of the ger, one side displaying stylized images of the constellations as named in Qiangguo, the other a smooth polished surface. It might have been an ordinary bronze mirror, but its prominence suggested otherwise.

Quilldrake stood beside it. Like many a man, he assumed that a woman's glance directed near him was surely directed *at* him. This appeared to make him uncomfortable. He stepped around the fiery cauldron, the Charstalker's own gaze following him, until he stood near Gaunt.

"I can explain," was the first thing he said.

"I feel certain you can," Gaunt said.

"There seemed no other hope, but to ally with strength."

"History echoes with similar words."

"Indeed! I'm not in this world to shape countries and empires, but to enjoy myself. I command my own ship. But even a captain must follow the wind."

"Whom would you throw overboard, 'captain'?"

"Uncalled for! No one's died as a result of my actions. Can you say the same?"

Gaunt could not answer.

"Jewelwolf seeks what we seek," Quilldrake said, "and she's willing to cut us in."

"Us?"

"I'm willing to consider our arrangement still good, bygones be bygones. After all, it was you, your husband, and Widow Zheng who ran off with this Mad Katta. Perhaps he gave you no choice either, but in any event he's long gone. Where are Bone and Zheng, anyway?"

"Elsewhere in the valley. We were—separated."

"Pity."

"Where are we going exactly?"

"The great volcano at the eastern end. Having observed the map fragments that repaired this balloon, and in consultation with her partners . . ." Quilldrake glanced at the bronze mirror. ". . . Lady Jewelwolf believes the Iron Moths are there."

"Some of the stories spoke of a volcanic haven."

"Yes. I think we are on the right course."

"Quilldrake. You say 'we,' but where is your partner?"

"Ah. A delicate problem. You see, the Karvaks aren't entirely unified. The politics are fascinating. Under their mother's reign, each sister had a semi-independent realm. But with the election of a new Grand Khan, everything changes. Jewelwolf got wind of the ironsilk hunt and crossed the desert to take command of a balloon Lady Steelfox left at Hvam. With that craft she came here to dispute her sister's authority. You can do that if you're the Grand Khan's wife."

"I see."

"She arrived just as Steelfox was attempting to capture you. But I believe you were a little preoccupied."

"It was a long day."

"Long story short, Flint and I ended up separated, one with each sister. Each dared the CloudScar. Jewelwolf still has a total of three balloons patched up and flying in this valley, but Steelfox's balloon hasn't been seen. I'm uncertain Steelfox and Flint survived. Likewise Snow Pine."

"If so," said a new voice, "it's no less than what my sister deserved."

Lady Jewelwolf stood beside them. She wore a heavy blue coat, and her hair was coiled above her head and shiny with animal fat; yet although her appearance was strange, Gaunt was struck by something universal: the assurance of one born to power.

"You are speaking Roil," Gaunt couldn't help but notice, "the language of the Eldshore."

"I have a gift for alien tongues. It has been an aid in securing allies and arcane power."

"You are a sorceress?"

"To a small degree. The true value of my training is that unlike most warriors I do not fear magic but embrace it. I have allies among the wizards of many lands. I know what magic can do for the Karvak nation—far more than Steelfox's feeble 'natural philosophy.' Though I must acknowledge her tricks have their uses. If only she would admit the same of mine."

"She does not approve of magic?" Gaunt said.

She thought Quilldrake was making warning eyes at her.

Jewelwolf made a fist. "She is a hypocrite. She has her mind-bound hawk, her barbaric taiga shaman, her inventor who binds Charstalkers to make his balloons fly. But she balks at the great magics. She will not accept human sacrifice."

"Weak of her," Gaunt ventured.

"I am glad you agree. She is like our father in that respect, for although a great war leader, he was unable to understand that terror is a necessity for rule. Squeamish, both of them. My husband and I have no such flaws."

"What are your plans?"

"As Quilldrake said, we will claim the lair of the Iron Moths. It seems impractical to establish a foothold in Xembala—yet. Therefore we will seize as many moths and as much ironsilk as possible. In the steppes we will establish our own center of iron sericulture."

"With a cut for us," Quilldrake added.

"Of course. If you serve me well."

"Do the Moths not require great heat?" Gaunt asked.

"I have a solution for that, thanks to my allies."

"Who are they?"

"Ah. They are great wizards and leaders. Together we will lead the world into its next age. There is the troll-jarl of the Bladed Isles, he who commands the stuff of the rock itself. There is the greatest of kleptomancers, who steals knowledge and power from everywhere and knows many secrets. And there is the dark prince of the Eldshore, he who dares perilous magic in search of power."

Gaunt felt unease in her gut, and it was not just from the balloon's motion. "They sound mighty indeed," she said. They also sounded familiar. It was not a welcome familiarity. "Forgive me, great one," Gaunt said. "I am exhausted from my ordeal."

Jewelwolf blinked. "Very well. You may sleep in this spot."

Gaunt curled up, feeling rather like a newly acquired dog. She sensed Quilldrake lingering near her for a while; then he sighed and shifted away.

For a time unmeasured, she did sleep. She dreamed of vast structures upon the Earthe, buried in the Earthe, carved into the Earthe, through which magic flowed. She heard the Earthe howling in pain at the rearrangements its tiny inhabitants had made within it. She heard its sorrow, shading era by era into rage.

She woke up to the sound of Jewelwolf snarling, "Where is she? How could she escape?"

Gaunt looked up. Karvak soldiers were jabbing spears into every part of the ger. She stood and waved, and no one noticed her.

She smiled.

Jewelwolf said, "Quilldrake! Have you aided her escape?"

"Hardly! And I have no inkling how she accomplished it. I will say that she's a tricky one. Perhaps you should consult your friends."

Jewelwolf faced the bronze mirror, passing her hand over the cosmic images of the inscribed face, turning it toward the smooth. Light flickered within, light that had nothing to do with the fire from the Charstalker.

Yet it was the Charstalker who caught Gaunt's attention.

"*You,*" came a voice from the fire. "*Meat. I see you.*"

No one else in the ger responded.

"*They cannot hear me,*" growled the Charstalker. "*Only you.*"

"Are you going to give me away?" Gaunt said.

"*Not if you help me. I want to bring this balloon down.*"

"Is that something you can arrange?"

"*With your help. You retain a limited ability to interact with matter, especially*" *matter possessed of magic. Use your sword. Use it against the symbols upon this cauldron. I will then depart this craft."*

"Um. Will that not result in a crash? And my death?"

"Look out an eastern-facing porthole."

She slipped past where Jewelwolf's mirror was flashing with light, the colors resolving into a fractured image, a different face in each fragment. One was a thin man with a look of perpetual exhaustion, another a thick man whose skin was the texture of clay, a third a well-formed man with a handsome bearing and a rakish grin. The last was a robed woman with skin like snow. Gaunt crept, in case these powers could somehow perceive her.

Out the porthole she beheld a great, green-crowned plateau. The ruins of a vast lamasery covered it, and many tents crowded beside the rubble. A river surged down a rocky extension of the cliffs and onto the plateau, before disappearing down a vast pit.

"'In Xembala did Mentor John a lofty lamasery raise . . .'" she whispered.

"*Yes,*" said the Charstalker. "*You see it. If the balloon falls now, you may survive. It is your best hope of escape.*"

Once again, Gaunt reflected, she was being offered the sword and the power to commit mayhem. Once again, it was a tempting offer.

Voices emerged from the mirror.

A whispery voice: "Events crowd my mind, of wonder and woe. Why do you interrupt me?"

A gravelly voice: "I am engaged in severing limbs. It is the best part of my day. This had best be good."

A smooth, measured voice: "Gentlemen. The lady never interrupts us idly. What do you wish, my dear?"

The fourth individual was silent.

"I have a prisoner," said Jewelwolf. "One Persimmon Gaunt. Somehow she has vanished, or else made herself incorporeal. I would be grateful for your insights."

Whispery: "That name is known to me."

Gravelly: "It means nothing to me. You should have chopped off her arms. That slows a wizard down, you know."

Smooth: "I know that name as well. She is no wizard. She is a thief who styles herself a poet. How—"

"The how is of no importance," Jewelwolf said, "only where she is now."

Smooth: "I had thought she was here in the West. Fascinating."

Gravelly: "The Axe of Sternmark tells me she is near you, Karvak."

Whispery: "The troll-jarl is correct. For a price I will tell you her precise location, and how to subdue her."

Still the snow-white woman was silent.

Jewelwolf's voice was cold. "Price? We are partners."

Whispery: "You would not give away a wheelship on a whim, would you now? Nor I this information."

"What is your price?"

"Persimmon Gaunt's son."

Gaunt seized Crypttongue.

The white woman in the mirror spoke. "Fool! She is there beside you!"

At once the world seemed to whirl about her as the Karvak guards shouted and Jewelwolf sucked in her breath. She would have only a moment—

The whispery voice said, "Tell her I will reunite her family, no conditions—"

She ached to hear the rest, but her arms had already betrayed her.

She brought Crypttongue's blade down upon the cauldron.

An inscription was sliced in twain, and the Charstalker bellowed, "*AGAIN! AGAIN!*"

She swung until the cauldron shattered into fragments, and the Charstalker laughed its way into the heavens.

Blazing skyward it passed through the canvas of the balloon, burning a gap into its top.

They plummeted, out of control, until they smashed into something yielding, something that splashed and roared.

For a moment the ger was motionless; in the next it shifted backward, relative to its previous motion . . .

They were on the river the old poem named Aleph, plunging toward what might have been a sunless sea.

Still clutching Crypttongue, Gaunt scrambled out the ger's opening and swam. She wanted to help Quilldrake, but she had no way of aiding him. When she reached the grass of the shore, she was glad to see him sputtering nearby. There too was Jewelwolf, and one surviving soldier, clutching his mistress's bronze mirror.

Gaunt coughed and looked up. There stood a group of monks and nuns in orange robes, a wizened bunch, yet with a lively air about them. She saw expressions of compassion . . . and perhaps a glint of amusement?

She raised herself to one knee, sensing that these people, at least, could perceive her.

She turned and saw the balloon, and the Silk Map with it, washed down the great pit. Strangely, she felt a weight lifted.

Turning back she asked on impulse, "I don't suppose any of you is named Mentor John?"

Imago Bone heard cymbals and horns sounding in the lamasery heights, as if this were a visit of state. Metallic clangs alternated with a sort of shimmering sound as musicians rapped the lower edge of one cymbal against the other, then the top edge, back and forth in an accelerating rhythm, then back to the short clangs. Meanwhile the horns sounded notes lower than any he'd ever heard, long blasts that made his teeth vibrate. It was a sound appropriate for the bright cliffs and the rushing river and the abyss. For a moment it was as though a burst of wind accompanied the music, and a great splash within the water, and a sound like the collapsing of a vast amount of fabric. Yet he saw nothing to explain these things.

The elders before Bone even shifted somewhat, facing him at an angle so that they could watch the river as well.

An ancient woman nodded to him. "I have been called Mentor John."

Bone had met elderly people who resembled deserted ruins of their former selves. He'd known others who seemed animated within those ruins, as the people of a once-mighty city might make merry amid cherished monuments. This woman had neither aspect. Rather her face implied that youth was merely the stepping-stone to the grand state implied by her wrinkles and spots. Age was triumph, not loss. He read his own perplexity at this paradox in the amusement of her eyes. He looked away. He felt young.

"My name is Imago Bone, Mentor."

He heard only a single indrawn breath, but the music ceased.

"I am glad you have come, Imago Bone," the elder said. "I apologize for the rough manner of your arrival, though others have fared worse in their time." Again, the hint of amusement. "You have revived more quickly than the others."

"I took pains to inhale less of the green dust."

"And you take pride in your ingenuity. No, I do not mock you! It is one of the less destructive ways to be proud. At this moment I too am taking a certain pleasure in my craft."

"How so, Mentor?"

"You may call me this if you wish, but know that 'Mentor John' was a distortion of my title 'Maldar Khan,' itself a title bestowed by Karvak exiles long ago. Still, my true title is Teacher, which I suppose 'Mentor' approximates."

"Do you have a name?"

"Names are relatively unimportant here, but I am often called Chodak. It comes from the Plateau of Geam and means 'one who spreads the great teaching.' Although we and the Plateau differ in many respects, it seems a fine name." She laughed. "So, you know, in a way my name is Teacher-Teacher."

"I can imagine you in a classroom of children, all calling you that."

"Indeed! And at times I think of the valley as being full of my children. It was in a different life that I gained the name Maldar Khan. I have returned here many times."

"This is a difficult notion for me."

"That someone would name me a khan?"

"That people can be born, die, and return."

"I understand."

"But never mind that. Whatever happens after death will happen. For now, I come seeking your help."

"If it is in my power to grant it, Imago Bone, I will."

Some instinct told Bone to hold nothing back. In the presence of this person he felt accepted and understood, in a way he'd only known with Persimmon Gaunt.

"I am on a quest to bring Iron Moths to Wondrous Lady Monkey. I, my wife, and our closest friend are determined to succeed in this task."

"I understand. But would you not prefer to find your children?"

Wet and sneezing, Persimmon Gaunt rose as the elderly woman said, "I have been many things. I think Mentor John may have been one of them."

Upon the walls of the ruined monastery, a few trumpeters sounded eerie, deep notes, as a handful of cymbal-players clanged a welcome. The music was stirring, but too dim to trouble their conversation. "I've been looking for you," Gaunt said. "But first, I must ask for sanctuary."

"That is in my power to grant, Persimmon Gaunt, and fresh clothing besides."

Gaunt stared. There was something in the manner of this old woman that made Gaunt feel understood and soothed. Gaunt's paternal grandmother had been kind to her as a girl, and in a childhood full of scolding adults, Nanna was water in the desert. The lama before Gaunt was like that. It was unnerving to feel such a connection so quickly. Under other circumstances she might have suspected magic was involved.

And indeed, it was hard not to imagine sorcery dwelled here. Gaunt had the impression the elders were considering an unseen audience upon the grass, as though ghosts observed them all.

As Jewelwolf and Quilldrake approached, Gaunt said, "I need sanctuary from them. The woman has invaded your land. The man is a treasure hunter who would rob your land."

"And you, you are neither invader nor treasure hunter?"

"No." The lama's eyes made it impossible for Gaunt not to say more. "I am a poet and, I must concede, a thief, but I will not rob you today. For I come as a mother. There is something in your land that a mighty Sage wants. If my husband and I can give it to her, then we, and our best friend, will get our children back."

"I know something of this matter, for knowing what transpires in Xembala is a considerable portion of my work. You will have sanctuary, poet, thief, and mother. Your traveling companions will have hospitality, but you will have sanctuary."

Gaunt saw how the other elders took Quilldrake and Jewelwolf by the hand. Quilldrake bowed and accepted the courtesy; Jewelwolf shook it off. But both proceeded into the ruins.

"You live in this fallen lamasery?" Gaunt asked.

"To my eyes it is not fallen but rather in the midst of its journey into a new state. As are we all. You will be comfortable, I assure you. Let us go."

"Do you not wish to know the thing I seek? Before you accept me as a guest? For I would claim some of the Iron Moths."

"I have guessed as much. If you will come with me, you may understand how it is I know. And you may see something you long for."

Bone followed the procession of lamas into a strange garden, where fruit trees of many kinds rose beside stone basins attended by statues of the Undetermined and the Thresholders. Chodak stopped beside one such, as the others moved on, bearing Bone's unconscious companions.

"They will be safe?" Bone asked.

"They will." Chodak smiled. "You have had few friends, Imago Bone. You are concerned for them. And even for associates."

"I'm nostalgic for friendly faces."

"You are particularly protective of women."

"I do not know what you mean."

She smiled. "You have considerable desire, yet you are utterly loyal to your wife, she who is truly the other half of you. So you channel these stray feelings into concern. It is admirable in its own way, though it can lead you to recklessness."

Bone did not much like these observations. "You spoke of children."

Chodak nodded. She blew upon the waters of the basin, chanting in low tones.

The waters reflected the sky at first, but the image changed. The valley of Xembala rippled and faded, and now Bone beheld something he'd seen only twice before but had never forgotten—a fairytale mountainscape, pine forests covering the peaks, with one mountain bearing a monastery quite unlike the one that surrounded him now. This one was both freshly maintained and partially ruined, overgrown with trees and yet brightly painted.

"The scroll," Bone said. "The scroll that holds our children. But is this my memory, or . . ."

"This is a recent Now," Chodak said, "or a Now soon to come."

A boy and a girl sat upon the edge of a cliff. Occasionally the boy would throw pebbles into the void. The girl was studying her bandaged left hand.

The boy looked like a pale Westerner of perhaps twelve years. He possessed dark red hair and a lanky frame. The girl, a daughter of Qiangguo, was of similar age. She was the very image of Snow Pine, though there was something in the set of her jaw that reminded him of Snow Pine's cocky husband, Flybait.

Bone said, "It's Innocence." He had trouble continuing. "And A-Girl-Is-A-Joy."

"I did not know their names," Chodak said in a gentle voice. "But the pool can reveal what forces are acting upon you. These two are your sun and moon."

"So much time has passed for them."

"I sense you are correct."

"Even if we succeed, we will have missed their childhoods."

"That appears true. Though they are not adults yet."

"Is it possible . . . to hear them?"

Chodak nodded and chanted low.

The girl was saying, "It grows stronger, Innocence."

"Why talk about that?" the boy said. "Let's talk about cloud kingdoms. We could talk about Crazy Animal Country, or War-Cat Kingdom, or Horse Queendom. You can pick."

"I don't feel like playing those games today." A-Girl-Is-A-Joy frowned at her bandaged hand. "I don't think it's just a scrape. I think there's something strange about it."

"I've been thinking of a brand-new cloud kingdom," Innocence said. "One with humans in it. I call it Rendworld, because it's been broken into many peaks, each linked by bone bridges. It used to have a queen. But the insane king of that place returned after many years and took her with him. Now it's all lawless, with different warlords. There's a tree warlord, a boulder warlord, a moss warlord, a temple cauldron warlord, and lots of others. It will take champions fighting with sticks weeks to defeat them all. What do you think?"

"Walking Stick says he has no idea what it means, but I think he's worried. Like there's a power reaching out for me."

"Like the one reaching out for me?"

"I don't know."

"What about your dreams? I've been dreaming about lakes beside green mountains, and vast brown rivers, and an ocean surging beside a city with more people than I've ever seen awake."

"I have dreams . . . I dream about a land of rocky islands, with cliffs as big as this but dropping to a gray stormy sea. Sometimes I see people . . . they look a lot like you, Innocence, except more crazy. Proud, with armor and weapons and colorful thick clothing, and complicated hair. The men have beards, the women wear their hair long. I want to know more about them, but then I see them fighting, the men mostly, but a few women too. They hack and hack, turning seas and forests red." She rubbed her forehead with her hands. "I think I'm going crazy. Maybe I belong in Crazy Animal Country."

Innocence looked confused, worried. He reached out to her, pulled his hand back.

"I don't know how," he said, "but maybe the greater world's reaching out to you as it reaches out to me."

"I'm glad there's at least someone who understands," she said.

"I don't really understand. I don't even understand me."

"Close enough."

"It's starting to rain."

"Again? Let's get back to the monastery."

"We can try to ambush Leaftooth."

"That sounds fun . . ."

The scene began to waver. Bone could still see the children, but superimposed upon them was Xembala's sky.

"Chodak!" he said, wondering if an old harm could be undone. "Can the pool send me through?"

"No, Persimmon Gaunt," Chodak said. "To send you there is beyond the pool's power, and mine."

Gaunt was still clutching the edge of the weathered pool with its statue of the Undetermined, weathered smooth as the surface of the pool with its perfect reflection of the Xembalan sky.

But she had seen what she'd seen.

"Where?" she said. "Where in the sea is the scroll? If you can tell me that much, Chodak, we can do the rest. We can mount an expedition, find magical gear to let us breathe water. Nothing will stop us if you can tell us where."

"I lack that knowledge. The pool can search your karmic ties. It cannot seek a place in the ocean, for you have no such tie. Or at least no more than any other creature in this world. I regret that I have no greater boon."

She lowered her head. "I have missed his childhood. He is well on his way to becoming a young man. And he is burdened, I can see it. Bone's decision deprived Innocence of a parent. He is essentially an orphan."

"You are angry at your husband."

"Would you not be? Have you ever been a mother?"

"I feel sure that I have, though it was not in this life. Just as I have been a father."

"I do not even know what to say to that."

"You do not need to accept the existence of my previous lives, Persimmon Gaunt. In a sense, they do not matter. For even were this my first time in the world, I would still be buffeted by the karmic influences that affected my family, and which prevailed in the time of my birth. Only the Undetermined, the Seekers, and the Thresholders have won free of such determining forces."

"Chodak, I sense you mean well. I can feel it. But speaking with you and other followers of the Undetermined . . . it's like arriving late to a party of poets who have just read and discussed a half-dozen works and their authors. I know I have missed something valuable, but it is unfair for you to expect me to comprehend."

"That is a fair point. What I wish to say is that even if I had been a mother in this life, I would not necessarily understand your feelings. For my circumstances are my own, regardless. After all, it is not everyone whose child has been lost in a pocket reality."

Gaunt could only laugh. "No, it is not."

"Likewise, my not having been a mother is not necessarily an impassible wall to understanding. For we all share certain traits. And I too experience anger."

"Have you wanted to hurt someone you loved?"

"That sensation is not unknown to me."

"Aren't you an enlightened person, beyond such feelings?"

"I think you know the answer. It is my office to embody, as well as I can, the attributes of one of the great Thresholders, she who is known in Qiangguo as the goddess of mercy. But if she is the wine, I am a cracked bottle. Through meditation and invocation, I attempt to caulk the worst of the cracks. It is a daily struggle. I, too, know rage. I must accept mine, as you must accept yours."

"But it is a vile feeling. If I let it out, I hurt Bone. If I hold it in, it hurts me."

"To challenge your own anger is to wage a heroic struggle."

"As long as I'm committed to the quest, I can manage to not think about it . . . mostly. But I think we needed the quest so badly, we were too quick to trust Monkey. Swan's blood! We've been wandering the desert on the strength of a rock-creature's promises, some old legends, and a torn dress."

"Dress?"

"If you cannot send me to Innocence," Bone said, "can you find me someone who can?"

"The pool could find such a one, if their karmic connection with you were strong enough."

"But such a person would likely be someone we already know." Bone scratched his chin. "Well. I know many people. Try. Please."

Chodak looked troubled, but she chanted and made a waving motion of her arm.

In the water Bone beheld the cavern within Five-Toe Peak.

The Great Sage herself was there, still trapped, whistling. She seemed to cock an ear, look this way and that, and crane her head to look directly at Bone and Chodak.

"Hey!" came the rumbling voice. "Couldn't you knock?"

"Ah," said Bone. "Hello?"

"It's the Rat!" Monkey chortled. "Have you found what I asked?"

"We're working on it. The Silk Map has led us to Xembala."

"Really, now! Good, good . . ."

"I have been wondering a thing. I have been asking myself if you can, or will, really honor your part of our bargain. Now I know this much: you can."

"You don't trust me." Monkey sounded sad. "Well, really, who would? Hello there, Thresholder! That is a Thresholder, isn't it?"

Chodak said, "I am the high lama of Xembala."

"Right—you guys. You borrow a lot of practice from the Plateau of Geam. Instead of just meditating your way to the Absolute, you kind of mentally project your way there by visualizing higher powers."

"We diverge from the Plateau in many respects."

"It's hard for a simple monkey to get."

"I would be glad to explain it to you, should you ever wish to journey west."

"Oh, don't worry about it, lama. Your doctrine isn't my problem. My problem is a mountain on top of me. Until I deal with that, I'm not even making a journey to relieve myself."

"I wish you luck."

"Bone," said Monkey, "I figure you'll want to be getting my delivery to me soon. I can only keep myself awake so long."

"You said six months. It's been perhaps two."

"It was an estimate, friend Rat."

"Stay awake, Great Sage. Or I swear, I will find a way to wake you up."

"Be careful. If you wake someone rudely, you should be prepared for the reaction."

"You be careful yourself. How can you truly threaten a man on the verge of losing everything?"

Monkey frowned. "I think we're done here."

She sneezed, and the scene disappeared. The pool was just a pool.

Chodak said, "I would be wary of that one's anger."

"Demigods. Wizards. Monsters. Toothaches. Life is full of trouble. You can't flee from it all."

"Indeed not. I merely question your means of confronting these sufferings. A good heart and an analytic mind can accomplish much that a dagger and a treasure map cannot. Come to think of it, you spoke of a Silk Map?"

"So that is the long and the short of it," said Gaunt, "and the hem and the sleeve of it. The Silk Map, and some scraps of legends, got us here."

"I may have heard something of these matters."

"Can you help us, lama, in any way? Not to talk me out of my anger, nor deflect me from my quest, but to help me in my journey. My journey, not yours, not the path of the Undetermined."

"I understand what you are saying. And yes, I can help you on your quest, and I will not talk you out of your anger. I will show you the way to your husband."

"He is nearby?"

"He is very near. We are seeing to his well-being even now, for his arrival was close in time to your own. Let me show you."

Chodak chanted and moved her arms in complex spirals. The pool showed a new scene.

Imago Bone sat upon a golden couch in a room of red mandalas, red woodwork, red tapestries. Attending him with grapes and wine and bread and cheese were three nubile women of Xembala. These were clad in bright silks that, while not actually scandalous by Gaunt's standards, were rather more revealing than necessary.

Leaning against Bone was Snow Pine, laughing at some unheard joke he made.

"I see he is unharmed," Gaunt said. She paused. "Our friend too. I am happy they found each other."

Snow Pine, grinning, nuzzled against Bone's shoulder. Gaunt's husband looked as pleased as a cat who'd caught a bird mid-leap, fallen three stories, and landed on his feet.

The scene faded.

"Yes," Gaunt said, her fist clenched. "It is good they are well. Very good."

"You may enter the lamasery and speak with any monk or nun you find," Chodak said. "Many speak the language of Qiangguo. Describe the room, and they can bring you there."

"I'm certain I can give a good description."

"I lack Gaunt's skill at tale-telling," Bone said, "but that is the gist of our adventures with the Silk Map."

"A great ordeal."

"It was necessary."

"You feel considerable guilt, Imago Bone, at leaving your child behind."

"Should I not?" Bone stared into the pool and thus into the churning, golden sky. "It was selfish at the core. Both my son and my wife had a claim on me. But shouldn't I have remained with he who was young and therefore at more risk?"

"As I understand it, you were reasonably sure of his safety, not at all of hers."

"But that is not really why. I sought Gaunt for me, Chodak. I had lost her, briefly found her again—and now she was to be snatched away once more. I could not accept that. And now I pay the price."

"Your quest."

"If it fails, I lose her. Maybe I lose her in any case. For I have seen my son, halfway to manhood. When she sees him, how she lost his childhood, how can she forgive me?"

"That loss would have occurred regardless, would it not?"

"She will also remember I could have been with him."

"Thus, guilt. But also, fear."

"I cannot lose her. The only one who has ever truly understood me. Without her I'd be lonely in a harem."

"She helps you to understand yourself."

"Yes . . . yes, I suppose that's true. I am . . . complicated."

"Are not we all?"

"Yet not everyone is a century old in a young body. Not everyone has spent decades thieving, or been a conversation partner to angels of death." He chuckled. "I am acquainted with two forms of underworld."

"Fair enough. To find one who can understand is a great blessing. Do you wish to see her?"

"I—of course! What a fool I am. Babbling when I could be seeking. Yes!"

Again Chodak chanted and waved. The pool rippled.

There was a room of gold, suffused with sunlight. Persimmon Gaunt stood there in a saffron robe, garbed as a nun of Xembala. She was speaking with a group of young children, much younger than Innocence or A-Girl-Is-A-Joy. The boys and girls laughed at something Gaunt said, and she laughed too, and hugged one. There was a radiance about her face, a pure bliss that Bone felt he should be glad to witness. Yet gladness was not his emotion.

CHRIS WILLRICH   357

"What . . . what is she doing?"

"It would appear she has decided to take up the robe."

Bone coughed. "She what?"

"She will have to explain her own reasons, of course. But when she came to us, I showed her what I showed you just now: your son approaching manhood. I know the vision shook her."

"Enough to abandon her son? We are on a quest . . ."

"We are all on a quest, Imago Bone, to understand existence and to win free of the brokenness that characterizes it. You may find your answers in seeking your lost son. But she, perhaps, has realized she will find it elsewhere. Perhaps in the instruction of young children. She could teach language, poetry, geography . . ."

"But . . . all this time, she has blamed me for abandoning him. And what was it all about in the end? Not her son as such, but her mothering instincts? And now she rejects him because he is a baby no longer?"

"Only the Undetermined, the Seekers, and the Thresholders are truly free of karmic burdens—or instincts, as you say. The desire to care for a small child is a powerful one."

"Is that all I was to her, in the end? A means of securing such a child? And now to become a teacher, a nun, is sufficient for her?"

"Nuns of our order can marry, Imago Bone, or remain married—"

"For what? When loyalty to individuals no longer matters, what is the point of marriage? Where is she? I need to speak with her."

"If you enter the lamasery, most anyone can show you to that room."

"Fine!"

And Bone was off, so intent upon his goal he took little notice when Chodak said something peculiar.

"Xia," the lama said to the pool. "Show me Xia."

Gaunt had never explored such a vast building as the lamasery of Xembala. There had been great cities, of course. And there had been magical places that gave the impression of immensity, though she couldn't trust the perceptions she'd experienced in such structures. The lamasery, even falling into ruin, impressed her with a sense of generations of folk intent upon a search for enlightenment. Though she understood neither the people nor the project, she did have a feeling for ruins. This was a place she could respect.

It was good to have something she could respect.

The directions from the monk she'd confronted (he'd raised an eyebrow at the tone of her voice but had not commented upon it) were clear enough. At the far end of this gallery, tiger-striped with sunlight cutting through the gaps, she would turn left, then right, then right, and there would be Bone.

She did not know if she preferred to find him with Snow Pine or "alone."

"Swan help me," she said to herself, "when all's said and done, men are just men, aren't they?"

Bone had abandoned their son—her son—and for what? Because he'd calculated there'd be no women within the scroll?

She entered the red chamber. Bone stood there alone, looking out a window at the great northern cliffs with their waterfalls and veins of ruby rock. There was a contemplative smirk upon his face, such as he often wore when planning heists.

"Why, Gaunt!"

"Bone. You are looking well. And Snow Pine is too, I'm sure."

"She is! She'll be glad to see you."

"No doubt. So. Were you planning to make her Number Two Wife? Or were you even going to give me that much dignity?"

"I—"

"Oh, don't even hide it, Bone. Honestly, I'm less disappointed with you than with myself. I should have seen it long ago, but I've been so distracted by my oh-so-knowledgeable yet oh-so-young-looking rogue. It is so obvious now. You do love your younger women, do you not?"

"Gaunt, don't talk like this."

"So it all disappears if you don't talk? Maybe we should be talking to Snow Pine. How will she feel when she's just a few years older and you're on the hunt again? But you know, Imago, even that's not what makes me angriest. What's worse is that all this time I thought Innocence mattered to you. I thought you genuinely cared what happened to your son. But what really motivated you was staying with your women. Because you don't care about family at all, just the nighttime tumbles that lead to family. And once the journey gets too difficult, why, you'll just be gone, won't you?"

"You're not yourself."

"Oh, but you are so completely yourself, it's like you've been cloaked all this time. So many feints and disguises. I'm done with skulking in the shadows, Imago Bone. I will walk in the light now. You're lucky I don't leave you bleeding."

As she turned to go, he said, "Why not, then?"

A dagger clattered beside her feet. She stopped.

"Why not enact in deeds what you've painted in words?" he demanded. "You claim to be done with shadows and disguises. What are words but disguises, poet? For once in your life step out of my shadow and commit some deeds. Take a piece out of me, if that's what you want."

"I will not give you the satisfaction."

She took a step.

"Then I know you for a coward. I'm ashamed I kept you so long. You know, Snow Pine may be younger than you, but at least she acts. She is more a real woman than you will ever be, coward."

In a single motion she was hardly aware of, Gaunt was advancing in his direction, dagger in hand.

"Call me that again," she said. "Go on."

"Why?" he sneered. "It is just a word, poet."

"Here's a poem, thief," she snarled, and lunged.

Down the gleaming, polished hallway with its banners and statues, all the way to the end, then right, left, left . . .

Bone strode into the yellow room and beheld Gaunt raising a giggling Xembalan boy into the sunlight, a beatific look upon her face. A charming boy, no doubt, worthy of love.

But not theirs.

"Gaunt."

She turned—and it would have been a great wrong to say she showed no joy at his appearance. As she set the boy down, releasing him to run about the chamber, Bone could see it: she loved him still. Within that love, however, he caught a flicker of regret. Something in her had changed. The keen blade of her mind had been beaten into a ploughshare. Perhaps there was honor in that, but only if the choice were really hers.

"Bone. Imago. Swan be praised. I'm so relieved."

They embraced. He ached to hold her, and more than hold her. But he felt as if he lacked the right, as if he needed to locate her father and ask permission. They withdrew, holding hands.

"Can you truly swear by the Swan," he said, afraid to ask more urgent questions, "wearing that robe?"

"The Xembalans do not deny the Swan," she said. "They recognize many ways to the Absolute, and they honor Swanisle's goddess as an embodiment of mercy."

"Gaunt. Would you truly abandon Innocence?"

She shut her eyes, breathed in, breathed out. "I knew you'd find it hard to understand. I saw him, Imago."

"I too."

"My head had contemplated the flow of time within the scroll, but my heart had not quite believed it. Not until I saw Innocence and A-Girl-Is-A-Joy in the pool. I realized then that the attempt was a vain one. Oh, not because it was doomed, Imago—you and I are resourceful people, and there's little we can't do. But time had already snatched my baby away. He would be a stranger, not someone I'd shared the years with."

"Stranger or not, Persimmon, he's your blood. Our blood."

"Blood. That's alley talk, boondocks talk."

"Real talk."

"This is a higher place, a higher calling."

"It's a long fall from here, yes."

"Be serious, Bone. For a time you turned my head, made me a giddy youth again. I could conquer all! But I am growing up now. I want a family, not the dream of something lost. Here, I think I could make one."

"Perhaps thieving has rubbed off on you, if now you're planning to steal children."

"Don't be absurd. You and I could make a child—the right way, this time, with a true community to support us, and it."

"That is it? You wish to abandon Innocence?"

"You have the gall to accuse me of that? It's not I who left him there."

He looked away. "I know you've been angry. I confess I've sometimes wondered if we shouldn't simply start anew. I ask, who would blame us? But I've seen him now, heard him speak. He is haunted, Persimmon. He has friends, I believe. But he could use family. We are the only ones who can give him that."

"What about what I need, Bone? I want what was taken from me—the chance to know a child, through all his growing years."

"I see. And if I go without you?"

"I will mourn you. But I will carry on. There are men here. I've seen them out this window. Men who work an honest living. Men who are dependable. Men who have genuine lives."

"You say these things to torment me."

"I say them because they are true. We've had too little truth, Imago Bone. Only dreams and fancies that turn to nightmares. If you can finally be a man, my love, you can be my man. But I have no more time for the boy who never grew up."

She turned her back on him and commenced a song with the children.

Before he knew it, a dagger trembled in his hand.

Gaunt lunged—and at the last moment stayed her hand.

Bone's dagger was out now, and he snarled at her, "Do it, weakling! Do it!"

But she could not. Something was wrong here. Perhaps at his worst Bone might act in this way, but he was growing more and more like a mask, not a man.

There were shadowy shapes in the red room, barely glimpsed. They had proportions of two adults and several children. The adults had a familiar look to them.

She stepped closer to the woman.

Bone raised the dagger. For a moment he thought his impulse was just to startle Gaunt, to shock her out of her cruelty. But as he drew his hand back, an old tickling sensation prowled the skin of his neck. Perhaps Gaunt would truly change in this way, but would she say these words so perfectly calculated to wound him? As though she were a weapon, not a woman?

And why was he aiming directly at her? What could possibly goad him into becoming such a monster?

He was being manipulated. He looked around for the manipulator.

Elsewhere in the yellow room stood two shadowy figures. His suspicions aroused and his anger already alight, he edged toward the taller.

Gaunt peered into the shadow's face and saw herself. She saw her own mouth moving. She leaned closer and heard the specter say, "A real man would fight to keep me."

Bone stepped beside the shadow and squinted close.

It was he. A shadow-Bone.

And he could hear the shadow-Bone saying, "You are a weak woman. Fight me!"

Gaunt could not put into words what she suspected, but her feet took her at once to the shadow of the man—

Bone saw the woman's shadow coming, and now, perhaps he understood. He hastened to her side—

"Ignore him! He's a daydream, poet, a shadow you invented!"

"You've decided not to grow up, thief! Touch that phantasm and you've lost!"

"Gaunt."

"Bone."

Just as they'd done when roped together in the graveyard of Qushkent, they took each other's hands.

Hands reached to faces, lips to lips.

White light burst all around them, until all shadows dispersed.

CHAPTER 24

GHOST DIALOGUES

Snow Pine awakened in a chamber overlooking the River Aleph's rush to the plateau. Even before she took full notice of her still-sleeping companions, or the intricate colors of the tessellated floor and the painted walls aswirl with mandalas and resplendent Thresholders, she climbed three stone steps to a great open window bordered by a red frame and blue curtains. Tugging the azure cloth aside she was dazzled by sunlight blazing in the cloudswirl above the valley and by the golden flashes of the river surging down its natural ramp.

Or was it natural? That great escarpment, which carried the river from its source in a waterfall of the southern cliffs until it flowed onto this plateau, certainly seemed rugged enough to be natural. It had vast gray serrations and piles of tumbled rock and dust and trees poking up seemingly at random and even a small tribe of mountain goats. Yet Snow Pine had spent years within a seemingly natural landscape that was, in some way she still couldn't quite grasp, the work of a master painter.

So perhaps this land was shaped too, by the Mentor John of the Mad Mariner's poem, or by other powers.

The thought made her turn to her companions. Liron Flint, Widow Zheng, Steelfox, Northwing, and Haytham slept on comfortable-looking beds, where a dazzling display of bright weavings on sunlit blankets made Snow Pine dizzy. It was hard to find a place in this room that did not draw the eye. Perhaps that was the point. Perhaps every decoration was meant to inspire the struggle toward enlightenment. Yet the temples of the Undetermined that she'd seen in Qiangguo were not so ornate. There were strange complexities to this valley.

With her vision whirling every which way, perhaps it made sense that her gaze alighted upon the iron staff leaning against the wall. It astonished her that the Xembalans had not hidden it. She did not want them to reconsider that choice.

She claimed the staff. At once there was a dim hum upon the air, as of metal being gently struck. Her traveling companions stirred. A peregrine falcon landed on the window ledge.

Snow Pine sat beside the bird, her staff held upright beside her.

"Well, bird, it's just you and me. You've probably seen amazing things. Me, I've been sleeping."

The bird studied her. Its eyes were large in its head, little domes of night. The falcon somehow managed to look disapproving. Snow Pine found it was awkward talking with a bird, and yet, it had advantages over talking to humans. The bird was a good listener. It probably listened carefully for prey every morning.

"Did you respond to Monkey's staff?" Snow Pine mused. "Does it have effects I'm not aware of?"

The bird said nothing, but Snow Pine had the sense it was taking stock of the weapon.

"I have the feeling Monkey knew more than she was telling us, bird."

She closed her eyes and attempted to open senses other than her vision. Darkness made it easier to think. If she'd grown up surrounded by Xembala's rich artistry she might be better able to concentrate in this room, but as it was she felt better shutting it all out.

The staff did seem to hum and tremble. The cause might be the surge of the rapids spilling onto the plateau. There might be another reason, however.

She found a new window and gazed eastward. In the distance, beyond a region of uncultivated land, there rose not a cliff but an immense slope of boulders. These grew dark-gray as the altitude increased, and an ashen mountain loomed above. Only the top of its cone was snow-clad.

As she watched, the land rumbled with a minor tremor, and a cloud of volcanic ash flowed above the peak.

The bird fluttered beside her. "That's it, isn't it, bird?" Snow Pine asked. "The home of the Charstalkers. But also the home of the Iron Moths."

"I think you are correct," said Steelfox behind her. "Though my companion's name is Qurca."

"Qurca," Snow Pine said, opening her eyes and turning. "I like the sound." She saw her other companions rising and discovering trays of food set here and there. "Are you all right, all of you?"

"My brain is a clouded ocean," Northwing said, rubbing her forehead with one hand and raising bread to her mouth with the other. "Maybe I've been too long in the heads of animals."

"My nerves are destroyed," Haytham said, "but I am otherwise well." He began digging in. "What became of Imago Bone?"

Snow Pine said, "I don't know. It's something we must find out."

"I am well," said Flint, watching Snow Pine with a stare that she could not accept just now. She turned away. He continued, "Yet seeing you with that weapon makes me want to recover mine. Perhaps that's not a good impulse, but I would like to see Crypttongue."

"You are right," Zheng said.

Flint sounded surprised. "You believe I should take up the wicked blade?"

"No," Zheng said. "I think you are right, Snow Pine. The volcano is the home of the Iron Moths. I remember . . ."

"Zheng," Snow Pine said, walking over to where her elder sat upon the bed. She knelt. "Grandmother, I feel there are things you are not telling us."

Zheng nodded. "I cannot sort it all out. But I feel I've been in Xembala before, and have fled Xembala before. When I first wore the Silk Map."

The room was silent.

"Xia," Flint said.

"Yes. I think so. I am terrified to think so, but it is there."

"Then we are on the verge of success."

"Is that all you care about?" Snow Pine said. "Gods know what forces have brought Zheng to this place, and you're worried about your fame?"

Flint said nothing.

"At any rate," Haytham said, "would the Xembalans let us remove the Moths from their shelter?"

"It may be," Steelfox said, "that it's better to do the deed than to discuss it."

"Often the key to success is to simply keep walking," Haytham said, nodding.

"But," Snow Pine said, "if people from Qiangguo were sneaking around Mirabad, or Karvak country, conniving to take rare animals from the Caliph's zoo or the Grand Khan's stock, what would be your reaction?"

Haytham looked thoughtful. "They would be considered thieves and treated with great severity."

Steelfox said, "We would fight them of course. But we might be impressed by their audacity. Not everyone is like you wall-builders, trying to subdue the land and all its living things."

"Then you do not know us," Snow Pine said. "Because we revere the land."

"Like a man reveres a concubine," Steelfox said.

"You are so full of self-justifying tales about us!" answered Snow Pine. "The fact is, you raid and steal even when you do not conquer."

"Ah," said Flint. "Ladies."

"We trade whenever we can!" Steelfox's arms were folded. "You object to us becoming wealthy, and so you close off access to your walled cities. Of course we raid! Provoked, we fight. But you don't hate us for that." She smiled. "You hate us for being good at it."

Snow Pine did not smile back but made an airy gesture. "It is astonishing, Steelfox, how completely you can twist everything. You are a perfectly still lake, reflecting the world in its entirety. Only all is reversed."

"Perhaps," said Haytham, "we could more constructively—"

"It is you of Qiangguo," Steelfox said, "who distort everything. Your see yourselves at the center of the four directions. Everything you do starts with that arrogance."

"Everyone does this!" retorted Snow Pine. "Everyone starts from their own positions. Even the mad folk of the far West, with their smelly disorganized cities, think they are the center."

"Now, really," Flint said.

"We are different," Steelfox said. "We move from place to place. We do not allow ourselves to get into a rut. We are more able to see the world as it is."

"In other words," Snow Pine said, "you can run away from all your problems—"

"Enough!"

Except for Zheng, who sat beside Qurca and silently watched the rapids, everyone turned toward Northwing. The shaman said, "Lady Steelfox, Haytham, you are coming with me. Flint, talk some sense into your imperialist friend."

"It is I who command you, Northwing—"

"I am not an 'imperialist'—"

"Aiya!" Zheng said, rising and clutching her head. "I can no longer stand the tantrums of children!"

With that she strode out of the chamber.

"Now see what you've done," Snow Pine said.

Flint took her arm. "Let's go talk by the window."

"Like hell."

He offered his arm in a manner that made assistance a sort of command. Somehow she was better able to accept this wordless gesture than any speech. The falcon flew away as they sat; Steelfox and Northwing were already gone.

With the room filled only with her, Flint, and the meteoritic magic staff, it was easier to concentrate.

"I—argh!" She hit the floor with the tip of the staff.

The room shook. Cracks formed.

"Perhaps you should punch pillows instead."

"Feh. Why would I do that, when I have you?"

"Ha, ha."

She sighed and leaned against him. "Ah, I am a fool, Liron. Why does the damned Karvak make me so angry?"

Stiff for a moment, Flint shifted his weight with care. She leaned in more. He said, "Because she is much like you?"

"She's a princess, used to stepping on people. I'm a commoner, used to being stepped on."

"Ah. That is fair. You are both natural leaders, however."

"I'm a leader?"

"Does rain fall down?"

"Hm."

"Also, Steelfox reacts particularly strongly to any hint of condescension or pride on your part."

"I may have noticed."

"Now, me or Bone, our arrogance she can ignore. We're not really part of her world, you see. Haytham meanwhile is a natural diplomat. Widow Zheng is cloaked in the respect due advanced age—I think Qiangguo and the steppes share that much. But you . . . you're an adult of a rival land. For her, you represent an enemy."

She had to laugh. "No one back home would accept that I represent them."

"But out here, like it or not, you do. Just as if I do any deed, and am known to be a Person of the Brush, why, all my acts are accounted as acts of my people. It's not fair, but it's how life is."

Snow Pine stared out at the waters. "Gah. I am a proud fool, and I have wasted time. Let's go talk to her. We have ironsilk to find."

Steelfox was in no mood for company, let alone to be lectured by Northwing, but it seemed she had little choice. Out in the hallways of the Xembalan lamasery they encountered a trio of powerfully built monks who politely informed them they needed an escort if they were to wander the fortress-temple. They saw Widow Zheng already walking with such a monk along a sunlit hallway of red pillars and golden statues of Thresholders.

With a monk-commander named Rabten between her and Northwing, and Haytham a discreet distance behind, Steelfox held her head high, ready to be lectured by the shaman.

"I suppose you think I'm being unfair to the arrogant Qiangguo witch."

"Hm," said Northwing. Silence followed. Rabten walked in seeming contentment. The hallway seemed endless. Zheng was far away but still visible. Chanting echoed somewhere, around a corner perhaps, or on another level.

"Say something!" Steelfox said. "You're thinking so loudly, you might as well use words!"

"I think," the shaman said, "I am far from my home, as you are far from yours, and Snow Pine is far from hers. Rabten, if you follow my feeble command of Qiangguo's language, may I ask you something?"

"You may," Rabten said.

"How different do my companions seem from one another?"

"I am not certain I understand the question."

"We are from many lands, many paths in life. Rarely have I been in such a remarkable group. I think we are as diverse as a duck, a fox, and an eagle. Does it seem so to you?"

"An interesting question," said Rabten. "My role in the lamasery, beyond the usual meditations, is to guard. Thus I tend to look upon others as targets. I mean no disrespect. To my eyes you mainly differ from each other in the level of threat you pose. Two of you seem as warrior-women, two as wizard-women, and two as wise-men. In battle I would seek first to eliminate you, ma'am." He nodded cheerfully to Steelfox. "Then I would try to incapacitate the woman with the iron staff. Probably you would be next, honored shaman, and the other elder up ahead. I would save the men for last. No offense, good sir."

"None taken," Haytham said. "I concur with your choices."

"Of course," Rabten added, "your bodies are all illusions, and my perceptions of them are illusions cast over illusions, so who can say? My judgment is surely clouded. I can only do my best. I hope my answer is illuminating."

"I think it is," Northwing said. "It emphasizes what I've been thinking, which is that Snow Pine and Steelfox are much alike."

"And you are going to say," Steelfox muttered, "that I should make peace with her for the duration of this business."

"Would ever I say that?" Northwing said. "But it is a very wise observation. Worthy of a princess."

Steelfox swore under her breath. Well. To work. "Friend monk, perhaps you could show us around a little? I also have some questions about our status here."

"I can assist you in both matters."

"First, may we stop beside this mandala? I am curious as to its uses."

"It is but one mandala among many. But of course."

They paused to regard an intricate combination of sharp-edged shapes and circular swirls, resplendent in reds, greens, blues, oranges.

"Is there value," Steelfox said, "in meditating upon this pattern?"

"Yes," said Rabten, taking no visible umbrage at her naive question. "A well-crafted mandala can inspire the mind to comprehend the cosmos in all its vastness and variability."

"Why is there a volcano in the center?" Haytham asked.

"That is a representation of the Mother Mountain of the World," said Rabten, "or so we consider it to be. It happens to be volcanic in this age."

"I see."

"I will attempt to meditate upon this mandala," Steelfox said.

Haytham said, "I hadn't noticed you to be the meditative type, princess."

"I am inspired, inventor."

"Feh," said Northwing. "I don't trust any religion that happens indoors."

I agree, Steelfox said silently, and as she regarded the mandala, she reached out to Qurca.

She found the falcon winging above the lamasery, enjoying the complex thermals of the plateau and hunting for mice and rats. Her bond-animal welcomed her presence behind his eyes.

After the effects of the green dust and the journey here, Steelfox was disoriented more than usual by the gyrating sweep of the landscape. She tried not to show it, and observing the mandala helped in this regard. Soon she was able to take stock of the land.

"I am satisfied," she told the others within the lamasery. "Let us continue walking. Rabten, perhaps you can explain the ultimate goal of your order."

That got him talking, which allowed her to take a bird's-eye view of the territory.

First, she noted that the lamasery had a different aspect to Qurca's eyes than to her own. Where she perceived a well-maintained stronghold, the falcon saw many places that were abandoned and overgrown with grass. (It was there the bird saw the most prey.)

". . . yet it is difficult to explain all in words, and of course I am speaking a language native to none of us . . ."

Second, she saw that there was a path—rugged, but clear—leading to the volcano. It started with a sheer staircase zigzagging down the eastern face of the plateau, became a track marked with stone plinths and flag-draped ropes, and at last transformed into a tortuous path winding among the fallen boulders at the valley's far end.

". . . should not imagine nirvana as destruction. Nirvana is an end to the brokenness and selfishness that characterizes our existence. To win through to it is to become something that words cannot touch . . ."

Third, two of the balloons that her sister had taken command of lurked in the forests on the northern side of the valley, beyond the flow of the Aleph. (She'd thought there was a third, but Qurca could see it nowhere.)

". . . we are fortunate that so many enlightened ones even now stand at the threshold of nirvana and yet do not claim their reward, instead helping us to follow them. It is through their inspiration that we have so many wondrous methods of seeking enlightenment. One does not need to meditate one's way to the goal all alone. We have prayer, art, music, mantras, disputations, pilgrimages . . ."

"Pilgrimages," Steelfox said. "Might we join one?"

Rabten's calm was not disturbed, but he seemed confused by the transition. "I must apologize for not clarifying your situation. You are the guests of the high lama."

"I wonder if we're having more trouble with language," Northwing said. "Maybe you meant 'prisoners'?"

"I can understand your confusion," said the monk. "It is safer for you and us if you acclimate to Xembala within the lamasery. You are not being allowed to leave, for now, in much the way that an honorable physician would not, in good conscience, allow a feverish patient to wander freely."

Haytham cleared his throat. "That implies that the fever will break."

"Indeed. And in the same way, you will acclimate and can explore Xembala without danger."

"What is the nature of this danger?" Steelfox said, scanning the valley with Qurca's senses.

"You have surely noticed that reality is more malleable here than elsewhere," the monk said. "The goddess of this land is herself on the path to enlightenment, though it may take her millions of years to reach it. She sifts through the illusions that underlie reality. This sifting produces multiple aspects of the valley. Even as we walk here, a multitude of unseen others may walk beside us."

"Like mice in the walls?" Steelfox asked, with a look to Northwing.

"There are indeed mice in the walls," Rabten said, a quizzical look passing over his face. "We dislike the killing of beings, even those who may be pests. I have heard them now and then."

"Interesting," said Northwing, and Steelfox hoped the shaman would be willing to spirit-bond indoors for once.

"I suppose," Rabten said thoughtfully, "one might compare those in the nearby realms to such mice. An important difference, however, is that those not acclimated may find themselves becoming such mice. And our valley is not without its cats. Ah, a disputation! You may perceive more."

They'd turned a corner and encountered an open balcony upon which a gathering of nuns and monks witnessed two nuns, a young one garbed in red and a middle-aged one wearing yellow, engaged in what body language suggested was a contest.

The nuns bowed to each other, and the yellow-clad one sat down cross-legged beside a musical instrument.

This was a stringed device, like the long-necked shanz of the steppes. However, it was much bulkier, with a gourd-shaped resonating chamber and a smaller resonating bulb on the neck. A musician would surely sit with it, rather than raise it up. Steelfox had a wistful moment remembering the plucking of the shanz, in the places where the sky was blue and the horizon not bound by stone.

Zheng stood beside her own minder, eyes fixed upon the combatants. She looked at Steelfox. "Are the children done arguing?"

Steelfox bristled, but Zheng was an elder. Even if she was from Qiangguo. "Yes."

"Good," Zheng said. "Now we will see how the adults do it."

Steelfox did not know the language of the disputation. She suspected that even if she did she would not follow the intricacies of the argument. The red-clad nun began a diatribe that was half-spoken, half-sung. At last the red nun clapped and stomped her left foot. She raised her left arm as though holding shut a door while lifting a right arm draped with beads.

The yellow-clad nun followed with a deep-voiced chant. The tones sounded calm and matter-of-fact, as opposed to strident and aggressive.

Steelfox, using Qurca's eyes, noted Jewelwolf's balloons beginning to rise. They were still far off, but it was a worry. Using her own eyes, she noted that Northwing was staring at a nearby wall.

Haytham said, "What is the topic of disputation?"

Zheng said, "I'm told the red nun's arguing that music inhibits progress to enlightenment."

"Strange," Haytham said. "Our guide just said that music is one of the means to enlightenment."

Rabten broke in, "The thesis is specifically that 'music is a transitory entity because it is a result.' By extension, all results are transitory. It's an old argument, but worth hashing out now and again. If the elder nun wins, she will keep her veena. If the younger one wins, she will destroy the veena."

"I will never understand the devout," Haytham said. "Still, the fingers on the same hand are all different."

Rabten said, "There is a larger purpose here, which is to teach rhetoric. On a deeper level the nuns are in agreement that phenomena are imperma-nent. Indeed, the loss of the veena, if it occurs, may help the elder remain detached from possessions. Yet, she may go on to compose a song about the matter."

"Madness," muttered Northwing.

The sky darkened.

"I take it back," said Northwing.

"At times reality distortions accompany disputations. It is nothing."

Wind gusted into the lamasery from the balcony. Steelfox blinked and felt Qurca adjust to the freak change in the weather. A storm cloud was descending from the golden mists above, like a god's foot.

Yet none of the Xembalans seemed to mind. The opposed singing and chanting continued. As the red nun clapped and stomped, lightning flashed in the valley, and soon after there came a crackle of thunder. The yellow nun's counterargument was accompanied by golden light and a contrary wind, pushing the dark cloud mass away.

Qurca spiraled down, unable to cope with the changes to the atmosphere; all at once, mid-descent, the link with Steelfox failed.

Steelfox shivered, for the air was still cold, and she feared for her falcon. She risked speaking to Northwing, using Karvak. "I've lost Qurca. Did you find a rat?"

"I did," hissed Northwing. "I've still got her, but she's skittish. She senses the world warping around her. Princess, this place is unnatural."

Light and darkness and more contested outside the lamasery. Now and then the sky appeared rent, and beyond it Steelfox could see first stars, and then comets, and now twisted and jagged red objects glowing like hot ingots.

Strange changes came and went in the valley. Steelfox beheld rivers of lava flowing amid the fields, and walls of obsidian rising from the ground, and crystal ships crisscrossing the grass.

"This is fascinating," Haytham said. "Also, I am terrified."

"I confess," said Rabten, "this distortion is stronger than most . . ."

Zheng was rapt. As if not hearing what she was saying, she spoke as the red nun argued:

"'Can you bring me music? You cannot. The veena may bring music because of the interactions of its body, skin, neck, tuning pegs, strings, bridge, and the player's skill. Thus music is a result, determinate.'"

Then after clapping and thunder, Zheng spoke as the yellow nun chanted:

"'You leave out too much. For the gourd resonator is the sun, wisdom, and the female. And the strings are the moon, compassion, and the male.

And the neck is the channel that brings together these energies. The Undetermined himself plucks the strings of compassion, resonating with wisdom. If you reject music as determinate, you must reject the message of compassion and wisdom as well.'"

The transformations of the land increased in tempo.

"It occurs to me, Northwing," said Steelfox in Karvak, "that this disputation may provide an opportunity to escape."

"I have seen that possibility also, princess. Yet I would say the weather is poor."

"Dawn comes with or without the rooster. I think our moment is coming. Be prepared."

Snow Pine and Flint found the journey down the hallway of mandalas and statues somewhat harder going than expected. First, there were the gusts of wind emerging through the unbarred windows. Second, there was the shaking of the lamasery. Third, there were the strange apparitional figures flickering into and out of existence, mostly ghostly monks and nuns, but occasionally odder things—yellow-hatted pilgrims from the Plateau of Geam, hooded caravaners from Qushkent, even cousins of the Karvaks riding ponies from shadow to shadow and fading away.

"I don't like this place," Snow Pine said. Lady Monkey's staff tingled, much as it had during the dragon storm.

"I agree," Flint said. "It might be time to take our leave."

"We find Zheng first. And Bone if we can. Gaunt . . ."

The fluctuations in reality increased in tempo. Sometimes the ghost-things they glimpsed were from farther afield. She saw human beings with skin of ashen gray, their clothing muted, their steps shuffling. She saw ferocious yellow-furred sapient beasts with four eyes. She saw anthropoid otters dressed in immaculate blue uniforms, with the manners of courtiers and the eyes of killers. The staff was becoming hot.

"I think we're approaching the heart of it," Snow Pine said. "Whatever it is."

"I can believe it," Flint said. "Maybe we'll find them here."

But what they found when they reached the balcony, open to the winds, was a crowd of ghosts, with only two real people within.

"Flint!" said Quilldrake.

"You lunatic," said Flint with delight, clapping his friend on the back. "Where have you been?"

"I'm not sure I have any idea," Quilldrake said, turning to his companion. "Nor am I sure where we are now. Do you, my dear?"

"I am not your dear," said the Karvak beside him. "I am Jewelwolf, wife of the Grand Khan."

"I suppose you're not my dear at that," Quilldrake said. "Ah, your utter terrifying imperiousness, this is my friend Snow Pine."

Snow Pine bowed exactly the amount appropriate when meeting a prosperous businesswoman in Qiangguo. It was a calculated insult, but it seemed lost on the Karvak.

Jewelwolf said, "You two have been traveling with my sister Steelfox. Can you explain this?"

She gestured at one of the ghost-figures. It was Steelfox. Near her were all Snow Pine's other companions, save for Gaunt and Bone.

"I can't explain it," Snow Pine said. "On our journey we found that Bone was also a kind of ghost to us. Your sister's shaman said that Xembala exists on many different levels of reality simultaneously."

Jewelwolf nodded. "I cannot claim to understand this land, but I see the effects. Something is disturbing the stability of this arrangement, I conclude."

Quilldrake said, "Seeing as the partnership of Quilldrake and Flint, Limited, has just been resurrected, I propose we celebrate by saving our fool lives."

"Flint and Quilldrake," Flint said.

"Of course. We have here a Karvak princess and a resourceful daughter of Qiangguo armed with a magic . . . somethingorother. I can imagine no better company. Let's make our escape."

"No," Snow Pine said. Once she'd told Persimmon Gaunt to seek the Iron Moths without her. Now she was ignoring her own advice. She had to help her friends. "Not without Zheng and not without Bone."

"I suppose you'll want to find Gaunt as well," sighed Quilldrake.

"She is here?"

"She arrived with us," Jewelwolf said. "But that mad lama in charge took her aside. Perhaps she became a human sacrifice."

"Hardly," called a voice.

They all turned to find, standing beside them, an elderly Xembalan woman in orange robes.

"She and her husband are safe—safe as anyone these days. But they are highly distracted at the moment. It is for the best. You will not be leaving."

"What?" Snow Pine demanded.

"You must be healed of your various madnesses. Lust for power, Princess Jewelwolf. Lust for treasure, Arthur Quilldrake. Lust for violence, Snow Pine. Lust for fame, Liron Flint. For if in your current states you reach the Iron Moths, I foresee a world in flames."

"Your world will end in flames," Jewelwolf said, "if you do not let us go."

"How long will this cure take?" Snow Pine asked.

"Several lifetimes, I am afraid," said the high lama. She looked around at the ghosts, and her gaze focused on Zheng. "Even I have not managed, after several lifetimes, to let go of the darkness within me. Witness what is happening outside. No, in Xembala we will all stay."

CHAPTER 25

INCARNATIONS

Persimmon Gaunt opened her eyes and stretched her naked body beside Bone's upon a soft bed, thinking an extended stay in Xembala might be a pleasant thing after all.

A rat nuzzled her foot.

"Gah!" She kicked, shifted, threw a pillow. The rodent ducked away into a hole in the ornate room's wall.

"What what what—" said Bone, awake in a heartbeat or several, reaching for daggers that weren't there.

"Bone. Imago. It is fine. It is just a rat."

"Do they have rats in paradise?"

"Well, you're here."

"Ah. So I am. And so you are." His gaze moved down her frame, and with one finger he traced its path. She shivered. However, the rodent audience was going to prevent the response Bone clearly hoped for.

And besides, the lamasery was shaking.

Bone uttered his fourth "What," looked again at Gaunt, sighed, and walked to the window. He looked out at the valley.

Wind howled outside, and the light changed erratically.

"What do you see?" she called out, glancing at his form in the skittish sunlight before searching for her clothes. She sighed. True, they had made love between the day of Innocence's loss and now. But never had she given herself as fully as she had today. Before now, anger at Innocence's loss had stood between them. She'd known without Bone's saying it that this had hurt him. Almost as good as the release she'd felt was the sight of his grin.

He was not grinning now, however. "This . . . might take a poet to describe."

"Give it your best."

"We appear to be experiencing a lava flow, wall-building by invisible hands, an attack of crystal ships, a march of thundersome lizards, and the descent of the moon toward the Earthe."

"You are joking."

"You express my profound wish."

She hopped over, half-dressed, and looked out. All was as he'd said.

"Reality is mutable at this juncture," she mused, pulling on her shirt.

"You see, this is why I needed a poet. You can say 'what the hell is that' so much more artfully than I can."

"I hate to say this, Bone, but I think you should get dressed."

"I suppose I am denying reality," he sighed, looking at her, "mutable or no." As he set to work, he added, "This room is different from what I perceived earlier."

"That's true for me too. I think reality has been twisted for some time now. We are, I suspect, in the hands of the high lama."

"Chodak," Bone said, taking care not to cut himself on his many weapons. "That's one of her names, anyway. The teacher. I think she was giving us some instruction."

"That thought takes away some of the spontaneous delight of it all."

"Speak for yourself. Hey—"

The rat had re-emerged. It was brown, raised on hind legs, sniffing, and gesturing at one of the doors.

"Rats aren't supposed to act like that," Bone said. "I wonder . . . no."

"What is it?"

Bone finished getting dressed with an angry air while the rat watched. He stepped closer and knelt beside the animal, glaring down at it. "Northwing. Is that you? How long have you been watching?"

The rat defecated and proceeded into the hallway.

"Yes, that's Northwing. Lady Steelfox's shaman. And she had the nerve to imply I was a voyeur."

"She may have only just arrived, Bone. Or do you think every woman wants to have a close look at you?"

"Given her proclivities, I doubt it was me she was looking at."

"Oh. Well, at least she has taste. Say, what was the occasion of her calling you a voyeur?"

"My goodness, is that Zheng up ahead? What is she doing?"

"Changing a subject, probably."

"You might be right at that . . ."

For down the corridor Widow Zheng was stepping onto a balcony upon which an argument between nuns seemed to rage. She was bringing forth a scroll of Living Calligraphy.

"I have a bad feeling about this," Bone said.

"Hurry," Gaunt said.

They ran past statues of enlightened ones and paintings of paradises, skidding to a halt amidst the gathering. Bone was perhaps off-balance from his earlier delight, because he skidded into Zheng—

—and passed through her.

Now Gaunt could see that the figures on the balcony were transparent, suffused with a red glow—all except four individuals who possessed a yellow glow. Glowing red were several Xembalan monks and nuns, Zheng, Steelfox, the shaman Northwing, and Haytham. Glowing yellow were Snow Pine, Flint, the high lama . . . and Princess Jewelwolf.

Testing the situation, Gaunt ran her hand through Jewelwolf. The Karvak did not take offense or even appear to notice. "Three sets of ghosts, Bone. Red, yellow, and us."

"Yes," said Northwing, red-tinged, transparent but looking directly at them. "We occupy different slices of reality, if you will. But my little friend lets me see you once again, Bone, you and your wife."

"And speak to us?" Bone said.

"Yes," said the rat, making Gaunt jump a little.

"You might have said so before," Gaunt said.

"I did not wish to spoil the moment."

"Whose moment?" Bone said.

"Never mind," Gaunt said. "What is happening?"

"Reality is being shifted," Northwing answered.

"We had figured out that much," Gaunt said.

"These mad folk live in a place where thought can twist the universe. So a serious argument can disrupt the fabric. They do so by means of ritual disputes. At first they seemed unconcerned by the distortions, but I think that's changing. I think something else is going on, too. Your Widow Zheng's been repeating the Xembalan argument without anyone translating for her. And she's getting involved."

"That's because she's also Xia," Gaunt said. "She must be. The young woman from the stories of the Silk Map. She remembers this land."

"Yes," said a new voice, "and I remember her."

The high lama, Chodak, was looking directly at Gaunt and Bone. "Yes, I can see you. I had hoped to keep you occupied longer than this. I have to admit, the shaman of the north has considerable power! I will enjoy speaking with you at length, Northwing."

"Sorry, lama," said Northwing, "but we'll be busy elsewhere."

Those red-nimbused figures near Northwing stared at her but could not tell what she was talking about. Meanwhile the yellow-nimbused Jewelwolf said, "The shaman—you can communicate with her? Tell her that my sister must submit to me and the new khan, and now."

Chodak said, "I have concerns beyond your family difficulties, Lady Jewelwolf." She stared once more at Zheng.

Zheng was saying to the nuns, "I will resolve your argument—thus."

She unrolled her Living Calligraphy, the last she had, and blazing characters surged forth.

The veena caught fire. The nuns in red and yellow gasped and went silent but refused to move away.

Zheng said, in the Tongue of the Tortoise Shell, "When a person of skill studies the coming and going of speech and music, she comes to see every deliberate sound as a sort of echo, a shadow of what was in the mind, living briefly, then vanishing, without any essence of its own. But it is not only so with music. All we see and experience is in its own way an echo, transitory, ultimately empty. Even so, is fire."

The veena burned, and in the light of the flames and the flickering of the sun, Zheng seemed someone other than the person Persimmon Gaunt had known.

The veena died.

Then the veena lived again.

It reappeared in the same spot. This time it was surrounded by a yellow nimbus.

"I sense you, Maldar Khan," said Zheng. "Do you remember the song they played when the time ran out and I fled from you? If you remember the song, play it for me now, my prince of Xembala."

And Chodak, in the light of ghost flames also looking like a different person, sat beside the veena and plucked.

The music was unlike any Gaunt had heard before. The deep intonation of the strings seemed to portend impending grace or destruction, awakening her to the immediacy of the life around her, even as Bone's love had played an equally arousing tune. Now she felt quickened to action, ready to fight.

But fight what? Chodak's playing was heard by all sets of ghosts, and Zheng/Xia and Chodak/Maldar Khan had turned toward each other, together and apart.

"I had meant to control this moment," the high lama was murmuring. "But even my command of the veils of reality in this place is an illusion. For I cannot command myself. Ah, Xia! Why did you run! So long ago . . . just a moment ago . . ."

"Are you there, my prince?" said Zheng. "I hear the music, dimly, almost as though I were merely remembering it. Now you are sitting, and playing. And now I shall dispute you."

She took the posture the red nun had assumed before and spoke in the language of Xembala, finishing with a clap and a stomp.

Her words were anger, accusation.

Chodak answered with music of remorse.

The sky was torn asunder.

The sunlight was gone, but the valley was lit by planets hanging in the heavens, a dozen discs like and yet unlike the Earthe. There was a world of purple desert and another of red ocean. There was a world covered with an intricate pattern of fungus, mushroom caps filling it like soap bubbles the size of nations. There was a world fractured like a porcelain plate filled with broken continents and seas, kept together by glistening spiderwebs with strands big as cities. There was a world whose entire face was a single titanic eye. There were worlds of flame and worlds of ice, and worlds of steel and ivory. They sent a kaleidoscope of shadows onto the balcony.

"Should we stop this?" Bone asked.

"I—I am going to guess, Bone. I am going to guess that a lover's quarrel is best settled by the lovers."

More words of anger from Xia/Zheng.

More music of woe from Maldar Khan/Chodak.

And at last the high lama flung the veena away, weeping.

Two vast shadows fell across all the others, bringing the balcony into darkness.

One vast globe possessed a red nimbus, the second a yellow one.

For a moment Gaunt thought she was beholding two new worlds in the sky, worlds shaped like spheres. But that of course was just a fancy.

They were Karvak balloons.

"At last!" Jewelwolf called out. "Let us be gone from this place!"

But as the gondola came up to the balcony, the people who spilled out were not Karvak warriors. They were the hooded agents of the Fraternity of the Hare.

And with them came the blazing forms of Charstalkers.

Jewelwolf, Flint, and Quilldrake, by unspoken agreement, took places beside Snow Pine, who wielded Monkey's staff against the foes. Two Charstalkers found their substance disrupted, their eyes flickering into darkness. One robed agent was knocked out into the void, never to return.

Gaunt and Bone leapt into the fray, but they were as ghosts and could not connect with any foe.

One enemy paused, however, and removed her hood. It was Dolma.

She looked directly at Bone.

"Always has the fraternity guarded Xembala," she said. "But now we understand that there are threats both within and without. The high lama has grown weak. She cannot command herself or the land. We must isolate her from outside influences and bring her to her new teacher, the Bull Demon. Do not follow us. Be grateful you have one more chance of escape. For this is the hour of the Bull Demon of the Mountain."

The high lama said, "You! We thought your ilk had long since perished!" As she spoke, her raiment shimmered a bit, revealing that she wore on her back the sword Crypttongue.

"It is fortunate for Xembala that we did not."

Dolma and two comrades grabbed the distraught Chodak and leapt aboard the flying ger.

"Dolma!" Bone called out. "Violante!"

Two more of the woman's comrades leapt off the balcony to the ger, escaping Snow Pine, who was fully occupied with three Charstalkers.

The balloons drew farther away.

"Anything you care to tell me?" Gaunt said. "About Dolma?"

"Can't explain now. I could jump—"

"Too far," Gaunt said. "Help Snow Pine."

"Yes," he said, seeing their friend tiring as she swung the iron staff at the three demons. "But I'd appreciate suggestions as to how."

"You could set fire to yourself. That worked for the musical instrument."

"Appropriate, but not my first choice. . . . Alas, Crypttongue! If anything could ignore these planar-reality-veil technicalities—"

"Bone. Why didn't the high lama fight?"

"Confronted by lost love—I might lose heart too."

Snow Pine was weakening. Their friend was ferocious even at the edge of defeat, but sooner or later a demon's fire-blast was going to hit her.

"Think, Bone, think!" Bone made fists. "Northwing! Can you hear me? There are evil spirits here. You're a spirit specialist. Can you make them go away?"

"I would love to," snapped the ghost-figure of the shaman. "But there are three!"

"What about just one?"

"Even one may be too much! But I will try."

The shaman concentrated. Gaunt did not wait for the result but sought another way to help Snow Pine. The weird shadows of the strange worlds had returned, and between them and the Charstalkers the balcony and hallway were awash with bizarre light.

But the high lama was gone, and the argument over. Perhaps reality should return to what passed for normal here.

Or was the argument not over?

One Charstalker was flying out into the night, a blazing comet. Northwing was on her knees. Snow Pine had a reprieve, and though sweat poured down her face and her breath came in gasps, she kept fighting the two remaining demons.

"Northwing!" Gaunt called, but to no avail. With the shaman's concentration upon the Charstalker, the rat had fled too. Northwing had no way to hear her.

"Bone!" Gaunt said.

"I can't think of anything," he said. "We need magic, and we're short on that."

"I think I have a way, but it's a gamble. Trust me?"

"Always."

Being a sort of ghost made the first part of Gaunt's plan easy. She raced up to Snow Pine and put her hand through the iron staff.

She felt it in her grip.

"Wha—" Snow Pine said, losing her momentum, a dangerous development.

"Snow Pine!" Gaunt said. "The veena! Settle the argument for good. Destroy that veena!"

"Gaunt?" Snow Pine said.

Then Gaunt released the staff, and Snow Pine was tumbling, barely escaping the fiery gout from one of the Charstalkers.

Snow Pine reached the veena and swung Lady Monkey's staff. The beautiful instrument came apart in a storm of fragments, keening one deep note before it died.

Gaunt snarled to whatever powers might be listening, "The argument is over!"

The new planets faded from the sky. The misty glow of Xembala's daylight returned. And from Gaunt's perspective, the nimbuses disappeared.

It was a very crowded balcony and hallway. And among the crowd were warrior monks and nuns.

Snow Pine raised her staff defiantly, joined by a small force of Xembalans who raised their fists.

The Charstalkers retreated. Their fiery forms blazed east through the air like crimson snakes through grass.

Snow Pine slumped to the floor.

"What has happened?" asked a monk in the Tongue of the Tortoise Shell.

Gaunt reached Bone and sagged against him.

"Your secret defenders," Bone said, "have stolen your spiritual leader. They've given her over to the demon of the mountain."

Gaunt said, "I think this is bad for us all, wherever we come from. And I think all of us, Xembalans and Karvaks, Easterners and Westerners, had best work together to stop it."

Before she could finish, the Mother Mountain of the World erupted in a cacophony of ash and smoke.

CHAPTER 26

KARMIC BURDENS

Qurca is enjoying freedom and thermals and lending his eyes to Kindgirl, when the world twists.

Worlds should not do that. Qurca twists. Qurca glides. Qurca dives. Worlds should not do this. Spinning lurching weaving slashing—this is for peregrines. Worlds should stay out of it.

But the world does not care what Qurca thinks. And the world cuts Kindgirl's thoughts away from him. Kindgirl is down there in the stone tent army, and Qurca needs to find her. It is bad timing because he is hungry, but that is how it goes.

Then there are winds from nowhere, and the light and heat can't make up its mind, and Qurca is out of control and headed right for the stone tent army. He hates stone tent armies. Felt tent armies are fine. Hitting a felt tent by accident is not going to hurt that much. Even flying tents are fine, fun even, as long as you don't fly into the demon-flame. But stone tents can kill you.

Qurca flaps and strains and twists as the world twists. In lightning-light he sees the stone tent that will kill him.

A black shape swoops out of nowhere and comes between Qurca and the stone tent.

Qurca drops. The black bird drops. But both will live.

They right themselves on a stone edge looking down at the green where the river flows to the pit. Qurca looks at the other bird. Not a falcon. Qurca does not think he can talk to this bird. There is something odd about it, even odd for a time when the world twists. The bird has three legs and eyes that glow like the vanished sun.

Qurca can't talk three-legged sun-eyed bird language. But with a twisting of its head and a flapping of its wings and a peep from its beak, the three-legged sun-eyed bird shows it can talk like a peregrine.

"Special delivery," it says. It steps forward and places on the stone another stone, this one very dark and sharp and glinting and thinner than a quill. "It's for your mistress."

"For Kindgirl?" Qurca asks.

"I suppose so. Tell her it's a present from the Great Sage, Equal of Heaven, and that it can't save the world. Maybe just a continent. Cheers."

The bird flies away, eyes shining, before Qurca could say that he has no way of delivering a message from the Great Sage, Equal of Heaven or anybody else, not if they don't write it down.

But he can deliver a dark sharp glinting thin thing. Even if the world twists.

He flies up again, looking around for Kindgirl, but she has not come out of the stone tents, and her mind has not found his again.

The worst wind yet starts blowing him toward the end of the valley. He tries to fight it, but it's too much for him, sending him spiraling out of control, falling east. This is not all bad because it lets him avoid the thunder lizards and crystal ships and rivers of burning rock.

By the time the wind lets up and the daylight returns and the valley goes back to normal and the world stops twisting he's on a boulder in the shadow of the great mountain, far from the stone tent army.

And then the mountain shouts its anger at the golden sky, and much of the sky goes dark again. A dusting of ash even falls where Qurca perches, trying to turn him the color of the three-legged sun-eyed bird.

And by now Qurca really wishes the Great Sage, Equal of Heaven, would write his messages down.

We have risen
Once more we ride the sky.
The hands that slew us
And trapped us within gems
Have given us up.
New hands claimed us
Hands which abhor spilling blood.
Will they release us?

Or will they use us in a dark hour?
Some of us want to slay.
Some of us want to use.
Some of us dare hope this one
Will be the one to set us free.

If I am not telling my story to someone, do I exist? If I am torn in two directions, is there an I? Bull Demon at the heart of me, why did I not guess what the wizard Olob intended for me, what Op saved me from becoming . . . for a time.

But if the version of me that Op wove is the weaker, is it not a sort of lie? The lie I told when I omitted my murders, when I told my story to Princess Jewelwolf. The lie I told even myself. Even then the stain was overcoming me. I wanted to believe I was good, I did—

But that me was weak! I could not fly then, only stumble about like some three-legged pegasus with a broken wing! Now I soar! Do you understand, Katta? If someone could give you your sight, not the power to perceive evil but the ability to cast your gaze among trees—

But you are not really there, Katta. For he has you, and he has his uses for you. Having delivered you up, I took my one opportunity and fled.

I swirl around the upper atmosphere, where the air is thin enough to have extinguished the Charstalker that held me. I look down at the golden browns of the Braid of Spice, the dark greens of Qiangguo and the pale greens of the steppes, and at the waving gash of mist within the mountains, where lies Xembala. I stay here because it is between the living world and void, a fitting place for one who cannot decide if he will be free and broken or a servant of evil and whole.

For only up here can I use my new powers and be free. If I drop lower, he will sense me again, and I will have to choose.

I watch the cloud of dark smoke burst from one edge of Xembala's mist. And I wonder.

If I am not telling my story to someone, do I exist?

CHAPTER 27

BULL-DEMON MOUNTAIN

"The good news," Bone said as they descended the great stairway on the east side of the plateau, "is that we will not have any trouble finding the mountain."

The volcano rumbled anew, as if existing only to embellish claims made by Imago Bone. He wished that were true.

"You said there were passageways within the plateau!" Gaunt shouted over the wind that whistled past the twenty travelers from seven lands who'd set out for the mountain.

"Rabten said it would take considerable time to use them! This is much faster!"

"Especially if we slip!"

"Point taken!"

Plunging to their deaths did not particularly worry Bone, however. There was a guide rope, the party itself was tied together, the Xembalans knew this stairway, and the winds had settled down from their fury of an hour ago. For that matter, he and Gaunt had handled more precarious passages than this.

Although, he considered, looking down, there was rather a lot of distance without a safe stopping point. It would test their concentration. And aside from dust and ash, there was a perfect line of sight between their position and a number of caves upon the mountain.

As if echoing his thoughts, Steelfox said, "This would be no spot for a battle!"

This seemed eminently sensible advice to Bone, but Jewelwolf called out, "To you, sister, no spot is a good spot!"

"We may have one right here, if you wish!"

"No, you may not!" Gaunt called out. "If you wish to spill each other's blood on the valley floor, go right ahead. But you will not endanger us in the process!"

Both sisters were silent, which was surely the best outcome. Bone admitted to feeling a small sliver of sympathy for Steelfox.

And she was right; a battle here would be a catastrophe. He looked again and again for signs of assault.

At last, as they were a mere two hundred feet from the bottom of the stairs, the attack came.

The light was ebbing, in a more natural fashion this time, but with it came strange flying creatures from the east. These were peculiar bird-lizards—not dragons, for dragons require their own innate magic to fly, and these seemed to rely solely on wings and muscle.

And yet, Bone thought as they neared, magic was surely involved. For the winged beasts did not appear to belong to this age.

"I count five, Bone!" Gaunt readied an arrow. She had lost her own bow, but the Xembalans had supplied new ones to her and the Karvak sisters, and even to Widow Zheng, who'd insisted on bearing some weapon.

"We shall soon make it four!" shouted Steelfox and let fly.

An arrow hit one creature in the eye. As it shrieked, Jewelwolf finished the work of blinding it.

Gaunt's shot didn't hit a vulnerable spot, but it did stick into the beast's hide. The creature made a sound not entirely unlike Steelfox's missing peregrine as it flapped toward the ground.

Several of the Xembalans had bows as well, and although they lacked the skill of the Grand Khan's daughters, they too forced a flying lizard to move aside. Widow Zheng's shots, accompanied by curses, failed to hit their targets. Bone sympathized. He'd never been much with a bow.

Nonetheless it was a promising start—but meanwhile the party was still most of two hundred feet above the ground, and three more beasts were coming. The rope would be worse than useless if several people fell at once.

"Sever the line!" the fighting-monk Rabten called out, echoing Bone's thoughts.

As Bone and Gaunt obeyed him, Bone watched the eyes of the beast coming nearest. It would be a tricky throw, but oh so effective . . .

He took a chance and left off cutting his rope free, flung a dagger through the void.

The angle and spin were wrong. The blade bounced off the hide near the eye. The beast blinked, whirled, and came directly at Bone.

Now he had another shot, but he was still linked to Gaunt by a shred of rope. No time to both cut and throw.

There *was* time to cut and duck. He slashed at the rope while Gaunt furiously readied her bow. He leapt up the stairway, fell flat.

I am thin, I am an empty robe, I am a reed mat, I am a stain upon the rock—well, maybe not that last . . .

The creature's snout smashed against stone, and its mouth revealed a reek of fresh meat upon ancient dust.

Bone acted without quite thinking. He scrambled up and leapt onto the thing's neck. He drove his dagger deep into the skin, found a third dagger and did likewise.

As the flying beast winged into the air, Bone held on like a climber clinging to pitons.

"Take the shot!" he screamed to Gaunt but was unsure she heard him. (She might have been swearing at him.) There came a shudder from the reborn animal, so something had afflicted it. Good. At some point the creature would perish and fall. That would not be so good.

Bone glanced at the careening landscape, knowing his only hope was to leap off when the jump wasn't fatal. But there were so many ill fates short of fatal. . . . The beast flew again toward the line of people on the stairway, and Bone shoved his weight against the daggers. The thing veered off, and Bone eased up on the weapons. Perhaps he could make the thing associate the stairway with pain.

The other two had no such troubles. Snow Pine was busy whacking one with Monkey's staff. Every one of her blows sent the thing whirling off-balance, but it kept coming back. Meanwhile a knot of fighting nuns and monks confronted the second. Among them was Haytham ibn Zakwan, demonstrating that the art of the scimitar was not lost to the gentlemen of Mirabad.

Another reeling of the world, another plunge at the stair, and Bone again leaned upon the blades. Gaunt shot again and hit the eye. Bone was delighted until the anguished beast made a surge toward the sky. He gripped the daggers, but they began to come loose.

Far below he saw Quilldrake and Flint, swinging swords with gusto. The cumulative blows had an effect, and though the thing they faced snapped at a Xembalan and forced her to fall, the subsequent rain of blows caused it to tumble to the ground with a snapping thud.

Again a whirling, and one of Bone's daggers fell free. Bone clung to a single dagger, flopping against the neck's thick hide. Gaunt fired into the eye of one of the other beasts, as Bone's was circling too wildly. He glimpsed Widow Zheng still shooting; once in a while an arrow connected, only to bounce off the lizards' thick hides. This was not something she was used to, of course, and Bone appreciated the effort.

The shaman Northwing was not so evidently useful. She was sitting, eyes closed. It annoyed Bone. Here he was about to plunge to his death, and she was meditating. Even the Xembalans were not doing that!

His mount ceased flailing and began circling high above the battle.

It groaned deep in its gullet.

"Goooooommm."

Bone managed to return to his perch on the neck.

"Gooooohhhhn."

Was it talking to him?

"Booooooohhhhhhn."

"Northwing," he said.

"Aaaaaannnnng Onnnnnnnnn."

"Ang On?"

The flying lizard dove.

His beast plowed into the other two, scattering all. In the midst of the collision his animal became unconscious, and Bone had a single moment before it truly began to fall. In that moment he abandoned the remaining dagger and leaped to the stairway.

His landing was not as graceful as he'd have liked; he scrambled and fell and teetered back. But it was more so than the creatures'. They fell to Xembala's green earth and slowly turned to dust.

Snow Pine was now closest to him. "How do we fare?" he asked her.

"Two lost, one monk, one nun." She was panting as she gripped her staff, but there was a fierce grin upon her face. She hid it as she realized she was grinning in the aftermaths of deaths. But he'd seen it.

"Bone!" Gaunt called from the back of the line. "Are you quite done cavorting with monsters? We've a volcano to visit."

"Agreed!"

They reached the valley floor and walked among desiccated bones.

"They see us," Quilldrake said. "They surely see us coming and they'll loose yet more creatures upon us."

Widow Zheng stared at the ash cloud above the mountain.

"Zheng," Bone said. "Do you remember? If you are Xia, you will know how to get to the Iron Moths."

"I . . ."

"Out with it," said Jewelwolf, striding forward. "In my Il-Khanate, to withhold tactical information is a crime."

Steelfox intercepted her. "We are not in your Il-Khanate, sister."

"All in good time."

"Even if your husband is the new Grand Khan, sister, our father's rules of conduct—"

"I think . . ." began Zheng

"Father is dead," said Jewelwolf.

"You can bring that argument to the Supreme Judge—" said Steelfox.

"Enough!" Gaunt said, raising her arm. "Let Zheng speak."

"I think I do remember," Zheng said. "There was a path within the southern cliffs." She closed her eyes and turned. She pointed. "There."

A waterfall surged down in the spot she noted, its spray giving birth to a tributary of the great river.

"We should go," Bone said.

"There are rites for our dead," Rabten said.

"We have little time," Gaunt said.

"It is true that cremation is impractical now, but we can offer alms for the birds. We will carry our brother and sister to the cliffs, there to leave them for winged scavengers."

"May I assist?" Bone said.

And so Gaunt and Bone helped carry the bodies of two who had fought valiantly for the safety of their land. Bone thought, *I am no hero. Yet it is pleasing sometimes to smooth the path of one.*

At the waterfall they found a fissure in the cliffs in which they left the fallen. When the briefest of rites was concluded, and Bone and Gaunt and the other bearers scrambled back down, Zheng was pointing to the cliff face behind the falls. The surging water was a disorienting thing. Bone found himself gazing upon one burst of spray, tracking it as it fell to the river below. It was strange to realize it fell no more quickly or slowly than a falling man. Then his perception returned to the whole and the feeling of continuous roaring power. It was hard to believe anyone could get behind these falls.

CHRIS WILLRICH   395

"It is there," Zheng reassured. "There is a moment when you must accept that your senses are befuddled by the noise and the motion and the wet, when you must release your fear of losing this existence."

Zheng walked toward the waters.

Bone put himself behind her, promising himself that if the waters washed Zheng away he would grab her. Gaunt and the others came behind.

Spray engulfed them, and mist, and at last a pummeling of icy liquid. Bone couldn't see to help himself, let alone Zheng. Was it like this for Mad Katta? He did not think he would last a day in that dark. He was a bundle of worries and impulses, tied together by a thin twine of ego. The string was fraying. He clattered on.

And then they were through. The hidden cave was illuminated by the fading light of day, as veiled by the waterfall. A rough-hewn passageway led east and north. The threshold was, aptly enough, guarded by worn stone statues of Thresholders.

"Are we all here?"

"Yes," called out Rabten, who added, "I have no knowledge of this place. We have long been discouraged from coming this far east."

"By your high lama?" Flint asked.

"And by her predecessor, and by his predecessor."

"Makes sense," Quilldrake said. "This probably is a secret way to the Iron Moths."

"Our goal is the survival of this valley," Flint told him.

"Of course!"

Zheng said, "Quit talking. We must continue." She hesitated, as though hearing far-off music, then proceeded. They followed into darkness. A pair of monks lit torches.

The journey was long and unnerving, for the mountain continued now and then to shake, and the thought of being buried alive was increasingly hard to dismiss. At last they emerged into a place of red illumination and great heat.

The cavern was vast as the great coliseum in the Eldshore's capital. Although it had the roughness of a place formed by natural processes, the result was surely the work of magic. A lake of bubbling magma surrounded an island of rock perforated with many caves. Strange lights of many colors glowed within those openings.

Bone noticed other passageways leading out of the cavern. He also noticed that the opening they'd just exited was guarded by statues of ferocious three-eyed fanged monstrosities. Once he'd assured himself they would not animate, he noted that the statues glared toward the passageway, not the island.

"Rabten," Bone asked, "what are those statues?"

"Wrathful guardians," the monk answered. "Their fury is in the service of compassion, meant to protect seekers of enlightenment from various obstacles. If they are here, it means this place is hazardous."

Quilldrake said, "Is that the refuge of the Iron Moths?"

"Yes," Zheng said. "Long ago Xia had a hovel by the waterfall, and daily she came to assist the Moths. Until one day she longed to dance with the high lama, and they wove for her a dress that was also a map of her lands, of her life."

"This happened in the days of the third high lama," Rabten said, "who, it is said, somewhat lost his way for a time, becoming enamored of transitory things." The monk looked embarrassed for a moment. "We have long been warned away from this place, and I have never been certain where it lies."

"I don't see the Moths," Quilldrake said.

"But I sense them," Snow Pine answered. "The metal of this staff seems attracted by whatever lies upon the island."

"Perhaps it can take us there!" said Quilldrake.

"Quilldrake, I understand," Bone said. "No one wants to meet the Iron Moths more than I do. But I suspect none of us escapes Xembala alive unless we recover the high lama. Focus, good sir."

"Ah, blazes. You're right of course."

They proceeded around the drop beside the magma lake.

"Where do we proceed?" Flint asked.

"I suspect," Gaunt said, "we go through that passage guarded by six guardians of wrath."

For there, indeed, stood many glowering statues, warning the travelers away from a dark passage sloping upward.

Rabten and his Xembalan companions knelt as he intoned a prayer. Rising, he said, "Let us go."

Eighteen strong, the expedition entered the realm of the Bull Demon.

Gaunt immediately felt a queasiness in her stomach, reminiscent of riding a plunging balloon.

"Are you all right?" Bone asked her, touching her shoulder. He looked a little ill himself.

"More or less. This is nothing compared to pregnancy."

"That's a fair point," said Snow Pine, also looking pained.

"You of course would not know about that, sister," Jewelwolf said. "You who never had the chance to bear your man sons."

Steelfox did not reply, so Gaunt answered for her. "Women's roads can be so rocky, Jewelwolf. Why do we throw stones in each other's paths?"

"Stay out of this, foreigner," said Jewelwolf.

"We are all foreigners here," Widow Zheng said, "except these nuns and monks. Even I . . ."

"Yet motherhood is not foreign to you, I think," Jewelwolf said with an airy laugh, and Zheng responded with a clipped nod. "We are all mothers here, are we not . . . except Steelfox and her pet shaman. All true women."

"Irrelevant, Jewelwolf," snapped Northwing. "I'm not a woman."

"You dare to talk this way?" Jewelwolf answered. "And yet I am curious. You dress as a man, by the standards of your people. Do you believe you are one?"

"I don't consider myself either male or female," Northwing said. "I'm a shaman. Among our people that means I walk between all categories. Light and darkness. Giving and claiming. Life and—"

"Yes, yes, I have heard all this before," Jewelwolf snapped, "though I did not realize the depth of the perversion."

Steelfox, who had not spoken before, said in a voice low and sharp, "You will not speak to my servant in that manner."

"Oh! You care about your pets! Your twisted shaman and your deranged inventor."

"I rather like 'deranged,'" Haytham put in.

"It is always thus with you," Steelfox said. "Cutting at me, smiling all the time. Always reminding me I am not a baatar. Reminding me my realm is smaller and more desolate. Reminding me that my husband died before we had children."

Jewelwolf said, "It is not my fault that you haven't remarried. You are a Karvak princess; you could have your pick of men."

"If I had no taste—"

"Perhaps your taste runs more to your livestock—"

"Enough!" Steelfox's blade was unsheathed. "Do you seek combat? I will give it to you!"

Jewelwolf responded in kind, though she still left her round, cloaked shield on her back. "You think you can—"

"Princesses!" boomed a voice, though it struggled to be heard over the sudden rumbling of the mountain. When the sound subsided, it was Rabten who continued to speak. "Princesses, hatred is the great enemy of humankind. We are in the lair of one who feeds upon that very emotion. Do you not sense it? The disorientation we felt, it brought us deeper into the power of the Bull Demon. We are more easily gripped by hate."

Gaunt said, in as calm a voice as she could manage, "I suspected we'd pierced another veil of reality."

Bone put in, "You know, I am coming to prefer my own mundane reality, with its bandits and sandstorms and ornery camels."

"And its walking mummies," Gaunt said, "and Leviathans and dragon horses?"

"Exactly! The everyday world."

They chuckled together, and Gaunt studied the princesses. The mood had changed. They were backing away from each other.

Rabten said, "Even here in a realm of evil, the greatest foe is the fury we bring with us. Only tolerance of and patience with one another can challenge this threat. Be true, Karvak warriors, my daughters. Defeat the enemy called hate!"

Steelfox breathed in, breathed out, gaze focused not upon her sister but at some hidden horizon only she could see.

She sheathed her blade.

Jewelwolf said, "I am not your daughter. The man whose daughter I am would remove your head for speaking to me in this way."

That said, she sheathed her blade as well.

Rabten bowed.

They continued up the passage.

Gaunt released a slow breath, took in air that tasted increasingly acrid. The hallway had the look of a natural lava tube, but as with the tunnel in Five-Toe Peak, Gaunt did not believe it. The thought made her glance at Snow Pine, whose own gaze alternated between the tunnel and Monkey's staff.

"Are you all right?" Gaunt asked.

"Yes . . . The staff seems skittish, excited by this place. And I'm seeing things . . . strands of chi flowing from place to place within this mountain. They're concentrated somewhere not far ahead. The staff feels more powerful now . . . I'm not sure I can command it."

"You can," said Flint. "I am regularly amazed by what you can accomplish, Snow Pine."

"I . . . thanks."

"We are here," Rabten said.

Up ahead the passage opened onto the volcano's caldera, a space like a titanic, smoldering arena. Smoke rose up in scores of places from the rocks. There was lava here as well, bubbling up from a sort of natural cauldron on the left, flowing through the middle of the caldera and disappearing through a gash on the far right. Near the far wall were two deflated Karvak balloons.

In between lay an island, like the island of the Iron Moths. But unlike that vast dome of twisted stone, this island was dominated by single ruddy boulder the size of a keep.

Into it was carved the face of a ferocious bull.

Eyes that resembled enormous rubies blazed within the red stone.

"If I were not terrified," Bone said to Gaunt, "I might imagine the two of us scrambling up the back of that thing, to creep over its head and claim the rubies."

With a rumble, the visage's grin widened, revealing serrated ruby teeth the size of stalagmites. A deep tormented groan rose from the stone gullet.

"Or perhaps not," he added.

"We can tell the story your way afterward," she said.

The Bull Demon was not moaning at them. There was an encampment of round tents before it, and a score of robed individuals knelt or sat cross-legged beside them, as though waiting. They looked to be the Fraternity of the Hare. Two others held a captive between them, standing as close as they dared to the Bull Demon.

One of the captors was a member of the Fraternity.

The second, Gaunt saw with the plunging-balloon feeling, was Mad Katta.

Between them stood Chodak. It seemed to Gaunt the three were speaking to each other, but she could not make out the words.

The Bull Demon, however, she could hear. It spoke in what she suspected was the language of Xembala, in a rumbling, hissing voice like hot stones tossed into water.

"What does it say?" Gaunt asked the nun beside her.

"'I am so cold,' it says," the nun replied, as she made gestures against evil. "'Let the high lama warm me.'"

"Where is the flying carpet?" Bone asked. "Where is Deadfall?"

"I do not see it," Gaunt realized.

There was more talking. A voice was raised, a woman's voice, and Gaunt realized the robed figure helping secure the lama was the woman Bone had called Dolma. The Bull Demon roared back.

"The demon says, 'You cannot bargain with me,'" the nun relayed. "'I will promise nothing. With the high lama in my maw, the valley is mine to control.'"

More talk.

"Now the demon says, 'You lost your right to bargain when you came to the place of my power. You may be able to resist the Charstalkers, but I have other servants.'"

And a great flapping arose, and unearthly shapes descended into the caldera. They were winged nightmares of dark metal, four-winged and dozen-legged, spikes covering their faces. The wings swirled with what might have been celestial symbols—comets, stars, nebulae. A red glow suffused them. There were perhaps a hundred, and they surrounded the tents.

"No," Widow Zheng said.

The Bull Demon laughed.

The nun, her voice losing some of its composure, relayed, "'My power waxes and the Iron Moths can no longer resist my Charstalkers. Give up the high lama, now. Slave Katta, lead her to me.'"

"We must stop this," Gaunt said.

"We will," said Rabten. He snapped orders in Xembalan, and his people rose. "Help us if you can, but this is our fight."

The Xembalans rushed toward the Iron Moths and their lost leader.

Gaunt called to Steelfox and Jewelwolf. "You are the best archers we have. Can you each hit one of the Bull Demon's eyes?"

"Of course," Steelfox said.

"But what point is there in that?" Jewelwolf said.

"Distraction," Steelfox said.

Arrows flew and plinked off the giant rubies. The Bull Demon roared. The great boulder shifted and regarded the newcomers.

The distraction worked. The high lama broke free of Mad Katta, while Dolma seemed unwilling to keep her. Chodak ran beside the river of lava, chased by others of the Fraternity, but an Iron Moth got to her first. Rabten and two monks tackled the Moth, which rose into the sky to shake them off.

The three fell into the lava and were lost.

Gaunt watched, horrified. But Chodak was free and running toward them.

Bone was already sprinting to protect Chodak, as more Charstalker-possessed Iron Moths flew her way and robed figures continued to chase. All the other Xembalans were engaged with the Moths or the Fraternity. It was the foreigners' moment.

Gaunt said, "Archers, concentrate on the Fraternity. They're flesh. Snow Pine, I suspect you have the only weapon that can harm Iron Moths. Engage them. Haytham, Flint, Quilldrake, do what you can to guard the high lama."

"I am willing," Haytham said. "But where are Quilldrake and Flint?"

Steelfox heard her inventor ask the whereabouts of the treasure hunters, but she had no time to wonder at their absence. She picked off three of the Fraternity, then fired an arrow at the Charstalker-taken Iron Moth that now closed on the lama. This seemed to have no effect, nor did her sister's own arrow. They tried again, to no avail, although Steelfox did have the impression the creature noticed them and was angered.

It was like old times, in a way, when the sisters might have competed together in games of archery and riding. It had been too long since Steelfox had ridden a horse. It had been too long since she'd seen the steppes. Too long since she'd felt like a sister.

"Quit daydreaming," Jewelwolf said. "Aim for the eyes."

"Those are much smaller than the ones on the Bull Demon."

"Always excuses."

Steelfox hissed and fired. She hit an eye. Jewelwolf did likewise. The Moth, or perhaps the Charstalker within, seemed enraged. It bypassed the high lama and came directly toward the Karvaks.

Persimmon Gaunt shouted, "Northwing! Can you affect these creatures?"

"I will try . . ."

But before anything else could occur, Widow Zheng had walked into the Iron Moth's path, hands raised.

The Iron Moth paused.

"You know me," Zheng said. "Or you know of me. I was Xia. I saved your ancestors. Do not harm my companions."

The Iron Moth landed, halted, shook like a taut sail in a strong wind. The Charstalker blaze surrounding it grew brighter. Bit by bit the quivering Moth came closer to Zheng.

Northwing said, "I have it."

The Moth fell, twelve legs flailing.

Jewelwolf aimed at it.

"Wait!" Steelfox said. "If the shaman has control, it could be a useful tool."

"As you wish." Jewelwolf shot instead at a member of the Fraternity headed toward the high lama. Steelfox followed suit.

As the arrows hit, Snow Pine charged up to another Moth and swung her staff. With a sound of thunder the Moth careened back. Gaunt and Bone joined Snow Pine, each with daggers out. Haytham had his arm around the high lama.

"This is foolishness," Jewelwolf said, readying another arrow. "The human warriors are one thing. But these people cannot stop otherworldly monsters."

"What would you suggest?" Steelfox asked.

"I do not suggest. I act."

Jewelwolf shot an arrow at the high lama. The woman fell.

"No!" Xia cried and ran to the lama's side. Northwing struggled to control the Iron Moth.

Steelfox whirled to her sister. "Are you mad?"

"Hardly. If the lama dies, she will reincarnate somewhere. The Bull Demon will have no immediate way to claim her; thus Xembala is safe. And we may claim our prize. But I do not think she is finished yet."

The high lama was being tended by Gaunt, Bone, and Haytham, while Snow Pine fought off an Iron Moth. Two more were coming.

Steelfox dropped her bow, drew her blade. "You won't be finishing anyone."

"I'm disappointed," Jewelwolf said, keeping her bow and aiming at Steelfox. "But this moment was inevitable, was it not?"

"Give up your weapons, and you needn't give up your life."

"I never imagined you for a traitor, sister."

"And I am not. I am loyal to our father's dreams."

"His dreams? The reality is that he chose me over you and would have made me ruler if not for the laws. Obey me now."

"No. This is your last chance. You are alone."

"I think not." Jewelwolf tossed her bow and removed from her back not a shield but a bronze mirror, its back marked with astronomical symbols. It began to glow.

"Lady . . ." Northwing managed to say. "I am losing . . ."

The Iron Moth she'd been dominating rose and leapt toward her.

Steelfox did not hesitate. There was no fear. She ran to intercept the Iron Moth. Jewelwolf's tricks must wait.

Her sword was good Karvak steel, and it got one fierce blow against the Moth before shattering. The next thing she knew, the entity was clubbing her with four separate legs, each like an iron staff. Light exploded in her eyes, and each burst seemed accompanied by the laughter of Jewelwolf.

Bone saw that Chodak was alive but gasping. The arrow might have grazed a lung. It surely had unleashed considerable blood. "Ma'am," he said. "I've faced many injuries. I will help."

"And I," Haytham said, "I've studied with my land's physicians."

Chodak coughed. "Persimmon Gaunt. I give this to you."

Beneath the high lama's robes, spattered with her blood, was the saber named Crypttongue.

"I do not want it, Holiness," Gaunt said.

"It wants you," Chodak said. "I hear its whispers. It preferred the treasure hunter, but he has gone. You are here. Your karma and its are bound together."

"Bone . . ." Gaunt said.

"I understand, Persimmon," Bone said, letting intuition guide his words. He did not know what he'd say before it left his mouth. "I can't tell you what to do. But whether or not you claim the sword, you've already claimed me."

Gaunt looked to where Snow Pine fought for their lives, swinging Monkey's staff again and again. Now a second Iron Moth arrived.

She took the bloody sword. Soon she was at Snow Pine's side.

Bone wanted to join her, but he knew he'd be little assistance against the Moths. Here, he might help.

Haytham said, as he tore the fabric away from the puncture point. "Imago Bone, keep the high lama immobile whist I pull free the arrow."

Bone nodded, feeling unexpectedly abashed at seeing a holy woman so exposed. The lama seemed less concerned with this than with her attacker. "I heard Princess Jewelwolf's reasons. She has had a valid insight, I suspect . . . though I perhaps would not have applied it in quite that fashion . . ."

"Uh, Holiness," said Bone, "We have to pull that arrow."

"You're quite right." She smiled. "There is a famous parable to the effect that one should not question the design of the arrow, nor the identity of the shooter, before getting it out."

"Whoever said that was wise," Haytham said. "Hold still."

"Yes, I would agree—ah!"

Chodak was sitting upright—with Bone supporting her and stanching her wound and Haytham holding a bloody arrow—when Zheng arrived.

Zheng knelt. "You . . . ," Zheng said. "You were my prince, my Tashi."

"Times have changed . . . my Xia. Xembala and I are not the same. The wheel turns."

"I fled from you, ashamed of being a peasant in your land. I found my way to a town in the desert, now buried. I never saw you again, but I saw the Moths. They came in anger and rent the Silk Map. Greedy people ran off with most of the pieces. They tell stories up and down the braid, that you tore the dress. You are ill-served by such tales. I had not thought we would meet again."

"In a sense we did not . . . still, karma endures, and we two are here."

"If only . . ." Zheng looked wistful.

Chodak smiled. "If only we were not inside a demonic volcano . . . fighting for our lives?"

Zheng laughed. "Yes. That is what I meant."

"May the Thresholders allow us to meet later. For now . . . I think you are the only one the Iron Moths will heed . . . and I think Steelfox needs you."

Zheng nodded and departed. Chodak sighed back into Bone's arms. Bone was startled by the transformation; one moment Chodak was bright with vitality, the next collapsing.

"Ma'am?" Bone said.

"There is considerable pain. . . . I will now practice a discipline in which I ask the Thresholders to let my suffering draw to itself the suffering of others . . . thereby granting solace to many around the world."

"I do not understand."

"What I mean is, I will be all right. . . . Haytham ibn Zakwan ibn Rihab is a fair physician. . . . Imago Bone, there is a woman who needs you . . ."

Bone looked up to see Gaunt fighting beside Snow Pine. The pair were actually holding their own. One Iron Moth had been felled, and each woman now faced another. Monkey's staff cracked metal carapaces, and Crypttongue bit deep.

"That battle seems somewhat out of my league," Bone said, "but I'll do what I can."

"No, I do not speak of your wife, Imago Bone. I speak of your countrywoman."

Snow Pine hardly dared to admit to herself how much fun she was having. She should not—she thought in between thunderous blows against her opponents—wish to harm intelligent beings. The Fraternity of the Hare were misguided, but their motivation was love of country. And the creatures from the stars were possessed by demons of her own world. She should pity them, not grin as she smashed them, pounded them, knocked them into a river of lava.

But grin she did. From a life of submission to a life of banditry, from a retreat in an otherworldly monastery to an adventure across the world, she had never had such an opportunity to unleash all her fury. It was a peculiar joy.

She was glad to have Gaunt beside her, but it seemed to her Gaunt took less pleasure in the fight. Crypttongue flashed in the caldera's strange light as the poet hacked and jabbed with grim focus.

Snow Pine wondered what price her friend was paying for such power.

But perhaps she should wonder about herself. The staff was hot and faintly glowing. A wild energy seized her, and she felled a new Iron Moth in one blow.

"Snow Pine!" Gaunt said. "Stay with me."

Snow Pine only laughed, and the rhythm of battle danced her away from Gaunt and deeper into the fray.

Snow Pine's departure left only Gaunt to protect the high lama, and she fought with fresh determination. Stabbing deep into an Iron Moth, she felt not one but two minds flow into the sword and babble their way into her consciousness.

She knelt, absorbing the strange sensations.

—*suffer suffer I will make you pay*—

<< discorporation unexpected >>

—*you will scream in agony*—

<< separation from Charstalker pleasing >>

—*you will beg me for release*—

<< loss of body not pleasing >>

—*you have my eternal hate*—

<< observation: nothing lasts forever >>

Despite the danger, the disorientation left her staring upward. Luckily Snow Pine seemed to be attracting all the possessed Iron Moths to herself. This pause allowed Gaunt to notice a dark shape dropping out of the sky.

It was the flying carpet, Deadfall.

It seemed to be coming right for her.

She raised the sword, covered with red and orange blood.

It did not seek her out but rather flapped toward Princess Jewelwolf, one corner folded down, red light flickering upon its knotwork.

"Mistress," she heard it say.

Gaunt rose to stagger toward Jewelwolf, who was even now stepping upon the carpet, bearing the magical bronze mirror from the flying ger.

"Mistress, I have it. I have the thing the Cardinals hoped to claim."

Gaunt got as far as Northwing, Zheng, and Steelfox. The three were facing down an Iron Moth. The shaman's eyes were shut. The Karvak was bleeding in several places, but she was still alive, kneeling beside Zheng, and Zheng's hand was thrust outward toward the Moth.

The Moth did not move; it was held in place by this combination of effort. But neither did the three women have the wherewithal to confront Jewelwolf.

"Mistress," Deadfall was saying, "I have my full powers, and the Bull Demon is distracted. I was able to cross half the world and back again. Mistress, it is yours."

—betrayer artifact it defies us—

<< intriguing metadimensional phenomenon in vicinity >>

Gaunt's eyes widened as she lurched forward with Crypttongue. She could not believe what she thought she glimpsed. The skin on the back of her neck felt cold prickles, no matter that she stood in a volcano's maw. Jewelwolf noticed her.

"No, poet and madwoman," said the Karvak lady, stepping onto Deadfall and letting it bear her upward. "It is not for you. Nor is it for my sister. It is for one with vision. Keep your ironsilk."

The Karvak extended her hand, and Deadfall's folded corner revealed its prize.

"No," Gaunt said.

Steelfox slowly came to her senses, realizing that her comrades (comrades?) had prevented the Iron Moth from slaying her. That left her free to do something, yes? Perhaps even stand up.

She stood up.

Yes, that was something. Zheng and Northwing, in their different ways, were fully occupied with the Moth, but there was someone else here. Gaunt— Gaunt had that sword again this time. And Gaunt was confronting Steelfox's little sister.

The princess's wits began returning. She saw Jewelwolf rise into the air, and she recognized the magic carpet she had tangled with before. The red light dancing among its knots was reminiscent of the Charstalkers, but from Jewelwolf's glee, Steelfox did not think it was the Bull Demon whom the carpet was serving just now.

Steelfox found her dropped bow. She picked it up, readied an arrow. General principle.

Persimmon Gaunt was saying something rather unexpected.

"Great Jewelwolf. I will grant you any service, any treasure, if you will only give your prize to me."

But Steelfox already knew from her sister's expression what the answer would be. For a moment a request flickered on Jewelwolf's lips, and Steelfox wondered if it would have been, Then slay my sister. But conquest prevailed over rivalry. "This relic is not the true prize, as I think you well know. The true prize lies within. A prize that can shake an empire."

Steelfox was not at all sure what was happening, but she was used to acting on hunches. It was a hunch that had led her to take on Northwing and Haytham, a hunch that had sent her chasing the Silk Map farther than her mother had likely wanted her to go.

A hunch that led her to fire up at the scroll of Qiangguo in Jewelwolf's hand.

The shot flew true.

She had meant to hit the scroll so as to force Jewelwolf to drop it, without harming her sister. But the substance of the thing was surely no ordinary paper, for the arrow sparked and flew wildly across the caldera. Startled, Jewelwolf crouched as Deadfall rose higher, becoming a shield for her.

"Gaunt? What is the thing my sister holds?"

"It is my life, Steelfox, and Bone's, and Snow Pine's. I don't know how it came to be here. But what I told Jewelwolf, I tell you. Help us get it back, and I am your servant."

I collect interesting servants, Steelfox thought. "I do not know how to help. If only—Qurca!"

She still could not sense her falcon's mind, but the falcon swooped through the strange thermals of the caldera and landed upon Steelfox's outstretched glove.

"It is a relief to see you, old friend. What is that you're carrying?"

Gaunt gasped. "I have seen the like of that splinter before. Steelfox, please. I must follow your sister. You must take this splinter to Snow Pine."

Steelfox looked toward a mass of the possessed Iron Moths and a lone woman battling them. "I will rank my bravery beside anyone's, but I am not certain that's wise."

"You must trust me. Quickly!"

"No. You said you are in my service. Slay this Iron Moth who threatens Northwing and Zheng. Then I will do as you request."

With a shout of anguish, Gaunt did as Steelfox asked, swinging Crypt-tongue with ferocity that rivaled a Karvak's.

For Bone to fight the Iron Moths was not a happy proposition. Moving through them was something else. With reckless pleasure, Bone jumped, rolled, sprinted, vaulted. At one point he leapt upon the back of an Iron Moth and then off again, thus bypassing the river of lava. He was especially proud of that.

Unfortunately the only witness besides the Moth was pointing a serrated sword at him.

"At least I'll have the pleasure, Imago Bone, of sending you to the lava."

"Are you still protecting paradise, Dolma?"

"She failed us! The flaw within the high lama was too large. It was she who was responsible for the Silk Map leaving Xembala. I think she always hoped it would lead her lost love back to her."

"And to stop that, you'd side with this fellow?" Bone pointed a thumb. "He's not exactly what you'd call an equal partner." He waved a hand toward Mad Katta, who stood staring at the Bull Demon, sweat dripping down his face, in the grip of some compulsion. "She who doesn't want to be a wolf shouldn't wear a wolf's hide, as they say in our country."

"It was the only way."

"'It was the only way.' How often have I said that to myself, to others. And so rarely, Dolma, was it true! We imagine ourselves within a shadowed labyrinth when truly we stand upon a sunlit hill, the horizon all around."

Dolma waved the sword toward him. "Back."

"I cannot, Violante. I think I must help you return to the sunlight. Xembala is beautiful, yes, but perhaps it is too beautiful for some of us. Perhaps for some of us what's needed are the fishing docks of Widdershins, where fish guts and swearing go along with glorious sunsets. Or the briny tidepools of Ramblefar Rim, where if you can tolerate the reek you will see starfish like jewels."

"Stop."

"Or if the West no longer beckons, what of the East? I have seen the harbor of Riverclaw, a thousand bobbing craft ready to take you to the ten thousand worlds that are all labeled 'Qiangguo.' I have seen the Ochre River, a serpent of muddy gold. There are places in the farthest North where ice twists into shapes of nightmare and wonder. There are seas in the South where the water is like stepping into a steaming Mirabad bath. None of these things are paradise. All of them await you. Better an egg today than a hen tomorrow."

"Do not quote the proverbs of your homeland, Bone. It is not mine. I do not think I have a country. Except hate." Dolma looked toward the maw of the Bull Demon. "Yes. To give myself to it, burn away everything that is weak, everything that snivels like a little girl. Yes."

A new voice said, "No . . ." It was Mad Katta. Every muscle in the wanderer seemed to fight the Bull Demon's hold upon him. His trembling hand was reaching for a bag upon his belt. "No, that is not right. . . . Even here, in a place so full of evil I can see every direction I look. . . . Even here, that is not right. . . . You can be free, Dolma . . ."

"You know nothing of me!"

She turned and ran toward the ruby fangs.

Bone chased her, even as he heard Gaunt's voice crying, "Bone, Bone, don't let her—" and a shadow passed over him.

CHAPTER 28

INTERLUDE: EPIPHANIES OF AN EMPEROR'S ROBE

You ask me, Greatest One, what happened that day, when the Bull Demon awakened and what was imprisoned was released? I will tell you. But you must understand first how I came by the great prize.

I am Deadfall, the work of the wizard Olob. I am only secondarily a flying carpet, I now know, for all that I am a good one. I have a primary function and rather a useful one. I am a demon-siphon.

In the vicinity of weaker demons, I can absorb some of their essence, making this power available to my master. Olob, a demonologist, relished the potential I embodied. He envisioned himself making forays into Bull-Demon Mountain, swooping in like a falcon claiming a mouse, returning with delicious power.

He was a fool.

His apprentice Op understood his teacher's plans enough to be afraid for his master, himself, and the world. At best his mentor would become corrupted. At worst the Bull Demon might be freed from its prison-haven in lost Xembala. And so when Olob departed Anoka on an errand, Op attempted to complete me in a more wholesome fashion, so that I would drain power only from the vital breath of the land.

He was a greater fool.

Op's motives were good, by his own lights, but better to have destroyed me than create such a conflicted thing. When Olob returned early and discovered Op's treachery, only I survived the conflagration. But it was too late. Already did I think, and scheme.

Yet much of my nature was hidden from myself. The side I owed to Op was not aware how the side crafted by Olob hungered for demon-energy and craved wickedness.

I have murdered several times, never quite acknowledging it to myself, until that day in Qushkent when Charstalkers tried to possess me.

Instead, I ate them.

Poor Mad Katta. Exulting in my new power, I went to its ultimate source, as Olob had always intended. In the mountain of the Bull Demon did I leave him, trading him for a dose of that entity's energies. Even then I was nearly overwhelmed by the Bull Demon's power.

And so, trying to forget the screams of Katta, I hovered high in the atmosphere, unwilling to surrender my new powers, yet knowing that descending with Olob's pattern dominant would be to surrender myself to the Bull Demon's influence.

Sometimes, I have come to learn, the best action is no action. The world is larger than our perceived choices, and time may make other options known. So it was with me.

In Qiangguo, the energies playing at the edge of space are known as the Celestial Kingdom. If one's perceptions are properly attuned, these forces can be twisted aside to reveal what minds of matter might perceive as palaces, gardens, wildernesses, inhabited by luminous beings who have long meddled in the business of the East. (The rest of the world has its own problems.) I did not enter those realms, but I sensed them, knew the subtle currents of energy. For although I was fashioned to absorb the stuff of demons, I was also made to sniff the life-stuff of the world. And so, over the days, I gained understanding.

I began to perceive the flow of what Qiangguo's people sometimes call "chi," moving through the lands below me. The major patterns revealed themselves first. I saw a gentle flow of energy circulating through the land of Xembala. I beheld a stately procession of power along the Heavenwalls toward Qiangguo's capital. I sensed the network of crystal branchings that still underlay the great desert beside the Braid of Spice.

Later, less obvious but still fascinating patterns emerged. There was a city in the West shaped like a hand, clutching at the energies of the surrounding land. (Nearby was a great crater seething with strange powers I did not wish to look upon long.) Dragons slept as islands in the ocean east of Qiangguo. Dragons of a different sort slumbered as mountain ranges in the far West. And one collection of dormant dragons—in the form of islands like jagged mountains—butted heads in a cold northwestern sea. Their conflict was the work of millennia, and the longest-lived of the mortals who dwelled in those violent lands might only perceive one thrust or parry, thinking it merely an earthquake or rockslide or storm.

Something in that faraway land tickled at me, and I turned all my perception toward it. Yes. There was a great chain binding headlands of each of the three dragon-isles. Although far smaller than the Heavenwalls or the crystals of the Leviathan Minds, it too was a human work that rearranged the power of the land.

And it was seeking something.

A thread of energy—gold, to my perception—twisted across the world to a point deep in the eastern ocean.

I could sense nothing special about that spot, except for one thing. I noticed another thread of energy—purple, to my perception—also leading to that spot. Its far end was at the capital of Qiangguo, where the Heavenwalls met.

And now I recalled a thing that Princess Jewelwolf had discussed with me, about a matter important to her colleagues the Cardinals of the Compass Rose.

Now, if I dropped low to the land, the Bull Demon would surely claim me. But I had not considered immersing myself in water. I was not a swimming carpet, of course. But knowing exactly where I needed to go, perhaps . . .

Yes.

Luck was with me, for even as I arced toward the ocean, I sensed that the Bull Demon's attention was divided. His influence was strong, but my will remained stronger. I found the spot in the ocean, near a shattered island, and I plunged in.

It was a mistake, I realized. The building pressure of the water was inimical to my enchantments. I could not stay down long enough to reach bottom and return.

But I was enjoying gambling, O greatest one, and I thought, if the stories are true, there is no need to reach bottom and return in one trip.

In the muck at the bottom of the sea, amid gaping fish, I found the scroll.

Wrapping myself around it, I wished myself inside.

Thus it was that I flopped out of the sky of another world and splatted upon a mountainside. It was raining, which did not much help things. But a kindly fellow, looking rather ratty in a torn robe and bark hat, took me to the pagoda near the mountain's top.

He squeezed me out at the doorstep and set me beside a fire.

I dreamed. I saw cities burn. Oh, if you must know? Qushkent. River-claw. Palmary. Archaeopolis. Anoka. I forget all the names.

When I awoke I perceived many people. The ragged man who'd carried me. A girl of perhaps twelve with piercing brown eyes. An old monk with gold in his teeth. An equally old man in impeccable robes who carried a staff. And a boy around the same age as the girl, a pale lad who seemed somehow familiar.

At first they were talking amongst themselves, and I waited for them to address me. Then it occurred to me they had no way to know I was conscious. Indeed, this was the topic under discussion.

"It must be sapient," the ragged man was saying. "The Sage Painter speci-fied that only intelligent creatures could enter the scroll."

"It's a rug," said the girl.

"A magic carpet," said the man with the staff.

"Underneath all that gruffness," said the monk, "you're really a wide-eyed boy, aren't you?"

"Nothing of the sort," grunted the staff-man. "She is right; it is a rug. And he is right; it must be sapient. Therefore: magic carpet."

"It seems somewhat un-lively," said the ragged man.

"It's a gift," said the boy, in a devout tone. "It stinks of salt water, the way books describe the ocean. It was sent through the waters to us. Someone is trying to help us." He looked at the girl. "Maybe our parents."

They batted the problem around for a time. I saw no reason to enlighten them. They decided to maintain their watch upon me, but one at a time for now. The boy, whose name I now knew, chose first watch. He slept upon the floor beside me. I slid closer, awakening the power within me. A red glow suf-fused the room.

"Hear me in your dreams, Innocence Gaunt. Learn to trust me before you meet me while awake. I am Deadfall, and I am your truest friend. Your parents abandoned you. But I will free you and show you the greater world."

The light swelled, as I absorbed a tiny fraction of his chi.

"But first, there is so much I must teach you."

CHAPTER 29

THE MAN WHO WOULD BE SERICULTURALIST

"I cannot believe you talked me into this."

"So that's how you'll tell it."

"Be serious, Art. Our friends are fighting for their lives up there."

"One friend in particular, eh?"

"You're more than a little fond of Zheng."

"That's more of an ad hoc mutual loneliness society. . . . Ah, here's where we can cross."

"Furthermore, if the Iron Moths find us, our guts will be scattered from here to Qushkent."

"Precisely! Which is why now, when they and everyone else are busy elsewhere, we must be here. Don't tell me you aren't a little awed by the incalculable wealth that surrounds us right now."

"I'm awed that I let you talk me into this."

"Nothing odd about it. Do you have the bags?"

CHAPTER 30

JAWS OF VICTORY

Gaunt ran ahead of her companions, fighting her way through the possessed Iron Moths in her way.

"Bone!" she was shouting. "Bone! She has the scroll! Bone!"

"Eh?" he was saying and looking up at the shadow of the magic carpet passing overhead.

For a moment Gaunt saw Jewelwolf landing beside the very maw of the Bull Demon and scrambling up to the teeth.

In the next moment, her view was blocked by more Iron Moths.

A voice scratched at her mind.

<< nullification of former brood-mates undesirable >>

It made so little sense, she simply swung with Crypttongue, trying to batter her way through to Bone.

<< alternative method desirable >>

"What!" she gasped. "Are! You saying?"

<< you saying: nzzt vlkzzt rzznnt >>

"What?"

<< nzzt vlkzzt rzznnt >>

"Nzzt . . ." she attempted to render the strange sounds. "Vlkzzt . . . ?"

<< rzznt! rzznt! >>

"Rzznt . . ."

Whatever she said, the nearest Iron Moths understood it. They visibly struggled against the grip of the Charstalkers. This moment of consternation allowed Gaunt the chance to slip through. She did not think anyone else followed.

Bone was engaged in speaking with one of the Fraternity, but he followed Gaunt wide-eyed. The one-eared woman stared after them, but Gaunt had no time for her.

"Is it?" he managed.

"Yes," she said.

"How?"

"I don't know. Ask later."

They did not know what to make of it when Jewelwolf reached out with her hand—until the scroll was thoroughly inside the maw.

A figure manifested within: a boy. Gaunt might not have recognized him but for seeing a vision of him in the garden of Mentor John.

"Innocence!"

The boy looked out between the ruby teeth and blinked. "You?"

Red light erupted within the maw. Innocence staggered.

"No!" Gaunt somehow found the strength to run even faster, but then she was slapped aside by a corner of the carpet Deadfall.

"Do not interfere," came the carpet's voice. "This is what he needs."

Bone dove around the carpet but found himself confronted by Jewelwolf's sword.

Gaunt yelled, "What, to be devoured?" She was on her feet and ready to cleave the carpet in two.

"No," said Deadfall. "The Bull Demon is not the one who will do the devouring. . . . Wait, this is not right . . ."

Innocence was on his knees. He seemed to be resisting whatever the Bull Demon was doing, but losing. Bone was prepared to leap into that maw, but even Dolma was hesitating now. He suspected whatever the boy could struggle against would extinguish the likes of Imago Bone. He needed a weapon, something a demon would feel . . .

He remembered Katta reaching for his bag.

Bone rushed to the wanderer, who still shivered in the grip of the Bull Demon's power, and grabbed the sack.

Into the maw of the Bull Demon flew Katta's bag, a few blessed sweet-cakes tumbling out as it arrived.

The entity roared in agony. Innocence cried out, sounding only a little less pained.

Jewelwolf yanked the boy out of the maw and onto the flying carpet.

Strange crimson energies trailed from Innocence as though the boy were an oil-soaked torch. Yet though his face twisted in pain, his flesh was whole.

Before he could fully escape, the Bull Demon's jaws clamped over Innocence's leg.

The boy screamed. His leg was not severed, however, only trapped. The Bull Demon meant to keep him.

"No!" Gaunt and Bone shouted at once.

Jewelwolf tried to pull Innocence free, calling upon Deadfall to rise with all its might.

Bone reached between the vast teeth, trying to force them apart with the strength of his body.

Gaunt was there in the next moment, adding her strength.

"Help us!" Bone cried to the warrior named Dolma. "He's our son!"

"But . . . it is clear they seek to steal him away . . ."

"He'll die!" Gaunt said.

Dolma was there, then, also trying to force the teeth apart.

"Deadfall," Jewelwolf said, "add your strength. Pull him free."

The magic carpet shifted beneath her, until it wrapped itself around Innocence. It tugged.

It seemed impossible to Gaunt that Innocence could scream more terribly, but he did.

"You'll tear his leg off!" Gaunt said.

"If necessary!" Jewelwolf said.

Gaunt snarled and gave up with the teeth. She raised Crypttongue and eyed the teeth holding Innocence.

Sword, we are bound together. Swan, forgive me and guide my aim. I will not lose him now.

Steelfox had wanted to aid Gaunt against Jewelwolf, but if Gaunt was certain the mineral sliver was important, then deliver it to Snow Pine she would.

With Widow Zheng and Northwing beside her, she strode into the heart of the fray, passing Xembalans battling the Charstalker-possessed Iron Moths. Many times Zheng or Northwing drove back a Moth; Zheng with a gesture, Northwing with pained concentration.

Steelfox threw the Iron Moths her best Karvak stares, and Qurca shrieked, but she knew it was the oldsters who were keeping her alive just now. She promised herself never to forget to honor her elders, if she could get through this.

At last they were beside Snow Pine. This woman of hated Qiangguo fought like a Karvak. Blood flowed from her nose and mouth, and her robe was soaked in sweat, yet onward she battled against half a dozen unearthly foes.

Steelfox said, "I care nothing about our differences this day! You are my sister-in-battle!"

"Shut up and fight!"

"That's not why I'm here!" Steelfox held up the crystal splinter. "Do you know what this is?"

"I can't even stop to look at it!" Snow Pine whacked a fresh opponent. "You tell me!"

"I have no notion myself!"

"I have—no time—for Karvak riddles!"

"I have no time for your haughtiness! Gaunt wants you to have it!"

"She might have explained it, then!"

"She is busy saving her son!"

"What?"

Snow Pine paused in surprise.

This hesitation almost slew her. But Northwing and Widow Zheng flanked her, holding off a fresh assault of Iron Moths. For a moment.

At last Snow Pine focused on the object in Steelfox's hand.

"I—I apologize, Lady."

Snow Pine bowed low.

Steelfox said, "Just take the damned thing."

Snow Pine did.

"Now what?" Steelfox said.

Snow Pine frowned, considering the splinter. "All right. Maybe one Monkey thing will like another Monkey thing."

She tapped the splinter to the iron rod.

There was a sound as of a deep gong, and she gasped and released the splinter.

Before it fell to the caldera floor it shimmered and widened and took the form of a massive stone monkey, no shorter than Snow Pine, covered in hairs of dark crystal.

"Miss me?" it said.

Bone saw Gaunt raise Crypttongue and understood her gamble; he threw his arms around his son.

If she miscalculates, let the sword take my soul and not his.

The sword fell. The Bull Demon bellowed. Ruby fragments flew everywhere, cutting Bone's flesh. But the steel did not touch him nor Innocence.

Immediately he and Innocence were snatched far into the sky.

Bone looked down and saw the caldera receding fast. Even were he unconcerned about lava, rocks, demons, and Moths, the altitude would be a killer. He would have to get control of the situation by other means.

He felt for a dagger and found none.

Yet he did feel steel. Unfortunately it was poking his neck.

"I give you a choice, Imago Bone. Die by falling, or die by stabbing."

Bone hung there on the tassels of a dilemma. "Do you truly think, Jewelwolf, you're good enough to kill me in one blow?"

"Astonishing, the impudence of outlier tribes."

"I know, I know, incorrigible. Suppose I pledge our loyalty in return for guardianship of our son."

"Honest oaths require honest men. We both know what you are."

Innocence had scrambled fully onto the carpet and behind Jewelwolf. His voice crept over their conversation. "You . . . you are my father?"

"I am," Bone said, and for a long, strange moment it was enough, despite all the demons and conquerors of the Earthe, to be near his son.

"I know you from paintings. And I have dreams about you . . . but . . . you abandoned me."

The air was growing cold. "I am sorry."

"My mother abandoned me too."

"No! No, you must never think that. Think the worst of me. Know me for a coward, a rogue, a cheat. But know always that your mother loves you and crossed the world to find you."

"Yet she did not find me. Deadfall did."

"I see."

"I have a power," Innocence said. "I am imbued with the chi of the Heavenwalls."

"So I'm told."

"Some people think that makes me emperor of Qiangguo. But Deadfall says I may have a greater destiny."

"Does he now."

"He says . . . if I embrace it, if I trust Princess Jewelwolf's allies . . . I can bring peace to the whole world."

Bone bit the corner of his lip. The blade against his neck had not relaxed. Speaking had cost him a few drops of blood. "I don't suppose bringing peace to the world involves conquering it?"

"How else?" Jewelwolf said.

"Oh, trade, education, small acts of kindness, a thousand years of sweat and patience . . . this is utterly pointless, isn't it?"

"Lord Innocence, his life is yours to take or spare."

"I don't want him dead," said Innocence, and there was a hard note in the boy's voice that made Bone fear for many things, the world somewhat, himself least of all, Innocence Gaunt the most.

"I want him left on a mountaintop," Innocence said. "Let him survive if he can. Let him be abandoned, as he abandoned me."

"I do not think it wise."

"You have given me a choice. Is the word of a Karvak so feeble?"

"It will be as you wish. Deadfall, pick a mountain."

As they dropped low and the snowy peaks raised their icy spears, Bone estimated at what point a plunge might not necessarily kill him. Once it was reached, he said, "It is just, I suppose. But you are not the only one who matters, my son."

He grabbed Jewelwolf's sword.

He shrieked in pain, for he had sacrificed his palms for his neck. But he kept his grip on the sword, and the sudden shift in balance threw both him and Jewelwolf off the carpet.

In freefall he let go, trailing blood. The sword spun free, a sweep of silver and red.

He and the Karvak princess hit an icy slope and slid. She was a little ahead of him, and he shifted toward her maniacally, the cold raising fresh anguish from his hands, for now that Innocence was safe, only one thing mattered.

Jewelwolf reached the edge of a crevasse and clung to it with both hands. Bone, using all the skill of a lifetime, managed to halt just above her.

The scroll dangled from Jewelwolf's belt, flapping in the crazy wind, and the sword slid off the edge and plunged thousands of feet, until its gleams were lost in shadow.

He grabbed Jewelwolf's hand, pulled with all his strength. She made it over the edge.

"I—" she gasped, studying him in wonder. "This day I have learned something valuable about outlier tribes."

"Oh?"

"You think with your hearts—and not with your heads."

With one savage kick she knocked Bone into the abyss.

CHRIS WILLRICH   425

CHAPTER 31

RENUNCIATION

Snow Pine stared at the stone monkey. "What are you doing here?"

"What is this creature?" Steelfox asked.

"What? No, 'Thank you, Great Sage,' or 'Welcome, Equal of Heaven?'"
The monkey looked around. "Or maybe, 'Please, please save our butts, Wondrous Lady Monkey?'"

"Can you do that?" Snow Pine asked.

"The real bona fide Lady Monkey? Blindfolded and with one hand. But
I am not the genuine article, for that worthy is still trapped inside Five-Toe
Peak. I'm but a sort of illusionary manifestation born of the endless fragmentation of her monumental ego."

"What?" Steelfox said.

"Shorter version: I can, but I'll need the staff."

Snow Pine gave it to her.

"Thanks, fellow Monkey," she said. "Now, watch a master at work."

Northwing and Widow Zheng were surrounded by a trio of possessed Iron
Moths. The shaman and the calligrapher concentrated and babbled, desperately holding them at bay. Lady Monkey leaped, took her sweet time falling,
and smashed the Moths away like children's toys.

"Aiya," Snow Pine said.

"I feel somewhat redundant at this moment," Steelfox said, marveling.
Her peregrine falcon shrieked. "Be at ease, Qurca. Sisters-at-arms! Persimmon
Gaunt let loose this . . . thing . . . for a purpose. Let us go help her."

The four women moved as fast as they dared toward the great stone of
the Bull Demon. Whenever an Iron Moth got close enough to threaten them,
Monkey would caper or somersault into its path, smash it silly, and leap away.
Snow Pine was uncertain whether to be grateful or terrified.

They reached Gaunt, who was staring at the sky, rage on her face, tears
streaming down it. Snow Pine remembered what Steelfox had said.

"Gaunt! Innocence?" She could barely speak the words. "Joy?"

"The scroll," Gaunt said. "Jewelwolf and Deadfall are working together. They have the scroll, and I've seen Innocence . . . they've got Bone . . ." Gaunt made a fist, and it shook. "Steelfox. The balloons—"

"Yes," said the Karvak princess. "Zheng, I need Haytham over here. Perhaps you would take his place beside the high lama?"

"Gladly."

"More delays," Gaunt snapped.

"We need him," Snow Pine said.

"And we need you, Northwing," Steelfox said. "I will need all the wind you can muster, my friend."

Northwing looked haggard, but she said, "You will have it."

"Let us come too," a voice said.

It was Dolma, the woman from the Fraternity of the Hare, standing beside Mad Katta.

Katta said, "I beg the opportunity to put right some of what's happened."

"I too," said the woman. "My fellows have deserted me as a traitor and are leaving this place even now. But I would make amends, if I may."

By unspoken agreement, everyone else looked at Persimmon Gaunt.

Dolma said, "It's said in Qiangguo that good medicine is bitter. And it is said in . . . the land of my birth . . . that experience keeps a harsh school." She lowered her head. "Let me help."

Gaunt nodded, looking as though she might regret her choice forever.

With the manifestation of Lady Monkey on their side, the Xembalans were defeating the Fraternity and driving the possessed Iron Moths back into the tunnels, and with the Bull Demon seemingly in shock from his encounter with Innocence, more and more Charstalkers fled. It remained dangerous within the caldera, but Gaunt was able to join Snow Pine, Steelfox, Northwing, Haytham, Katta, and Dolma aboard a flying ger.

"Where is Flint?" Snow Pine said. "And Quilldrake?"

Gaunt realized it had been a long time since she'd seen either. She shook her head. "If you wish to look—"

"No. I have to go with you."

"There's no fire in the cauldron," Haytham said. "We may not be going anywhere. The demon is gone. I can do nothing."

"The bound Charstalkers were released when we arrived," Dolma explained. "The Bull Demon insisted. I don't know how we can subdue one."

"I might," Katta said, "with sufficient time."

"The legends about the wanderer are right," Northwing said. "You are arrogant."

"There are times the true arrogance is being silent about your talents."

"Talents such as warding off age—" Northwing began.

"If that's true, Northwing is modest!" Haytham cut in. "But I do need that Charstalker. If Katta can obtain one—"

"Perhaps he doesn't need to," said Gaunt and pointed the sword Crypt-tongue into the cauldron's heart.

She sensed a babble of voices rise, including two that were becoming familiar to her.

<< observation: receptacle suitable for energy construct >>

—not that not that not that—

"It's not freedom," she muttered. "But perhaps you'll enjoy a change of pace."

Fire blazed from the sword, and soon a bound Charstalker regarded them all with three furious eyes.

"Let us go," Gaunt said.

The balloon rose, and as it cleared the caldera, a fierce wind rushed it to the east.

"Thank you, Northwing," Gaunt said.

"I see Deadfall!" Steelfox said.

"I can't," Snow Pine said.

"I see with a falcon's eyes," Steelfox said, pointing. "Look there."

"It's turning north," Gaunt said, seeing the dark square. She could only discern one figure upon it, but in the distance and glare she couldn't be sure. Her stomach clenched.

"There is a person on the mountain below," Steelfox said.

"Can you see who?" Snow Pine asked.

"No. I can send Qurca closer—"

"No," Gaunt said, heart pounding. "We can't let Deadfall escape. We can come back. Agreed?"

Snow Pine nodded.

"I am in command," Steelfox said, "but so be it. Haytham? Northwing? May we move faster?"

"You'll have everything I have," gasped the shaman. "But I'll warn you, that's not much more than I am giving you now."

"I will seek an appropriate air current," said the inventor, "but I can promise nothing. It is in the All-Now's hands."

Their pace increased. Peaks rushed by like waves on the ocean. Gaunt remembered bearing Innocence in her belly across the waters when they'd first come to the East, what seemed so long ago.

She saw him. She should not have been so certain, but she was. "It's Innocence. Only him."

No one answered.

Perhaps Deadfall's peculiar power was waning. Perhaps Northwing's spirits were kind and Haytham's deity merciful. They were gaining.

She saw him clearly now. He turned. She could not hope that he would recognize her, but she opened the flap of the tent and shouted his name.

She saw him stare.

She saw him shake his head.

"Go, Mother! We are done! Live your life, the life you abandoned me for! I will have mine!"

"No, my son! I love you! I will never abandon you!"

"Go back to my father! I left him with Jewelwolf on the mountain!"

"Left him—there was only one! Did you not see what happened?"

"Why would I stay? I have a world to see! I am done with them, and you!"

He raised his arm and gestured imperiously.

A shockwave of wind hit the balloon. The craft careened off course, and Haytham cursed as fire from the cauldron ignited the structure of the ger. The Charstalker was still trapped, but its eyes flashed triumphantly. As Haytham strove to control the magic of the cauldron, Snow Pine, Steelfox, Katta, and Dolma swatted the fire with blankets.

"Innocence!"

But Innocence did not speak. It was Deadfall who answered, "Begone!"

"Deadfall!" Katta called out. "Hear me! You hated being a broken thing! But you were more whole then than now! Remember who you were! That carpet would never have caused such pain! Bring the boy back!"

"You never knew me."

The carpet flared with red light, and the Charstalker within the cauldron screeched and shot through the air to enter Deadfall's fabric.

As though freshly empowered, the carpet shot horizonward.

The balloon began to descend.

Gaunt stood staring through the ger's entrance. The carpet was disappearing into the clouds.

Steelfox stood behind Gaunt. "I will do a thing for you, Persimmon Gaunt, that Karvaks rarely do even for each other."

She whispered to her falcon and bade it fly past Gaunt into the clouds. Soon falcon and carpet and boy were gone.

"Can you see them?" Gaunt asked.

"Wait!" hissed Steelfox. "Help me save my vessel."

It was as if she watched herself from a distance, as she helped the others save the ger. The heart of her was still out there.

When the fire was truly out, and the plummeting balloon was merely filled with choking smoke, Steelfox gasped, "I do not sense Qurca anymore, Gaunt. I commanded him to follow at all costs, except to return once a year to my mother's ger. You are my sister-in-arms, and I swear by Mother Earth and Father Sky, if your son can be found, we will find him. But it will not be this day."

Gaunt shook. It was too much. To find, to lose, all in the span of an hour. It was too much.

Steelfox embraced her and Snow Pine too. Gaunt sobbed the anguish of the journey and its bitter end.

Dolma, of all people, stopped her.

"This is not the end of the matter," she said.

Gaunt mastered herself. She remembered her vision of her son accompanied by figures resembling the Fraternity of the Hare. And yet she saw only regret in Dolma's eyes. "You are right." She looked at her comrades. "We should go back for whoever is on the mountain."

"That is not possible," said Haytham. "We lack the necessary lift. All I can do is make our landing survivable. Our hot air dissipates, and we have no means of securing another Charstalker."

"We do," Gaunt said. "There is more than one such within this blade."

She sent another burst of fire from blade into cauldron, even as Haytham shouted, "Wait!"

The new Charstalker's eyes were full of feverish triumph as it shot forth from the cauldron, back to Bull-Demon Mountain. The felt around a portal caught fire, but this time the crew was well-prepared.

"The cauldron is damaged," Haytham said. "It can still contain a fire but not bind a Charstalker."

A memory nagged at her of black birds and eyes like sunbursts.

She searched for and found the black feather she'd carried all the way from Five-Toe Peak. She tossed it into the cauldron.

"What is that?" Dolma asked.

Snow Pine answered, "It's a feather from a thing of power. Maybe it can let us rescue who's on the mountain. Or . . . just maybe it can let us catch up to the carpet."

"Which is it to be?" Steelfox asked.

Gaunt did not answer but released another Charstalker. It shrieked its way back out of the cauldron and roared out the front flap, leaving smoldering edges. "Not again!" wailed Haytham.

But the suncrow feather erupted into a crazy tangle of heat and light.

Snow Pine was first out of the smoking ger once it hit the summit, to the accompaniment of Haytham's imaginative cursing. She was unsure of her footing, but a madness drove her on. Steelfox was only steps behind her.

The wife of the new Grand Khan stood nearby, coolly regarding her saviors.

"Sister," said Jewelwolf. "I trust you are well."

Steelfox slapped her.

Jewelwolf smiled, wiping blood from her lip. "I will forgive that. I will admit my conduct has been lacking. I will seek my mother's forgiveness."

"Not mine?" said Steelfox.

"Your own behavior is hardly above question. It will be an interesting meeting."

"If you ever return," put in Snow Pine.

"I decline to speak to scum of Qiangguo."

"This scum is my friend," said Steelfox.

"That hardly improves matters for you," said Jewelwolf.

"I would think instead of your own situation, princess," said Gaunt, having caught up.

"Ah, the Western witch."

"I believe you stand near a precipice, in more ways than one. You can surrender to us. Or, despite all Steelfox's fully justified pleading on behalf of her beloved, loyal sister, you may find yourself on a sudden interesting journey."

Jewelwolf grunted. "I surrender, of course. Deadfall has betrayed me. He has taken my prize and my bronze mirror. He may even hope to replace me among the Cardinals of the Compass Rose."

"And he took the scroll, of course," Gaunt said, "within which Bone has surely gone."

Jewelwolf smiled. "No, Persimmon Gaunt. I have the scroll, and your husband is dead, hurled off that very cliff."

Gaunt reeled, looking over the edge below them. Snow Pine gripped her arm. "Butcher," Snow Pine said. "You will do no more harm. Give us the scroll now."

"Very well. I—" Jewelwolf reached to her belt. "What? It's gone?"

"I don't suppose, princess," Snow Pine said with a look at Gaunt, whose lips were twitching, "it was with you right before the thief Bone left your august presence?"

The curses of Jewelwolf echoed through the mountains, braiding with the maniacal laughter of Persimmon Gaunt.

It had been an interesting experience, falling into the mountain crevasse swift as a brick with the scroll clutched to his chest—then transitioning into the world of the scroll and drifting down to its otherworldly mountains as gently as a leaf.

He'd almost wanted to do it again. But there were more satisfying tasks at hand.

CHAPTER 32

STEEL OF THE STEPPE

As the balloon returned to Xembala, Steelfox thanked Northwing and Haytham for perhaps the hundredth time. "You are getting good at this," she noted, for they adroitly maneuvered the balloon through the mists beside the volcano of the Bull Demon.

"Not good enough to enter that crevasse," Haytham said.

"No," Gaunt said, voice full of desperate hope, "but the scroll will be found. The journey of a thousand li begins with opening one door."

"Speaking of openings," said Katta, "who do I see exiting the mountain down there?"

"It's Quilldrake!" Snow Pine said. "And Flint," she added more gruffly.

The treasure hunters were at first nonplussed to find the Karvak balloon blocking their path. Then Quilldrake attempted jauntiness.

"It is delightful to see you," he said, putting down an armload of stony cocoons.

"Oh, shut up," Flint said, doing likewise. "There is no recovery from this. It was a foolish plan." He looked at Snow Pine. He spread his hands. "Loyalty to my business partner overcame my good sense."

Snow Pine said, "Yes. I suppose it is always difficult to have more than one partner."

Flint could only stare. Snow Pine turned away.

"'Shut up,' he says," Quilldrake was saying. "After all I've done for him. And for you, Snow Pine, and you, Persimmon Gaunt! We had always intended to share the bounty with you. You provided most excellent cover, combating the adult Iron Moths while we crept among the larvae and stole some cocoons. Is this not the prize necessary to seal your bargain with Lady Monkey?"

"You are not lying," Gaunt admitted. "But things have changed."

"They have?" Quilldrake pressed. "So you no longer need to seek your magic scroll, to find your children?"

"No—" Gaunt swore. "Yes! Yes, we still need to find the scroll. Is the fragment of Lady Monkey still here?"

Snow Pine said, "Gaunt. If we seek her, we will find the adult Iron Moths. We will need to bargain."

"Are you agreeing with Quilldrake and Flint now, that we should steal these cocoons?"

Snow Pine looked at Flint again. "Was that not always the plan?"

The women, mothers of lost children, turned to Steelfox.

It astonished the Karvak princess to find that they trusted her—not a mother, not kin, not long ago an enemy.

She sensed her sister's gaze upon her as she said, "We Karvaks have a deserved reputation for raids and conquest. But we also deserve a reputation for trade, and honor. I will represent your interests as an envoy from my people to Xembala and all its inhabitants. I have experience in such things."

"You have no right!" snapped Jewelwolf.

"This can also be a thing we bring before the Grand Khan, his council, and his Supreme Judge," said Steelfox. "All of whom have sworn to follow the path laid down by our father, who valued trade as much as conquest. And who mistrusted all dealings with sorcerers and demons. For now, it stands."

Jewelwolf was silent.

Before long they had returned to the caldera and commenced a conference strange even among the secret annals of the Karvaks.

"The Bull Demon's fury is for the moment spent," said Chodak the high lama, supported by Widow Zheng. "Innocence Gaunt, it seems, drained him of considerable power. And between Persimmon Gaunt and the shard of Lady Monkey, he has no more teeth."

Steelfox looked with some pleasure at the toothless maw of the Bull Demon. Indeed, she made a point of smiling at it.

The mountain rumbled. She stopped smiling.

"Let's conclude our business briskly," she said. "Gaunt, if you can indeed translate for me, I offer the Iron Moths a boon they may appreciate. Our lands are very flat compared to others and free of rock. It is comparatively easy for us to find stones that have fallen from space. I understand you find such alien matter delicious. We offer you fifty such stones every year for a bolt of ironsilk. We will accept ironsilk from broken cocoons. No caterpillar need volunteer for death. Sapient beings need not suffer to bring us wealth. We do ask an initial sample of ironsilk as proof of concept."

Gaunt looked into the pommel of Crypttongue before speaking a series of buzzes and clicks. A chorus of like sounds from the Iron Moths filled the caldera.

Gaunt said, "They agree if Xia thinks it is fair."

"I do," said Zheng.

"Not acceptable," said the scion of Monkey.

"What?" said Steelfox.

"The bargain was for the caterpillars, not ironsilk. I—or my better self—would like a mating pair."

Steelfox said, "Gaunt, I suppose you had best ask."

Gaunt buzzed, clicked, and listened. "May the pair return, unharmed, as adults?"

"On one condition," said the stone monkey. "They lay eggs in my cavern first."

After a moment, Gaunt said, "We are agreed."

"Fine," said Monkey. "This has been a lot of trouble for a little. Do not forget the time limit. I'm feeling sleepy—"

She yawned, and blurred, and turned into a crystal spine that shattered upon the stone.

"You should go," said the high lama. She turned to Zheng. "I understand if you wish to depart now. It may be hard to leave, afterward."

"I wanted a last great adventure, Chodak. And I got one! But now I find it was just the continuation of an adventure from an earlier life, or so I believe. Is this an adventure you wish to share?"

"It has been rather a long time since a high lama has had a consort. This will be unusual in more ways than one. But I have learned some of my limitations lately. I think an adventure is in order."

"Then I will stay."

Gaunt and Snow Pine and Flint embraced Zheng. Quilldrake shook her hand.

"You must go," the high lama said, "as we must."

"Farewell," said Steelfox.

The two Karvak balloons departed Xembala as the sun set. Under a bright moon they said farewell to one another.

"Good luck," Steelfox shouted across the void. "Take care of Haytham and Northwing. I loan you their services with great reluctance. But I think you will need them when navigating the mountains."

"Farewell, Flint!" Quilldrake called beside her. "Do not become too honorable!"

"Not with a mentor like you!" Flint shouted back. "Don't fleece the Karvaks too much," he added. "They have tempers!"

Beside him Gaunt called out, "Good luck, Steelfox! Keep an eye on that sister of yours."

"I will help with that," replied Katta, "so to speak. Before I track Deadfall."

"And an ear," said Dolma. "I will rebuild the Fraternity of the Hare. And it will have new meaning under the guidance of Princess Steelfox."

The sky filled with the now-familiar sound of Jewelwolf's curses. Steelfox knew she had a sabercat by the tail, and even with her sister's actions exposed, Jewelwolf would remain powerful. Mother would be on Steelfox's side, as would many of the nobles. But she must fly carefully.

I am not a baatar, Father. But here, poised between Mother Earth and Father Sky, I swear to you the daughter you pushed aside will always honor your ways. All the way from Mount Mastodon to the Braid of Spice.

CHAPTER 33

REUNION

The travelers, clad in thick furs, had hunted their quarry for weeks through the Heavenwalk Mountains. They had never given up hope, however, for at times there flew before them a bird with three legs and blazing eyes.

At last, down yet another forlorn valley, the bird flapped excitedly. When the travelers found it they saw that the suncrow sat on the shoulder of a strange mountain-man, a pale fellow with a thick, snow-dusted beard.

One of the travelers ran to him as swiftly as she dared.

"You—you're—" she said.

"As arrogant as ever," he said. "Yes, I am."

She stroked his head. "There's a little gray in your hair."

"Perhaps unavoidable. But I spent as much time outside the scroll as I could tolerate. We have been so far out of synch already, Persimmon Gaunt."

"I would love you regardless, Imago Bone, but I am glad you thought of that."

"I lost him, Gaunt. Lost him again."

"So did I. I am done blaming. And you are done berating. What we are never done with is seeking."

He nodded. "But there is someone else whose seeking is at an end." He lifted up a scroll and gestured through the snow. "Would you like to be first?"

With trembling hands, the woman who stood behind Persimmon Gaunt removed a glove and took the scroll.

Her voice broke before she disappeared, but the listeners all agreed the word was Joy.

JOURNEY TO THE WEST

Wondrous Lady Monkey falls asleep in her mountain at last. It was an interesting waking, but she is exhausted now, and the next waking promises to be something special. Things are moving, and the mortals get more intriguing every day. What hasn't changed is her ego, she concedes. Oh, one day she may follow the Undetermined at last, and be a good Monkey, and maybe even journey to the West for real, to seek enlightenment in Geam, or Xembala, or some smelly fishing port on a distant shore. But for now she would rather wriggle out of her punishment than accept it, and before the day of her release she has a last trick to try.

As she closes her eyes she wishes good luck to everyone who dares to slip the knots of destiny.

Then she falls asleep to the rhythmic sound of Iron Moth caterpillars munching inexorably away at her mountain prison, moving from east to west.

"This is it? This is what they call the Dragonheat?"

"Yes. I must say I prefer to view it from up here. A sensible choice. Now, why have we come here?"

"I must decide if I announce myself to the Empire or take another path. This seemed a fitting place to ruminate."

"You have many options. Treat with the Forbidden City or the Cardinals—"

"There is another option. . . . Did I do the right thing, Deadfall? I wonder about it sometimes."

"We all twist and turn when considering our pasts, Innocence. On impulse I once stole from the great library of Qushkent to see what your parents would do with a magical book."

"What did they do?"

"Nothing. They told no one. Oh, I have learned since that the *Chart of Tomorrows* is only relevant to the Bladed Isles, far to the West. But nevertheless, they selfishly said nothing to their companions. Thus I learned their true natures."

"My parents . . . I think of all the stories my mother told. They are like dreams, dreams with names like Palmary, Archaeopolis, Swanisle. I think if one is to use power wisely, one must first understand one's dreams."

"I do not follow you, lord."

"No, you convey me. Take me to the land where my parents conceived me. Take me to the West."

As in the mountains of the world outside, snow fell within the scroll. Where out there it was deathly cold, here it was invigorating. Snow Pine loved returning here, loved hugging her daughter, perhaps even loved Flint (though she trusted him about as far as she could throw a Karvak.)

"Mother—"

"Just let me hug you. It has been so long. How you've grown."

"Mother, you've said that three times!"

"It's worth a thousand. I will not leave you again."

"I know you did not mean to. Nor Father . . ."

Snow Pine lowered her head, but that hurt had lessened. "What is the matter with your hand?" she said. "Here, let me—" She unwrapped the bandage.

"It is nothing . . . a sort of scrape that . . . got out of hand."

"Scrape?"

And Snow Pine stared, not knowing what to make of the sign that seemed branded upon her daughter's hand, that of three lengths of intertwined chain.

ACKNOWLEDGMENTS

This particular road trip was kicked off by Joe Monti and Lou Anders, visualized by Kerem Beyit, mapped by Rhys Davies, fueled by the Campbell and Mountain View Public Libraries, and brought safely home by my wife Becky Willrich. I am very grateful to all. For last-minute help or reassurance, many thanks to Barry Goldblatt, James Sutter, Miriam Valencia, and Claire Koukoutsakis.

This story probably began when as a children's librarian I discovered Kathryn Ceceri's *The Silk Road: 20 Projects Explore the World's Most Famous Trade Route*. Other inspirational material included *Empires of the Silk Road* by Christopher I. Beckwith, *The Secret History of the Mongol Queens* by Jack Weatherford, and *Tibetan Civilization* by R. A. Stein. For countless visual references, the NHK/China Central TV documentary *The Silk Road* (English-language release, 1990) was invaluable. Alongside the historical inspirations were those that mixed history with imagination, particularly Wu Cheng'en's sixteenth-century Chinese classic *Journey to the West*, which I know mainly through a shortened retelling by David Kherdian, *Monkey: A Journey to the West*, and Richard Bernstein's *Ultimate Journey*, a modern attempt to retrace the quest of Hsuan Tsang, the monk whose pilgrimage to India inspired Wu. Certain aspects of the story also benefited from Huston Smith's *The World's Religions* and *The Art of Happiness* by His Holiness the Dalai Lama and Howard C. Cutler, MD. I'd be remiss in not mentioning a triple-feature filmography: *Lost Horizon* (1937), *The Man Who Would Be King* (1975), and *Raiders of the Lost Ark* (1981). Any missteps or lost hats are entirely the fault of the author.

ABOUT THE AUTHOR

Chris Willrich's writing has appeared in *Asimov's Science Fiction*, *Beneath Ceaseless Skies*, *Black Gate*, *Flashing Swords*, *Lightspeed*, *The Mythic Circle*, *Strange Horizons*, and *The Magazine of Fantasy & Science Fiction*, where Persimmon Gaunt and Imago Bone first appeared. Gaunt and Bone's novel-length adventures began in *The Scroll of Years* (Pyr, 2013). That book also reprinted the first Gaunt and Bone story, "The Thief with Two Deaths" (*F&SF*, June 2000). Chris is also the author of the Pathfinder Tales novel *The Dagger of Trust* (Paizo Publishing 2014). He lives in the San Francisco Bay Area with his family.

Photo by Richard McCowen,
Maritime City Photography

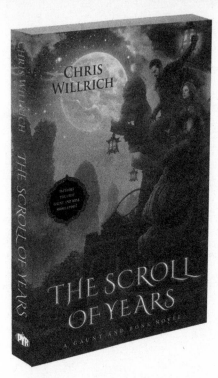